Three Lords scheming - soon to die
Two hearts frozen - soon to melt
One nun imprisoned - soon to be free
One angry King - forgiving

Mela Ells

Willow Pond Press

Willow Pond Press
www.WillowPondPress.co.uk

Paperback ISBN: 9780995492103
Ebook ISBN: 9781783019038

Printed and bound in Great Britain by Clays Ltd, St Ives plc

To

A, R and MW

You know how important you are

Hugger-mugger was a phrase used at the time of this novel. It means something that is secret, clandestine or done in secrecy or concealment.

Prologue

Southern England, January, Twelfth Night, 1515

THE POST-HORSE was frisky. He'd been held at the back of a dark, musty stable for too long and was glad to be back on the open road. His rider was not. He'd left Southwark on the southern bank of the Thames, just south-east of London, in pre-dawn darkness. Mercurial steaks of silver sky had guided him east but they'd been quickly smothered by dark, heavy cloud and the light had never really lifted. That was hours ago; seemed like a week.

He'd coped with the temperaments of more horses than he cared to remember, suffered as many saddles, negotiated potholed roads, muddy tracks, howling wind followed by sleet and snow. His coarse, leathered face braced the elements, his hands smarted from controlling wet reins, his legs ached from difficult mounts. He was tired, irritable and longed for the end of his journey.

Delivering post was his job, it had been since he'd returned last year from King Henry's campaign in France. It paid the rent, kept food on his table, bought his ale, paid for women. None of that made it any easier. It was a lonely job and on long, dark days like this his mind wandered back to the army. The camaraderie, the raucous banter, the drinking. Then he'd remember the terror of the battlefield, the stench of death, the smell of blood, the spewing of guts, the cries of agony and tell himself not to be so stupid. He was lucky to be alive. Many hadn't had his luck. He was alive and his injuries healed. He was fit for work and not just for begging. He chided himself and took it out on the sides of the horse.

Canterbury was edging closer with every stride. He dreamt of what was to come as he took hedges, jumped ditches, egged and urged the horse on to the next stabling post. There would be twelfth night revelries to mark the closing of Christmas-tide. Music, dancing, ale, lust and larks. He would get out of these saturated clothes and enjoy himself. Perhaps this black, evil sky would even oblige with the dangling of a cheery star or two.

It was through heavy torrential rain that the large heap in the road ahead loomed up. Violently he yanked his horse to a sudden stop, the beast swerving into the hedge. A young wench ran to him, her clothes and hair stuck to her.

"Please 'elp mister, please 'elp," she screeched, pointing to the mound which he now realized was a horse with its rider laying beside. "There's bin an accident, I fink ee's dead."

The rider ran to the man, lifted his head, felt for a thumping in the neck. It was there. There was no blood, no visible wounds but the legs were contorted. After a long minute the man groaned pitifully. The rider tipped a few drops of pomace from his wineskin into the man's mouth. He always kept his cheap fruit brandy with him, ever since his army days. He cradled the man's head in his huge hand and slowly the groaning stopped and the eyes opened.

"Me 'orse slipped on mud, we bofe went flyin'," he mumbled, taking a hand to his head. The rider looked at the horse, its eyes weren't wild, it wasn't startled. Its head was low but only because it was being held by a short rein which the fallen man clenched tightly. The rider released the grip and coaxed the horse up. It quickly responded and like the man had no visible sign of injury. It was soaked, trembling but certainly not lame.

The wench took the reins and led the muddy horse to dry safety under a mighty oak. She stroked it tenderly, spoke soothing words, the rider noticed and was glad for it. Even through the rain he could see she was a handsome woman. A full bosom tumbling over loosened laces, thick hair that now clung in wet tendrils around an inviting neck. What were these two really up to? The rider mused and smirked to himself. Seemed the man's thoughts weren't on steering his horse!

"Let's get you to that cottage over there," the rider snapped, noting his own unease. His instincts were rattled. The situation didn't feel right. He could see the glow of candles through the trees and assumed they meant occupancy. "Can you walk that far?" He was irritable but trying not to show it. He didn't need diversions from his task in hand, he wanted to get on, hear cathedral bells and be rid of saddles!

The man nodded and together they walked, the rider taking the man's heavy weight, his own body bending under the strain.

"I's got the 'orses," the wench called, securing the rider's reins, too. "Don't be worrying about the beasts."

The cottager was welcoming, the man could rest there for as long as he needed and within minutes the rider returned to his mount, eager to resume his journey. The wench had lifted the hem of her skirt and was wiping his wet saddlebags. Was she touching the buckles?

"Hey! What yer doing woman? Get away from them bags, they's private."

"I's just wiping 'em. They be soaked," she said, smiling coquettishly. "One of 'em buckles was loose, I's fixed it, you don't want rain getting in."

"Stand away!" He pushed her aside and took the reins. "Leave 'em be, they's private!" Those buckles weren't loose, he thought to himself, I'm sure they weren't. He ran his stubby fingers over the contour of the bag, he could feel the package inside, everything was still there and anyway why would a wench steal documents. She'd want money. Mayhap he was being overly suspicious.

"Anyfing else I can be helpful with?" She leant provocatively against the sturdy trunk of the tree. Her question hung in the air. He couldn't help but gaze at her, so hot and welcoming on this cold, miserable late-afternoon. For a moment he was tempted but then he remembered the urgent missive that lay in his saddlebags. Can't keep an Earl waiting! This incident had already stolen too much of his time and there'd be plenty more wenches in Canterbury.

"Another time lass," he called, reluctantly, "although you's pretty enough to tempt a monk."

"O I does," she laughed, "quite reg'lar."

The rider mounted his horse smiling, blew her a kiss and headed on to the cathedral city.

Chapter One

Richmond Palace, near London, England
Early spring 1515

SO. HERE HE was again. A tremor she couldn't put a name to shuddered through her. She tried to stop it, she failed. She concentrated on staying calm, remaining composed. She lay her book in her lap.

"Lord Melbroke, m'Lady," her maid announced. She heard his footsteps enter the room. She didn't respond. Didn't speak. Didn't turn around to greet him. As before he had avoided the usual method of Court procedure. He had avoided the usher or the page and had sought out Annie. As before he wanted to keep his visit known to as few as possible. The maid left and closed the door. Silence. Then she heard his footsteps walking towards her. Deliberate, bold steps. The steps of a military man, a man of bearing, of status, of courage. The steps too, she knew, of a strikingly handsome man. Tall, broad shoulders, high forehead, intelligent face. Confident in his attraction to women, experienced in their ways and wants. A man with a reputation.

When he first visited, some five weeks ago, she had told Annie that he needed guidance, advice, on a prenuptial surprise he was planning for Lord Pierre, her groom-to-be. Already he had her lying.

As before he stood behind her, placed his hands upon her shoulders and kissed the top of her head. A little tremor flickered through her. There was no point in stopping him, no point in saying he should not make so free with her. No point in reminding him she was the daughter of an Earl, that her family held sway at Court, that she was a Lady. He knew all that and he didn't care. His ranking was higher; he shared blood with King Henry. Her reminding him hadn't worked before, she knew it wouldn't work now.

He threw his heavy cloak over a chair, she felt its waft of air brush her cheek. He lent over her shoulders and drew the heavy drapes across the window, eliminating the morning sun that had been giving light for her reading. His closeness took her breath away. Now just candles lit the room. He loosened her golden hair from its snood and let it tumble over her shoulders allowing the candles to catch its glints. He kissed her neck, teased her ear with his tongue, nuzzled his face into her curls. She could feel his breath on her cheek and a weakness flushed through her.

"Hello again my beautiful lady," he said. She wanted to tell him she wasn't his, he had no right to call her 'my' anything. Lady Frances of Blean was betrothed to another. She wanted to tell him his behaviour was outrageous, that he was a cad, a rake but she didn't. She wanted to stand up and challenge him, to call for help, to broadcast his shame but she didn't. She couldn't risk a scene that could escalate to a scandal that would ruin her reputation, not his.

She was trapped by his ungentlemanly behaviour but she would call upon her inner strength, it had helped her before, it would now.

She could handle this, she told herself, safe in the knowledge that she would soon be far away from this place. Soon she would be in Kent, preparing for her wedding. Soon this would be a distant memory and Alban, the Lord Melbroke, would have to divert his attentions elsewhere!

He tilted her chin, lifting her face upwards and made free with her mouth. His lips were soft, sensual; his tongue hungry and penetrating. She surrendered to his strength, to his want of her and tried to fight the heat that in little waves was simmering through her body. His touch ignited her, she couldn't fight it but she wouldn't show it. She had never known the like before, it both frightened and excited her. He stroked the soft rise of her breasts. Her book fell to the floor.

"Loosen your bodice," he whispered. She obeyed. The first time she hadn't, she had objected most strongly but his clumsy tugging had torn her dress and explaining that to her maid had been difficult. Today she was wearing a simple morning dress, a long velvet skirt with a silken bodice fastened at the front. She loosened the ties as he kissed her neck and made her tremble like a wave on water.

He slid his two hands over the smooth skin of her shoulders and down into her bodice. He'd done this before, before him no man had ever touched her. She tried to fight the sensation but her body wanted to respond and she couldn't stop her head from pressing back against him. He gently caressed her as the very smell of him enveloped her. Something evocative, woody, sandalwood mayhap or cedar. She struggled to stifle any groan of pleasure. She was fighting the feelings that were overwhelming her, they were wrong, she was to be married in four weeks' time, this must stop but she was young, she was inexperienced and she didn't know what to do.

"Stop," she pleaded. He ignored her.

"Stand up," he commanded. She did and her bodice fell open. He turned her around and looked at her. Her nakedness was beautiful, it caught his breath. She quickly grabbed her bodice and held it over herself. Her shoulders were as smooth as a white sea shell, her cheeks flushed, her body trembling. She was his for the taking, they both knew that but he didn't want this to be the place.

He grasped her waist and lifted her on to a nearby table. He pushed her knees apart and stood between them, her skirt and petticoats now the only defence of her maidenhood. He pulled her to him, his impatient breath burnt her cheek, his kisses skimmed her shoulders. "I want you so," he implored. "This...you...you're driving me mad."

He stepped back from her. Her face now flushed, her hair tousled. She looked ravishing and he wanted to ravish her. "Tonight," he said. "It must be tonight. The King sends me to France in a few days, I must have you before I go."

She sat silent, her mind in turmoil.

"I will come to your rooms at nine o'clock, make sure you've dismissed your servants." His determination stunned her. The passion in his eyes alarmed her. He looked deep into her sapphire-blue eyes seeking approval, he saw none but neither did he see dissent. She was silent, speechless. She didn't reply.

She watched the broad shoulders, the strong legs, the powerful presence as he turned from her and made for the door, swinging his cloak around himself. She felt a mix of bereft, unfulfilled need, of humiliation but most of all of anger – at him and herself. He let the door slam behind him.

Quickly she secured her bodice, scrambled between

furniture to retrieve snood and book from the floor and was just about respectable when her maid re-entered. "Annie, please go immediately to my sister, bid her come at her very earliest convenience."

Annie made to open the curtains.

"Leave them, I have a headache. Lord Melbroke kindly drew them for me. Just go to Lady Margaret, quickly, 'tis urgent." That was her second lie to this faithful servant who had been with her family since before she was born. She knew who to blame for her feelings of shabbiness.

Panic was rising in her chest. Her breathing was rapid and shallow, her hands were shaking, her mouth dry. She had to get away. She had to be a virgin on her wedding night. If she weren't the shame and scandal would rock two good families. Even King Henry would hear of it. She shuddered just thinking of the ramifications.

She also knew that if she were in her rooms at nine o'clock then Melbroke would have his way with her, she would be powerless to stop him. She knew already how he could make her will dissolve like ice in flame. How she weakened in body and resolve at his touches. He had awakened a want in her. This couldn't be. She had to get away or be ruined.

FRANCES' MARRIAGE to French aristocrat Pierre, Marquis de Champagne, was the merger of two important families. King Henry had given his blessing. Queen Katherine, to whom she had been lady-in-waiting for two years, was thrilled. She and Pierre had been introduced over a year ago and they got on well. They shared common interest in literature, card games, dancing. She thought they would be happy. "Passion will come," the Queen had assured her. Frances hadn't known what that meant. She did now, except it was with the wrong man!

The wedding had been long in the planning. The heavily embroidered wedding gown was made. The feast planned. The music, entertainment and dancing organized. The guest list very long. Frances was to stay at Richmond Palace until a fortnight before the wedding when her father would escort her to their ancestral home near Canterbury for the nuptials. She was simply changing her departure date! That's all, she told herself and Margaret, who was obviously bewildered at her sister's sudden need to depart early and her demands that she accompany her.

"Whatever you say sister," Margaret agreed with a sigh, "but why? This really is most perplexing." Margaret, at twenty-three, was four years older than Frances. Similar in looks but with darker hair and hazel eyes.

"I'll explain later, right now I just want to leave. Now!" Frances' usual calm demeanour was alive with urgency. Her eyes had panic in them and were set in a pale, now strained face. Margaret could see all that. As her hand reached for the door Frances called: "You must go yourself to the stables Margaret, don't send a servant."

"O Frances, really..."

"No one must know we intend leaving...and I can't go, I mustn't be seen."

"Mustn't be seen! What are you talking about?"

"Later, Margaret, I will explain all later..."

"All right sister, all right but it had better be soon."

Frances was praying that no one would expect two women of the royal household to be riding a long distance on horseback. Two gentlewomen alone would be unusual but not unheard of. Once on the road they would pass as ordinary wayfarers. Her brain was racing. Her good brain in the academic head that had conquered Latin, loved literature, understood music. Her head was ruling right now, she was making sure of that.

DUST FROM the tiltyard was swirling over the yard wall as Frances, on her favourite white mount Lunar, headed away from the Palace stables. It was just gone two o'clock, she'd heard the Palace chapel bell a few moments earlier. Two lonely clangs that belied the lavish decoration over which they rang. By her side rode Margaret on her usual chestnut mount. They were two proficient horsewomen who'd been introduced to a horse's back almost as soon as they could walk. Today, they were in plain riding clothes, no feathers nor finery. A deliberate decision to be less noticeable on their travels. They had money, a few personal requirements and good boots.

The jousting was well underway. The shouts and claps and whoops of excitement banged Frances' ears as she pulled Lunar toward the open country beyond the Palace. Queen Katherine was there, she knew for she had helped her dress earlier in the day. She'd be watching her champion now, his horse bedecked in her Aragon colours. Melbroke was there too, she could see his green and red pennant flying high, fluttering in the breeze along with the many others that stood proud above the yard wall. He too was jousting, then. Defending his reputation. He certainly cared not for hers! Would his mind wander at all to what he planned for himself tonight? Was he thinking of her as much as she was of him? Or was he too busy with his current sport! Angrily she pushed him out of her mind.

She'd sent a note to Queen Katherine, explaining her sudden departure. Had she yet read it? She hoped not, for if the Queen objected to Frances leaving Court earlier than planned she would send a messenger to bring her back.

"While the wedding preparations go well," she'd written, "my father hath sent message earnestlie requesting that I return quicklie to Canterbury. A few unforeseen but thankfullie minor problems, have arisen and he needs my guidance. He hath commanded that my sister, the Lady Margaret, accompany me. I am sorry I did not speak with Your Grace before I left but I determined not to interrupt your enjoymente of the joust. I pray, your Majesty, that my absence a fortnight earlier than wee did plan will not cause any inconvenience and I beg your Majesty's understanding and forgiveness. I am, as always, your Majesty's most loving servant..."

As she'd sealed the wax she'd prayed the untruths would never be revealed. She nudged Lunar's sides and moved from walk to trot and into canter. Margaret followed suit and soon they were covering good ground. Soon the stone and brick rectangular palace, with its three floors and long windows, its inner courtyards, its pepper-pot domes and jungle of turrets and chimneys would be well behind them. She was angry at being made to leave but mainly relieved.

They would keep to the Thames' south bank until Greenwich and when the King's favourite Palace, his birthplace and where he'd married Katherine, came into view, they would turn south-east. They would keep well away from the beautiful gardens that cosseted the great courtyards where both their King and her predator had played as boys, they would spend one night in a Greenwich inn then they would head into deepest Kent. Depending on how many miles they could manage each day Frances anticipated arriving at her father's home at sunset the day after the morrow. It would be hard going, they would become tired, they would need to build in rest, they would need to find safe places to eat and sleep. Under other circumstances it could have been a happy adventure, right now all she wanted was to be safely ensconced behind her father's walls.

The afternoon sun warmed their backs and the river sparkled as if diamonds floated upon it. She felt Lunar's strength and power beneath her, it made her feel secure and safe. "I'm away," she called to the heavens in gleeful relief, her speed lifting her sentiments upwards and the wind dissipating her words as they floated to the clouds.

She could only guess how his Lordship would react when he found her bed empty. Her head didn't care, it knew she was doing the right thing. The King was sending him to France, a diplomatic mission no doubt. Very soon the Channel would be defending her virginity. He could touch her, no more. Arouse those feelings, no more. Once she was married to Pierre he wouldn't dare.

Chapter Two

EARLIER THIS DAY two brothers had met in the piercingly cold dawn. Their rendezvous, just a few miles north of Richmond Palace. The more manly of the two had arrived first and in the knife-sharp wind and under a breaking, silver-streaked sky he'd pulled a heavy cloak around his fighting-man's body and waited. A hoar-frost ate into his bones. Early crows were already cawing, their wings flapping like black rags in the stillness of the white world.

The other brother, as thin as a reed, weakened from a sickly childhood, dainty in his ways, appeared within minutes and they embraced eagerly, slapping each others shoulders with gauntletted gloves. Both French and English by birth they spoke each language with no accent. As brothers they couldn't be more different. One strong, sturdy, broad, handsome. The other willowy, boney, his face featureless, his eyes startled, his mouth mean.

They'd settled on hard rocks by the side of the dilapidated hut, once a gamekeeper's sanctuary, now theirs. No one at the

Palace must know of their connection. Secrecy was vital to the plan. This dark place, with its warning in the rocks and ears in the trees, a short raven's flight from those they planned to attack, those they were already deceiving, was where they always came. A sharp crack yanked their eyes wide. The strong brother stood, his hand shooting to the hilt of his sword. Just a passing animal, they relaxed.

"'Tis the meek who shall inherit the earth," the weak man said bitterly, his whole body shivering in the cold. "Are we meek enough do you think," he asked, expecting no answer, his face grimacing in contorted disdain. "Our plan must work or we've lost everything. Almost already have."

"We'll make sure it works. And remember brother," said the stronger man, "the meek don't want the earth, neither do we, just our bit of it. Meekness doesn't pay. Ask and you won't be given. Fight and you will. We are doomed to our fate, we have no choice."

Dark glassy eyes watched from the frost-rigid branches. The cawing had ceased, even the crows it seemed were stunned by the cold into an uncanny silence. They perched like sentinels, witnesses to the plots, gatherers of evidence they could never reveal. The iron-cold earth crunched beneath the brothers' heavy boots as they banged warmth into their feet. A light snowfall fluttered around them, their thoughts so deep in their plans they were unaware of the beauty of a world turned silver. Spring shoots might be struggling forth but winter was reluctant to give up its vice-hold.

"Our die is cast," the weakling asserted. "Too late to change our minds now."

"Indeed. Too late. Now we begin to reveal ourselves."

"We stalk our prey like the wolf, we devour like the raven, we get back what is ours. Agreed?"

"We already are, now we step up our plan. 'Tis time for

the bear to roar," the handsome brother agreed, knowing that if it came to fighting it would be he who danced the sword. His weak brother was the schemer. Together they were a good team. They stood and embraced.

"Back in France we will celebrate."

"May God walk with us," the strong man said, his arms tight around his comrade in crime, his face sad. "And may God forgive us."

Their horses snorted, the vapour from their nostrils floating upwards like released steam in the gathering day. A tug on the reins and the two men parted, their horses hooves almost silent on deep leaf-mould as they moved between trees. A Marquis and his brother, joined in blood, united in intent, now to be divided by time and space. They would cast their fates to the winds, it's what courage is all about. Trust and hope. Hope and trust.

ACROSS ENGLAND robed figures knelt in supplication for the final religious office of the day. Through the dark night the bells of Richmond toned the Compline hour. In the Palace a handsome man strode along an empty torch-lit corridor, his cloak pulled tight around him, for even inside the Palace the night was chill. His ears were alert for approaching footfall, even the rustle of a skirt he would note. His eyes honed, like an animal on the prowl, ready to deal with approaching shadowy shapes if they danced on the walls. Ready to smile benignly.

At nine o'clock Melbroke knocked on Frances' door. The wall torches flickered along the empty corridor, their light bringing a sheen to his shoulder-length, thick, brown hair, loose now, dancing about his collar. His deep, dark eyes shone like polished conkers. No answer. He scanned the corridor, left and right. It was still empty. Luck was with him. He knocked again, banging his knuckles more forcibly, feeling the contact of bone on oak. Again no answer. Again he knocked. He was getting irritable now.

He had bedded many women, none had captured him in wedlock, it was unlikely any would. He was the eldest nephew of an Earl whose own son had already produced heirs, there was no pressure upon him to wed anyone.

He had lusted but never loved and had no intentions of so doing. The life he led was ideal, he believed, for a warrior-knight when his King called him to battle and a courtier-agent during times of peace. Anyway, love was a sham, why people chose to seek it he had no idea.

The jousting had exhilarated him. He'd hoped Frances would have been there, he'd have taken her ribbons but he couldn't see her in the throng so he took those of Lady Elinor although his interest in her had long waned. His new armour had gleamed like a sun. He'd won his fights, knocked his opponents clean over. The applause had rung around his ears. Even the King, himself a champion jouster, had shouted his praise. His blood was up, his self-esteem soaring.

Still no answer. He would wait no long. He wrenched at the handle and stepped inside. Darkness. He grabbed one of the corridor torches from its sconce and shone it around the entrance room. Not a servant in sight: no chatter, no voices, just silence. Good! He strode from one room to the next and finally to the bedchamber but only continued darkness greeted him. No candles, no fire. An empty bed. His anticipation turned sour and his irritation to anger. Where was she! He slammed the side of a clenched fist against the wall. He was sure she wanted him. He had felt the arousal in her. This was a first - no woman had rejected him before! "Damn the woman," he said, out loud. "Damn, damn, damn."

He snatched back the drape and saw the moon was full, the night windy. He would go to the river, walk off the need that had already built up within him. The cold night air, the sleety rain in the wind should do it. He would walk along the Thames bank to Ham and back. Curse Frances, Lady of Blean.

UNBEKNOWN TO the angry Lord Melbroke, the Lady, around whom his rage now swirled, was settling herself into her first night's stopover in Greenwich. Their first day on the road had been hard. While they had left Richmond in bright spring weather the temperature had plummeted as they travelled and fat, floating snowflakes amid a biting wind had welcomed them into Greenwich. Now at least they had glass in the windows and a fire that roared. The Red Lion was safe and respectable, or at least, as safe as any inn could be for two women travelling alone.

"Come sister," Margaret had urged, as she lay on the large, low bed they would share. The room, one of the more expensive on the upper floor, was small and the candles gave it some cosiness. "My patience is spent. Come next to me and tell me what all this is about."

Frances was embarrassed. She realized in the telling, that she should not have been so submissive. It was all right now looking back but at the time she had been bewildered.

"Do you love this man?"

"No, of course not," Frances snapped, shocked.

"Then why do you tremble when you speak of him?"

"He frightens me. The whole situation frightens me. When I think how close I came to losing my reputation...hurting Pierre... father...it frightens me."

"You've done the right thing, I understand everything now.

So will father."

"No! No!" Frances exclaimed, pulling herself out of her sister's embrace and sitting bolt upright. "I don't want father to know!"

"Why? Why not expose this man for what he is. Why do you want to defend him? After all, who knows how many other young women he is doing this to. Let father quietly deal with him."

Margaret was more privy than Frances to Court gossip, most of which came from her husband. Melbroke was known among the men for his lascivious exploits. Yes, he was strikingly handsome, charming, witty, provocative and sensual in his dealings with women. Many women at Court were 'moistened' by his passing attentions. He cared not if the women were married or not, if they made themselves available he took them.

Margaret's husband William, Lord Runmore and Melbroke were good friends. They had been tutored together as children. They'd learnt the art of the sword, the knife and the shield together. They had fought for the King and in peace were his loyal servants. "He's a law unto himself," William had told Margaret after their betrothal. "He's a good friend to men but not women." His meaning had been clear.

"No! I don't want father knowing, I'm too ashamed," Frances insisted.

Margaret smiled tenderly, she understood, she would say nothing. Frances' wedding was so close, soon she would have a husband to defend her and this situation would quickly slip into murky memory. As a nearby church bell chimed the eight o'clock they headed for food, both starving, both hoping the innkeeper had kept something for them.

THEIR CORNER was dingy. Good! The place was packed with noisy drinkers, some already drunk, some looking for trouble. Swirls of smoke from the fire lingered in low corners and the stench of beer hit the back of their throats. Apart from the inn's serving wenches, Frances and Margaret were the only women there and the dark corner gave them cover.

Recognizing they were Ladies it was with over-egged courtesy that the innkeeper had escorted them to their table, adjusted their chairs and changed the smelly tallow candle for beeswax. Their choice of food was jugged hare, spit-roasted chicken or pigeon stew, all left over from midday. A basket of chunky home-made bread greeted them. They hoped they could eat unnoticed. Sadly not.

Many eyes immediately sought them out. Men jostled and nudged each other as heads turned to stare. Crabby faces, tired and lined from the hard lives their owners' lived, suddenly sparkled. Blank expressions became leers. Bent backs straightened and eyes roved. One man in particular was making Frances uneasy. He was tall, bulky, in rags and with a long woollen scarf wrapped around his head, the end secured across his face so that only his piercing eyes were showing. He was set apart from the others, they either didn't know him or didn't want to. He was standing in a corner, a long staff propped by his side. He seemed unable to take his eyes off her.

They ate ravenously, the ride had worked up an appetite and they were part way through when the ragman headed in their direction, leering and mumbling under his breath. As he passed their table he stumbled and fell on to Margaret, rocking the table and spilling the wine. The innkeeper rushed to assist, swore at the man and in no genteel manner shoved him ceremoniously out of the rear door, his long staff flying out after him.

"Drunk! He be a stranger to these parts Ladies, no idea who the scoundrel be," apologized the landlord, shooting the bolts so the troublemaker couldn't creep back in.

"That's it," said Margaret, "back to our room. Now!" She quickly spooned the remains of her stew and was up from her chair and away before Frances could quite finish hers. Up a steep flight of wooden stairs, across a landing, up a second flight and back into the privacy she yearned. Frances hurried just a few steps behind, a chunk of gravy-soaked bread in her hand.

Margaret wedged a chair under the handle of the bedroom door and begged God to allow morning to come with no further incidence. They removed their top coats, riding hats and boots and agreed that was all they would remove. Frances, the first to clamber under the feather-filled coverlet, felt calm and confident. She had put a good few miles between herself and Melbroke. She was being the logical, commonsensical young woman her father would be proud of - whether he'd be proud of the situation she found herself in was another matter.

The sisters lay hand in hand in their strange room, miles from all whom they knew and trusted. Frances listened to the sound of the strong wind, of the tree branches knocking at the window, of a fiddler playing a haunting melody somewhere in the distance, of the rhythm of the tip-tapping rain on the window. Margaret was more concerned about the perils that surrounded them: the lusty eyes, the raucous noise, the miles ahead, the strange taste in her mouth and the growing discomfort in her stomach.

MELBROKE WAS always an early riser, the next morn had been even earlier than usual. With the first crack of light in a heavy, iron sky that hovered low over Richmond he'd sort comfort in the freedom of fresh air. Still irritable, still unable to accept rejection, he'd ignored the food his servants had prepared and headed out into the Palace grounds. Another cold morn. A bitter wind tore off the Thames, a flurry of snow blew into his face. Only those that had to be were out this early. He'd gathered his long fur-lined coat around him, pulled the fur collar up around his neck and braced his hatted-head into the wind.

As always the Palace at dawn had been busy. Chamber servants were lighting fires, preparing hot water. Kitchen staff, who had been baking bread by torch light, were now slicing meats for breakfast as dawn cracked into life. Butter was being churned, milk strained. For the midday meal pastry was already being rolled, pies mixed, meats into roast, pots on to stew. King Henry and his Court were big eaters!

Melbroke was hardly noticed as, for a second time in less than twelve hours, he'd wended his way back to Frances' private apartment. He wanted answers! His pride had been affronted but he was also aware of a feeling of unease that was shadowing him. Again her rooms had been empty.

Now he was strolling through the Palace yard, a sagging, sullen sky above and disappointment near-mastering him. It wasn't an emotion he was familiar with. He scolded himself. Dwell upon it he would not!

A stream of horse-drawn carts trundled past, their clatter breaking into his rambling thoughts. They were bringing daily provisions to the Palace: hay for the horses, fresh milk from the herds that roamed the surrounding pastures, casks of wine, cages of wild geese and duck still flapping and quacking their anger and fear.

Out-staff from the nearby hovels were heading in. Charmaids, washerwomen, general labourers, gardeners. All dodging carts and horses' soil as their meagrely-clad feet trod the rock-hard mud. Men shouted and marshals barked orders, their bone whistles blasting to maintain some kind of order amidst chaos. The sweet-sour smell of dung pervaded.

Gingerly Melbroke pushed through the pandemonium and made for the Thames that skirted the Palace and churned like a grey-brown snake as it went about its business. This cold morn it looked threatening and powerful, a mist still clinging to it like a thin, mean, shroud. 'Twas where he oft went to think, to mull, to clear his thoughts.

He was just edging his way around the back of a rattling ass-drawn cart when two scruffy men barged into him. Suddenly fists and feet were flying. A blow to his abdomen, another to his side, a kick to his shin but the men weren't trained fighters, their blows winded but didn't injure.

He landed hefty return blows and managed to prise from his chest the cur that seemed hellbent on attaching himself to his person. He grabbed his shoulders and tossed him to one side. As quickly as it started so it ended. The two attackers scampered away, darting between passers-by who hadn't even noticed.

"God rot 'em! Rot 'em," the waggoner growled. "You 'urt m'Lord?"

"No...thank you." Melbroke stood bent, hands on his knees, catching his breath. "Did you get a look at them?"

"No, I didn't, m'Lord. All happened so quick. And look," he said, pointing to one of the cart's wheels, "broken, split down the middle, must 'ave landed it an almighty kick."

"Probably meant for my shin! Damn their eyes," he cursed. He brushed himself down and fumbled for a coin. "Here take this, get the wheel mended."

"That's mighty generous but t'wasn't your doing, me Lord."

"Mayhap not but for some reason I was the target, not you."

Melbroke strolled away from the cacophony to his favourite stone bench. What on earth was that all about! The day was brightening but still bitterly cold. The frost had left its freshness, the air off the river was cool and clean. He sucked his grazed knuckles, cursed the clay-brains that caused them and stretched his arms upwards as he faced the weak sun that was now penetrating the cloud. A watery golden disc it may be, spring's new-born sun as the crones would say but his face could feel a little of its tender warmth and his flattened spirits were being seduced just a little by its cheer.

This time next week he'd be in France. He was looking forward to the freedom of the sea crossing, the excursion into a different culture, the chance to practise his French. Getting away from the strictures and formalities of Court life every so often suited him. He would immerse himself for a month in the King's affairs, ask the questions the King needed answers to, do his duty. With that done mayhap he would stay even longer. There would be good food and wine, re-aquaintance with old friends and some new women to tumble. Hell's teeth Melbroke, he chided himself silently as he sat watching the sun reluctantly shine upon Surrey, why are you so bothered about the Lady of bloody Blean.

Chapter Three

THE VOICE WAS strange to him. "Lord Melbroke, I believe," it said, its owner lifting his hat as he bowed low, allowing its flighty feathers to sweep the ground. His hose clinging to boney legs. His dainty, ladylike, free hand flicking the air in deference as he bowed.

Melbroke reluctantly rose from his riverine bench. "You are correct my Lord, may I assist?" This intruder was an extra irritant to his bad humour. He had wanted to sit alone, think about the attack, divert his aches to the pleasures of his upcoming French foray. He managed a smile.

"I am Pierre, Marquis de Champagne. Bonjour. We have never met but I know of you, my Lord, of your esteemed position in Court." He was bowing again. His English perfect with not a hint of a French accent.

"And I of you Lord Pierre. Please, sit for a moment," Melbroke said, indicating the bench. "'Tis a good spot, you can see the comings and goings of the Palace, I often come here."

Hell's blood, Melbroke was thinking, this is what Frances will marry! A boy of a man! Disbelief soared through him, he wouldn't linger upon it, the situation demanded politeness. "My belated congratulations on your betrothal."

"Thank you. Yes, the wedding is only four weeks now." The Marquis sat, hugging himself with a fur-lined cloak which swamped him, emphasizing his willowy thinness.

They were closer now and Melbroke could better see the young face. The eyes were permanently startled, the lips just thin colourless lines on a face that was pale, cold and apart from a long pointed nose was uncannily featureless. A man in age mayhap, it was difficult to age him, there was no sign of a need to shave. His skin was soft, his cheeks flat, his chin dimpled. He ventured: "Have you seen Lady Frances this morning?"

"No. I have only just arrived from France. I escorted my mother to England...for the wedding you understand."

"She's in the Palace now?"

"No, she stays with her sister in the Manor at Mortlake. She will be staying for the summer. She is English, my father died last year, I look after her now."

In the flimsy cheer of the weak spring sun they watched the busy river with its continual, endless string of boats bringing passengers, goods and messages from Greenwich, Westminster, Hampton Court and beyond. The Marquis was fidgety, Melbroke noted his ill-ease. A rash of skiffs jostled. Wherries with their short sails now strapped to stubby masts, bobbed around wooden jetties as the watermen, just some of the thousands who plied the river, waited to deliver their cargo. Strong arms and legs resting after hours of rowing. Heads lolling forward in weariness. Lamps that lit the way in the darkness now extinguished and needing fresh oil. Spent, like their owners.

"I thought to take a boat from Mortlake." Pierre broke the silence with a slight giggle. "Until my mother gave me the gifts she has brought for their Majesties." A broad boyish grin swept his face. "I needed a carriage, they were too much for a boat, it would have sunk I think." He laughed childishly. Melbroke made the gesture and smiled. His thoughts were all of Frances, he cared not about gifts nor boats. It wasn't his place to tell the lad that his betrothed appeared to have vanished from before nine o'clock last night and anyway how could he explain he knew that! "I expect you will be going to Lady Frances soon?"

"She usually rides in the mornings, I will see her later. I have an audience with His Majesty...to give him the presents...my first, I am a little worried." His pale cheeks lifted in a brief, tortured attempt at a nervous smile.

It was Melbroke's cue to give a few tips on how to deal with his cousin but it wasn't the King who was on his mind. "Lady Frances, is a good horsewoman?"

"O yes, excellent. Better than me. I was sickly when I was young, my parents were very protective of me, I never really took to horses. I am forced by circumstance to use them but never out of choice."

"But you joust?"

"Good Lord no! Don't even like to watch. Too violent."

Inwardly Melbroke groaned. "Are you also nervous about the wedding?"

"A little but Frances and I are good friends."

"She's a beautiful woman, you are a lucky man."

"She is? You think so? We have got to know each other well over the past year, we have become good friends, that is what matters to me. My mother has grown to love her, she says she is right for me, I believe her."

Dismay rose in Melbroke's throat threatening to choke him. In four weeks this boy would have free rein over Frances' body. Had he truly not noticed how lovely she is? Had he not traced her curves in his mind's eye, not imagined what touching her would be like? Was he really not lusting after her? He believed he knew the answers. No times four.

He had, though, revealed a clue. She is an excellent horsewoman and was probably now out riding. That, though, would not account for her absence last night. Where did she go? And why did he care!

Melbroke, lost in his thoughts for a few seconds, was suddenly aware of the French Lord's piercing eyes upon him. The space between them had changed. Become icy. The eyes stayed steady, staring, as he turned to meet them. They held his gaze, looking straight at him, into him, rigid and unblinking. In an instant the mood had turned sour. The innocent face had turned into a sly, lupine mask. A strange mocking twist played on the Marquis' mean mouth.

"Look what I just found," he said cockily, drawing Melbroke's attention to a gold, pocket sundial that snuggled in his dainty, cupped hand. He stared at Melbroke, all sign of courtesy gone. His face and voice suddenly harsh, hinting at danger. "Some whoreson must have dropped it. Who would do such a stupid thing d'you suppose?"

Melbroke recognized it immediately. A gift to his father from his mother on their tenth wedding anniversary. He had inherited it upon his father's death and kept it with him always. He most certainly had not dropped it.

"'Tis mine, my Lord."

"You may make that claim but is it true?" A contemptuous sneer settled across the Marquis' face. "You could, after all, be claiming something that isn't yours. Are you? Do you do that sort of thing, my O so noble Lord?"

Melbroke stiffened his back. "I don't lie! If you look on the back you will find ten small diamonds sunk into the base."

The French Lord turned it over. "You are correct. It would seem you have identified your property. Such a beautiful piece, so delicate," he sneered, locking Melbroke's eyes, daring him to look away. A harsh sneer played around cold, penetrating eyes revealing an unexpected side to this flimsy man. There was menace in his voice and contempt in his gaze. "It deserves to be better looked after, wouldn't you say?" He waited for an answer, none came. Melbroke was taking his time, assessing both man and situation. "A man might kill to own something as beautiful as this. Almost as precious as a beautiful woman, wouldn't you say?"

Hostility pervaded, all civility gone. "My sundial, if you please," Melbroke demanded, extending his hand. Without taking his eyes from Melbroke's the Frenchman tossed it into the air, making sure it hit ground not hand. Thud!

"So careless," the Frenchman tutted. He leant inwards toward Melbroke's face, his eyes still icy and now far too close. "I would kill whoever took something as beautiful as this from me," he hissed.

Melbroke could smell the garlicky breath but he didn't move. Anger was claiming his spine. Clearly the varmints had picked his pocket during the melee by the cart. Dropping it was a bit careless if they were thieves. Or had someone paid them to rob him? This French Lord mayhap? Questions but no answers and he certainly wasn't about to discuss anything with this unpleasant stick of a man. The chapel bell rang out the seven o'clock and broke the sinister spell between them.

"I hope you will excuse me," Melbroke said, rising from

the bench, "I have arranged to meet a friend, I should be on my way." He lied but it was a good excuse.

VOMITING, OR rather, trying not to, was all that was on Margaret's mind when she awoke the next morning in Greenwich. Her night had been fitful. Her stomach ached, her head throbbed, her body shook. All still did. Outside the window there was banging and men's raised voices. Horses whickered, cartwheels grated, whips cracked. New stocks for a new day. Next to her the bed was empty. Frances had gone ahead to break her fast, unaware of her sister's uncomfortable night so deeply had she slept.

Back at last night's corner table but this time in the shaft of weak morning sunlight, Frances ate lightly and alone. Last night's fire-smoke still hung in the corners, tiny open windows did little to bring in fresh air and the place was stuffy and stale. Empty too, with only a cleaner's humming breaking the musty silence.

Her appetite was minimal and she couldn't face the thick porridge of vegetables and beans, nor the heavy, brown bread. She drank some whey and picked at a boiled hen's egg. Eager to get back on the highway she gathered up some food for Margaret to eat in their room, took bread and cheese for their journey and returned back up the narrow wooden staircases. What she found shocked her.

Margaret was on the side of the bed being sick into the wash bowl. She was clutching her stomach. "Frances I feel terrible. I'm shaking, my head is pounding. I can't continue our journey, I am too ill."

Frances concentrated on compassion but with difficulty. It would be too self-centred to dwell on how their travelling plans would be affected but in shameful truth that was uppermost in her mind. "Don't worry," she managed to say. "We will rest here for a few hours. You are over tired, mayhap we rode too hard yesterday, we obviously over did it."

Margaret tried to smile, her hands rubbing her tender stomach. Mayhap Frances was right, mayhap not. Frances suggested brandy, Margaret declined. She did though want a lackey to get the fire going again. "I'm cold to my bones, I need some warmth." She pulled the feather coverlet around her shaking shoulders.

Frances yanked dry straw out of the mattress, stirred the embers with the long poker until sparks showed themselves and used the straw to tease them into flames. Logs atop and the fire was soon roaring in the grate.

"Exactly where did you learn to do that?"

"I've watched the servants," Frances replied, wiping the dirt from her hands. "It pays not to be completely helpless." Frances closed the flimsy curtain. "Rest now, dear sister. I will tell the innkeeper you are not to be disturbed and then I shall check on our horses."

FRANCES HEADED for Greenwich market. It was alive, noisy, its colour and confusion exciting. Servants did her shopping and anyway her father would never permit she frequent such places. "Full of wolves," he'd bark, meaning the cutpurses, drunks, tricksters and worse. If she had to fill a few hours while Margaret rested, then at least this place was entertaining.

Here, in this throb of life, nobility and peasants mingled. Rich and poor shared rare space. Gentlemen and merchants bartered. Stallholders who travelled from one market town to another nestled aside locals. Many had money aplenty, others had spent last night poaching duck, hedgehog, badger for the chance to make a few coins. They risked death if they were caught; judged by those who bought from them.

Beggars loitered, some maimed from birth, some victims of soldiering for their monarch. Frances stepped around and over them, trying to avoid their eyes. They were a pitiful sight among the counters loaded with beef, crane, boar and other mouth-watering offerings they could never afford.

In the muddle of the crowd her attention was caught by a huge hand coming down upon a small child. They were huddled in a corner. The large broad back, rounded by life and belonging to a brute of a man, almost hid the girl. No more than twelve years of age she had a flock of pale hair and eyes the colour of honey. She stood flattened against the wall, her chin rigid. The man was angry, red-faced, remonstrating. His slaps drew neither tear nor whimper. Even her passivity angered him. He yanked at the rope he'd tethered to her wrist and whipped her legs with its loose end. Still no response. The girl seemed immune to feeling.

A small man with greasy, grey hair and filthy hands, the worse for ale and looking for a bargain, punched a coin into the big man's hand. It was less than a man would usually have to pay but the girl had riled her owner. He looked at the coin, spat on the floor and relinquished the rope. The small man tugged and the girl followed mutely.

Frances groaned, her eyes unable to leave the girl as her small back disappeared into a dingy alley. For several seconds Frances' attention was not on her own steps and she bumped into the corner of a stall specializing in all things feathered. A large, hanging swan knocked her shoulder, the weight of it surprised her and she would have stumbled but for the strong hand suddenly about her elbow.

It was a rat catcher, she'd noticed him earlier, ambling

between the stalls, his head and face wrapped in a long, woollen scarf against the cold. His eyes, peering through a slit in the scarf, were permanently looking down. He steadied her step, averting his gaze from hers. Silently he brushed two white feathers from her shoulder. It unnerved her, she pulled away and he released his grip. He moved off, a dozen or so dead bodies dancing from his staff in rhythm with his step. His staff boasted his busy morning but he wanted more. No one acknowledged him, ignored by all except the rats who scurried.

She continued on, her eyes caught by sellers of beer, besoms, salt, herbs, spices. The world, it seemed, had come to Greenwich bringing its exotic smells with it. The place filled her senses: its noise, aromas, abundance, poverty. She threw one man a coin, his filthy gnarled hands grabbed at it. The smell of him wafted around her and she turned quickly away, her gaze falling again on the rat catcher. He'd followed her. His eyes, still peering though the scarf's protection, were now staring straight at her. She gasped as suddenly she realized it was the man at the inn last night, the one that bumped into their table. He nodded cockily, knowing she now recognized him. He bowed in mockery, his dead rats swinging. She shuddered, averted her eyes and walked on.

She comforted her hands around a warmed beer while pondering a newly-thought problem. Swan might well be bought by servants from Greenwich Palace and mayhap someone would recognize her. She had stayed at Greenwich many times with Queen Katherine, she didn't want to be spotted by wagging tongues! The privacy of the inn called.

THE NEWS ricocheted through Frances like a pick through ice. "We'll have to go back," Margaret said, as soon as Frances entered their room. "I can't continue on, I'm too weak."

Frances had no intentions of returning to Richmond Palace, it was an impossible thing to ask and suddenly the panic of yesterday was back. To travel on alone would be better than returning, protective Margaret wouldn't like it but that was exactly what she would now have to do.

"I'll speak to the landlord, he may have a carriage we can hire," she said. "You set about preparing yourself."

Her heart was beating fast. She was about to behave in an appalling way, she would not be proud but it had to be done. Fate for a second time had placed her in a situation from which she had to extricate herself and yet again she would have to call upon her inner strength.

The innkeeper was prepared to loan his carriage so long as it was returned on the morrow but was less happy about losing Ned his stable lad to drive it. Frances' coins soothed his reluctance. Noon was fast approaching as she helped Margaret into the carriage, tucked a blanket around her legs, kissed her on the cheek and quickly stepped back on to the cobbles.

"Frances, what are you doing, where are you going?"

Frances prayed that her sister's natural decorum and desire not to make a scene in public would prevail. "I am not returning with you. I'm sorry but I cannot. You know why, you know..." Her eyes appealed to her sister whose wan face was now etched with concern

"Frances," she snapped, "get straight back into this carriage."

Frances shook her head. "You know I cannot sister, you know the position I am in."

Margaret, too weak to argue, managed one final command. "Frances, you wait here today, keep to your room. I shall send

William to escort you on to father's. Do you hear..."

The horses were pulling away. Frances could see the anxiety on Margaret's face. "I hear sister...I hear." She didn't like deceiving but events had conspired around her and she must do what was necessary. She had no intention of wasting time in Greenwich. She would hit the highway as soon as she'd paid the bill. She was alone now. The lanes and tracks to deepest Kent lay before her. The saying 'needs must when the devil drives' came to mind. She shuddered as if someone had walked over her grave. She knew exactly who 'the devil' was and right now she hated him.

A VOICE rang out as 'the devil' made his way across the central Palace courtyard. "Well met Alban. All well with you?" Melbroke turned on the spot to find William, Lord Runmore, just a few paces behind. The two men embraced. Strong arms around strong shoulders, equal in build and stature, both fighting men, both now with friendship lighting up their faces. "Well met, Will, wonderful to see you. You've been away...up North was it?" His deep chestnut eyes met Will's bright hazel.

"Yes, up North, four very long weeks, just got back, about an hour ago." Tiredness etched his face but mainly Melbroke saw anxiety.

"Everything all right, Will?"

"Not sure. Got this note," he said, waving it in the air, "it concerns me." Runmore turned on his heel and bid Melbroke join him in his rooms. William and Margaret's apartment was on the sunny side of the Palace and impressive. Eight rooms including a nursery for their one-year-old. It was at a musical evening here that Melbroke's eyes and lust had first settled upon Frances. His attraction had been immediate. He'd struggled for some time about the civility of pursuing his friend's sister-in-law but in the end lust became a craving which became larger than he could control and he had tossed courtesy aside.

William's servants had prepared a fine midday meal on a large table by the window. The two men ate well, exchanging their news between mouthfuls of jellied meat and salted fish. Eventually Melbroke asked: "So, Will, what's this note that causes such concern?"

"I may be overreacting, I'm not sure. 'Tis from Margaret. Her maid had been instructed to give it to me immediately upon my return."

"And?"

"You know her sister, Frances, marries in a few weeks?"

"I can hardly not, everywhere I go people are discussing the implications of the two families uniting."

"Politics! I keep well away," Will interrupted, squinting his eyes as an unexpected burst of sun pierced through the window, lighting up his short, fair hair. He broke a large chunk of crusty bread and dipped into freshly churned, soft butter. "My loyalty is to His Majesty, I care for little else."

Melbroke grinned as he nodded agreement. The King despised sycophants but demanded subservient loyalty. He and Will walked the divide uncannily well. He knocked his goblet against Will's.

"Margaret writes that she and Frances have gone to their father, near Canterbury, 'twas urgent. Complications with the nuptials, apparently. Says she will explain everything more fully when she sees me."

She's what! Melbroke swallowed his shock and maintained disinterested calm. "So? What's wrong with that?"

"I also returned to a letter from her father, going over

various wedding loose ends, no hint from the Earl of problems. On the contrary, all the plans seemed to be going perfectly well."

"Strange?"

"Plus, he's a very polite man, do you know the Earl?"

"Of him yes but never met him." Melbroke broke into a fresh pot of brawn.

"He's an absolute stickler for manners and correct procedure. He would never usurp my position as husband, he would have asked me if Margaret could return to Canterbury. He's that courteous. And why didn't she take her maid?"

"And you glean from all this?"

"The note doesn't ring true. It concerns me, something's not right about it."

Melbroke quaffed the last of his wine, slammed his napkin on the table, pushed back his chair. He, of course, knew exactly what was wrong with it. It was a pack of untruths. The Earl hadn't summoned Frances, she'd fled, run away from him, taken her sister as company. Why? Why are women so contrary!

"Right," he said, "the first thing we must do is go to the mews and find out when they took their carriage."

RUNMORE'S FACE noticeably ashened on discovering his wife had left with no carriage, no servant, no male escort, no protection. She and her sister had left alone and on horseback. In the stables and as the head groom answered his questions, Will paced in anguish. Melbroke shuffled guiltily. Hell's teeth, both men were thinking, any manner of rogue haunts the highway. What are they doing!

"There's only one course of action," Will eventually said, his hands on his hips, his forehead lined in crippling puzzlement. "I must go after them."

Melbroke's heart sunk. Will was right and while it was the last thing he needed, he couldn't let his friend go alone. While Will was anxious, Melbroke was angry. The Blean woman was proving to be too much trouble but he'd see to his honour and support his friend.

"They've got a near-day's start," said Will, "mayhap I'll never catch them."

"Yes, you will or rather we will. I'm coming with you." Will opened his mouth to argue, Melbroke raised a hand. "No arguing, I'm coming. And anyway, they are women, they ride slower than us, they would only have ridden for a few hours yesterday afternoon, they would have tired quickly. We can ride all day. I take it you know the route to Canterbury that they'd have taken?" William nodded.

Melbroke, with great inner reluctance, turned to the groom. "Prepare our horses for a speedy departure, we must leave immediately."

William's hands went to his head in anguish. "Damn! Damn! I can't! I've been summoned by the King, I've to see him today, to talk about my Northern trip." His face was contorted with tortuous pain.

Melbroke slapped his friend's shoulder. "Don't worry. I'll go straight away, you follow as soon as you can." The two men embraced. "It'll be all right Will, we'll catch them." Failure didn't even cross his mind. He couldn't leave his friend's wife in such a perilous situation. As to the other woman, he'd have a few well-chosen words for her!

THE GROOM walked Melbroke's stallion out of the stable. He was an impressive beast and was lifting his hooves in happy anticipation of his outing. He was tall at seventeen hands, strong, powerful, black as jet. He loved galloping, he loved cross country and his brave temperament suited his owner perfectly. Galahad and Melbroke were made for each other.

Melbroke knew as he mounted that he wasn't dressed for riding. His silk shirt, its pleated collar and fancy cuffs, his velvet doublet, were completely unsuitable. He'd even left his fur-lined coat in William's apartment so had no extra warmth for what would be a long ride. He wasn't though, about to waste time changing. He pushed his velvet hat into the front of his doublet and tightened the chord holding back his thick, brown hair. He beamed a reassuring smile to Will and waved a hand in farewell. Inside he was fuming. Couldn't remember when he'd last gone into Kent, nor when he'd even wanted to.

"I'll be right behind you...as soon as I've seen the King," William called. "God give you good speed."

Melbroke tapped his heals on Galahad's sides and they were off. He too had upcoming business with the King who wanted to see him before his departure to France. He'd got to be back at the Palace within forty-eight hours. He'd got to get this Blean business sorted and sorted quickly. He and Galahad must fly like the wind.

As Galahad got into his stride Melbroke realized that he was actually frightened for Frances. Margaret too but it was Frances' face that filled his mind's eye. Damn the woman! She'd done to him what he'd done to her – she'd aroused feeling that he wasn't used to. Damn you Frances, Lady of Blean.

Chapter Four

NOT LONG AFTER his 1509 coronation Henry, the eighth of that name, then 17 now 23, had sent out an edict that the nation's iron production should be increased. His father, Henry VII, had lived haunted by the ongoing hatred that seeped into his reign following thirty years of the Plantagenet Wars. The red rose against the white had racked the nation, slaughtered much of the aristocracy and ended when some 28,000 men fought on an open field in Leicestershire one summer morning in 1485. Two hours of fierce battle which ended by noon saw England's future change as the rebel army of Lancastrian Henry Tudor took the Crown from Yorkist Richard III at the Battle of Bosworth.

That Henry had set about re-uniting the nation, including marrying Elizabeth of York, niece of Richard, the man he had beaten at Bosworth and whose crown he had stolen. The union in effect united the red and white roses but anger, hatred and claims that he was a usurper with no right to the Crown, abounded.

England was not a contended place. That Henry was always looking behind.

Young Henry's birth, six years later, of a Lancastrian father and Yorkist mother helped heal the nation and his coronation on that happy June day, when he paraded with his Spanish wife, Katherine, by his side, was a new beginning for the monarchy and for England. The astrologers predicted a caring king, sensitive but strong-willed and protective of his people and his country.

Henry VIII didn't have to look inward or backward as his father had. This Henry had his eyes trained outside of England and he wanted to make the English throne the most respected and influential in Europe. He was concerned, therefore, that the nation's arsenal was running low.

His elder sister Margaret might well be the widow of one Scottish king and mother of another but that hadn't made the Scots a friendly nation and just across the Channel there was hostile France. He'd already been at war with them for two years, Scotland had sided with the enemy and had invaded northern England knowing the English army, with its King, was elsewhere engaged. It was only the Earl of Surrey's quick command of the situation, his raising of an army and support from the Regent Katherine, that saved the day and made a widow of Henry's sister. Henry was already thinking the Scots had got to be ruled by England.

More cannon was needed, more swords, more daggers, more armour, knives, halberds, shields, chains, nails, pike blades, more horse and wagon paraphernalia. More of everything made of iron that regiments of Foot and Horse needed. Production must be increased. The Weald of the South was proving to be fertile ground.

It was with this in mind that the Earl of Blean, a Lancastrian supporter during the Wars and now an ardent supporter of the young Henry had diverted his interests into iron and was today making a visit to his first works near Grinstead.

"How are your bones, m'Lord?" Bellowes was steadying the horse for the Earl's dismount. As the work's founder, Bellowes was the man in charge. He hired, fired, supervised and harangued. He kept the furnace burning and he met production deadlines. He made sure the works made a profit. It was this that the Earl was here to check.

"Aching as usual. Me spine's collapsing, me buttocks numb, me clothes mud-splattered, me stomach empty. Age is catching up. These monthly visits are becoming a nightmare."

"Your stomach, m'Lord, we can do something about." Bellowes smiled as he tied up the horse and led the Earl into his office where beer and food had been set out on a covered trestle alongside the books and ledgers the Earl had come to inspect. The linen table cloth and matching napkins were an idiosyncratic touch of elegance in this otherwise spartan world and had been provided by the founder's beloved wife, who'd also put the food hamper together.

The office was a wooden structure, rain and windproof but cold, bare and uninviting. Comfort did not exist in this place, not even for Bellowes. Most of his men either worked outdoors in all weathers or close to the lethal heat of the furnace and molten ore. Men dug wide shafts by hand and pickaxe, going deeper and deeper as the iron called them downwards. Ladders were propped against steep, deepening walls and the diggers moved up and down with baskets of heavy ore. From daylight and fresh air they descended to gloomy staleness some twenty-five feet below. Their legs were strong, their feet agile on the ladder, their hands callused from friction and toil as they smashed the earth to reveal the treasure they were after, the pick of the axe continually landing perilously close to their scantily protected feet.

Above ground the iron ore was roasted on burning logs to prepare it for the furnace which roared day and night from October to the end of April, sometimes even into May. The burning pervaded the works, its smoke, its sootiness, its smell. It was a hard place to labour, dangerous and dirty but it was a new industry. It was the start of a golden age. The King wanted it for it had the potential to make England mightier. Swathes of Kent and Sussex were believed to be full of iron ore, getting it out of the ground was the new mission. Only a few iron works were already functioning and the Earl had plans to open his second very soon.

"We've had a good month since last we met, m'Lord." Bellowes felt proud as, alongside an Earl, he took of his own midday repast. He was an overweight but refined man, careful in his manners but years with iron had blackened his hands, its brand upon him now so entrenched in the creases that no amount of scrubbing by his beloved could rid its ownership of him.

"So I see...yes, I see," the Earl grunted between long gulps of beer as he flicked over the pages. He used his cuff to wipe his mouth. "I needed that, most welcome." Bellowes pushed some food in the Earl's direction, along with a napkin. "Should make a handsome profit. Keep this up and there'll be another bonus at the end of the year. You're doing well." Two complimentary whacks descended upon the founder's back; his stomach and chins wobbled.

Bellowes was pleased but not taken aback. He'd grown used to the Earl's generosity. He'd never been treated so well by any other employer. Yes, the Earl barked at folk, was irascible, demanding, never shied at pulling rank but was always fair and honest. It would do Bellowes.

"This profit will go towards reimbursing what I've invested on the Blean estate," the Earl said, chewing on a cold cutlet. "Cost me a lot of money, hell of a lot but if it produces returns like this I shall be mightily pleased." He pushed his silver hair off his face and reached out for more meat. In a minute he would turn his eyes to the crusty sweet pies.

ALMOST AS soon as Frances rode away from Greenwich light rain appeared as if a phantom from what had been a perfectly cloudless sky earlier in the day. She wouldn't let it dictate to her, she decided. Truth was she had no choice. Keep riding and get damp; shelter and lose time. She chose the former.

She was a mix of emotions. Thrilled to be back on the road, every one of Lunar's strides taking her a little closer to her home but anxious, too. She was alone now. Lunar was noticeably not as sprightly as she had been. She wasn't picking up her hooves in her usual high fashion and the prospect of rain making the roads under-hoof even muddier was worrying. Her only companions were hope and commonsense. She had plenty of both but was praying for luck, too.

A monk, in a long white habit, his face obscured by a deep-pointed hood, had bid her 'safe travel' as she'd left the inn. He was from a silent order, just one of thousands of pilgrims who trod the route from London to Canterbury every year. He had scribbled "God bless you both" on a slate and made the sign of the cross on Lunar's muzzle before striding out, strong and erect, his walking pole slamming purposefully into the ground as he'd waved goodbye. His strength and calm had strangely reassured her; made her feel less alone.

About halfway to Rochester the spasmodic showers turned into persistent sleety rain. The wind was biting, a bitter air pierced her nostrils. Almost instantly she became very wet and very cold.

Lunar was suffering in conditions she wasn't used to and was being unco-operative. Frances pulled her to a halt by a stream but the horse refused to drink. She was used to palace rain water that was collected in huge barrels. She took against the fast-running stream and reared away. Her hooves were caked in mud, she was tired and fractious. "There, there girl. We'll get you some lovely oats at Rochester and rain water. I promise."

In typical spring fashion the clouds cleared and the sun returned. She removed her wet riding coat and laid it over a field gate to dry. A nearby oak offered a dry patch under its spreading branches, she sat down, opened the linen parcel that contained her cheese and broke her bread. She drank a little from her wineskin. Now she was more worried about Lunar than herself. She was only used to short canters around Richmond Palace, she had never spent so long on the open road and there was still plenty of that ahead of them.

Truth is, she mused angrily, it doesn't matter how intelligent you are, or how much commonsense you are blessed with, if you embark upon something you've never done before then you can't foretell the problems that may arise. She wished she had though, for now she was guilt-ridden as well as wet and miserable.

When she returned to the gate to fetch her riding coat it had gone. The shoulder bag she'd hung on the gate's post had also gone. Alarm grabbed her stomach. She looked around her, the lane was empty, not a soul in sight. "They can't have walked away," she groaned out loud to the air.

With dismay consuming her she refilled her water-skin from the stream and remounted a very irritable horse. Together they journeyed on, slowly but purposefully with Frances constantly leaning forward to whisper re-assurance into Lunar's ear. For a few miles they travelled through thick trees that gave them protection and for a while optimism returned. It didn't last. As they put the wooded area behind them and turned into open country so the heavens opened again, this time with vengeance. March it seemed was even angrier than usual. This time it was torrential rain that fell, each drop icy cold, stabbing her face like hailstones. Within minutes her riding gown was soaked and Lunar again distressed.

The wind blew up as if from nowhere, played games until it had stolen her hat and snatched away the net that secured her hair. Very quickly long bedraggled strands of what were usually golden tresses were whipping around her face like rope. She looked around, there was no shelter, she would have to press on. Lunar whinnied and bucked, it took all of Frances' strength to control her and all her skill to remain mounted.

Another mile farther and Lunar stopped. Refused to go another step. She ignored Frances' encouraging words. Just stopped. Her hooves were as if nailed to the ground. Frances dismounted and stood beside her. The ground was now a rider's nightmare. Deep, sticky mud squelched under foot and hoof. Chances are Lunar felt unsafe. Frances led her to the lee of a tatty, long-forgotten haystack and together they stood and waited for the heavens to quieten.

As far as she could recall she had never been out in such cruel weather. Never felt so exposed and frightened. She watched the hard, relentless drops as they struck tree and leaf and earth. Their rhythm like a relentless drum pounding out a pending doom. She watched the puddles getting deeper with stormy tops and splitting sides. Was this how Noah felt? Did he peer from his ark and wonder if it would ever stop?

Never had she felt so lonely, so abandoned by life, so full of hate for one person who right at this moment she wished the full wrath of hell would descend upon. Little did she know that as she cursed him he was galloping toward Greenwich. She turned her thoughts to Pierre. Kind, considerate, Pierre. The man whom she had discovered over the past year was a perfect gentleman. He had never treated her with disrespect. He would make a good husband and father. He pleased her heart, he didn't excite it but she could see that life with him would be secure and safe. If this is excitement, she thought, I can do without it.

Horse and owner stood for what seemed an age. Frances kept her arms around Lunar's neck, stroked her strong muscles and whispered calming words in her ear. The two of them were bitterly cold and deflated. When eventually the wind subsided and the rain eased they set off at a gentle trot, Frances unaware that with every second she'd dallied Melbroke was getting closer.

On a good day her back ached, her knees throbbed, her ageing hands stiffened. On a bad day her pains kept her abed. Today was a good day. She thanked the Lord for allowing her to experience suffering and asked Him for help in her struggle with self pity.

When Sister Magdala first started growing herbs she had a small patch, about twelve feet square, now it was huge. What had started as an interest was now an obligation, one that Mother Superior Esme resented and used against her whenever she had the chance. Magdala had carved an important niche for herself in the convent; Esme felt it undermined her authority.

At first her herbs kept Magdala sane, helped quell her mind from its rages, helped give some creativity to the repetitive religious order. Now they were her reason for being. She gave them her body, her energy, her love and some of her soul. Most of the latter two she tried to give to Jesus but it was a struggle. She hadn't been a willing nun and her relationship with our Lord was strained.

She stood up slowly, giving her creaking bones time to renegotiate their upright stance. She rubbed her earthy hands on her long, coarse apron then took them to her lower spine. She allowed her head to fall back and she gazed up at the weak, blue sky. The magnificent vastness of it made her head spin and she allowed her thoughts to travel back to her childhood. She used to gaze at the sky then, find patterns in the clouds, catch the sunbeams. For a second she was back in her father's home, his little girl, so dearly loved.

She was the only one in the herb garden today, usually at least a couple of her dozen-or-so helpers would be with her but a sickness had spread through the nunnery. She had escaped it, most hadn't. Even Mother Esme was being forced to be grateful for the potion the apothecary was giving her that had been made from Magdala's herbs.

Chapter Five

THE SUN HAD long gone by the time Rochester appeared on the horizon. Silent, still and wet the city lay beneath the night sky and never before had Frances been so glad to see habitation. Any moonlight was stolen by heavy icy-rain cloud which hung menacingly above the thatched and slated rooves. Lights were flickering like twinkling stars fallen to Earth and her heart lifted. It was a welcome sight to a rider cold right through, wet and miserable.

The first inn she saw looked reasonably smart, not as dirty or rundown as some and she dismounted with great relief. Her head felt frozen, her wet hair hanging like seaweed, her ears and nose numb, her teeth chattering. She was shivering, bedraggled, exhausted.

"Yep, we got both. Money up front," replied the innkeeper to her request for a room and stabling.

"I will pay when I leave! As is the custom," she retorted, not the least bit in the mood for this man's cheek.

"Up front or yer goes elsewhere." She hadn't the strength to argue so went to Lunar's saddlebags to fetch her money purse. It had gone! She hadn't realized.

"My money...it's been stolen," she gasped in dismay. The innkeeper shrugged. "My coat and bag were stolen some miles back, I didn't realize they'd taken my money, too."

"No money, no room."

"Please, you needn't worry, I am the Earl of Blean's daughter."

"And I's the Holy Roman Emperor," he smirked.

"I do not lie, I am who I say, as soon as I arrive at Blean I will have the money sent to you."

"O yea! 'Tis why yer looks like a drowned rat, yous no money and yers travelling alone. No Lady travels alone luvvie. Now begone wiv yer, I's a busy man."

She struggled to control her emotions, her morale so low it was near impossible. "I do not lie," she implored, "I began my journey with my sister the Lady Runmore, she became ill and could not continue. I've been robbed, my horse is exhausted. Please, you can trust me. I need some help or I fear my horse and I will become ill."

He could see she had genteel hands, he noted her refined accent, her polite turn of phrase, he saw the fine cloth that her now drenched gown was made of. "You can put yer 'orse in the stable and you can stay wiv it. 'Tis best I can offer."

She knew not to argue. She knew not to bother trying other inns, they would all say the same. "Thank you," she said quietly, heavy-heartedly accepting that a stable roof was better than none. She yearned for hot water, a feather bed, hot food, a roaring fire. Not for her though, not now. The day had been as an eternal twilight, its darkness now further deepening. The innkeeper took

Lunar's reins. "Follow me." He led them across a muddy cobbled yard to the stables.

"There's wa'er for the 'orse in there, hay and barley." "Thank you," she said again, desperately hoping he would offer food for her. He did not.

"I wants yer gone by sunrise, d'y'ear me? Gone! Or I'll take yer 'orse as payment."

"Yes," she said quietly. "We'll be gone."

ONE LIT lamp in the stable gave little light. There were no other horses, that at least was a blessing. Her ice-cold fingers struggled to remove Lunar's saddle and bridle. In the corner she found a couple of smelly blankets, she used one to dry off Lunar and the other to wrap around herself. She was just pondering where to lay and sleep, for sleep she sorely needed, when a noise at the door startled her.

"I's the innkeeper's wife, me luv," the rotund woman said, beaming as she entered. "Ignore me 'usband, we've had trav'llers wot cheats us, sez they'll pay la'er, never does. E's a gooden really."

She placed a bowl of hot pottage and some bread atop a bale of hay. "Eat this me luv, 'twill warm yer up. Lady or lackey we can't 'ave yer catching yer death, now can we."

The woman's kindness finally triggered tears. Hot, uncontrollable tears that tumbled down Frances' face. "I'm so sorry," she said, picking up her skirts to wipe them away. "But this has been the worst day of my life."

"Now, now, yer'll be safe in 'ere, no one will bovver yer 'ere." The woman hung another lit lantern on a hook, shadows danced as it swung, adding to the eeriness of the place.

Frances sank atop a pile of bales and surrendered to her emotions. The woman's kindness had overcome her. "Come on girlie, nuffin' can be this bad." She wrapped a chubby arm about Frances' shoulder and rubbed her back.

"O it is. I don't lie, I am who I say. I am travelling to my father's estate near Canterbury. I was chased out of Richmond Palace by a rake who was forcing his attentions upon me. My sister who was accompanying me was taken ill which meant I had to travel on alone. My coat and money were stolen, I lost my hat in the wind, I'm soaked right through and my horse is suffering because of the strain I place upon her. Now I must sleep in a stable."

"O dear missy, we is feelin' sorry for ourselves. Weren't our Lord born in a stable? And don't some folk always suffer? Aren't some folk always cold, always 'ungry? If what yer sez is true then yer'll be back in yer luxury soon and all this will be a bad memory. Some folks can't escape."

Frances took a damp handkerchief from her pocket, wiped her eyes, now red-rimmed and sore and blew her nose. She felt ashamed. "You are right, of course. I am behaving atrociously. My father would be ashamed of me."

"Now, now. Don't go being too 'arsh on yerself. Yers tired, worn out. All I'm saying is, keep it in proportion. Come on, eat the pottage, 'twill warm yer frough." Frances did as this motherly figure bid her. "Would yer like more? I's got plenty." Frances nodded. "Good. I'll fetch another and get you some warmed beer while I's about it. Get ou' of those wet cloves while I's gone, I'll find yer somefing dry."

Such kindness. Frances wouldn't forget it. She would come back later and repay the woman. She stripped off - even her chemise was damp - wrapped the blanket around her naked self and finished the pottage while she awaited the woman's return.

"Here we is luvvie," the woman said, just moments later as she placed another steaming bowl on the pile of bales. "And this'll fit, 'tis me daughter's." She held up a grey, drab dress with a high neck and long sleeves. "'Tis wool, will keep yer warm. And look, I've brought one o' me shawls. Now try and get some sleep. Everything'll look different in the morning."

The dress fitted well. Frances used the blanket to dry her hair best she could then wrapped the shawl around her head and shoulders. She put her hands around the warm lamp and flexed her fingers. Slowly they were coming back to life as her circulation improved. She was beginning to feel human again. At least her feet were dry in her sturdy riding boots.

Lunar had drunk and eaten and settled down in the corner of the stable. She looked peaceful, at last. In hindsight, Frances realized, she would have done better using hired horses that she could have changed every few miles. In her haste to escape Melbroke she hadn't thought that part through properly. It was too late for regret now. Here they were. Two exhausted females a long way from home. In a way Frances was glad she was staying with her over night. Leaving her alone in a strange place would not have been kind. Mayhap this was one of God's mysterious ways.

AS FRANCES had entered Rochester so Melbroke galloped into Greenwich. William had been right. Even on this pitch-black night The Red Lion was easy to find and the innkeeper helpful.

"They woz 'ere yer Lordship. Arrived last night, left earlier t'day. The older Lady took ill, borrow'd me carridge and one of me stable lads, 'e's taken her back to Richmond Palace."

"And the younger Lady?"

"Left on her own 'orse...'twas about midday."

Melbroke's heart found a new low. So now Frances was on the road alone! He felt his anger and anxiety rise in equal measure.

If she hadn't been attacked, raped or murdered - and it was a big if - she was probably in Rochester. He was right of course, she was. Not attacked by the threats he feared but beset by anguish nevertheless. "Do you know what ailed the older lady?"

"Weak apparently and vomiting."

" God on His cross! If she's sick because of me..."

He couldn't dwell on possibilities, he decided, as he walked Galahad to the stables. The facts were worrying enough. The side of the inn was unlit but he could see torches at the rear and he headed toward them. A stable lad walked forward to meet him.

"He's tired," Melbroke said, as he handed over the reins. He needs a good groom, your best barley and oats, water and plenty of it." He pressed some coins into the lad's hand.

"I shall be leaving in a few hours, before midnight, leave his saddle close by, I will saddle him up myself." The lad nodded and led Galahad away.

"Afore you go," Melbroke called, "where can I buy a riding coat and some sturdy boots at this hour?" His shoes and hose were now caked with mud and his doublet wet. He needed better protection from the elements. He also needed the feel of steel about is person, he had foolishly left Richmond unarmed.

"Market's long since packed up m'Lord but yer could go to the clovier's 'ome. Don't 'spect he'll mind yer calling at 'is cottidge, not if yous buying. 'Tis the thatch by the stream, one in the middle of free." Melbroke pressed another coin into his hand.

It was not his intention to stay the night. He would buy what he needed, eat immediately, rest Galahad for a few hours and be away again in the hope of catching up with Frances before she left Rochester in the morning. He found the clothier easily, bought a heavy, leather riding coat, knee-high riding boots and a pair of strong leather gloves. A large dagger was now tucked into his right boot.

Back at the inn he took a roast capon, a hot piece of pie, bread and warmed wine to his room and threw himself on the bed. He was too tense to sleep but just incase tiredness overcame him he'd instructed the innkeeper to knock on his door at eleven o'clock. His head was swimming with concerns: worry for Margaret, anxiety for Frances, the reaction of Will if, when, he discovered the truth.

Presumably the Lady of Blean, he was thinking, had also found somewhere to eat and sleep by now. Assuming she was still alive! At least off the road she was less vulnerable. Stupid fool! Had she given but one thought to the number of evil rampallions that surrounded her? The cut-throats who could shadow her? How every bird song, every crack of twig could be their sign to each other as they stalked her with goodness knows what intent? Had her brain given but cursory consideration to the perils of the road? Stupid! Stupid woman! He hoped to make Rochester by sunrise and catch her before she left. By God he was going to give her a piece of his mind!

Having eaten and drunk some wine he closed his eyes. He was getting used to his anxiety for Frances, it hovered in his being like an annoying wasp. He was though, still mystified as to why? Why! She'd laid guilt upon him, that was why! That angered him. He allowed his thoughts to stray for a few moments upon her beauty. The scent of her golden hair, the softness of those perfect lips, those bewitching, sapphire blue eyes. He found himself smiling, just for a few seconds before his brain reminded him of his anger.

He turned his thoughts to William. He'd have seen the King and be well on the road by now. Had His Majesty asked for him? He would certainly be assuming that this loyal servant was making plans for his mission to France not chasing an annoying woman across southern England!

IT WAS two pecking geese scrabbling around her feet that awoke Frances. That and the honking from the rest of their gaggle outside in the yard. Exhaustion had given into deep sleep and she'd found warmth between bales of hay. She opened her eyes and stared at the unwelcoming wooden beams above her. Her senses were immediately filled with the smells of the stable as her awareness came back to reality. They hit her nostrils first then her stomach; nausea waved over her. Her bones reminded her of how close to the ground they were and she stretched her body gingerly as her back, shoulders and hips ached as she had never known. The innkeeper's words, "sunrise, or I'll take yer 'orse," came flooding back.

She would leave her still-wet clothes for the woman and daughter. Mayhap, when the fabric had dried, they could sew themselves something. She placed them in a neat pile to indicate her intention to the cheerful soul who had shown such kindness and with which Frances, right now, had nothing else to thank her. She cupped water into her hand from the horses' bucket and rinsed her mouth, she wouldn't risk swallowing although she was mighty thirsty. She needed to refill her waterskin, the next stream would do.

A choir of birds greeted her as she led Lunar out into the courtyard. She imagined the rising sun over Canterbury, shining down on her father's home. She imagined what they would be doing, how the house would be stirring, fires being lit, the kitchen springing into action, her father drawing back the bolts to let out the dogs. She had no food and her mouth salivated at the thought of hot bread and melting butter. She hadn't brushed her hair or washed since rising in Greenwich and she felt stale and fusty.

How was Margaret? With shame she realized she hadn't given her sister a second thought for a long time. She would be back in Richmond now. Back in her own bed, safe with her husband by her side.

She used an empty barrel as a mounting block and lifted herself on to Lunar's back. She hooked her hair behind her ears, wrapped the woman's shawl tightly around her body back-to-front so that her front had the most protection and gave Lunar's neck a loving pat. "Come on girl," she said, into her pricked ear and together they headed into the morning gloom.

SHE ENDURED a ride of constant drizzle, biting wind and intermittent weak sun. Promising white clouds were nudged away by dove greys which scurried apace across the sky by an unrelenting wind. The elements it seemed rejoiced in sprinkling her woollen dress as if teasing it and her. She pressed on. Rochester was a good few hours behind when the weak sun finally lost its battle with the darkening sky. Low clouds, the colour of iron, triumphed and threatened yet another soaking.

She saw the barn off in the distance. A small compact building on the side of a mud-and-stubble field, it stood on staddles with ducks from the nearby pond darting under and out again. She steered Lunar to the left, past the pond with its rattling brown reeds and trotted her up a narrow muddy trail. The ice-cold drops started, at first intermittently but becoming heavier and landing on her head like little daggers. As she got closer she saw a horse tied to a tree. Good. She could seek permission to shelter until the rains passed. She secured Lunar under shelter and made for the barn door. It was jammed. She tugged, pushed, banged - no movement.

A soft tap on her shoulder startled her. It was the White Monk. The one who had blessed her in Greenwich. The surprise presence of a figure, the swish of robes that fell in folds to the ground, the closeness of him, took her aback. She stepped away, her hand reaching to the barn's side to steady herself. He placed a hand on her shoulder as if to calm her. She caught her breath: "You made me jump."

He was tall, his hood was hiding his face and he quickly walked away from her, beckoning her to follow him around the side of the barn to a smaller door. He extended an arm, indicating she should enter first. She wasn't accustomed to being alone with strange men but she told herself he was a man of God, there was nothing to be fearful about. She smiled. "Thank you" she said, passing him, still unable to see the face hidden by the hood.

Chapter Six

THE BARN SMELT dank and of animals but the several ready-lit lanterns hanging from beams gave a touch of bright welcome to a needy soul. There were empty cattle pens at one end and straw strewn over the floor and in tied-bales around the edges. It felt chilly but it would keep her dry - just till the rain eased.

She was no sooner through the door than a heavy thump landed on the middle of her back and sent her flying into the interior. She let out a scream as she lost her footing and landed painfully on the hard floor.

"Get up whore," the monk shouted, as he stood over her. He kicked her leg. "Get up! Get up, whore that you are."

She struggled to her feet. In those few seconds the monk had whipped off his habit. She immediately recognized the heavily-built imposing frame, the handsome face. "Pierre!"

"Yes, me. Your beloved, your betrothed. The man who would share your life in a few weeks' time."

"What are you doing? What are you talking about?" She was bewildered and frightened.

He stepped toward her and gripped the tops of her arms as if with an iron vice. "This is what you like, isn't it?" He growled, forcing his mouth on hers and running his hands over her body. "Like it do you whore?"

She struggled to push him away and after a few seconds he allowed his grip to slacken. She ran from him, putting several yards between them. "So, you run from me but not from him!"

"Pierre, what is all this about?"

"And to think I showed you respect, treated you as the Lady I believed you to be and all the time you wanted to be fondled and groped."

"I don't. What are you talking about? I don't understand."

"I saw you. I saw you...with him."

"Who?"

"Melbroke! In your rooms. Kissing you, touching you and you letting him." His voice broke with angry emotion and he turned away from her. Frances paled and weakened. She sunk on to a bale of hay.

"Pierre, I'm sorry, so sorry."

He spun around. "I don't want to hear sorry. It's too late for all that. You betrayed me, degraded me. Degraded us!" His exasperation, his pain, clothed his words. "Do you think I want you now? Soiled goods? And soon to be soiled reputation? No. Never!"

"Pierre, let me explain."

"There's nothing to explain. Melbroke's reputation goes before him. He's a charmer, women can't refuse him apparently... well my betrothed certainly couldn't." His hollow laugh drowned her.

"He forced himself upon me."

"Not true. Don't lie Frances, don't be a liar and a whore."

"He did!"

"I saw for myself. You sat passively, you undid your own bodice, you welcomed his hands upon you. You were in his arms willingly. You're a slut, a whore." He was distraught and full of rage. "I hate you...now you must pay." His voice tapered off, emotion overcoming him.

She rushed over to him. "Pierre, please." He grabbed her again and pushed her against the barn wall. He slapped both sides of her face then kissed her savagely, painfully, spitefully. He pulled up her skirt and roamed over her thighs. She wriggled to stop him, used her knees to try and push him off. He relented and turned away. "You fight me Frances, anyone but me can touch you, anyone but the man you agreed to marry." He grabbed some rope and dragged her to one of the barn's props. "Stand there and keep quiet!"

"What are you going to do?"

"Quiet!" he bellowed in her ear. She shrunk away, her head spinning. She was trembling with fear. He was white with rage. He pulled her arms behind the prop and tied her wrists.

"How is it you are here?" She knew her question risked another slap.

"I've been following you from Richmond," he said, yanking the rope tighter. "Remember the rat catcher?'

She nodded incredulously. "Put the scrapings from the hen house in your sister's stew, that got rid of her. Got you all to myself then," he laughed, viciously.

"It was you who stole my things?"

"Yes it was me." He gripped her chin and spoke into her face. "I'm not proud Frances but then 'tis you that's reduced me to this. Reduced me, me a French Marquis, to sneaking around the Palace, peeping through doors to watch you. Reduced me to stealing. Seems both of us has a side the other didn't know"

"How did you know I'd come into this barn?"

"I didn't, I slept here last night, seems luck's on my side. Now shut up."

"Pierre, please, let me explain." She spoke quietly, hoping not to enrage his temper even further. He slapped her face again. "Quiet I said. I'm not interested in your explanations. Explanations from a whore are worthless."

His every word was stabbing her pride, her self-esteem. Every turn of his vengeful screw was hitting home. She was humiliated. Ruined. "Anyone but your betrothed it seems."

"Not anyone..."

"O just Melbroke then! Special was he?"

"I didn't mean that..."

He slapped the other side of her face before she could reply. "Don't even think to speak, I don't want to hear it. You've degraded me and made a mockery of my family's title and reputation. All I want to do now is kill you. Restore my honour. You treat a French Marquis in this way, you pay!"

His eyes were wild. She could feel his breath on her face. Hot. Vindictive. Determined. "But not before I've had my sport with you. After all, everyone else has. Why should I be denied what would have been legally mine."

"Pierre don't, I'm begging you."

Another slap across the face. "Quiet, I said."

She wriggled her tied wrists. Pointless. The rope was tight, her wrists already grazed, the prop rigid against her back. She couldn't move, she was helpless. Pierre drew his dagger and used the tip to tease her neck. It forced her head back and he traced the outline of her trembling chin. He ran the blade down her throat to the top of her dress and with one skilful flick he cut the neckline without marking her skin. He ran the sharp edge down the front and the wool succumbed like snow in sun. He stepped back, his eyes fixed on the long, narrow strip of bare, porcelain-white skin running from her neck to her navel.

She screamed and felt another slap. "Quiet!" Her face was burning. Did he really mean to rape her? To kill her? She was helpless to defend herself. She could barely breathe from sheer fear. She was trembling from head to toe. "We'll have some sport whore, you and me. We've plenty of time. There's no rush but be assured, by nightfall you'll be dead."

He undid his sword belt, threw it to the floor and loosened his hose. "Now let's see what Melbroke found so alluring that he kept coming back."

"No, please, don't," she begged.

He grabbed the torn dress and was about to force it back over her shoulders when an almighty bang startled them both.

"Get away from her," came the commanding voice that had just burst into the barn. "Get away or I'll kill you." It was Melbroke.

THE BADLY lit barn was all Melbroke had in his favour. That and the element of surprise although he was ill-equipped for it. Pierre reacted quickly, retrieved his sword from its sheath and was now ready for whatever was to come. Melbroke had no sword, he would need to use fleet of foot and dance in the shadows. He quickly freed his arms from his heavy riding coat and claimed the dagger from his boot. The two men stood at opposite ends of the barn waiting for the other to attack. Sizing each other up. Patrolling like panthers. The weight of Melbroke's dagger in his hand no comfort against a sword. He was at a disadvantage, no point now cursing himself for not travelling properly armed.

He quickly looked around, checking out the stage. Seeing what could help him, what could hinder. He was used to the battlefield, this was different. No military strategy would work here. This was down to instinct, strength, quick thinking. Whoever had the greater would live. Already the blood was pounding in his head, the thrum of arterial flow filling his ears. Already the brutality of self-defence was whirring. He would need to be the lightening and the oak. Quick and strong. Faster and stronger or he would be dead.

His eyes fell on Frances. Reduced, embarrassed, shaking, frightened. Keeping a rigid eye on his opponent he made toward her, the dagger alert and ready for action. He went behind and cut the rope from her wrists. "Get right away," he shouted. "Go!" She grabbed the shawl and scuttled off into a dark corner.

"Well, well, if it isn't the great Lord himself," snarled Pierre. "I was coming for you later but I don't mind who I kill first. You, then the whore, that'll do me nicely. Once I've had my fun with her but then you know all about that you bastard!"

Melbroke was not about to be drawn into conversation. He had no idea who this man was or what he was talking about. He could see though, even in this bad light, that he was a strong man. Tall, heavily built, a strong upper body. A trained man who held his sword's weight like a quill. Melbroke grabbed a milking stool in his left hand as defence. Instantly Pierre's sword came down on it like a bolt from hell, smashing it to smithereens. Melbroke's hand was an inch from becoming a stump. He jumped back in surprise as the force thudded up his arm to his shoulder. Pierre laughed and in that second Melbroke thrust his dagger into his left upper arm immediately drawing blood. It drew a cry and an angry response as the sword swung again, this time around Melbroke's head, as if trying to decapitate him. Melbroke ducked, brought his dagger up from a low position straight into his adversary's abdomen.

Pierre staggered backwards, aimlessly swinging his sword. It caught Melbroke's upper arm before spinning out of his hand and into the bales of hay. Melbroke struck the Marquis, his clenched fist slamming into his opponent's jaw. The Marquis' head rocked backwards, his legs buckled, he staggered then fell to the ungiving ground. Melbroke was on him instantly, a knee on his chest, punching his face, one side then the other. Yield! Yield you whoreson! Blood ran from the Marquis' nose, beaten only in velocity by the torrent of abuse from his mouth.

Quicker than Melbroke noticed Pierre's hand reached out, found his sword in the hay and garlanding what strength remained he swung it with all his might at Melbroke's back. The broad side dealt a severe blow, had it been the sharp edge Melbroke would be dead. The blow winded him, sending agonizing pain down and up his spine. His head jarred on his shoulders, his spine juddered and in those few weak, unguarded seconds the Marquis wriggled out from under his legs.

Cleverly Pierre had seized back the advantage. Now he was on top. He stood above Melbroke grinning, his face and doublet covered in blood, his sword held in two hands above his head. These were Melbroke's last seconds unless he took action quickly. With a deep-throated war cry he charged the stranger, butted his head into his chest and thrust his blade through ribs and straight into his adversary's heart. One experienced, fluid action had saved him.

The Marquis froze, blood gushed from his mouth. He clutched his chest and sunk to his knees. The sword flew through the air and clanged to the ground. For a startled moment Melbroke watched, held in time. He hadn't expected it to be over so quickly. He hadn't wanted to kill him. He'd been given no choice. Blood oozed from the man's mouth as he fell backwards on to bales then slid helplessly to the earth-solid ground.

Melbroke strode over to the body, sunk to his knees and stared at the lifeless frame. There was no doubt the soul had fled. The face was held in agony as if it had just peered into hell. Melbroke was breathing heavily, his brow glistening with sweat despite the cold. His back and left upper arm throbbed. Shock, that reminded him he had never before killed a man off the battlefield, sent a shiver through him. He wiped the blood off his blade on the Marquis' clothing then rammed it back into his boot.

"Frances." he called, "you can come out now."

A FRAGILE, shaking figure emerged from the shadows clutching the Marquis' fallen sword. She had reassembled her dress and again tied the shawl across her front, this time for modesty. Her every limb was trembling. Her heart was pounding and with the threat now over, tears were pouring from her eyes. Hot, burning tears that she couldn't control.

"Thank the Lord you are unharmed," Melbroke said, stepping toward her.

"Stay away from me," she screamed, lifting the sword, pointing it at him. She put a good ten feet between them. "Stay well away from me, you...you beast! Don't you ever touch me again."

"Frances?"

"'Tis Lady Frances to you...you monster."

Melbroke was stunned. "Lady Frances, I have just saved your life."

"Only because you put it in danger in the first place."

"What are you talking about?" He was bewildered at her accusations and concerned about a sword being in the possession of a near-hysterical woman. "Please, Lady Frances give me the sword, it will be needed as evidence."

In truth, it was getting increasingly heavier in her grip and she was becoming increasingly weaker. The ordeal was overcoming her. "Only if you promise to keep your distance, stay away from me."

"If that is your wish," he replied, placating her but not knowing why.

She knelt by the body, rocked back on her heels and screamed to the heavens. A loud desperate scream, like an injured animal. Melbroke didn't understand what he was witnessing.

She dropped the sword by the body and for a moment stared at the man she would have married. The full implications of the situation began to reveal themselves. New shock waves flushed through her. Still trembling from head to toe, her legs still weak, she had trouble lifting herself back to standing.

He saw her stagger. "May I assist?"

"Stay away..." Her startled eyes threatened him, forbade him to come nearer. She could pick up that sword in a second if she had to!

"I will keep to my promise but I am very confused Lady Frances. May I remind you that I have just saved your life."

"And may I remind you, Melbroke, that neither myself, nor Pierre, would have been in this position if you hadn't forced yourself upon me."

Melbroke was stunned. "I never forced myself upon you. And what has Pierre got to do with it?"

"You've just killed him. That's Pierre," she shrieked, her trembling arm pointing at the body on the floor, her voice cracking.

"That's not Pierre. I met him in Richmond two days ago. He's skinny, effete, nothing like this man here."

"Melbroke, please allow me to know the man to whom I was betrothed. That is Pierre, Marquis de Champagne. The man you met sounds like his younger brother but why you should think him Pierre, I don't know."

Because he told me he was, thought Melbroke. Suspicion jangled through his mind. There's a plot here. This doesn't smell right.

"So why was he attacking you?"

Frances was slowly calming down. The trembling was stopping, the tears quietening. Her face was still sore from the slaps but she was slowly regaining some sense of composure.

"Because he saw you come to my rooms," she said quietly, her voice full of contempt. "He watched through the open door, saw you...what you did."

Melbroke sank on to some bales of hay. Her accusations, her blame were coming at him like hail in a storm. His upper arm was now throbbing badly, the arm getting noticeably weaker. His hand went to the wound and was quickly wet with blood. His doublet was soaked.

"He refused to let me explain that you had forced yourself upon me," she continued.

"That is the second time you've made that allegation. I did not force myself..."

"Yes you did! I asked you to stop," she hurled at him, raising her voice again. "The first time you tore my gown. Every time I said 'stop' and you ignored me."

Melbroke couldn't believe his ears. He had never forced himself on a woman in his life. Never had to. "I just thought it was nerves because you weren't used to the emotions."

"That is partly right, Melbroke. I certainly wasn't used to the emotions: the anger, the humiliation, the feeling of being belittled, abased, soiled..."

"But you groaned with pleasure, I felt you..."

"I was gritting my teeth, just praying you would get it over with and be gone."

"Gritting your teeth!" He was standing now, his back aching. In the fight his shoulder-length hair had come loose from its usual tie at the nape of his neck. He raked his slender fingers through it, pushing it straight back from his high, intelligent forehead. A forehead that was now creased in bewilderment and annoyance. Well, another first, he was thinking, no woman had to grit her teeth before!

"You certainly didn't give me that impression," he snapped, surrendering to a searing juvenile need to defend himself. "You enjoyed me touching you, why are you denying it!"

"I didn't and anyway I wasn't yours to touch, you had no right and you should have heeded my request to stop, in fact you should never have been in my rooms at all."

His whole being ached, physically and emotionally. His injuries were worsening by the minute and her words cut into him as sharply as Pierre's sword. "I had no idea," he said, allowing his face to flop into his hands.

Neither spoke for a few moments. Neither sure what to say. It seemed an age. Eventually Melbroke broke the silence and looked straight at her. "I apologize most sincerely. I had no idea, I obviously completely misread the situation. I thought you welcomed my visits."

"I did not."

"I can only apologize again, I am not the man you have thought me, I can assure you of that." He waited for a response but got none. "You must surely realize now that neither was the Marquis the man you believed him to be. He was going to...well, I think you know what he was going to do..."

"He was going to rape me. You don't have to spare my blushes Melbroke."

That was the fourth time she hadn't given him the courtesy of his title. It reflected her obvious despising of him and it angered him.

"I may be inexperienced but I know what men do to women. I've had a taster of that from you!"

"Frances, I..."

"Lady Frances! Your familiarity with me is at an end. Do you hear?"

O he heard and he nodded.

"So," she went on, sarcastically, "if I'd been in my room at nine o'clock as you commanded and said 'no' you would have stopped would you?" There was mocking contempt in her voice. "You never did before, why would you once you were actually in my bedchamber. I don't think so, you would have forced yourself upon me. I had to get away...get away from you!"

Again Melbroke was stunned into silence. Again he ran his hands through his loose, thick hair. God's truth, he was thinking. She was almost right, of course. He did intend taking her that night. But rape? No!

"And my running from the Palace has led to all this. I've been through hell, all because of you," she said, pointing a finger at him. "You!"

She looked so fragile and vulnerable standing there in her skimpy drab dress, her hair matted from the rain, her face pale but her cheeks bright red from the slaps and the wind. Despite the vitriolic attack he couldn't help but admire her. He felt broken from her accusations, her cruel words but mostly because he was beginning to realize they had truth in them. He was used to being regarded as a rake but this was something else. She was right, he should have heeded her words. No woman had ever said 'stop' before but then he wasn't used to virgins.

Truth was he usually avoided them but her beauty had drawn him to her. He hadn't realized she actually meant it. He was filling with his own rage, rage at himself for being so stupid, so arrogant, so vain. He also felt deeply ashamed.

The lanterns were guttering, new candles would soon be needed but there were none to be seen.

"How is it you are here at all?" Her voice was calmer now. It took him a few seconds to reply, she thought mayhap he hadn't heard her and then he coughed to clear his throat and spoke very matter o' factly.

"Your sister left William a note saying you and she had gone to your father's to sort out some wedding problems," he replied quietly, unable to look at her. "William knew this to be untrue because he had just received a letter from the Earl in which problems weren't mentioned. We made enquiries, discovered you'd taken two horses, that you had no male escort, it all seemed strange, we were both concerned for your safety, we decided to follow." He was speaking without emotion, just relaying the facts, his voice weary from events. "I came first because William had business with the King, he intended following as soon as he could. I saw your white horse tethered outside the barn..."

She moved her attention from his voice and allowed her eyes to settle upon him. What was left of the lantern light was catching his rich brown hair with its deep auburn lights. Shadows were outlining the strong jaw, the now sorrowful, deep chestnut eyes. For the first time she saw the subdued, gentle man rather than the strutting peacock. He must have ridden through the night, she was thinking. He must be exhausted from his travels, the lack of sleep and the fight with Pierre. He looked pale, pain was etched on his face. Her heart went out to him. She snatched it back.

"You realize," he continued, "Pierre would almost certainly have killed you after he'd..." He couldn't say the word, his sentence tapered off.

"Yes. He told me I would be dead by sunset."

"He would have had no choice, kill you or be executed for the assault. His family's honour would have been ruined."

"I know. Despite my anger, I do appreciate that it was a miracle you arrived when you did. You saved me, I know." She took a deep breath, it was true, she did owe Melbroke her life. "My gratitude to you is greater than you can ever know," she said, trying to pull herself together. "I shall, of course, give witness to the Sheriff and you will always have my sincerest thanks."

"I don't want thanks!" he said, incredulously, taking a step toward her without thinking. She put up a hand to bar him.

"What do you want?" She asked, believing she knew the answer.

"I want you," he was going to say, "to forgive me" but Frances didn't let him finish his sentence.

"'Tis as I thought," she mocked, "You think you can have any and every woman you lust after, well not me!"

"No, I wasn't going to say that..." but he couldn't finish, for at that moment the barn door burst open again. This time it was William. "Thank the Lord you are here," she cried, as she ran over to him and fainted into his arms.

Magdala yanked off her wimple, a grave sin but there was no one to see and she allowed the sun to bless her naked head. How warm God's touch was, how reassuring. A breeze blew strands of her wispy white hair into her face reminding her it must soon be shorn again.

Just as she had done as a small child she turned around on the spot. Round and round, faster and faster until she felt giddy then she quickly lay on the ground, her back and outstretched palms flat against the earth and imagined she could feel the very planet spinning. She opened her eyes and all she could see was sky. From ear to ear nothing but blue dotted with white smudges. In her mind's ear she could hear her mother laughing, she could feel their dogs' eager wet kisses on her face. She could feel her brother's toe as he nudged her side and chided her not to play dead.

"Leave her alone," her mother would call. "She's floating on air."

"No she's not," he'd argue, "she's laying on the Earth."

"And what do you think the Earth is doing?"

She and her mother would smile. Hugh was older than she but not as quick or as imaginative as the two females in his life. He'd huff and walk away, feeling ganged up upon. She'd have to find him later and hug him and allow him to tickle her 'til she screamed so that he believed he had won whatever it was he needed to win. For a few moments she was in another world as she remembered innocent bygone happiness. Then the reality of her life crashed in, she was ashamed of this but she couldn't help it. Her brother had in the end won everything. Taken everything.

Chapter Seven

FOR A FEW peaceful seconds Frances had forgotten where she was, then it all came crashing back. Sharp tips of straw were digging into her neck and scalp. Something heavy, smelling of leather was laying over her. For the first time in what seemed an age she felt warm but her wrists were sore, her cheeks burned and her lips bruised from Pierre's savage kissing.

She could hear men's voices: "It's Pierre!...You killed him!...I can't believe it!...Tied her up!...Slapped her face!...God's truth!" It was as if the owners of the voices were on another planet, distant, remote from her. They weren't, of course, they were just a few feet away and it was her they were talking about!

She stirred and lifted herself on to her elbows. "William," she called quietly. The two men rushed over.

"Frances, how are you? You passed out, do you feel a little stronger now?" She nodded. "Melbroke has been telling me what's happened here, or some of it at least."

"Please no more, I can't take any more, not now."

Melbroke turned to William. "There was a reasonable looking inn about a mile back, we should all go there, rest up for today and continue on to Blean in the morning." William nodded agreement.

"Frances," William asked tenderly, "can you ride for just one more mile?"

She nodded and made to stand, Melbroke's coat falling to the ground as she did so. He picked it up. "Please, keep the coat," he said, offering it to her. "It will keep you warm. And you can ride with me on Galahad if you feel too weak."

Was he a lackwit? Her contemptuous glare said she thought so. Had he heard nothing of what she'd said? She didn't want anything of his anywhere near her. Not his coat, not his horse and especially not him.

"I can ride Lunar," she said, throwing him daggers with her eyes. She made for the barn door with care. Her legs were shaky but she could manage one more mile, ten if it meant not being close to Melbroke.

THE SECOND iron works was to be on the Earl's own huge estate near Canterbury. A specialist surveyor from Southwark had visited before Christmas, had taken soil samples and in an authoritative report delivered on Twelfth Night had declared that the Blean land was iron rich and a new works would inevitably prove successful and financially beneficial.

Initially the Earl hadn't wanted industry so close to his home. Hadn't wanted lands that had been farmed since before the Conqueror to be blackened and scarred but his King wanted iron so iron he would give him. The Grinstead works was running well, he was confident he could give Bellowes more trust and only visit quarterly. This freed him to divert time and energy closer to home. It also rested his ageing bones.

He reined his horse to a halt, relaxed his tired back in the saddle and surveyed the site with pride. An early riser, he was out just before dawn, a time of day he loved. He watched the veil of night lifting as the morning sky lightened, the sun's rays chasing night away, streaks of straggly cloud dissipating playfully. The night had seen a silent snowfall which crunched under foot and hoof. The air was bitterly cold, he took a few deep breaths, the sharpness made him cough and he pulled his heavy cloak more tightly around him. He was imbued with a great sense of satisfaction as he recalled the effort, the organizing, the money that had gone into the venture that lay before him.

The new works with its twenty-foot tall stone furnace, looking surprisingly like a church tower, nestled in a valley by a small river at the northern edge of the Blean lands. It was a good thirty-minute canter from the house and once functioning would be well out of sight, sound and smell. The new forge would turn the molten iron into long bars, most of which would be sold to the blacksmiths at the Tower of London, just as the Grinstead bars were.

There were plenty of trees for charcoal burning. Plenty of water from the river to swell the twenty-acre pond which would turn the large waterwheel that would control the huge bellows that in turn would feed the flames and keep the furnace at a heat that could scorch a man's lungs. Both nature and the earth's resources were playing their part in abundance and had, along with the surveyor's report, encouraged the Earl to invest heavily and expect a good outcome.

He dismounted and strolled in what, for the moment, felt

like a theatrical stage set. Right now it was a ghost works, pristine and new but if he closed his eyes he could conjure up the noise, the smells, the activity. Here was to be different to Grinstead. Once it was up and running the Earl wanted minimum hands-on dealings. This site he would lease to others who would pay him for the privilege. He would visit, if and when he chose but would not shoulder the main responsibilities. The annual fee would increase as the lessee's profits increased but never fall below the initial figure, not even if they didn't turn it into a going concern. He couldn't lose, the only bridge remaining to be crossed was to find the lessee. Word had already gone out.

"Bonjour Monsieur," a voice called from behind him. The Earl, yanked from his daydream, turned on the spot. "Une belle journee, n'est pas?" It was Pascal Blanc with his usual curtain of greasy, fair hair hanging lank around his narrow shoulders. A Frenchman in his thirties, skin and bone, his shoulders no wider than his hips, his back slightly rounded, unshaven, scruffy. He was the expert from near Dieppe who had made himself indispensable as Bellowes' under-founder at Grinstead. He had contacts in iron on both sides of the Channel and along with the Earl's lawyer, Blanc was also spreading the word of the available lease and the potential of considerable wealth.

"You think so Blanc?" He queried, sarcastically. "It's bloody cold and the wind's blown down two beech trees. It's bloody well not a beautiful day."

"Pardon, Monsieur, when you 'ear my news you will agree today iz indeed magnifique."

The Earl raised his eyebrows, annoyed his peace had been disturbed. "How did you find me?"

"Your steward zed you were 'ere Monsieur. I have news, bon news, tres bon news!"

"Get on with it man."

"Deux Monsieur Harwykes have contacted me, they are interested in, 'ow you say? Ah, oui, leazing your works."

"Two Harwykes. Brothers or father and son?"

"This I do not know. They 'ave asked to meet with your Lordship, I tell zem I will explain to you. This iz why I am 'ere."

"Well as you are here Blanc, you can set about filling in this pit, must be ten feet long, could've broken me ankle. 'Tis bloody dangerous."

"Non, non Monsieur! This is part of the production. To take molten iron as it flows from the foundry. This pit we call 'sow'. You see theze channels," he said, pointing precisely to where the Earl, just moments before, had nearly stumbled, "theze take the overflow, into theze smaller pits." He was moving agitatedly now, flinging both his arms around to eagerly show the Earl how the molten ore would travel and then solidify. "Theze small pits we call 'pigs'."

"Ah! Hence pig iron?"

"Exactement," the Frenchmen grinned. "We make ironmaster of you yet."

"No thank you Blanc, not interested. But I am interested in the Harwykes. Get them over here, seven o'clock the morning after tomorrow."

"I attend also my Lord, if you are agreeable?"

"Indeed I am, you can answer the technical questions." The Earl turned to his mount, his thoughts now on a hot breakfast. "If you're hungry go to the kitchens at the house, tell cook I said to feed you."

"I am not 'ungry my Lord, too early for me. I need to return home to sleep but merci," he called, as the Earl cantered off.

AS SOON as the three very weary travellers arrived at the inn Melbroke arranged for a message to be sent to the Kent Sheriff asking him to visit first thing the next morning. The innkeeper knew who owned the barn and could make sure the body wasn't touched. Luckily there were just two vacant rooms. Frances took one; the men would share the other. All three intended sleeping until supper.

Frances' room was small but had everything she needed: a roaring fire and a comfortable bed. She pulled off the woollen dress which she was now glad to be rid of. Its itchy, rough wool directly upon her bare skin had chafed badly and she now had sore, red marks at points where the dress had rubbed. It was now useless anyway, Pierre's blade had seen to that. She threw it into a corner of the room.

She'd asked for two large jugs of hot water and two bowls. She washed her body and hands as best she could and splashed her sore face. The warmth was heaven and the rough towel invigorated as she rubbed herself dry. The second bowl she positioned on the floor at the fire end of the bed and poured the second jug of hot water over her feet. They'd been imprisoned in sturdy riding boots since leaving Richmond, she was glad to flex her toes in the warm freedom of the water. She was sitting naked on the bed, feet in the hot water and using her fingers unsuccessfully as a comb through her tangled hair when William knocked on her door.

"Are you all right?"

She quickly swung the bed cover around herself. "Yes, come in."

He peered round the door. "O sorry," he said, making to quickly leave.

"William please, stay," she called. "I've been through so much this past day my brother-in-law seeing me like this is the very least of my worries."

He smiled and stepped into the room. "Is there anything you need, anything I can get you?"

"You might wish you hadn't asked," she said, trying to raise a smile, "but I've no dress, no undergarments. No comb. I haven't even got a shift to sleep in."

"Ah!"

"I can't arrive at Blean in this state. I must buy travelling clothes from somewhere and a comb but my money's been stolen. I've got nothing!" The pain was back in her voice.

"Don't worry about any of that, I have money on me," he said, trying to calm her from across the width of the room. "We can sort that out in the morning before we leave. I'll go now and speak to the innkeeper. You won't be the first traveller to arrive with no luggage. He's bound to have a wife or daughter who can lend a shift and comb."

"Thank you." She smiled but her face was wan and tired.

"Your nerves are shot, you look exhausted. Your father will be worried to death if he sees you like this."

"What on earth are we going to tell him? We can't tell him the truth?" Her voice cracked with anxiety.

"Leave that with me and Alban. We'll discuss it later, after we've slept, we'll eat and talk ."

"I won't be able to join you, not without a dress. And anyway I don't feel able to talk about it, not yet."

"Of course. Tomorrow, we'll talk tomorrow. The rest of today and tonight are for resting." He turned to leave.

"How's Margaret?"

"I've no damned idea!" William turned back, anger now in his eyes. His voice had hardened, his annoyance on show. "I left the Palace afore she returned. I go now to send message that I've caught up with you and that you are safe."

"Good."

"Yes, 'tis good," he snapped. "Good and very, very lucky. God only knows what the pair of you thought you were doing. But I won't press you for explanations now. The time will come soon enough."

MELBROKE WAS splashing cold water on to his arm wound when William got back to their room. There was nothing he could do for his back which was now seizing up in occasional, agonizing spasm. He settled uncomfortably on to a stool with his back to the roaring fire hoping its warmth might help. He was bare chested, his doublet around his shoulders, a goblet of wine in his hand. He hooked his thick, brown hair behind his ears. "Is she all right?"

"Not really," William replied curtly. "We won't be seeing her 'til morning. She's exhausted."

"She doesn't want to eat with us later?"

"Can't! She's no clothes!" He glared at his friend, then turned his eyes to the dancing flames. "I've just had to ask the innkeeper to lend her a night shift. She'll eat in her room, I've arranged a stew and some wine. Probably best anyway, her nerves are in pieces, she's been through a hell of an ordeal." His angry eyes were back on Melbroke who winced inwardly. His fault! His blame!

William poured himself some wine. "So now Alban, tell me, exactly what has been going!" William wanted answers and he wanted them now. "Margaret's been put at risk, I demand to know why!" He was uncharacteristically raising his voice. "What's all this about!"

Melbroke covered his face with his hands and for a few seconds sat in silence, his elbows on his knees. His back pain seared into him as if hot irons burned his bones. He straighten up slowly and took another swig of wine. "I'm not proud of what I am about to tell you Will, indeed I am sorely ashamed."

William waited.

"Pierre wanted to rape and murder Frances and then kill me."

"What!" William couldn't believe what he was hearing. He sat down on a stool near the window. "What on earth are you talking about...and why? Why!"

"Because he saw me. With Frances. At Richmond. Over past weeks. In her room." He was talking staccato fashion, hardly able to string the sentences together. Barely able to confess the terrible tale. As if telling it in short bursts would make it less shameful. "I've been calling at her apartment. Kissing her." His back pained, he tried standing. William too was back on his feet. "You didn't..."

"No! Definitely not. It was just kissing and mayhap a little touching..."

At that, William landed a hefty blow on Alban's jaw. "That is for the Earl who is too old to defend his daughter and this," he growled, as his second fist smashed into the other side of Alban's face, "is for Margaret. She would be devastated if she knew."

Melbroke reeled from the blows, took several steps back but didn't fall to the ground. He put up no resistance nor did he strike back. He knew his friend was in the right.

"I deserve your wrath Will, I know that." He allowed himself to lean back against the wooden wall; pain shot down his injured arm and up into his shoulder.

For a few seconds both men were silent. So much of Melbroke's body now ached he could hardly differentiate which part pained the most. Part of William wanted to beat his friend to a pulp the other half wanted him alive to answer questions. Melbroke steadied himself and clutched his injured arm, his hand immediately blooded.

"I can well understand," William went on, "why Pierre would want to kill you but why Frances? And how did he know?"

Melbroke rinsed his mouth with wine, spat out some blood into the wash bowl and sat down.

"The first time, apparently, was by chance. He was in the Palace making his way to visit Frances and just happened to see me heading for her rooms ahead of him. He followed and watched through the door." He stood again. There was no comfortably position for his back and anyway his restlessness was governing him. His hands, in anger, were clenching into fists as he recalled his own stupidity. "I heard the maid close it. It was definitely shut! He must have opened it very silently, just ajar, just enough to watch. Then he began to secretly keep watch, no one even knew he was in the Palace, not even Frances."

"How do you know, about him watching you I mean?"

"He told Frances, in the barn..." His voice tapered off as he remembered her tied up, trembling, dress ripped, frightened out of her life.

"Go on. I want it all Alban."

"Because he thought Frances was welcoming my advances he branded her a whore, not worthy to be his bride. If she were a whore he would treat her as such and then murder her. He had it all planned."

"And was she welcoming your advances?"

"I thought so at the time but she tells me today that she was not."

"By God man, she either was or she wasn't!"

"She told me to stop but I didn't think she meant it. I was

wrong..."

"The lady said stop and you ignored her! You are a disgrace, an absolute disgrace. And she fled the Palace to be rid of you?" Melbroke stared silently at the floor, William could read the answer. "You've put my wife at danger and her sister, all because you wanted some sport. You think of nothing but your own pleasure." And with that another blow landed on Melbroke's face. He reeled from the force and this time his nose streamed crimson, the heat gushing down on to his chest. "I won't fight you Will. I know you are right, I take full responsibility."

The two men sat on their narrow beds. Melbroke full of remorse, the blood matting on his skin; William full of anger, the deep pink of his rage spreading from his neck and face to his head, visible now through his short-cut, fair hair.

Melbroke's body felt racked. "What the Marquis didn't expect," he continued, "was me becoming concerned for Frances' safety when I discovered she was on the road with no male protection. The last thing he expected was me to follow. He was shocked to the core when I burst into that barn."

"Just a minute! What's this I'm hearing. The great debaucher, the rake who thinks women are there for the taking, talks of caring. I don't believe what I'm hearing."

"Go on mock, just about everything else has happened to me today."

"You'll be telling me next that you love Frances."

Melbroke side-stepped the accusation. He didn't know what he felt and chose to ignore the suggestion of love. What was love anyway! Something to be avoided, that much he knew. It was a fact though that he couldn't get the blessed woman off his mind and that when he saw her so vulnerable, so scared, he was prepared to risk his own life to save her. All this he would banish from his mind, immediately! The metallic taste of blood was back in his mouth, he rinsed and spat it out.

"You must pardon me Will, I must lay back on the bed. I feel a little unwell, my wounds are a little more serious than I'd realized."

William snatched at his friend's open doublet and saw the serious gash in his upper arm. It was still seeping blood, it was deeper than either man had realized and the blood was slowly journeying down the arm to the floor. The herbed rushes were already blooded.

"That needs a tourniquet," and with that William ripped the clean sleeve from Melbroke's discarded shirt and tied it tightly around his arm.

"So, you have feelings for Frances. I don't know whether to laugh or hit you again,"

"Please do neither," Melbroke said risking a smile, not sure how William would take it. "I have just saved her honour and her life. If that could be taken into account I would be most grateful. And I didn't say I had feelings for her, I said I was simply concerned. I was concerned for Margaret too, for both of them."

"Yes, in a situation of your making! I want to beat you to within an inch of your life."

"I'll not fight you Will, you're my closest friend. 'Tis I who is in the wrong, I have no desire to injure you on top of everything else."

"And I won't fight a man who won't fight back, I'll have to let hell take you!"

The two men remained in silence for a few moments, each in his own thoughts, his own anger. Melbroke lifted his legs off the floor and gently settled his back on the softness of the bed's feather pillows. He covered his sore, swelling face with his hands and let out a long groan as the rawness of pain scorched through him. His arm was throbbing even more, his face was bruised, one eye was closing, his nose, luckily not broken, was caked with blood and his back ached as he'd never known.

"You don't need me to tell you how stupid you've been," William ventured.

"No"

"But all this for a few kisses! Yes, it was wrong, you were your usual disgraceful self and Pierre certainly had the right to be angry, even call off the wedding but rape and murder? Was he insane?"

"I know nothing about him."

"Nor me really. Only met him once, at the betrothal banquet the Earl gave last year. He seemed a cultured man. His mother is very charming. But it seems there was obviously more, a lot more."

"Yes, a dark, vicious, vengeful side, it seems. Any man that plans to murder a woman must be deranged."

William was being forced to privately consider that mayhap his friend's behaviour had saved Frances from a disastrous marriage. "We're both exhausted," he said. "We've got all afternoon to sleep, then dine, then a good night's sleep. You look terrible, let's hope tomorrow sees all three of us in better shape."

"I feel terrible. I was thinking, if you don't need me at Blean, I'll head back to Richmond in the morning."

"As you wish but let's see what the morning brings."

"Is Frances all right?" Melbroke asked.

"You've already asked me that and yes, she's coping. Hopefully sound asleep by now."

"Do you think she hates me?"

"I wouldn't be surprised..."

"I don't hate you Melbroke," a quiet voice announced from the open doorway. It was Frances. She had pushed wider the door that was only ajar. In agony Melbroke, with William, stood. He quickly swung his stained doublet around his naked shoulders as Frances entered the room. "To hate you would be to suggest you have the power to engender feelings within me, you have no such power, I have no feelings for you whatsoever."

Her carefully-worded dagger was well aimed. It pierced into Melbroke causing pain that was a stranger to him. "Lady Frances," he said, "you must pardon my bad manners but I must sit, I feel a little unwell."

"And you must pardon my appearance, I have no clothes as your Lordship knows." She spoke with a hint of sarcasm. She was barefoot, clutching the bed cover around herself like a cloak. A borrowed night shift was underneath and she had done the best with a borrowed comb. Her beautiful vulnerability took Melbroke's breath away and he turned his eyes from her.

"What's the matter with him?" She addressed William as if Melbroke wasn't in the room.

"He has a bad sword wound, Pierre caught his upper arm, it is deep and still bleeding. He also has an injured back, again from the Marquis' sword."

Frances had caught a glimpse of the deep gash and the tourniquet and the blood-matted, strong chest as he'd swung his doublet around himself. Now she saw his ashen face, the gore, the swollen eye.

"What's happened to his face?"

"I hit him."

"Why?"

"Because of what he did to you at Richmond."

So the truth was out. Melbroke had confessed.

"Do I have your permission to tell Margaret?"

"She knows."

Melbroke looked up. Who else knows!

"She's promised not to tell father," Frances continued. "You won't..."

"No I won't, don't worry. We must discuss all this in the morning. But why aren't you asleep?"

"I needed to ask about Lunar, is she well cared for?"

"Yes, she's with our horses in the stables. We've instructed they be well groomed, reshod, fed and watered. She is fine. Now no more worrying. Back to bed." And with that he took her arm and steered her back to her room across the landing.

Melbroke swung his legs on to the bed and allowed his head to sink into the soft pillow. William, still angry, returned and replenished their goblets. Melbroke, in agony from the head down, lay in thought, churning things over in his mind. "Have you ever met the Marquis' brother?"

"Yes, once, at the betrothal dinner."

"A slight, weak, boy of a man?"

"That's him."

"He introduced himself to me at Richmond, day afore yesterday, as Pierre."

"Why on earth would he do that?"

"I think to provide an alibi for his brother. Pierre couldn't be at Richmond and elsewhere killing Frances could he? They were in it together."

"Hell's gates! Well 'tis certainly true that few at the Palace knew what Pierre looked like and probably none knew his brother." William went to the door and called for more wine. "They spent most of their time in France. When he came to England he stayed at his aunt's place in Mortlake."

"I think we can assume they would both be heading back to France tonight, escaping capture, had their dastardly plan worked." He eased himself up from the bed. The caked blood in his nose was making breathing difficult, he splashed cold water on to his face, the relief was temporary, his nose throbbed. He tested his back, extended his arms upwards, the pain soared through him, he stifled a groan and cursed silently. Both men removed their boots and laid atop their beds.

Melbroke covered himself with his coat and surrendered to his body's yearning for rest. His mind wanted to turn off, turn away from the past day's events. Frances had warned him off, told him to keep his distance. That suited him just fine. He would do nothing that could cause her any more distress and he would put miles between the two of them as soon as he could. The innkeeper had been instructed to wake them when he was serving the evening meal. They had the rest of the day to sleep and he was glad for it.

Chapter Eight

FRANCES FOUND THE pile of clothes outside her door. It was William's gentle tapping that had awakened her from a deep, dreamless sleep and she'd shuddered from both memory and chill as she swung her scantily dressed body off the bed. The room was cold; the fire had long since died. Her face was still sore, her body aching, her wrists now showing bruises, her nerves still raw. She did though feel better than she might have expected and she was ready to face the inevitable. She would have to talk about yesterday's events.

'Hope these will suit,' the accompanying note read. 'Keep shift. Come break your fast. W.' A jug of steaming hot water was by the side.

The dress and coat were plain but warm. Shades of oatmeal and tan with dark brown velvet trims. Made for a matron. Dull but respectable. Her main concern now was her appearance when she met her father, these would do. He'd got much to hear that would shock him and his heart was weak. What had been done to her and what she'd been through, she would keep from him. These clothes weren't of her choice but they would give her cover, in more ways than one.

The brown velvet hat was too big but that too was good. She would hoick her tangled mass of hair into it. She could do nothing but hide it. She had no net, no snood, no choice.

THE TWO men were talking intensely, immersed in their plans. She could see them through the open hatch between the corridor and the eating area. William looked his usual smart self. Shaven, washed, fresh faced. Melbroke did not. He hadn't shaved, his face was too sore. He was haggard and pale save for bruising around his jaw and the deep bluish-purple around his swollen eye. His nose had bled no more but was painful to touch. He was dressed again in his blood-soiled doublet but with no shirt. He had removed the tourniquet on his arm, the bleeding appeared to have stopped but the shirt sleeve was in his pocket, just in case.

The men rose as she approached the table, Melbroke's back objecting strongly. She saw pain shoot across his face.

"You look much better and the clothes fit, thank goodness," said William, kissing her cheek.

"A little big mayhap but father won't notice that. Where did you get them?"

"There's a seamstress in the village, I called first thing, they were ready for collection by a customer, I paid her double."

Another woman I must thank once I get my life back to normal, she was thinking.

Melbroke poured her a cool water, it came straight from the inn's own well. "Would you prefer wine? Warm beer?" She shook her head, not even glancing at him. There was hot boiled beef on the table, along with cheese, butter, freshly baked bread and slices of cold mutton.

"We think we've devised a story that will sound true for your father," Melbroke ventured. "We don't want to tell too many lies, 'tis too easy to get caught up in them, so we'll stick to the truth wherever we can."

"And of course," added William, "there's the Sheriff and the Coroner to think about. We need our statements of events to be the same for both."

"There'll be an inquest!" She was alarmed. "This will become public?"

"Probably not an inquest," Melbroke said, "the cause of death is obvious but the coroner may be involved."

William nodded. "We must get our story straight and stick to it."

Frances remained silent. Anxious. She wanted neither her father, nor the world, getting even an inkling of the truth. "How on earth do we explain how we three just happened to all be in the same barn in the middle of Kent at the same time?" Anxiety etched her face. "And how will we ever explain why my betrothed wanted to kill me?"

"We don't," said Melbroke. "You weren't there. We'll keep you right out of it."

"How? 'Tis all about me!" Her angry eyes looked at him incredulously.

"It needn't be," William said, placing his hand over hers in reassurance. "We've come up with a story that we think sounds feasible"

Frances was listening. She relaxed her back against the wooden chair and waited.

"When the Sheriff, or his men, get to the barn," William continued, "they will find Pierre's body, your coat, your money, your bag with its personal things inside."

"Yes, that was stupid of me," she said irritably. "I realized after we'd arrived here last night that I'd left everything behind. Stupid!"

"No, it doesn't matter, in fact 'tis good. They can't be identified, they could be anyone's. And of course, they'll also find a monk's habit."

"Yes..." she said, slowly, not yet understanding where this line of thought was going.

"We've used them to make a plausible story," Melbroke added.

"Go on"

"I was on my own," he continued, "the heaven's opened, I needed to take shelter, I saw the barn. As I approached I heard men shouting. One man, who turned out to be Pierre but I didn't know because I've never met him, was accusing a monk of being a thief and a fraudster. He had his sword at the man's throat and was shouting that the man had taken his money. I watched for a moment, didn't intervene at first but then Pierre began cutting the man on his hands and arms and threatening to kill him if he didn't return his money. The man was screeching with fear, terrified.

"Thinking him to be a man of God, I went to his defence. I fought with Pierre, I'll describe it as it truly happened. I didn't mean to kill him I only wanted to defend the monk. Your father and the Sheriff will see my wounds, my arms, my injured face. I killed Pierre in self defence."

"And the monk?"

"When Pierre fell to the ground I went over to try and revive him only to find he was dead. I was shocked. My alarm stole a few seconds and when I took my attention back to the monk he had gone. He'd abandoned his habit. I saw him running across the field. He was a fraudster! He was a highway robber and he'd fled for his life leaving behind his habit and cache of stolen items, including your shoulder bag and money."

"Why did he take off his monk's habit?"

"So he could run faster, he was after all running for his life, or so he would have thought."

"That's excellent," Frances beamed, "and a story that will be believed at Court."

Melbroke nodded. "We think so." He continued: "I was just preparing to leave the barn when William caught up with me, having ridden all night. He saw Galahad outside the barn and came in. From there we tell the story exactly as it happened but without your presence."

"But why are you two on the highway?"

"We can give a truthful answer to that question," continued William. "I returned from the North to Margaret's note saying you had both gone to Blean. I was concerned for your safety, you had no male protection, I knew I'd got to follow. I told Alban of my concern and he insisted on helping me."

Frances flashed a sarcastic glare Melbroke's way.

"I had to see the King first so Alban went on a head, I was just a few hours behind."

"A bit of a coincidence though that you both ended up in the same barn in the middle of Kent, don't you think?"

"No, not at all," winced Melbroke. His whole body was again screaming to be allowed to return to bed, it couldn't be. "Before we left the Palace William gave me the route you would take, that is actually true. He said it was the route your family always took."

"Yes, he was right. But how will you bring me into it, I'm here after all."

"William and I headed for this inn and by lucky coincidence you were already here, resting up for the day because the travelling had exhausted you."

"And Lunar, she was exhausted, too."

"That's good. A woman's concern for her horse is a nice touch. Rings true."

"It is true!"

"Because of my injuries and your tiredness," continued Melbroke, "all three of us stayed the night."

Frances thought for a moment. "The Sheriff might question the innkeeper, he knows we arrived together."

"We can sort that," said William. "Last night at supper smoke from the fire kept billowing back into the room. The innkeeper was cursing the rooks, they've nested in his chimney tops for so many years they've near blocked them. Alban is offering to pay for all his chimneys to be cleaned, if he will assist us."

The three sat quietly, eating slowly, thinking, running it all through in their minds, looking for errors.

"My father will reimburse you," Frances eventually said, her voice barely above a whisper. She didn't want to be beholden to Melbroke any more than she already was. She wanted nothing more to pass between them, she was determined to keep their relationship distant.

"There is no need,"

"O but there is Melbroke," she snapped. Her frostiness was palpable, even William could sense it.

"Your father cannot reimburse Alban," William said soothingly, "it would mean explaining why we had to bribe the innkeeper. I will pay."

"I am only trying to repay some of the pain I have caused," Melbroke sighed, raising his eyes to the dirty ceiling above.

"'Tis not necessary. You saved my life but you have no responsibility for me." She turned to William. "There's one more thing, why was I on the road? Why was I riding to Blean? And what about Margaret?"

"You tell us Frances. Why were you on the road?" Both William and Melbroke waited, eager to hear how her explanation would sound when she told the Sheriff.

She thought for a moment. "Because I was getting nervous about the wedding. Everyone at the Palace was talking about it, kept asking me questions, wouldn't leave me alone. My nerves were getting on top of me. I had to get to father's for some peace. I asked Margaret to accompany me."

"That'll do nicely," said Melbroke, "and stick to the truth."

"Don't presume to give me orders," she snapped, turning her face to his, her eyes cold and glaring. "I know what I must say."

After a frosty moment she continued. "Margaret was taken ill at Greenwich and returned to Richmond, I travelled on alone."

"Indeed," said Melbroke nodding, not prepared to allow himself to be subdued by her. "'Twill also give some unsubstantiated reason as to why Pierre was on the road. Perhaps he had heard of your departure, was worried and followed. He's dead, he can't say but it might quell the Sheriff's concerns."

"And father's."

"That's settled then," said William as he slapped his friend's shoulder in triumph. Melbroke winced out loud; they both heard it. "Is your arm no better?"

"'Tis fine."

"No it isn't," Frances argued. "You're sitting with your left hand in your lap, you've hardly moved that arm at all."

"'Tis a little painful, 'tis true but it will heal, might take a day or two more, that's all."

She should have looked at the wound, she was thinking. At least made sure it was clean but she was so exhausted herself yesterday and so full of anger and shame that she just didn't think.

"Which brings me to the next thing," said William. "Frances, I think you should journey on from here by carriage."

"But that will take so long! No, I can ride, truly," she replied.

"In a carriage, with Alban," he insisted. "You are too fragile to ride the distance."

"No!" Closeted closeness for many hours to this particular Lord was the last thing she wanted.

"Alban can't ride Galahad with that arm. He's a stallion, a powerful beast, he needs controlling. Nor could his back take hours in the saddle. You two go in the carriage, I'll take your horses."

"Absolutely not. I'm riding and that's final. What Melbroke does it up to him."

A lackey approached their table, bobbing a shallow curtsey. "Scoose me Lordships, Lady, the innkeeper asks if he could speak wiv you, Sir." She directed her request at William. He left the table and followed the girl.

"Don't trust yourself in a carriage with me?" Melbroke grinned.

She stared coldly at him. "I don't trust you anywhere. Do you blame me? 'Tisn't your horse that needs controlling, 'tis you!"

"I am not a monster, madam!" he challenged, his eyes angry. "I have explained already, had I realized you meant 'no', I would not have..."

"You understand now that I mean it?"

"You have made your views perfectly clear."

"And you don't feel I am beholden to you because you saved me, that you have a claim on me, that I owe you something?"

He swallowed hard as her words cut into his dignity. "Mayhap, to be on the safe side," he said coolly, his eyes flashing but his demeanour controlled, "and just incase my lust overcomes my injuries, you should ride in the carriage alone." He was being sarcastic, she realized that. She could also see his controlled anger. Her words had duly wounded. Her low opinion of him fuelled his annoyance of her and the situation. He was a gentleman, especially toward ladies. He had never forced himself on any, nor did he choose to. A tumble was only delightful if both were enjoying it. It occurred to him now that a virgin wouldn't understand that.

Neither spoke for a few moments. Eventually Frances asked: "Will you take a carriage?"

"No, I shall ride, I can manage with one arm. But I'm not sure I shall come to Blean, I would like to get back to Richmond."

They sat in silence. Frances relieved and confident that the story they had concocted would convince her father; Melbroke in pain from his injuries but trying not to show it.

William returned. "It was a messenger with a note from the Sheriff. As he has to be in Canterbury urgently on other business and as we are travelling that way, he will call on us at Blean. Well, that seals it Alban, you've got to come to Blean, you've got to see the Sheriff."

"Seems I have no choice," Melbroke agreed.

Frances felt guilty. Melbroke clearly couldn't ride all that way. She was concerned too for Lunar.

"Well in that case," she said, "and on the strict understanding that you keep your distance from me, I would appreciate your escort. 'Tis true I am weakened by events, I would prefer a carriage."

Melbroke bowed his head mockingly. "My Lady, is too kind. But wise I think. We wouldn't want anything else happening to you, would we?"

She bit her lip at his condescending words but knew he was right. Even with just one functioning arm and a bad back he was still a lot stronger than she.

William chose to ignore the ongoing hostility between them, he had more pressing matters to concentrate on. "The Sheriff's sending a constable to the barn, to survey the scene. If and when he and the Coroner are satisfied, when they've got our statements I presume, he will arrange the appropriate authorization for burial. I've sent a return message saying we'll expect him at Blean, about midday the day after the morrow. I've also given him Pierre's mother's details in Mortlake."

"O, good Lord," uttered Frances, "I had forgotten about his mother. She only lost her husband last year, this will be devastating news for her."

"At least with our story," William said, sympathetically, "she need never know that her son was clearly deranged. That he planned to murder two people."

GOD'S WOUNDS! A thought like lightening struck Melbroke just as he and Frances were about to enter the carriage. I am supposed to be seeing the King today, to talk about my trip to France!

"Lady Frances, you must excuse me," he said, giving her no chance to object. "I have forgotten something most urgent." Before she could respond he'd gone. She arranged cushions. He ran back into the inn, his back screaming in excruciating pain with every footfall on the uneven cobbles. With luck the London-bound messenger hadn't yet left. "Can you go to Richmond Palace?" The man nodded. He bade him wait while he wrote a missive to his monarch. He kept it simple, gave a rough sketch of the story they'd hatched, outlined his wounds, explained where he was heading and offered his deepest and humblest apologies to his much loved cousin. He borrowed the inn's sealing wax and pushed the small ring he wore bearing the Melbroke crest into its molten blob.

"All speed," he commanded. "'Tis an urgent message for the King." His Majesty would receive it later today. Melbroke could only hope he would think kindly toward him. It was a big hope!

CANTERBURY CATHEDRAL came into view, way off on the horizon, just as Frances opened her eyes from a shallow sleep. It was late afternoon, the sun was now behind them and she had pulled back the curtain across the glassless window. Tucked under a blanket she had been drifting in and out of sleep while Melbroke had slept nearly all the way, save to pay the various tariffs when the horses were changed. William had gone on ahead with Galahad and Lunar on lead reins, she wished she'd thought to ask him for some money, it was a silly oversight which had put her completely in Melbroke's control.

"I shall reimburse you," she'd said, several times.

"If you really feel you must," he'd replied, tiring of her constant objection to his basic kindness.

At first they had made small talk. "We were lucky to find such a busy inn," he'd ventured, at the start of their journey. "One where messengers congregated."

"Indeed. And one that had a carriage we could use. Even if poor William did have to pay a king's ransom for it."

He'd ignored the barb. "Is everything comfortable for

you?"

"Comfortable enough, thank you."

She spoke civilly but coldly. Shock and dismay still ruled her and probably would forever, she was thinking. She knew it was unedifying but for now she didn't have the strength or the inclination to be any other way. "Don't feel you must keep me in conversation all the way to Canterbury," she'd said. "If you wish to sleep I shall not be offended, indeed I shall probably sleep myself."

It was his release to give up trying to be civil. For a few moments he'd looked out at the passing countryside, then rested his head back against the upholstery and closed his eyes. The horses had got into their rhythm and the carriage followed suit. It moved gently, rocking is occupants. It was soothing and Melbroke, with his back well padded against sudden jolts, was soon slumbering.

He was sitting cross-legged with one ankle over the other knee. His doublet was open at the neck, its left sleeve now heavily blackened and stiff from the stain of dried blood. No shirt, she noticed. He hadn't bothered to buy one. Just a bare, strong neck leading down to the top of his powerful, broad chest. The open doublet, the stubble, the movement of his thick hair as it swayed to the dance of the road, mesmerized her for a few seconds. Then her eyes fell on his tan leather boots, her gaze followed them up his legs, over his knees to the strong thighs that were rocking to and fro with the rhythm of the road. Thighs that could control a powerful beast in the joust or galvanize its power on the battlefield. I expect his women are taken with those thighs, she thought.

She couldn't take her eyes from them, they held her gaze, commanded her fascination. Then she realized he had opened his eyes and was watching her. Had he sensed her eyes upon him? She saw an illicit smile flicker on his lips as he raised his eyebrows and a questioning wave of acknowledgement was directed at her. She blushed as embarrassment claimed her.

"There is much blood on your doublet Lord Melbroke, has your wound begun to bleed again?"

"Your concern is appreciated Lady Frances, my arm is well."

"'Tis not," she snapped. "You can barely move it."

"'Tis painful, 'tis true, all sword wounds are. But no worse than I would expect."

She felt she had been put in her place. She gazed at the passing scenery for a few seconds and then closed her eyes. She was pale, her complexion drained. He noticed shadows under her eyes, her furrowed brow as she rested tensely, her pale lips. He thought how pleasing it would be to bring colour back to that face. Then he dismissed the thought as quickly as it had occurred and closed his eyes, too.

This is how they had carried on for the many hours it had taken to get to Canterbury. Civil snatches of unnecessary conversation, followed by sleep interrupted by horse changes. He had offered her refreshments, she had declined. He had taken wine.

"Please eat," Lord Melbroke, "if you so wish, don't let my needs govern yours."

"Eating is difficult today," he'd smiled. "Your brother-in-law defended you well!"

"That is why you ate little breakfast?"

"Indeed. My jaws are very painful."

She looked down into her lap. "I'm sorry," she'd said quietly. It took him aback.

"You're sorry! I thought you would be delighted."

"Please Lord Melbroke, I am not a monster either! You saved my honour and my life, I would not choose to have you injured."

Their eyes had locked. Her beautiful sapphire eyes were his for the briefest of moments. Any other woman and he would have stepped across the gap that separated them and kissed her. Not this one. This one was complicated, he didn't need it. A second of intimacy and then they'd both looked away.

He'd stretched his body along the short seat, manoeuvred cushions for the umpteenth time to bring comfort to his back and allowed his long, booted legs to jut into their shared middle space. He'd thrown his riding coat over himself and slept as Kent passed by.

IT WAS her excited voice, hours later, that drew him back from a place that had been free from pain. As sleep slipped from him so agony returned. "We are nearly home," Frances called. "We are nearly at Blean."

He stirred, opened his eyes, swung his legs gingerly to the floor.

"Look, Canterbury Cathedral," she said, pointing to the right. "'Tis only a few miles now."

She was full of excitement, relief. Happiness radiated from her. God, she's beautiful, he thought. He envied her the love of her family home. "I look forward to meeting your father."

"You will love him, everybody does."

"I'm sure I will."

Where she had been sleeping, her head against the back of the seat, her hat had been jogged by the carriage's rhythm and some of her hair now fell in matted tendrils about her neck. Should he tell her? Was it too personal? Would it add to her irritation of him?

"Lady Frances," he ventured boldly, remembering that her appearance to her father was paramount, "may I mention that before you greet your father you may wish to attend to your hair, it has come a little adrift."

Her fingers worked quickly on the loose strands. "All right now?"

He gazed at her neck as she turned her head for him. One side then the other. Her beautiful white neck, the neck he had kissed and teased. Swanlike, elegant. He remembered the scent of her hair, the softness of her skin. "Yes 'tis fine now," he said, turning away and forcing his thoughts to the passing daffodils.

The sickness that had ravaged the convent was waning and the demand for apothecary cures was returning to normal. The past few weeks had taken much of Magdala's time and energy. Many of her usual herb-growing chores had been put aside to concentrate on the fever and now the apothecaries of both the nunnery and the adjacent monastery, where the fever had also taken hold, were complaining that their shelves needed replenishing.

With the senior apothecary's eager urging and Mother Esme's begrudged permission, Magdala would now be spending more time outside tending, sowing, planting and renewing the herb supply.

The monastery had its own herb garden and theoretically the herb growers of convent and monastery were not supposed to converse. It was forbidden, a sin. Nevertheless they did. Like-minded folk have a tendency to gravitate to each other, even in religious orders. Magdala knew it to be a need of the soul and vows of obedience were put aside to fulfil the hunger for companionship, for discourse. She certainly recognized it in herself. All that apart, her herb garden was better than the monks' and they frequently asked for supplies.

She enjoyed her furtive talks with the men and much of her early knowledge had been gathered this way. She had to be careful though, eagle eyes were always watching. Shrivelled souls, very often belonging to the most pious, were always ready to report and spoil.

Her helpers were on a rota and like her had to attend Offices and do Mother Superior's other bidding. In fact Mother had insisted that Magdala do as many extra hours in prayer as she was doing in the herb garden.

"Your work makes you too egotistical, Sister. Ask God to return you to humility," Esme had ordered.

No protestations had been able to soften her command so now her knees were really in trouble.

"I shall trust to your honesty, Sister," Esme had said haughtily. "I know you to be an honest gentlewoman, a true servant of our Lord. Lie to me and you lie to Him." Magdala hadn't needed reminding.

A gentle night's rain had softened the ground so turning the soil and yanking the weeds was easy. She never pulled rank, she bent her back along with the others for as long as they did. She twisted her trowel and planted the seedlings at as rapid a pace as any of the younger nuns and with them sang along to their favourite melodies. Sometimes on a still day they could hear the monks singing too. Sometimes they sung alternate verses in a strange act of human contact that surely even Esme would have trouble finding evil, should she have heard, which she never did. They made sure of it, just in case.

Chapter Nine

HIS VOICE WAS stern. "I hope, Lady Frances," he said, as their carriage turned into the tree-lined drive toward the house, "that you will allow me to assist you out of the carriage, if only for appearances sake. Your father will no doubt meet us."

"Of course. My anger and your behaviour are matters between us. They concern no one else."

"Two other people now know, I suggest we keep it that way."

"Do you honestly think I would want anyone else knowing!"

"No. Nor I."

"Really? I'm sure that amongst men your story would raise a great laugh."

"And your obvious despising of me will be noticed. It could undermine our story," he retorted, trying not to raise his voice.

"I don't see why, you have just killed the man I was to marry. Even in our fabricated story, you've done that!"

"Will you be able to control this anger, this dislike of me, once you are safe in your family home?"

She flashed an angry glare at him. Even her emotions he criticized! "Don't worry yourself my Lord. I don't need lessons on manners or behaviour from you!"

As far as he could recall, he'd never been the subject of hatred and anger from a woman. Men, yes, many times but never a woman. It made him very uncomfortable although he couldn't help but admire her spirit. It would seem, though, that she did not intend to humiliate him in front of the Earl, he'd be thankful for that.

"I pray to God that I will come to forgive you," she said, her voice lower now. "But I am struggling with my frailty in this matter."

"I have apologized, I hope you are able to accept that apology."

"I am and I have. But you have also killed Pierre."

"But he was going to..."

"Yes, I know what he was going to do! But I have to consider that I drove him to it. You drove him to it! Aren't all men, even the mildest, capable of violence if they are driven by circumstance." It was rhetorical, she didn't want his answer or his opinion.

They looked away from each other, she emotional, he considering she may possibly be right. She continued: "I know too, that I should be grateful to you but I am very confused. I have thanked God for sending you when He did, it was indeed a miracle. I suppose I can't quite believe it has all happened. Pierre was always so courteous and kind."

"Did you love him?"

"I don't know. I liked him well enough. I'm not sure what love is."

"Nor I. What I've seen of it always seems to bring pain."

"You mean, all those women and you never loved one!"

"Never. Nor do I intend to."

"But you told them you did of course," she scoffed, "in order to have your way with them."

"Never. I have never told any woman that I loved her. Nor ever needed to lie!"

"O, you're so handsome, so charming, they fall at your feet I suppose."

"Something like that," he said, turning his grinning face to the dusky parklands they traversed. She flashed a contemptuous look and turned her eyes away from him. They continued up the drive in silence.

THREE LARGE mastiffs encircled them, barking with excitement at having a visitor, wagging their tails and leaping. The Earl, elderly but erect, white hair framing his kindly but firm face, stood waiting. His steward Gates a few steps behind.

"O father, I'm so glad to see you," she said, falling into his outstretched arms. Melbroke strode to their side. "Father allow me to introduce Alban, the Lord Melbroke." Melbroke bowed low as befitted the Earl's rank, his back screeching in objection, his teeth gritted. The Earl tipped his head. "Honoured young man. I know of you of course. Fought with your father at Bosworth against the Yorkists. Wonderful man, loyal, brave."

"Indeed he was my Lord."

The Earl slapped Melbroke on the back, he absorbed the pain without a wince. "We haven't had royal blood in the house for many a year."

"'Tis an honour to meet you my Lord. Only a little royal blood I'm afraid, I am but a distant cousin of his Majesty."

"And how is it you two know each other?" He put an arm around his daughter and not waiting for her answer, continued: "You look pale my dear and you, Sir," he said, turning back to Melbroke, "have been in a fight. Has anyone looked at the wound that I assume lies beneath the blood on your doublet?"

"No my Lord. And I confess it is very painful."

"Right, well go tend to it. William's already here, we'll meet in two hours in the library. Cook knows supper will be late tonight. I want to know what all this is about, every jot and dot." With that the Earl called his dogs and headed off into the grounds. He to enjoy his last stroll of the day, the dogs to hunt rabbits for tomorrow's pot.

Frances turned to Melbroke and smiled. It surprised him. "Well my Lord, what do you think of Blean?"

He gazed up at the impressive house, its leaded lights glinting as inside lamps were being lit, its ornate chimneys reaching for the sky, several of them already smoking, the grey trails playing against the amethyst hue of twilight. The parkland around rolled into the contours of Kent with curves and dips that looked as though they held secrets. Forest was way off on the horizon and he could see the Earl with his dogs heading toward a stream that shone like a silver ribbon in the dying moments of what had been a long, trying day.

"'Tis very beautiful," he replied. I can see why you love it here."

Gates led the way through the imposing main door and into a tiled reception area. "My Lord, if you would care to follow me."

Melbroke turned to Frances: "I'll see you later, my Lady."

"Indeed my Lord, I look forward to it. And please be sure to soak that arm in hot water. I am concerned about it."

Gates led Melbroke up two flights of oak stairs. His room, on the floor above Frances', was large with impressive perpendicular windows giving views over the stream. A fire roared in the grate. The four-poster looked comfortable and welcoming, he longed to get into to it and sleep for days. Is she really worried about my arm, he wondered.

"A servant will be up to fill the bath, my Lord," said Gates, pushing open a door that led to an adjoining dressing and wash room. "And there is wine and light food under the napkin."

He followed the steward's gaze to a side table. It looked inviting, his stomach was telling him it had been an age since his sore jaws had allowed him to eat. He poured a wine and lifted the cloth. Sliced meats and little pink cubes of something melting and sweet. Perfect.

"The Earl has instructed me to give you clean clothes, my Lord. He was of similar size to your Lordship in his younger days. A maid will bring them shortly." Gates bowed and left.

Melbroke looked around the room. Warm, nurturing colours of bronze and deep red. Outside the tall thin windows the sun was setting in a sky with not a sign of rain clouds. Amethyst was turning to mauve and in the distance he could see birds swirling in large flocks. He was in the west side of the house. The sun's last rays, along with this sumptuous room, cheered his bruised soul. The room was warm. It felt like a sanctuary from the world. He would rest here until tomorrow, give his statement to the Sheriff and be off to London and the King. He didn't want to stay a moment longer in Frances' home than he had to. He knew she would be glad to see him gone and like those birds he would fly to new adventures.

LATE EVENING by the gamekeeper's hut just north of Richmond and a weak, thin, effete man waits for his brother. He paces the leaf mould, kicks the rock in impatience. He throws a stone at gathering black birds and their wings scrape angrily at the air to lift them up and away. The brother is late and the sky is darkening. The first stars are like pins on a blue cushion heralding another bitter night. Already night chill prevails. He goes into the wattle-walled hut to be away from the elements but can still see the sky through the roof of branches, the turf that laid above them long gone. This wraithlike, albeit well-dressed man, bangs his hands together and blows warm air between them. Where in hell's name is he!

The crows are now conspicuous by their absence. The brother, with his startled eyes darting and thin lips purpling from cold, is alone. Discomfort pervades and his nerves jerk at every crack or rustle from the undergrowth. He is surrounded by trees still in skein, there is little cover, even inside the hut he feels exposed. He is irritated by his brother's absence, his mood blackening with the menacing fall of night. He will wait until he can no longer see the tallest branches then return to Mortlake, mayhap there will be a message. Little does he know, on this cold, crisp even that penetrates his very bones and bites at his nose, that he will never see his brother again. He will now be forever alone.

FRANCES STOLE Melbroke's breath as she walked into the library. She was wearing a gown of soft green silk trimmed with velvet. The silk was heavily embroidered in a shiny thread and the neckline decorated with emeralds. Her tiny waist was emphasized by the full gathered skirt and lacy, golden underskirts danced around her ankles. Her hair was freshly washed and fell in curling cascades from a small golden cap which also twinkled with emeralds.

As she'd descended the stairs she'd heard her father's booming voice. "Dead? God's body! I can scarce believe it!" They had started without her. She didn't mind. They had the lion's share of the story to tell. She felt better now. Safe now she was home, warm now she had soaked her aching limbs but still tired, her mind still churning over events she could scarce believe had truly happened.

The three men stood as she entered. Melbroke bowed, his painful back a little more supple from his hot bath. "My Lady." She didn't respond. She declined wine, kissed her father and took a seat by his side. Melbroke settled away from the fire, near the window. He was wearing the borrowed doublet, shirt and hose. He had shaved and looked the better for it. His freshly-washed hair, tied again at the nape of his neck was gleaming and catching the candlelight. She could see its glints dancing on its richness. He still wore his knee-high boots, now polished and shining. Again he sat with one ankle over the other knee. Why did that pose affect her so? He looked so strong; so confident. It was his way. Tonight though he felt neither, although none present realized just how bad he was feeling. He made sure of it.

"My dear," said her father taking her hands, "Pierre dead. I can scarce believe it."

"Tis a great shock, father. William has explained, I hope, that it was self-defence, Lord Melbroke had no choice, he didn't mean to kill him."

"Yes, yes, all has been explained. But why did you leave the Palace?"

They had obviously left her part until she arrived.

"Of course, I wish now that I hadn't but everyone was going on and on about the wedding. My nerves were building up, some days I felt sick with nerves. I wasn't sleeping for worrying. I decided I'd come here, get away from all the gossips, enjoy some peace before the day."

He stroked her hands. "Poor girl. Poor, poor girl. And presumably," he turned to William, "the Marquis heard about it and chased after her."

"Presumably Sir, yes. We have to assume that. There is no other reason for him being on the road to Blean."

"But why," the Earl asked, "didn't you tell Pierre you were leaving?"

William and Melbroke held their breaths. It was a question they hadn't anticipated.

"I thought he was still in France," she quickly answered. "I had no idea he was at the Palace, he hadn't been to see me." The two onlookers relaxed.

"And you, Melbroke," he said, turning to the other side of the room, "you didn't even know whom you were fighting?"

"No, Sir. I had no idea. William saw my horse tethered by the barn and arrived on the scene just minutes after the fraudster monk had fled. It was he who told me whom I had just killed."

"Terrible, terrible business."

He paused for a while, absorbing all that was being told to him. "And Frances, I hear you got soaked to the skin, near caught your death! And Lunar was fractious. Why on earth didn't you use the Blean carriage?"

Again Melbroke and William held their breath. Another question they hadn't anticipated.

"I left the carriage for the servants who have much to bring for the wedding, I didn't want to wait for them to get everything packed up. Anyway, I was happy to ride, the weather was fine when I left, I certainly didn't expect it to change so. "

"Very sensible of you to stay awhile at that inn. And luck for me that you did, at least you had two strapping men to bring you on to Blean."

"Indeed father. I was very glad to see them both."

"So you know Lord Melbroke?"

Again the onlookers tensed.

"Just a little father. I have seen him around Court but I was first introduced to him by William and Margaret, at one of their musical evenings last year."

"And how is me daughter, William?" Thankfully the Earl changed the subject.

"Sir, I fear I cannot say. We crossed each other. She heading back to Richmond by road as I headed to Greenwich cross country. I sent a message that Frances is well and that I was escorting her to your safe care."

"Right, William," the Earl said, slapping his thigh. "First thing in the morning send another message. Get her down here. You all look worn out. You can stay here for a few weeks. Tell her to bring the staff she needs and Frances' maid."

"And Smiley," Frances added.

"Yes and the blimmin' dog, if that's what you can call such a weedy thing on four legs!" He kissed his daughter's hand, grinning. The son-in-law nodded. "And William, after supper you and I must discuss how we are to handle the ramifications of this situation."

"Sir?"

"The wedding! We've got to inform over two hundred guests, including the King, that the wedding is cancelled because the groom is dead! We shall need help." Almost as an afterthought he added: "And I must send condolences to the Marchioness.

There is a lot to do. We must get cracking after supper. What time is the Sheriff coming?"

"I instructed after midday, my Lord."

"Good. I've a meeting in the morning but then we can begin to get this behind us. Then I want you three to concentrate on recuperating."

"My Lord," ventured Melbroke, "I feel I would be intruding. I intended leaving after seeing the Sheriff."

"Nonsense! That arm needs care, so does your back. I've had sword wounds, caught a very nasty one at Stoke, fighting with our King's father, they don't heal in a hurry and the muscles in your shoulders and fingers are probably affected. Don't deny it!" He was right, Melbroke had great trouble tugging on his long boots, the pain had shot from his fingers to his shoulder while his back had competed and nearly won. "You're staying here, if not for a few weeks at least for a few days. No arguments, do y'hear?"

Melbroke nodded with resignation. At least Frances had heard her father insisting and he would, if truth be told, be grateful of more time to rest. "I must send another message to the King in that case."

"We'll get scribes over from Canterbury in the morning, set them in the lower hall. We'll get messengers over as well, there's going to be a lot leaving Blean on the morrow, can't keep sending staff traipsing into Canterbury."

THE SUPPER table groaned with food. Frances walked into the rich, oak dining room on her father's arm. The two men followed behind, through the high stone arch, its heavy studded doors anchored open to reveal the room's splendour.

"Can't take your eyes off her, can you?" William whispered.

Melbroke ignored him while watching the roll of her hips, the flow of her skirts and her hair, fresh and golden, falling nearly to her waist and gently bouncing as she walked.

A fire roared in the impressive, huge, stone fireplace and a stack of logs stood ready on the hearth. Above them gold-leaf angels danced between red and white tudor roses carved high on a wood and plaster ceiling, its fashionable blyse blue bringing even more richness to this impressive room. Heavy tapestries adorned the walls, crystal twinkled on the oak dresser, silver shone.

Cook had provided Frances' favourite saddle of rabbit with garlic. There was also stewed beef with herbs and spit roast birds. The meal was a quiet affair, punctuated now and again by another question from the Earl. As the evening progressed so the pains in Melbroke's body increased. His arm felt worse since its long soak in hot water. He had noticed the flesh around the wound was pink and tender to touch. He ate with one hand and chewed slowly, his face was also still sore. His back, now showing heavy bruising could find no comfortable position.

"Father, perhaps in the morning we could go to the chapel and pray for Pierre's soul," Frances said quietly, her eyes looking tearful.

"Of course my dear. It is the least we can all do. The poor man, such a courteous soul."

They all remained silent. Let him believe that, they were all thinking. Why ruin his opinion of the man he thought was to be his son by law. Generosity was needed here, for the Earl and particularly for the Marchioness.

"Now to the withdrawing room. I've some newly delivered Port," the Earl announced, when the meal was over.

"If you don't mind," said Melbroke, "I feel I would do well to go to my bed. My arm is very painful, I would not be good company."

The Earl had noticed how little his guest had eaten, how quiet he'd been, how pale he was. Frances too was ashen.

"Off you go then, both of you. William, too. You all look worn out. We'll reconvene in the morning. Early, damned early. Do y'hear?" All nodded and left the table.

Frances and Melbroke walked up the stairs together, Frances leading the way. On the first landing she turned to him. "I shall say good night here, my Lord. I hope you feel a little better in the morning." To his astonishment she lifted her hand and offered it to him.

"But you've forbidden me to touch you."

"You can when I permit it."

He took it gently and bent to kiss the back of her fingers. A sweet smell filled his senses, the softness of her skin graced his lips and for a brief second he was unaware of the pain in his spine. She noticed slight beads of perspiration on his forehead, had he been too close to the fire?

"Good night Lady Frances, I look forward to seeing you on the morrow."

"You will come to the chapel?"

"If you would like me to."

"I think you should. You are his slayer after all! You could pray for your own soul, too." Her words snatched away what he thought had been a moment of softening hostilities.

"Would you have preferred me not to have saved you?" He snapped, irritably.

"No, of course not."

"Then perhaps madam, you would desist from using his death as a weapon against me."

"My hand please, my Lord," she said, snatching it out of

his grip. "Before we break our fast. If my Lord can spare the time!"

Chapter Ten

THE MOUNTED EARL sat at the top of the valley and looked down. The ridge he was on was higher than the tree tops. He was surveying skeletons. Mighty oak and their hardwood neighbours, all good for charcoal. Erect they stood, waiting for the surge of new growth, the younger trees amongst them unaware that the recent equinox had been their last. It was the younger trees, with their slimmer trunks, that were earmarked for charcoal. Their destiny was not to be ancient. They wouldn't be rustling their messages across the centuries as their forebears had done. To his right a clearing cut like a sore into the vista, he hated the look of it and turned his eyes up into the moody, dawn sky.

The cutting of the greenwood had started weeks ago, while the sap was down, the wood destined for the burners that would produce the charcoal on which to lay and burn the iron ore. The furnace ate charcoal and the suppliers were making sure they didn't fall short of their contract. A huge pile of trees lay like felled soldiers awaiting their fate.

Thirty-five acres he'd given to this works, a mere pimple on the northern side of his multi-thousand acre estate. Nevertheless there was a sadness that he couldn't shrug off as he thought of those proud trees. His nose caught the smell of freshly cut wood. Usually it was sweet and pleased him, today he hated its brutal witness. He grunted and turned his thoughts away.

He walked his horse down the side of the valley, sticking to his familiar track, leaning back in the saddle as the downward path became steeper and the horse trod gingerly. The soft air of morning became more intense as he descended. Under-hoof the ground was spongy and the aroma of damp leaves caught the breeze. The cold dew dripped. A late owl hooted its final call and took to wing. The smell of wood-smoke lingered in the thick of the forest, in the deep secret darkness of shrub and holly and yew that escorted him on both sides. He could hear the scurrying and warning calls of animals and birds unused to human activity at this early hour. In the distance the flow of the river, tumbling over ancient stone as it swelled from recent rain, gave background rhythm to his ride. God how he loved the country! This country!

He could hear men's voices as he approached the works. Laughing and chatting as though they had known each other for years. He dismounted and led his horse towards the group. Pascal Blanc was on good terms it seemed with the Harwykes, or perhaps it was just the French way, over familiar, a different understanding of boundaries than the more reserved English. Whatever it was, the Harwykes seemed to like it and much slapping of shoulders was going on.

Blanc saw him first. "Ah, my Lord, bon jour. Comment allez vous?"

"Never mind how I am Blanc, just introduce me to your

friends."

Arthur and Samuel Harwyke, who could have been twins they looked so similar but were actually born one year apart, proffered a begrudging bow. They cared not for deference. Approaching forty, the Earl surmised. He saw daggers at their belts and he didn't like their cocky felt hats with brims that formed bills at the front. They had worn, boney faces, flabby skin that hung in folds and small, mean eyes. Their hands weren't stained like Bellowes' and Blanc's. They weren't gentlemen's hands either. They were rough and callused but they weren't stained.

"Know much about iron?" His manner was brusque as he took an instant dislike to them.

"We are learning," said Arthur, the older of the two who sported a short, pointed beard. "We were just asking Pascal if we could buy his guidance."

"He's in my pay! You ask me!" The Earl was in his oft-irascible mood. He noted they were already on first-name terms.

"Our sincerest apologies," said Samuel Harwyke obsequiously, stepping forward and settling too close to the Earl. "'Twas idle talk whilst we awaited your arrival, my Lord, we should have thought." The Earl snorted and moved away.

"You know the details of the lease? You can afford it?"

The Harwykes nodded in unison.

"Where's your money coming from?" Not a question he would ask his own class but an instant distrust of these two was nagging at him. Was their source solid, reliable? These weren't gentlemen, they didn't even look like merchants. They looked like two scoundrels who'd bought decent dogaline coats especially for this meeting. His eyes fell to their now muddy shoes and ridiculous gaiters tied with bows down the fronts, the lower ties now also covered in mud. Completely unsuitable for visiting an iron works in the middle of a forest during a cold, wet spring.

"Had an inheritance, my Lord," explained the fawning Samuel. The Earl raised his eyebrows. "From an uncle." Aha, thought the Earl, probably bought the new clothes. "My brother and I wish to invest it sensibly, 'tis what our uncle would have wanted."

"You like the works?"

"Indeed we do. We hope to get production going as soon as possible."

"Should produce a ton o' pig iron a day, wouldn't you say Blanc?"

"Indeed I would Messieurs."

"That good enough for you? Think that a good investment? What say you?"

The brothers bowed in affirmation.

"Right. Get your lawyer to contact mine, Blanc's got the details and we'll get this sorted quickly as we can. You could be digging shafts within the week. No point in hanging around."

The Earl turned and made for his mount. "Come to whatever arrangement you like with these two," he called to Blanc, from the saddle. "But keep me and Bellowes informed, can't have too much of your time diverted from Grinstead."

With that the Earl turned away and prepared to walk his horse back up the valley. He hadn't liked the Harwykes but this was business, what did it matter. Once the contracts were signed he need have little truck with them.

THE CHAPEL was small and intimate. Dozens of chubby and slim cream candles flickered around the high stone walls and made the altar shine and glint in its goldenness. The Earl hadn't summoned the priest, it was to be a short, private affair. Just those who knew Pierre, kneeling in his memory and saying a prayer for his soul. Frances wouldn't be going to the funeral. She and her father had discussed that earlier. It would probably be in France, he didn't want to travel and he didn't think it appropriate she went without him. If it were in England then William would represent the family. This was her goodbye.

For a few minutes she remembered the poet, the musician, the civil Pierre, not the one that hit her, bruised her mouth, threatened her life and worse. She could see the kind face in her mind's eye, hear his voice, see his smile, his sparkling eyes so full of life and hope that her guilt in this matter stabbed her heart. When the brutal reality threatened to creep back in she pushed it away. There would be time in the rest of her life to remember that, if she so chose. Right now she knelt in prayer for Pierre's soul, may it rest in forgiving peace, she asked God.

Occasional drifts of perfume from the spring flowers she had placed around this holy place, surrounded them all: William and Margaret, her father and herself. Their fragrant, sweet aroma soothed and calmed her thoughts. For a while she was lost in troubled memory, unaware of the chill of the chapel, the growing ache in her knees. She contemplated the man she so nearly married; she relived some of their times together. She remembered his charming mother. How close she had been to being part of that family! Alarm began to rise, she denied the shudder and took her concentration back to prayer. Later she would write her thoughts in her day book, first though she wanted to see Melbroke. He hadn't bothered to attend. She was disappointed, angry. She wanted an explanation!

NO RESPONSE to her banging on his bedchamber door. Angrily she banged again. She heard movement and then it part-opened. Melbroke looked gaunt, pale, weak. He had thrown his riding coat around his shoulders. She had obviously awakened him, his eyes were hardly open, his hair ragged.

"You forgot or you just couldn't be bothered! Which is it?" Their eyes met. Hers angry, contemptuous; his near lifeless. She made no effort to hide her anger and glared at him awaiting his answer. He didn't respond. His hair was damp, as was his forehead. She pushed the door a little more open. It hit his injured arm. He groaned in pain and fell back against the wall. "Are you ill?"

"I fear I am. I feel a little giddy," he said, grabbing the door which she had to steady.

"Get yourself back into bed, quickly! I will return with help."

Somehow he did as instructed and lay back within damp sheets, his head on a soaked pillow. He had been sweating all night. His hair, brow and neck were drenched. Within minutes he heard footsteps hurrying back upstairs, William and Frances entered, they were alarmed at what they saw.

"I must see his arm, that wound," she said, to William urgently. He rolled up the sleeve of Melbroke's night shift and revealed a gaping wound. A clear liquid oozed from it and for a few inches all around the arm was bright red. She pressed the inflamed area, he winced, bleeding began again. "I am sorry to cause you pain," she said, softly, "but I must see how bad things are."

She bid him flex his fingers which he did with some difficulty. She bid William place his hand on Melbroke's shoulder, gently press it from the nape of the neck to the top of the arm, this he did and the patient winced repeatedly. She bid Melbroke lift his arm outwards from the shoulder, this he could do but with difficulty.

When she asked him to lift his arm straight up, he couldn't.

"What does all this tell you?" His eyelids were heavy, yearning to close, his voice barely more than a whisper.

"That you have a very nasty wound, deeper than you thought but it doesn't appear to have completely severed your muscles and tendons, which is good. You may have lost the use of your arm if it had, possibly even the arm. The redness tells us the wound is infected. Your sweating tells us you have a fever."

The Earl entered. "Father, Lord Melbroke's wound is more serious than we thought. We need the apothecary from Canterbury, can you send message for him, 'tis urgent."

"Of course, anything else you need?"

"Tell Gates to send a lackey with a bowl of hot water, one of cold and plenty of clean cloths. And fresh bed linen. And quickly."

"William you do that," the Earl commanded, "I'll get the apothecary."

"Thank you," Melbroke said quietly, once they were alone, "and I'm sorry I missed your service for Pierre."

"I confess I came here to scold you but I am truly saddened to find you like this. Despite our..."

"History?"

"Yes, despite our history, I would not wish you ill."

Two servants placed bowls of water and clean cloths on a table near the bed. Frances soaked one cloth in cold water and placed it on Melbroke's hot forehead. "We must get your temperature down, this should help." With the hot water she bathed the wound. With every touch he winced. She cleaned away the dried blood and the globules of transparent goo and could then see how deep the wound was. "This needs a proper poultice, the apothecary will do that. In a moment I shall get you garlic."

"Ah, yes, garlic…" His voice tapered off, the little strength he'd mustered was draining.

"'Tis an antiseptic, it will start to fight the infection."

While she went to the kitchen his heavy eyelids closed, he struggled to keep his mind alert to the surrounding noises in the house and gardens but it was a battle. By the time Frances returned he was gently slumbering. Not fully asleep but not awake. He felt her by his side. He felt her gently tuck his shift sleeve farther up his arm. He forced his eyes to open and watched as she pressed the garlic paste into the gaping slash and covered it with cloth she had torn into strips of bandage. It stung like hell, he gritted his teeth and remained silent.

"I have brought a towel, may I wipe you dry?"

He nodded. She opened his shirt and wiped the front of him, his upper chest, his throat, neck and face. Blood again caked his nose, she dabbed it away. She ran her hand behind his shoulders to coax him into a sitting position. He stifled a yelp as he leaned forward but he could not keep the pain from his face. She pulled back his shift to wipe his back and was aghast at the extent of the blue-purple bruising that stretched a double sword's width from one side of his body to the other.

A servant appeared to collect the water bowls and a maid appeared with clean sheets. The top sheet was quickly changed, the bottom would have to stay, damp as it was, he was too ill to move or roll.

"Go immediately to Gates, ask him to come here urgently," she ordered the maid, who normally would not dream of approaching the steward of the house. "And more cold water. Now."

Frances lay a fresh cold compress across Melbroke's brow. "Drink this," she said, offering a vessel of hot liquid to his good arm. "'Tis warmed wine with herbs, it will help the fever." He took a few sips. "Are you hungry, can I bring food?"

"No." With that his head flopped back on to the soaked pillow, his sweat-matted hair laying across red stains from overnight nose bleeding.

Within minutes steward Gates arrived, entering the room quietly, staring at the patient in disbelief. "This is sudden m'Lady. How may I help?"

"Please set the housekeeper to find all the spare pillows in the house, I need a regular supply, probably three or four a day, mayhap more. Dry and clean, if you please."

The patient didn't hear the final orders, his body had demanded more sleep, he was incapable of denying it.

The herb garden was enclosed by a sturdy brick wall that gave shade to herbs like celandine with its eye-soothing properties; lily of the valley, a good tonic for the heart; nightshade used as a sedative; and feverfew, Venus' herb for women. Along its high top ran cramp-curing woodbine and over its shaded sides grew ivy for ulcers, burns and scalds.

There were hundreds of herbs in her garden from the sun worshippers like thyme to the impressive angelica which at six-foot was nearly as tall as the wall and came to mankind to combat the plague. Some called it the herb of the Holy Ghost, others simply angelica because of its angelic virtues.

Magdala knew them all as friends and was as knowledgeable now as the apothecaries as to their various uses. Not that she was allowed to make tinctures or ointments or poultices. That was skilled work that needed long training. She was just a gardener.

Her one concession to her age was to allow herself to work

in the shade. At turned fifty she was expecting to meet her maker soon and an occasional pain in her abdomen, that was worse on some days than others, told her that day may well be nigh.

As long as life endures, she thought to herself, stabbing the seedlings into rows of holes and using her earthy, arthritic fingers to bed them down. As the Sext bell rang for the noon worship some of her helpers left and others returned. On the None bell at three she left to begin three hours of prayer. She owned nothing, not even the clothes she stood up in. Even her wedding ring had been taken from her. She had no rights, no say, no status, no love. Even Magdala wasn't her real name.

If she were lucky Mother Esme would share short, swift, unfulfilling conversation with her. When Mother was absent she would take the opportunity to talk, sometimes even laugh, with the other nuns. It was snatched happiness with the shadow of disapproval hanging over it. True pleasure and happiness she shared with her herbs.

"Put nothing before Christ" Saint Benedict had said. Twenty years from her forced entry into convent life and she was still struggling with exactly what that meant.

Chapter Eleven

A SHORT, FAT monk, dressed in the black habit of Canterbury's Benedictine monastery was whispering in his ear. "My Lord... can you hear me?" The patient stirred and opened his eyes. For a moment strange thoughts sifted through his mind, his vision was misty around the edges, he felt disorientated and the slightest movement sent pain spinning through him.

"My apologies my Lord, 'tis late but I came as soon as I could." A well-fed voluptuous face with kind eyes and a full, gentle mouth was looming over him. Melbroke looked enquiringly toward Frances who was standing by the monk's side.

"Brother Thomas is the apothecary, from the monastery."

"Please my Lord, may I examine you?" Melbroke nodded.

The monk removed Frances' bandage and looked at the arm-wound. He felt the hot forehead. He held Melbroke's wrist to monitor the pulse and then lowered his ear to the Lord's chest asking him to take deep breaths. Running his hands over his patient he felt strong legs from thigh to shin, a solid chest and hard stomach. He examined the back; Melbroke groaned.

"You have done well," the monk said, turning to Frances. "To soak the wound in garlic was a very good emergency measure but I think now we can do something more specific."

He went to his case and with surprisingly nimble fingers for such a large man he mixed up a thick, unctuous paste. A pungent smell pervaded the room, curiously it was both unpleasant and reassuring and it gave Frances hope that now this man was here all would be well. The monk lit a small oil lamp with a dish in a frame above it and warmed some of the paste, the smell getting stronger with the warmth. It filled her senses and she surrendered to the confidence it gave her.

While the paste warmed the monk took quill and ink and marked the edge of the red area on Melbroke's arm. He then plastered the hot salve on to the wound, pushing it deep into the gash. Melbroke moaned slightly, turning his head on the damp pillow but had no energy to object.

"This wound may need stitching," the robed physician muttered, quietly to himself. He was both apothecary and surgeon; his calling having trained him in the first, the battlefield the second. Infection that poisoned the blood had forced him to amputate many a limb, the screams of the men still haunted his dreams. He had learned the hard way to leave the wound open, concentrate on fighting the infection, sometimes limbs, lives, could be saved that way. His slender fingers worked fast as he rewrapped the bandage to hold the salve in place. He ground herbs from little packets with a small pestle in a small mortar, tipped them into a liquid he had brought with him and poured into a bottle that laid on its side. He then poured a little into the empty wine goblet by the bed. "My Lord, drink this." Melbroke obeyed. The monk gave Frances the bottle.

THE EARL was waiting impatiently at the foot of the wide, oak stairway. "Well, will he live?"

"The next forty-eight hours will tell us that, my Lord," the monk replied.

"Is there a risk he may not?" Alarm was in Frances' voice.

"He has a very bad wound which is infected. If that poison gets into his blood stream he may well succumb."

"Good grief," exclaimed the Earl, now regretting his cavalier question.

"He is a strong man, he is in good general health, he is well nourished. I have seen men on the battlefield with worse and survive." He turned to Frances. "My Lady, are you prepared to continue the nursing?"

"Yes, of course. Anything." Despite their 'history' she couldn't abandon the man who had saved her, not now in his hour of need.

"Very well, you must do three things. First, I want him to sleep, 'tis the greatest of all healers. The bottle I have given you contains sedative, valerian, mistletoe, camomile and others. It also contains opium poppy, a strong painkiller. Give him two spoonfuls every time he awakens. Only two, no more. If he wakes and appears to be drifting back into sleep then leave him. If he appears fully awake then give him the draft again. But no more than two spoonfuls every three hours. I want to keep him permanently asleep, day and night, is that going to be possible?"

Frances nodded. "Yes, I can remain with him all day."

"And I'll stay in his room at night," William offered, having just joined the group. Like the Earl he couldn't believe what he was hearing and was shuffling from foot to foot, wanting to pace out his anxiety but governed by civility not to.

"The second thing?" Frances asked.

"Is the poultice." He handed her a bowl full of the unctuous mixture he had already plastered on to the arm. "A small dollop of this must be heated and spread into the wound every four hours, day and night."

"Very well, 'twill be done."

"The third thing is keeping the fever down. In one respect the fever is good. It tells us his body is fighting and that he is strong enough to fight, although we can see that for ourselves from his general, excellent physique. But if his body temperature rises too high that can become a threat to survival. We prevent that with cold compresses every hour. Again my Lady," he said, turning to Frances, his body wobbling in rhythm with the action, "you did well to apply the cold compress, it was exactly what was needed."

He turned to the Earl and William. "We keep up this routine for forty-eight hours and then we see how he is."

"What of his back? No treatment for that?" Frances' eyes appealed to the monk.

"His back is severely bruised but 'twill heal itself. 'Tis best he is disturbed as little as possible at the moment, sleep is the priority."

"Food?"

"Not necessary. A man of his size can go several days without food. And anyway a fast will be good for him. His body can concentrate on fighting the infection without being diverted to digest food. He can have liquid if he is thirsty." He turned to William.

"Lord Runmore do you have the o'clock?

"It is just after seven."

"Very well, I will return at seven in the morning."

THE EARL took charge. "Right," he said, as soon as the monk had left. "We had better get the servants organized, you two will need some help." He summoned Gates, the cook and the head gardener. "I don't expect all of you to stay up all night but make sure you have staff available, I'll leave you to work out a rota."

"My Lord," asked the puzzled head gardener, "what is expected of me?"

"Constant cold water, man," the Earl barked. "And I mean cold, cold as ice. 'Tis needed to combat Lord Melbroke's fever. When cold water is called for I expect it to be immediately available. Not luke warm, not tepid but cold as the devil's heart and not in ten minutes time. Got it?" The gardener nodded.

"Cook, have someone in the kitchen to warm the poultice every time 'tis needed. And light food, day and night, for me daughter and son-in-law, they also need to keep up their strength."

The Earl turned to Gates. "Please be your usual well-organized, reliable self," he appealed, with a sigh. "Make all this work, the poor fellow's fighting for his life." He clicked his dogs to heel and headed for some air in the gardens.

WILLIAM AND Frances worked out the timings for the poultice: seven, eleven, three and seven. Day and night. William took the first shift and watched his friend sleeping silently. The patient never moved, the medicine had literally 'knocked him out'. Frances rested in her room. Her eyes were closed but she couldn't sleep, she was too worried. He might die! She felt sick to her stomach. She regretted every harsh word, every look of disdain, every comment that indicated she despised and disliked him. She was worried to her very core and was glad when the six o'clock church bell chimed, releasing her from a fitful night of anxiety and regret.

"He hasn't moved all night," said William, as she entered the sickroom to begin the day shift. He emerged from the bedding he'd laid over himself on a hard, ungiving chair. "I've been changing the cold compress hourly and the poultice at eleven and three, he didn't even know I was doing it. 'Tis as if he's unconscious."

"Just drugged, the apothecary knows what he's doing. We've used him for years, he's very wise." The patient was damp again, the pillow soaked. "Go have some food William and then get to bed. You must be exhausted and this could go on for several days."

She lifted the compress and laid the back of her hand on Melbroke's forehead, it was still burning hot. He stirred, his eyes flickered open. He lifted his arms from under the covers and looked around. He looked confused, bewildered.

"'Tis I, Frances, you are at Blean."

He widened his eyes and focused on his surroundings. His good hand instinctively went to his injured arm.

"No don't disturb it, we've been applying poultices all night."

"All night?"

"Yes, William slept in this room with you, changed it every four hours, now I'm here to be with you during the day."

He tried to smile but every effort was monumental. "I feel terrible," he said, "what's happened to me?"

"You've a fever, caused by the wound on your arm. Do you remember the apothecary visiting last night, the monk in black?"

"No."

"'Tis he who looks after you."

She went to the bottle the monk had left and poured two spoonfuls into the wine glass. "Now drink this," she said, supporting the top of his back to help him lean forward. His face screwed in agony.

"My damn back," he cried out as the pain tore into him, shuddering up into his head and down into his lumber.

"Your back apparently is the least of your worries. The apothecary says it will heal in its own time. 'Tis your arm wound that he is worried about."

Melbroke swigged back the medicine. "Hell's gates, what on earth was that! 'Tis disgusting."

"A strong pain killer and a sedative to help you sleep."

"I don't need any more sleep. The King's calling me, Galahad could get sick from the dogs..." He was rambling. "All I need is..." As he spoke so his eyes closed and he was gone again into his silent world of healing.

The barking of the Earl's dogs, followed by the tread of a heavily-built man upon the stairs, announced the monk's arrival. He puffed up the two flights and gratefully sank into the chair Frances had placed by Melbroke's bed. He unbandaged the arm wound. "Excellent."

"Excellent? But it is still bright red! And he's been rambling."

"Well, we mustn't make presumptions, 'tis early days but the infection hasn't spread past the ink lines, hopefully this means his Lordship is winning the battle."

"We've followed your instructions, Brother, to the letter."

"Yes, I can see that. Now bear in mind he's more likely to wake in the day, now the moon has sunk and the sun is high. The body wants to wake, it will fight the medicine but just remember no more that two spoonfuls every three hours."

Frances nodded.

"And don't worry about the rambling, if he is to live 'twill pass. I'll be back at seven tonight."

SOMETIMES SHE read, sometimes she did her sewing. Sometimes she sat thinking about the past days' events. She had escaped a seducer, been soaked to the bone, had a knife at her throat, been tied up, nearly raped, seen Pierre killed, lied to her father and was now probably the main topic of gossip at Richmond and Greenwich. Sometimes she felt overcome by the enormous mix of emotions and was glad for the peace of the sickroom. Oft times she just sat looking at Melbroke's strong face, now ashen and drawn. Oft times she allowed her mind to ponder - was it truly only Melbroke's fault? She had time to think now. Quiet, lonely time. Mayhap too much time. Thinking though, she was.

Every time she changed the compress she checked his forehead. He seemed to have stopped sweating or was she imagining it. She didn't seem to have to change the pillows so often but again, was she just too eager to see good signs.

She had taken to holding his hand, cradling it between her two. Stroking the back of it. Silently urging him to recover, to keep fighting. She changed the poultice again at eleven o'clock, changed his cold compress for the fifth time and had just settled herself down by his side when he opened his eyes.

At first she didn't notice. She sat with her head bowed, stroking his hand, extending some of her strokes farther up his arm. His strong, powerful arm that was now so badly injured that he might die. She lifted her head and realized he had been watching her. Their eyes met. Neither spoke. Eventually he asked: "Why do you look so sad?"

"Because you are seriously ill and I feel responsible."

"You haven't hurt me, Pierre did this."

"But if I hadn't panicked, if I hadn't fled from the Palace he wouldn't have hurt you."

"Yes, he would. It was his intention to murder me. Both of us. And who is responsible for that? Me! You are not to blame, truly, I brought this upon myself." His voice was stronger, the rambling had passed but he was still pale and riven with injury. His face was an artist's pallet of colours as bruising healed at different rates. One eye was still partly closed from the surrounding swelling, his nose still prone to slight bleeding, his knuckles raw, his back blackish-purple, his arm throbbing.

"But my panicking has led to all this."

"You are not in the wrong, I am," he insisted.

"I reacted badly. 'Tis not enough for me to say I am inexperienced where men are concerned, 'tis true but I allowed my fears to govern my reason. You are being very gallant in taking all the blame to yourself."

"I tell the truth, that is all. It is also true that if you could please continue to hold my hand I would get better much quicker." He tried to smile but she could see his eyes were still haunted with pain.

She returned his smile and cupped his hand in hers. "Just while you are ill, you understand."

"I understand. Now tell me please, just how ill am I?"

"Your wound is badly infected, should the infection get into your blood stream you could die." She knew this fighting man, who had seen more carnage on a battlefield than she could even imagine, would want the blunt truth.

"And do we know? Is it getting into my blood?"

"The apothecary came this morning and said you are no

worse, your body is fighting but we won't know for sure until at least another twenty-four hours."

"And my treatment?"

"We have to apply hot poultices to your wound, cold compresses to your forehead and give you medicine when you wake."

"We?"

"William and I. He's doing the nights and I'm here all day. Staff have been up all night."

"I will have a lot of people to thank when I recover."

"You most certainly will," she beamed, trying to lessen the tension of the seriousness. "Father's even got the head gardener burying water in the grounds to make it ice cold for your compresses. Cook has staff up round the clock to warm poultices and provide William and myself with food day and night."

"So much." He allowed his head to flop back on the new pillow, he could feel its crispness. His eyes wanted to close again, he could barely fight it.

"Even father's helping. I saw him earlier exercising Lunar and Galahad. Lunar likes Galahad, I could see, even from a distance."

"I wish her mistress could find it in her heart to like Galahad's master."

"No more talking," she side-stepped. "The monk says you mustn't waste energy on anything but fighting this infection. Are you thirsty?"

He nodded. She gave him fresh water from Blean's well, he sipped slowly. "Now take this," she said, handing him his medicine. "'Tis very strong, it contains opium poppy and various other things to help you sleep."

"Ah, that's why my arm feels less painful." He downed the

foul draft in one. "Will you hold my hand while I return to sleep?"

"If you wish."

"I do wish, 'tis very comforting."

FRANCES HAD just heard the two o'clock chime when her father's raised voice began vibrating around the house.

"No Malins you cannot talk to anyone. We've a family crisis."

"I arranged it with Lord Runmore..."

"Yes and you're a bloody day late!"

"Unforeseen circumstances kept me, I apologize my Lord."

"And unforeseen circumstances have occurred here. Lord Melbroke is gravely ill, he can see no one. Now go...go," he said, flapping his hands as if he were shooing chickens.

"Father, what on earth is going on?"

The caller turned to Frances. "Your Ladyship. I am Malins, Sheriff of Kent. It was arranged that I call. A man is dead, I must speak with the eye witnesses." Malins stood proud in a billowing red velvet coat. The chain of his office lay on his black doublet. Large black hat in hand, he bowed.

"Of course Sheriff. Father why don't we take Sheriff Malins into the library, we can explain everything to him there." Her eyes tried to calm her father, they'd got to face the Sheriff at some stage.

The Earl hissed. "If we must!"

Events had conspired then. The task of explaining their story fell to her. She spoke clearly and slowly. The Sheriff listened intently.

"So, you believe the Marquis was following you. That is why he was in Kent?"

"In the absence of any other explanation, we have to think that."

"And Lord Melbroke didn't know whom he was fighting?"

"No. He knew the Marquis by name, of course but he'd never met him. And it is the injuries he sustained in the fight to save the monk..."

"Who wasn't really a monk at all..."

"That's right, that now threaten his life. One of his wounds has become infected, he has a high fever, he is in a deep sleep induced by drugs. If the infection gets the better of him he will die." She was trying to stay strong, be authoritative with the Sheriff, give their story gravity but she couldn't conceal the crack in her voice.

"I must speak with Lord Runmore now your Lordship," he said, turning to the Earl.

"Well you can't man! He was up all night sitting with Melbroke and is now abed himself. I will not have him disturbed."

Malins was noticeably irritated. "Lady Frances, has a physician seen Lord Melbroke?"

"He's under the care of Brother Thomas, apothecary from the Benedictine monastery."

"So he could verify this story?"

The Earl exploded. "Verify the story! Are you accusing me daughter of lying? How dare you! Get out of me house, now, this instant."

"My Lord I have to conduct inquiries. A man is dead. I must have statements from all concerned. The Coroner must be kept informed."

"And you will get your statements but not today. Now come on man, lift yourself out of that chair. Me daughter has to get back to her patient and I'm a busy man. We'll send message to your office when the crisis is over and Lords Melbroke and Runmore can speak with you."

The Earl opened the door. "Come on, leave," he bellowed. "Now!"

Gates escorted the Sherif off the premises.

"Father really, you can't speak to the Sheriff like that."

"O yes I can, I appointed the blaggard."

Chapter Twelve

FOUR SCRIBES ARRIVED from the Canterbury Scribes Office, as summoned by the Earl. He and William had penned a letter that would now be copied and sent to all the wedding guests. Assuming most were married couples it meant that at least a hundred missives had to be hand written by the scribes and delivered around England within the next few days.

The scribes were in the lower hall, watched from the walls by huge paintings of Blean ancestors. They were in the Earl's way! He wasn't happy. The manager of the Scribes Office was arranging the post-horses so that at least, was one thing off his shoulders.

William had written to Margaret bidding her come to Blean. The Earl had written a personal condolence note to the Marchioness and was now sitting in the withdrawing room with a big goblet of wine and food on a tray. He was irritable and angry. His whole world was turned upside down. Violence and tragedy had touched his family and he could do nothing about it. The scribes, he had instructed, were to be out of his house and sight by nightfall. They'd better be! He was in no mood for laziness!

THE MONK visited at seven that evening and seven again the next morning and each time saw him more satisfied with his patient's progress. Frances was just changing the three o'clock poultice, concentrating on the bandage, when a hand touched her cheek. "You look pale and tired," the voice said.

"O, you made me jump!"

"I can't allow this any more, it won't do."

"What won't do?"

"I'm not allowing you to make yourself ill over me."

"I'm not."

"You look exhausted."

"That is nothing to do with looking after you."

"What is it to do with?"

"Worry. We're all worried about you. None of us is sleeping properly. Wait 'til you see William, he's gaunt. Father's going round barking at everyone. Servants have been up all night. You're probably the healthiest of us all given the attention you've been getting." She laughed, she realized for the first time in days but it was hollow.

"I feel much better, please thank everyone. Are they still burying water?" She nodded.

The afternoon sun was breaking through cloud and filling the room with its cheer. Raindrops on the panes of the mullioned windows glistened like dew, her patient had regained consciousness and suddenly the world seemed more hopeful.

"I'm very glad to hear you feel better but you are not recovered. Not by a long way. And you needn't think you are getting out of that bed." He inwardly smiled and the fact he now had the energy to imagine her laying next to him was all the confirmation he needed that he was going to live.

Frances went to pour him a dose of his mixture.

"No, no more."

"But you must."

"No."

"I'm nurse and I say yes. Yes!"

"Not 'no' any more then?" A grin struggled across his still-painful face.

"I can see you are getting better, my Lord," she scolded. "I can see I shall need a chaperone in here from now on. For your information it most definitely is still 'no'!"

"I apologize. But you must agree that the fact I can again appreciate your beauty must mean that I am recovering well."

"Behave and drink this. Even when you're ill you are lustful."

"No more of that stuff. I refuse to be rendered unconscious anymore. I feel much better." He took his good hand to his wound and gently pressed. "It still hurts but not as much."

"That is due to the medicine you are now refusing to take."

"I want to be fully awake when the monk visits this evening, so I can talk with him. It also gives me a few hours to see if the excruciating pain returns or not."

"Very well but you have become a very difficult patient."

"I apologize for that," he said, taking her hand. "Please sit and hold my hand, as you were before. I'm sure 'tis that alone that has made me better."

"Certainly not," she said, freeing herself from his grip. "You have declared yourself recovered, you no longer need my hand."

He allowed his head to flop back on the pillow. "What a terrible, cruel nurse you are." She ignored him.

He took the compress off his forehead.

"Leave it!"

"No, I want to test myself. Just until the monk gets here, see what he says."

"I think he'll say you've been fooling us all," boomed William. "Alban, my dear friend, how wonderful to have you back with us. How do you feel?"

"Much stronger, I think you'll soon be rid of me." He watched for Frances reaction.

"Not yet we won't," she said, sternly, showing no emotion.

"Yes, my friend, you're getting ahead of yourself. You may feel better, it doesn't mean you are. In my opinion it will be a good few days, mayhap even a week, before you can even think of leaving."

"In that case I must write to the King. Give him a progress report."

"Has been done," said William. "The Earl wrote as soon as we had the apothecary's prognosis."

"Any reply?"

"No, nothing"

Christ's wounds, Melbroke agonized. No reply means he's angry and the Royal wrath always explodes eventually. William turned to Frances. "I'm going for a ride, blow away some cobwebs, give Galahad a gallop."

"Why don't you both go," Melbroke ventured. "Get some fresh air. I will be fine on my own." It suited him to have some time alone, time to think about the wisdom, or not, of writing again to his cousin. Frances protested, he insisted. "Take as long as you like, I'm fine."

As soon as he was sure they had descended the stairs he slowly lifted himself from the bed. It wasn't easy. He felt a little giddy and his back protested angrily but his determination would not be deterred. He reached for his long riding coat that hung in a small closet just a few steps away and put it round his shoulders. Now he was using his wounded arm it was throbbing again. His head began to spin and quickly he lowered himself into a chair. A hard, spiteful, wooden chair that his back objected to most strongly and suddenly his body was racked again with pain. He breathed deeply and slowly, determined not to let the pain get the better of him. It was a futile task.

IN AN upstairs room at the Manor of Mortlake a lanky, effete, bewildered brother brooded. Downstairs his mother sobbed. He sat, he stood, he wailed. The loss of his brother's strength diminished him, the anger at his loss strengthened. His mother read and re-read the letter of condolence from the Earl. It sickened him. From grief, to revenge, to fear, to sorrow, his emotions soared and plummeted in seconds. He was ravaged by events. Their plans in tatters, soon the family would be in the same state.

It was down to just him now but did he have it in him? He paced the floor, exasperation racing through his veins. He threw his goblet at the wall. The blood-rush to his head drove him on. Yes, he could do it. Would do it! Pierre's life must be avenged. The family must be saved. It might be the old straight track to hell but he would walk it. He would, could, conquer this sudden loneliness that threatened to drown him. His apprehension, his fears, his self doubts would all be sweetened by the success of revenge. He sat quietly by a writing desk and began.

THE VOICE boomed: "What is this!" The patient woke in a start. "Get back into that bed immediately!"

The short fat monk, puffing from the stairs and red in the face from rage, was shouting at him. "Bed. Now. Or I shall leave this house and not return."

Melbroke was outraged. "Brother, do you know to whom you speak! Where is your courtesy, Brother?"

"I care not who you are Sir, not even if you are the King himself. We are all equal in the grave which is the very place I have been attempting to save you from. If you are too high and mighty to take advice then I shall cease to advise." He made for the door but turned, his face still red, his breath still short. "I have been apothecary for thirty years, I have trained under the best in Europe, what is the point, Sir, of me trying to save you from death, if you do not follow my instructions. Bed. Now! Or I leave." He slammed his case on a table and stood hands on hips, eyes glaring. Melbroke did as commanded. Angry but resigned.

"Where is your nurse?"

"I sent her away, I am feeling recovered."

"I will be the judge of that."

The monk unwrapped the poultice and examined the wound. He mumbled in what seemed an approving manner. He lay his ear on Melbroke's chest and tutted. He felt his forehead and sighed. A refreshed Frances entered. "Brother, I didn't hear you arrive. Is all well?"

"No! All is not well. The patient has taken his recovery into his own hands. I arrived early and found him out of his bed. He has ignored my instructions."

She scowled at Melbroke and shook her head in disbelief.

"His heart is racing," the monk continued. "He has raised his temperature, his forehead is hotter than when last I examined him. His wound however is responding well. The infection is receding."

He turned to Melbroke. "Now my Lord. Are you going to heed my instructions or not?"

"What are your instructions Brother?"

"Another twenty-four hours bed rest and I will assess the situation again tomorrow evening."

"I will stay abed, if you insist," he snapped, "but I am not being rendered unconscious any more."

"I was not going to suggest you should be." He turned to Frances. "The poultices will continue at the same frequency, so too the cold compresses." He turned to his case and fetched out a different bottle of medicine. "This, my Lord, is a strong pain killer that I have prepared especially. It will not sedate you. It is to be taken night and morning and up to three times during the day when you need it."

"Is he out of danger Brother, that's all I...we, want to know?"

"He is my Lady, so long as he doesn't trigger a relapse by taking his recovery into his own hands for a second time." He glared at the patient and turned on his heel. He had no intentions of debating the treatment with Melbroke, it was up to him whether he wanted to live or not. "I can see myself out, may God grant you good evening." And he was gone.

An angry Frances turned to Melbroke. "So, you've raised your temperature! Why are men always such bad patients?"

"Mayhap because we are doers not sitters! Hell's gates. Another day!"

"Just one, that's all, one more day of bed rest. Regard it as a test of your patience," she said, pasting on the next poultice and rebandaging his arm. "The wound looks very much better by the way. Healing is slow but the red infection is now pink and only half as bad as it was."

"Thank you. And I apologize for my temper." He reached for her hand but she pulled away.

"'Tis not me you should apologize to."

"I know. I shall speak with him."

Footsteps on the stairs told them William was coming for the night. "Do you think that's still necessary?" Melbroke asked Frances.

"Yes," replied William on entering, happiness radiating from him. He was light of foot, his face freed from all earlier signs of exhaustion. "What did the monk say?"

"You look disgustingly happy Runmore, what's up?"

"I've had message from Margaret, she will be here on the morrow. I haven't seen her for over four weeks, feels like four months." His excitement was palpable and an unusual stab of envy hit Melbroke's stomach.

"Well, come on, what did the monk say?"

"Our patient has been chastised. He got out of bed when we went riding, he's raised his temperature, his heart is racing but the wound is healing well."

"So overall is that good news?"

"It is. So long as he now does what he is told," she said, angrily flashing her eyes again in Melbroke's direction.

William sat on Melbroke's bed. "Thank the Lord, dear friend, you've had us all very worried."

Melbroke leant forward and took a hand of each of them. "Thank you both, you have saved my life it seems, I am indebted to you both forever."

"'Tis what friends do," Frances said, pulling her hand away again, "and anyway, it was the monk who saved you."

"He had the knowledge but you both put it into action. I might have died without you both."

He turned to William. "If you insist on spending another night here..."

"I do. Your poultice and compress must be changed."

"Then how about we play chess...until we are ready for sleep."

IT WAS about ten o'clock when Melbroke felt his eyes closing. William gave him the pain-killing draft, snuffed most of the candles and settled into his makeshift bed. "Not sure I'm going to get any sleep tonight, too excited about Margaret arriving tomorrow."

They lay in the near dark. Silence. The house was still, the birds asleep. Just occasionally there was a scuffle and a squeal, probably badgers. Melbroke used to joke with William that he was crazy to tie himself to just one woman. His life was far better for a man's needs, he'd say. Different women, different sport, no responsibility. Just lust and freedom, what better! Now he found himself haunted by Frances and he didn't like it. No woman had ever haunted him before, never. Couldn't even remember what most of them looked like. Why now then, did he envy William his happiness? What was happening to him!

He was confused and very aware that while he could please a woman very well in the bedchamber he didn't know where to begin out of it. He was a complete novice when it came to courting and wooing and understanding their ways. What are you thinking! He chastised himself as he successfully turned on to one side. He didn't want to woo or court anyone, he didn't want to understand women's ways!

It was true though and he couldn't deny it, Frances had

taken up residence in his thoughts. This couldn't be. For now he was captive to his injuries but as soon as he could he would get away. Get away from her.

An hour later he felt William changing the poultice and he felt the ice cold of the next compress cover his brow. He kept his eyes closed, William believed him asleep. Just out of interest he would watch William when Margaret arrived. He would study how he behaved with the woman he loved. He would listen to the language, watch for the small courtesies, the lover's attentiveness, the passing tenderness. He wasn't really interested but it would be an amusing exercise to relieve the boredom of his confinement.

How long had it been since she'd known joy? Magdala couldn't remember. She settled these days for peace. Apart from Mother Superior there was plenty of that.

It was early morn, her favourite time and she had come to the herb garden with dawn's light. She was sitting on the grass, allowing her hands to run through the morning's dew. She allowed the fresh aroma of her loyal friends to fill her senses and she came as near to joy as was possible these days.

Human reaction to sense and things sensual wasn't encouraged in the nunnery and she craved affection, an arm around her, a kiss of tenderness, a sign of human love. In the early years she had been able to close her eyes and see her beloved husband's face. Not the pained face as they had taken her from him but the tender face that had gazed at her in deep love. For theirs had been a love match and their only son had been born in love.

She used to be able to see both their faces, feel their bodies against hers, recall their voices, hear her son calling 'mama' and her husband's sweet words of love as they lay together. No more.

Memory failed her these days and had done for many a year.

Her husband and her son were like ghosts to her now. Powerful ghosts who could make her heart thrill some days and sadden on others. Ghosts in that she could give them no shape, no features, no personalities. First anger and hatred had taken them from her, now time and age had taken over. She knew they had loved her, she clung on to that in her darkest moments but on a bad day she didn't even know what human love was any more. It certainly didn't abound in the convent.

Little human tenderness lived here so instead she let the perfume of her herbs caress her senses. She plucked a sprig of starflower, the expeller of melancholy and the bringer of joy. She tucked it under her habit so it was close to her lonely heart and thanked God for its comfort. Just then the six o'clock bell summoning her to Prime clanged into her thoughts and claimed her back.

Chapter Thirteen

THE SHERIFF ARRIVED several days later, just after the midday meal. He had received message from the Earl that the two Lords were now able to give their statements. With him was a diminutive clerk, a portable writing desk hanging around his neck, his limbs trembling with nerves. They were shown into the library by Gates.

Melbroke was now recovered save residual bruising to his face, a back that still resisted exercise and a permanent scar on his upper left arm. The latter didn't both him at all, it joined the others that blades had given him. Both the former remained prone to tenderness but were manageable. He was eager to return to Court for fresh instructions. His trip to France could be delayed no longer. The King, it seemed, had shown uncharacteristic patience over recent events but the silence from on high was causing Melbroke concern. His antennae and experience were sensing hostility.

"Please gentlemen, be seated," invited Frances, as she,

Melbroke and William entered the library. She signalled a wooden chair to the clerk who readied himself for his work, his portable desk now open revealing quills and ink and blank parchment.

"You want our statements," said Melbroke, "but I'm not sure we have much to add beyond what Lady Frances has already told you."

The Sheriff, still standing, shuffled. He coughed, cleared his throat, fiddled with his hat, dabbed his damp brow. This April day was warm but it was discomfort that troubled him. "I'm afraid my Lord, there has been a development."

"Go on."

"The Marquis' brother, Lord Jasper, has alleged that you murdered the Marquis."

Frances gasped, William was immediately on his feet. "Utter nonsense."

Melbroke stayed calm. He leant forward placing his elbows on his open knees. He steepled his hands. "Pray Sheriff, continue. On what grounds is this accusation made?"

"Lord Jasper claims that on the death of your father your mother was left impecunious, that she borrowed money from many people including from his family." The silence in the room was palpable. It seemed to steal the air and Frances found her breath deepening. The Sheriff continued: "The late Marquis had been content to leave the debt unpaid but when he died last year Lord Pierre, the new Marquis, had been seeking repayment."

The Sheriff's discomfort noticeably increased, beads of perspiration now glistened above his top lip. He was accusing the King's cousin of murder! The seriousness of this he realized. He was in the devil's trap. He must do his job, the wheels of justice must be seen to turn but he feared it could be he who met the inside of a dungeon!

Frances and William were stunned into silence. Melbroke remained calm, rigid, unmoving and unmoved. He noted the Sheriff's predicament and smiled understandingly. "Pray continue and please, fear not, I know you have a job to do. Pray do it."

It was the begowned man's cue to continue: "Lord Jasper claims you refused to pay m'Lord. That arguments ensued, that you threatened to kill his brother if he didn't desist from hounding you for money."

Melbroke stood. "You repeatedly use the phrase 'Lord Jasper claims'."

"He has made a written statement to the Sheriff in Surrey. A copy has been sent to myself."

"I would like to see it."

The clerk jumped up and handed him a rolled scroll tied with cord. The accused went to the light of the window to read it. All remained silent, embarrassed on his behalf. After a few moments he began. "If your man is ready Sheriff, I will reply to this accusation." He returned to his chair and spoke clearly and slowly, leaving regular pauses for the diminutive, still nervous clerk, to keep up.

"When my father died he would have left my mother an extremely wealthy woman. Unfortunately, she was no longer within the family. She had left six years earlier to carve a life for herself elsewhere." He turned to William and Frances and quietly said: "My father was a broken man, cuckolded, humiliated." Words not meant for the statement.

Melbroke's face was etched with a sadness Frances had not seen before. Being dragged back into memory and having to tell the Sheriff such intimacies was obviously very difficult.

Melbroke had no intentions of telling them how as a young ten-year-old he had been awoken at dawn by horses hooves. How he'd seen a strange man enter the house, heard shouting then seen his mother willingly leave. How in the early morn the man had held his mother's waist and lifted her on to his horse, his arms about her as they trotted away. Such intimacy! How he had watched her shape until it became an outline and then the mists stole her. How he had never seen her again.

Later he'd asked where his mother was and his father replied: 'She's gone away.' When he'd asked why, his father simply said: 'Because she had to. She's gone, she won't be back.' He'd embraced his boy but said no more. His father's face had been riven with pain, he had aged overnight, his eyes had died, his love of life gone. Even at ten years of age the son had known not to keep asking.

He had no intentions of sharing how every morning he raced down the stairs hoping she had returned. How some days he stood at the gates of their long drive for hours watching left, then right, then left again, praying God would bring her back. How his father's steward would fetch him in, an arm around his shoulder to comfort him. How eventually his father had sent him away to his cousin Harri Tudor, the current King's father. The boy could grow in happier surroundings, would get a good education under royal tutors at Richmond and Greenwich and would be safe behind palace walls.

Melbroke had no intentions of revealing to the world how his father hadn't coped, had become a sad recluse who'd turned to drink and shunned his friends. He had seen his father broken by love and betrayal. His sadness of that was second only to the sadness in his own heart. When Melbroke was sixteen his father died, it was then that he had sworn to himself that he would never love a woman. That women let you down, that love is too painful, that he would never marry. He would avoid both and be free and happy.

He turned back to the Sheriff and continued: "My father never knew where she had gone, he was therefore never able to tell me. He died from a broken heart. The late King, in familial loyalty and care, put an officer of the Court at my disposal to oversee my finances."

Only the scratching of the scribe's pen could be heard in the heavy, choking silence. Frances was hardly able to breath. Melbroke paced the room, agonizing over being made to relive a time he had buried deep within himself. His voice though remained confident, assured.

"He was privy to all my family's financial affairs. He knew what my father had owned, the substantial wealth I inherited, where our income came from, how different monies were allocated and he oversaw the running of our estates. He performed this duty until I came of age, then I took on the responsibility."

Frances was bewitched by his calm delivery. She now understood why he never spoke of his home, his family. He was galvanizing his thoughts with no pre-warning nor rehearsal. He was calling on all his inner resources of control and strength. He couldn't have put his case more clearly and succinctly. She, on the other hand, found herself terrified for him. She was the one person who was an eye witness to the true events. Only she knew he hadn't murdered Pierre and she could say nothing.

Melbroke continued: "My family has had no debts at any time. We have borrowed from nobody. The King's officer is still at Greenwich Palace and would give a statement confirming mine. If it becomes necessary I can also ask his Majesty..."

"Really, Sheriff!" William interjected angrily, unable to listen to any more. Having known Alban since childhood he was the only other person privy to part of his background, although he hadn't known it all. Nobody had, until now. Now he knew more he was overcome with a desire to defend his friend. He stood, his face etched with annoyance. "Lord Melbroke can even get a supportive statement from His Majesty. You surely realize this is all poppycock!"

The Sheriff cleared his throat again, shuffled again, dabbed his damp face again. This situation was bringing him even closer to the King! "I trust your Lordships understand that when a murder allegation is made I have no choice but to investigate." His voice was agitated, his eyes alarmed.

"Fear not," said Melbroke, trying to bring calm to the man whose face was now florid. "This allegation is unfounded, do your job well and there is no reason the King need ever hear of any of this."

The Sheriff bowed in thanks. Melbroke took the finished statement to the window and read it slowly, several times.

William was pacing. "Is this the end of the matter?"

"No my Lord, I'm afraid 'tis not. Further investigations will have to be made. I shall attempt to speak myself with Lord Jasper who is, of course, now the new Marquis. I fear this will take at least one more week."

"But he wasn't even in the barn," said William angrily, "how does he know what happened?"

"I realize that my Lord. This is not an eye witness statement just an allegation but it must be investigated. A man is dead."

"'Tis all right, Will," sighed Melbroke, "let the Sheriff do his duty. But Sheriff I must inform you, I leave Blean on the morrow and leave for France on the King's business in a few days' time."

Frances' heart was gripped with pain. Only she could save him. Only she knew he wasn't a murderer.

"I must ask you not to leave, my Lord."

"You must make your request to the King, I will not disobey him."

The Sheriff shuffled again, weighing up his options. "How long will you be in France?"

Frances didn't look up but was listening intently.

"I would imagine no more than four weeks."

William stepped forward with three documents. "We have all written and signed our statements as to the true facts of that day," he said, placing them in the Sheriff's hands. "It was a tragic day which none of us will ever forget. But it did not include murder. This is a fabricated allegation, for what purpose I do not know but it is malicious and totally without foundation. There really is nothing else to be said."

"Not for now my Lord, I agree." The Sheriff bowed and left, his clerk shuffling behind.

THE THREE sat quietly, shocked and embarrassed by what had just taken place.

"Why?" William was pacing again.

"He wants to damage me."

"Why?"

Melbroke turned to Frances. "I'm sorry but I have to refer back to..."

"Please," she interrupted, "just say what needs to be said. There is no one in this room who doesn't know the real truth."

He turned back to Will. "'Tis obvious. It is because of what occurred between myself and Lady Frances at Richmond. I ruined the marriage, his brother is dead, he is determined I shall pay."

"Have you executed!"

"He knows it won't come to that but he can damage my name. If he can do nothing else, he can do that!"

"I'm the only person who can prove you didn't murder Pierre," Frances said quietly. "We shall have to tell the Sheriff that I was there, what Pierre did to me, how you saved me." Her voice was quivering. "We shall have to!"

Every sinew in his body wanted to go to her, hold her but he knew it wasn't welcomed. "We can't, we've just given our signed statements to the Sheriff, we would be seen to be liars and perjurers. And anyway, I'm not having your name, your family, brought down by me."

With that Frances stood up. She was ashen and clearly emotional. William went to her, put his arm about her shoulder but she pulled away. "Leave me alone, I just want to be alone," she said, choking back tears. She gathered up her skirts and ran from the room, the door banging behind her.

"Go after her then," William urged.

"What?"

"Go after her."

"But she wants to be alone."

"Good God man, she doesn't mean it. She weeps for you. Go to her."

"Weeps for me?"

"Well 'tis not for me you idiot, is it! "

MELBROKE FOUND her on the terrace. A lonely figure, sitting on an ornate stone bench, her head in her hands. She wasn't precisely sure what she was emotional about. Was it the threat that now hung over him or the fact he was leaving or the possibility that the truth may have to come out. It was probably all of them. She only knew she had an ache in her heart that never used to be there and an enveloping sense of loneliness that disturbed her. He sat down next to her. "Thank you for offering to help me."

She turned toward him and looked appealingly into his eyes. "I'm the only person who knows the truth, you must let me speak."

"No. I won't allow it. You mean too much to me." There! He'd said it. Without his planning, the words had slipped through his lips. He looked into her face for a response and saw tearful eyes, pools of blue with pain and anxiety in them. Her cheeks were stained from the tears. She looked so beautiful, vulnerable, fragile. "Am I allowed to touch you, to wipe away a tear?" She nodded.

He moved closer and lifted her chin toward him. She felt a tremor of panic tremble through her but she didn't resist. He felt her tense as he gently kissed her cheeks. She felt his lips move across her skin so tenderly. He tasted the salt of her tears and it thrilled him. He looked at her mouth, full, soft, slightly trembling, lips slightly apart. What was she saying? Did she want him to kiss her? He so much wanted to but he didn't. He would do nothing to risk frightening her again.

Instead he took her hands and raised them to his lips. "Thank you for wanting to help me but nothing will come of these allegations, I am confident."

In a flash she brought herself back to the real world. Remembered the man in Richmond, his actions that had started all this trouble. She pulled her hands out of his, stood up and quite sternly, said: "I will be guided by you for now but if this matter escalates then I shall speak whether you allow it or not."

"It won't," he said, smiling and standing. Her spirit was back! "Jasper has no evidence because there is none. This will go no further."

"I hope not. Despite everything I wouldn't want your head on a block."

There was silence between them, just for a few moments then she said, coldly: "So you leave tomorrow then?"

"Yes, I decided this morning. It would not be wise to test the King's patience any longer and this trip to France won't go away. My wounds are all but healed, I have to go."

She turned away, he extended a hand to her upper arm. "Will you miss me?"

She pulled back, out of his reach. "I shall miss you upsetting the usual Blean calm, I won't miss forever having to be on guard against your lust." Before he could respond she turned and went back into the house leaving him feeling crestfallen and herself saddened that tomorrow he would be gone.

THE EARL'S lawyer George Jarrett hauled his heavy black leather case on to his knees and pulled out bundles of parchment tied with ribbons. The Harwyke brothers fidgeted nervously and the Earl bid them sit. He still didn't like them. Under normal circumstances he wouldn't have the like in his home but his leg pain, the legacy of his wound at Stoke, was playing up this week and it saved him riding into Canterbury.

Wearing exactly the same apparel as last time, still not removing their billed hats and still wearing daggers at their belts, the brothers settled uncomfortably on the two backless stools the Earl had indicated on the opposite side of his desk to himself. His lawyer, the overseer of all Blean legal affairs for many a year, sat by the Earl on his side of the desk.

The Earl's arm stretched to an hourglass on the corner of

his desk. He flipped it over, its white sand now cascading through blue glass. Jarrett knew the sign: the Earl wanted this pair of jarring scuts gone by the time the sand met its equilibrium. "Let's get on with it," the Earl said, his eyes roaming over the two dull specimens that sat before him. "Any questions?"

His daughters and Runmore were visiting friends, Melbroke was out riding. He wanted these two gone before anyone returned. The brothers shook their heads, Arthur the older of the two, scratching his short beard with one hand and brandishing the surveyor's report with the other. "No my Lord, we have the report, we are content with its findings."

"And you have no legal representation?" Not for the first time lawyer Jarrett queried this.

Again the brothers shook their heads. "We trusts his Lordship," said obsequious Samuel.

"I'm sure his Lordship, like myself, would prefer you to be legally represented."

"Our choice is ours," said Arthur, looking sternly and directly into Jarrett's eyes, as if to say 'don't challenge us'. Jarrett averted his gaze.

"So, no questions then." It was rhetorical. The Earl was getting bored, he wanted the matter completed and signalled to Jarrett to press on.

"Very well, gentleman." With that he produced two contracts, one for the bothers to sign, one for the Earl. The agreement being struck was for the leasing of the Blean iron works, the annual lease price and the profit-share agreement. The brothers had agreed to all the Earl's demands on the strength of the Southwark iron expert's glowing report. All were expecting to make money.

Formalities over the Earl immediately rose. "Get mining

and good luck," he charged. Each brother extended a hand, the Earl ignored them. Gates who, as instructed, had been loitering outside, immediately entered the room and escorted the men at a pace from the premises.

"Don't like 'em," said the Earl to Jarrett, pouring two glasses of deep red wine. "Can't put me finger on it, just something about 'em."

"I know what you mean. And no legal representation concerns me."

"Saving money I suppose, although they seem to have plenty."

"I several times felt, when they came to my office with questions, that they were deferring to someone, I assumed it to be their lawyer. Mayhap I imagined it, I'm probably wrong. Strange though, to make such a major commitment in life without legal guidance."

"A pair of cocksures, think they know it all," scoffed the Earl.

"Lackwits if you ask me," said the lawyer, knocking back the last of his first wine. The Earl's hand went to the flask. They were in for a session and some serious reminiscing.

SUPPER WAS a silent affair. The events of the day had seen to that.

"William tells me you leave in the morning," said Margaret, in an attempt to bring some conversation into a dull evening.

"'Tis true, the King calls."

"Your arm is strong enough for riding?"

"I think so, it will ache I expect but I shall manage."

"Sorry to see you leave Melbroke," the Earl uttered, joining the conversation.

"I also, my Lord and no words can truly express my gratitude for the kindness and care you have all shown me." He noticed Frances was being very quiet. She was hardly touching her food. "Lady Margaret," he continued, "if a man wanted to buy a lady a gown how would he go about it?"

"Would this be locally in Canterbury or in London?"

"In London."

"London has plenty of dress shops or he could go to a dressmaker and have one designed especially for the lady."

"Which is best?"

"I think the latter. Then the lady has a dress that is unique."

"Right Melbroke," called the Earl, wanting to take the conversation away from dresses. "You can do me one last service."

"My Lord?"

"Take the dogs for their evening walk, me leg's playing up tonight."

" My pleasure."

"And when did that dog of yours last get a really good run Frances? Poor thing, always cooped up in your bedchamber. 'Tis a lovely April evening, take him out with my three, remind him he's a dog, not just a toy.

THE SKY was tinged with apricot and gold as Melbroke, Frances and four dogs walked away from the house. The sun was setting somewhere over the western edge of England. There had been a light shower, the grass was slippery and as soon as the dogs had bounded off Melbroke offered his arm as they strolled toward the stream.

"Do you have a mistress in London?"

"What on earth makes you ask that?"

"Because you wish to buy her a gown."

Inside he groaned. "No. I have no mistress. The gown is for you."

"Me?"

"As a gift for nursing me back to full health."

Why did relief flood through her! "There is no need, truly. 'Twas my pleasure. And don't forget William helped, too."

"And I shall buy him a gift, also. And your father, for allowing me to stay here." After a pause he asked. "Do you have a favourite colour?"

"You choose."

"This is a heavy responsibility."

"I'm sure you have impeccable taste."

They strolled in silence for a while then she asked. "But you have had mistresses?"

"No, Never."

"But all these Melbroke women that people refer to."

"They weren't mistresses."

"So what were they?"

"Passing fancies."

"There's a difference?"

"O yes, a very big difference."

He was desperate to get her off this subject. These were his last few moments with her for goodness knows how long. He didn't want to waste them. They threw sticks for the dogs for a while and walked farther on to the bluebell wood on the eastern side of the house. He ventured an arm around her shoulder.

"You haven't scolded me for touching you without permission."

He noticed a flicker of a smile cross her face. He would try just a little more boldness. He turned her to him, cupped her face in his hands, gave her time to pull away, she didn't. He gently brushed his lips on hers. Warm, soft, moist, welcoming. She closed her eyes and let the feel of him rush through her. His tongue traced the inner contours of her lips. She could feel his hot breath, so close it was stealing hers. A wave of thrills went through her, cascaded down her body to her very fingertips and toes. She gasped as the world seemed to spin. It only lasted seconds but she was thrown into a confused whirl before her brain took over and she pushed him brusquely away.

"No, Melbroke, no!"

The dogs came bounding back to their side, the moment was smashed.

"They look tired enough, we're going in now," she snapped, cross with herself for showing even a hint of weakness. He offered his arm for the return stroll to the house, she declined.

Her thoughts were racing. He knew how to turn women on and off, that's what he was doing with her. He lusted after her, she knew that, in fairness he had never denied it but that wouldn't suit her. Her pain when she learned he might die, her pain now that accusations had been made against him, disturbed her. She was slowly coming to realize that she wanted more, more than a man like him was prepared to give. She would have to pull herself together and get him out of her mind. It was good he was leaving, give her time to come to her senses.

Neither spoke on the way back. He angry with himself for being impatient; she angry with herself for her weakness.

"I bid you farewell. I shall retire early," he said, civilly. "I have to pack my things and prepare for the morrow. I shall be gone before you break your fast."

"Good night then Lord Melbroke, may God give you safe

journey."

IT WAS a little after dawn when Melbroke and William saddled their horses.

"She asked if I have a mistress. She clearly thinks very little of me."

"Rubbish. She was obviously jealous."

"Jealous!"

"Of course. It would have taken her courage to ask. Why else would she ask if she didn't care?"

"Care?"

"God's body, Melbroke. She cares for you. Thought you knew about women."

"Turns out I don't."

"Well you've had enough of them."

"Yes, well, we didn't get to talk too much. It wasn't their emotions I was interested in. And anyway I didn't love them." It was out before he could halt it.

William stopped what he was doing and turned to him square on. "What's this! You love Frances?"

"It seems I do."

"And your intentions are?"

"None. You know my background. I couldn't bear to go through what my father went through. Love for my mother killed him. She betrayed him and abandoned me. Women can't be trusted."

"Your background isn't common, my friend. Truly it isn't. Look at the Earl and his wife, me and Margaret. Many couples we both know are happy together, having a good life. You are denying yourself something wonderful. You're being a fool. Would your mother want that?"

"Couldn't care less what my mother would want. She certainly didn't want me!"

William couldn't argue with that but he did now better understand why Melbroke was such a womanizer. Fun and frolics but no commitment. "'Tis a hollow life you lead, my friend. Believe me love and marriage are wonderful."

"I'll think about it," he mused, buckling some final straps.

William clasped his friend's shoulders and pulled him to him. "Come here you ol' devil. So you've finally been tamed. Margaret will laugh her head off when I tell her."

"How wonderful to know I'm a source of such amusement."

"And we'll both help, do whatever we can."

"Well, apart from not referring to 'all my other women', I'm not sure there is much you can do."

"On the contrary. You're like a fish out of water. You've no idea how to read a woman have you? How to understand what her words really mean? Her wants? Her needs?"

"Apparently not."

"I will help you. I'm very good at this sort of thing, comes from having three sisters."

"Just one problem. I'm off to France and anyway, I'm not sure that I want your help. Miles between myself and Frances may be a good thing. Mayhap I'll forget her. Come to my senses."

"And no doubt you'll be consoling yourself with a few romps?"

Melbroke ignored that last remark. He didn't know what his plans were, not beyond getting away and forgetting a certain beautiful face. They walked the horses into the courtyard. "Where are you going?"

"Greenwich. Margaret and I want to move from Richmond,

be closer to Blean. Need to make the journey easier."

"Good, we can ride together. Is His Majesty happy with your move?"

"Don't know yet, thought I'd see the apartment first, then raise it."

"Well he goes between the two palaces so regularly, probably spends more time at Greenwich actually, can't see it matters which one you're in."

"Nor you come to that."

"Meaning?"

"It might not be long before you're looking for a larger apartment closer to Blean."

"Drop it Runmore! I've confided in you, please now forget everything I've said. I don't think Frances even likes me."

"Believe me she more than likes you."

"She did let me briefly kiss her last evening, very briefly."

"What more proof do you want? Women don't allow themselves to be kissed by men they don't have tender feelings for."

"O yes they do Will, loads of them do. That I do know, only too well."

"Not ladies like Frances."

"Mayhap you're right."

The two men mounted their horses and walked them down the long drive.

"So, she's let you kiss her, you must build on this. She is behaving like a woman whose emotions are in flux."

"She is?"

"God's truth! Yes, Melbroke she is," said an exasperated William. "She wept for you, she showed jealously," he said, counting them off on his fingers. "Three, she worried herself sick when you were ill. Four, she is prepared to have her reputation ruined to save you from the executioner. S'truth man, she has feelings for you. 'Tis obvious as day. Now I agree, that because of all that's passed between you, she may herself not yet realize it but believe me she does."

They passed down the drive in silence, Melbroke churning over his friend's theories, his head spinning in disbelief that he was even having this conversation.

"Well, well. Melbroke's in love," mocked William, leaning across the gap between their horses and slapping his friend on the back. "Melbroke's in love."

"Shut up Runmore!"

They pulled their horses to the right and headed for London.

Chapter Fourteen

PARIS WAS AS always. Busy, hectic, noisy. It was a confusing place for a new visitor but Melbroke wasn't that. He spoke and read French, which was precisely why the King frequently dispatched him there and why he felt so at home. Of course, the King had his official representatives in the French Court but Melbroke was unofficial, informal and loose tongues often spoke out unguardedly in his presence.

The King valued his older cousin's skills at subtle diplomacy, his ability to be friendly with untrustworthies and his analysis of Anglo-French relations based on experience of humankind rather than ecclesiastical or political training. He was also confident of his loyalty. This time though, their parting had not been cordial.

Henry was angry at Melbroke's long absence from Court, his late departure to France, his seemingly putting his Sovereign's demands second to his own. "By Judas' stretched neck! I've run the country with sword wounds!" The King had snarled, rage reddening his face and neck, spit spraying over Melbroke. The accused man not flinching, not reacting. His cousin's patience exhausted, his concern for this insubordinate, good-for-nothing's health, diminished.

They had been in the Presence Chamber, a room Melbroke knew well but this time he did not enjoy its magnificence. He kept his eyes down, away from the sumptuous tapestries, away from the carved panelling, away from the rich, golden splendour that left no visitor in doubt they were inferior to its owner. He remained silent, head bowed.

Silence had descended upon the room. His enemies enjoying the spectacle, his friends willing it over. The King ranted, Melbroke listened. Charges of insolence, laziness, unreliability were hurled at him. Betrayal no less! No chance to respond was given, nor expected. The meal they always shared was not offered. The private evening of talk, the game of chess, was denied. None of the usual affection was shown.

"Begone with you. Out of my sight!" With that Melbroke had bowed low and remained bowed until he had backed from the room. A secretary had given him his French tasks and itinerary. He returned to his rooms, packed and was gone within the hour. The King's badge nestled within his luggage, its authority hidden but available should he need it.

He had arrived at his usual Paris stopover in good speed. The journey went well, the Channel had been calm and having indulged in a fine midday meal he arrived at the home of friends where he had permanent leave to stay.

"Ah monsieur," beamed the tall, seductive chatelaine, throwing her arms about his neck. "My favereet Engleesh gentleman."

Yes, they knew each other well, today though, he smiled as he removed her arms. "Not now Madeleine, I have no time for your charms today, as alluring as they are."

He was amazed with himself. Frances was confusing him, damn her. With annoyance he realized he couldn't stay here, he didn't want such temptations. He would sleep elsewhere. What on earth was happening to him!

"Is the Comte at home?" He asked, knowing full well he was not.

"Non, Monsieur, he and the Comtesse are away."

"Please tell them I called." He kissed her hand, promised to see her when next he visited Paris and returned to his hired horse. He never unnecessarily took Galahad across the Channel, didn't want to inflict non-vital sea crossings on him. This horse was good, he'd do.

He walked the horse through the streets of Paris. Narrow, grubbier streets than even in London. Busier and even noisier with more beggars and more thieves. He breathed in the foul air and loved it. He listened to the hubbub, the song of the French language, the smells of food peculiar to Paris and with joy he felt at home.

He made his way north of La Seine, past gardens where beggars loitered, past alleys where worn-out souls huddled, past rows of washing that hung limp on this damp April day, the women who'd pounded it snoring in snatched rest, their tatty children playing nearby. Eventually the air turned sweeter, the vista greener and the large detached house of the English Ambassador came into view. He'd stay here, the Ambassador couldn't refuse the King's cousin.

His immediate plan was to execute the King's business at the French Court, this were paramount. The list of tasks was now far longer than he had expected, he assumed by way of punishment for his neglect of his monarch. His stay may have to be longer than he'd first thought, the Sheriff would not be happy. He may even have to venture to the Loire Valley, another seat of power within French politics, he would see how things went. He didn't mind. It was beautiful there. He wanted space to think. Paris or the Loire were ideal.

At some stage he would take time to order Frances' gown then track down the effete Marquis. Parisian contacts would help him, indeed the Marquis may be in Paris. He wanted the 'murder' statement withdrawn and a full apology issued to clear his name. If neither was forthcoming he intended threatening legal redress for damage to his reputation. Commonsense told him it wouldn't come to that. Once 'little Jasper' knew he was after him he felt sure the Marquis would acquiesce. If Jasper wasn't in Paris then he would have to go to the family's estates near Reims. God only knew how long that would take.

TWO SURLY men called at Blean three times in one week. Frances, who was now alone with her father, saw them. She watched them arrive by horse, spend time in his study then leave. She didn't like the look of them.

They were brusque, lacking in breeding. Both dressed in tunics, secured with leather belts, leather gaiters tied by bows down the fronts of their legs and brimmed hats that peaked at the front like bills. They didn't remove their hats in the Earl's presence and they carried small daggers at their waist which they didn't remove when entering the house. They were uncouth; she was concerned. After the third visit she asked her father who they were. He brushed her query aside. "Just business acquaintances. Just business."

But her father had no business. He was a landowner with a huge estate to run and staff to oversee. He also had a weak heart and had no business having business. She also noticed how their visits left him dark and moody.

Apart from this concern, life at Blean was back to normal. Queen Katherine had written to offer condolences and had ordered Frances not to hurry back to Court. Margaret and William were organizing their move from Richmond Palace to Greenwich and May stretched into a promising summer like a golden ribbon dancing towards the horizon. Was she happy? No.

True her days were her own. She read, walked Smiley, ate with her father, shopped in Canterbury, rode Lunar, visited friends but never a day passed without the handsome, commanding, towering figure of Alban, Lord Melbroke entering her mind. She chastised herself regularly but it did no good. She couldn't free her thoughts of him and when on her knees in Canterbury Cathedral or Blean's chapel, it was for his safety that she prayed. Please don't let the arm become re-infected. Please let him travel safely. Please don't let him be with other women. The last prayer shocked her. Yes, she was jealous at the thought of him with other women. Yes, remembering when his lips last brushed hers still re-ignited the same overwhelming feelings.

Every time a messenger came she went to the hall to check the deliveries. Nothing from France. He had been gone a month, surely soon there would be some news.

She busied herself by preparing the Earl's surprise party. His birthday loomed and William and Margaret intended announcing that his second grandchild was on its way. She spoke with cook about food, with Gates about hiring musicians, tumblers, jugglers, fools. She devised a guest list and then sent an urgent missive to Margaret seeking approval of the details. The next day the reply was back.

No, William hadn't heard from Melbroke, Margaret wrote. Yes, she did think he was well and his arm would be holding up. No, there was no cause for concern because William hadn't heard from him. Why, dear sister, Margaret asked, do you care so much? Finally, your party plans are perfect.

THE GOWN arrived a few days before the party. Soft blue silk, a full skirt that fell into a short train, a wide, square neck on a tight bodice adorned with hundreds of small crystals. No message, no letter. He knew she would know whom it was from.

No, she thought, putting the lid back on the box. 'Tis beautiful but no. Her thoughts were racing. He had replied to William's invitation that he would attend the party, she wanted to wear it but he may think it a signal that she accepted his advances. Indeed wanted them. No!

At five o'clock the first guests began arriving. The musicians struck up on the terrace and the torches around the grounds flickered in a kind, gentle, early-summer breeze. William thought Melbroke would ride directly from France via Dover. She tried to show scant interest but inside she was tense.

Guests were giving the Earl their presents, talking, laughing, catching up with each others' news but she felt strangely apart from it all. She saw William and Margaret usher the Earl away from the main party. She watched as the Earl raised his arms in delight. He embraced his daughter and slapped William on the back. She was deep in her thoughts when a voice broke into her consciousness.

"You're not wearing my gown." The voice was rich and warm. Jocular but disappointed. That was not to say its owner didn't like the peach gown that she was wearing. Peach decorated with pearls, a headdress of pearls and a rope of them wound around her waist as a loose girdle. She looked up.

"My Lady," he said, bowing low. "How wonderful it is to see you again. And such a lovely party."

Her heart immediately raced, she couldn't control it. His face was happy, his eyes shining on her. He was immaculately dressed in black and deep reds. The light of the torches danced on rubies and caught the shine of silk. Six weeks it had been, it had felt like six months. He must have arrived earlier she was thinking, he clearly hasn't just dismounted a horse. He extended his hand, she laid hers upon it and stood up. He dipped his head and before she knew it he was curling her fingers over his and kissing them. His woody smell enveloped her, her heart pounded in her ears.

He wanted to ask why she hadn't worn his gown, instead he said: "Am I allowed to say how beautiful you look tonight?"

He intended saying so much more. The past long weeks had given him time to think. He'd done nothing but think. His feelings for her hadn't diminished, Paris hadn't been as far away as he'd hoped, indeed she had travelled with him everywhere he went. He now longed to tell her how he felt. William's words about his hollow life and how he was a fool to dismiss love and marriage had haunted him. A knot tightened in his stomach.

She nodded, her smile cracking his heart.

"Did you not like my gown? Is it not to your liking?"

"Oh indeed it is. 'Tis beautiful. It fits so well, how did you manage that?"

"Let's just say your sister helped me. But you don't wear it tonight?"

"Tonight is father's night and he likes me in this. These are the Blean pearls," she said, showing him the girdle. "Six feet of them. They were my grandmother's."

"They are beautiful indeed," he said, relieved at her reason and using the excuse to gaze at her slender waist.

"I don't feel I deserve your gown."

"But I do and that's an end to it," he said, playfully sternly. "Anyway I owe you a replacement for the gown I ripped at Richmond." Why had he said that! He was immediately angry with himself. The last thing he wanted was to remind her of his atrocious behaviour.

"Please, let's put those days behind us. It heralded a terrible time but as events turned out I think they were for the best."

"You do?"

"I have grieved Pierre's passing as best I can. I try to remember his good side but I did not love him, I realize that now. It makes me shudder to think I would have been married to him now."

"Why now do you realize you didn't love him?"

Because I love you, she was thinking. She blushed. "Intuition I suppose and the fact that I wasn't exactly heartbroken when he was killed."

He said nothing, not knowing what to say. She continued: "He wasn't the man I believed him to be. I used to think that you were a villain and he was a perfect gentleman, I know now that I got that completely the wrong way around."

Had she really just said he was perfect and had he realized? O yes, he'd heard and he'd made the decision not to react even though his heart was racing.

"It would have been a disastrous marriage," she went on. "In the most perverse of ways you have saved me from that. She smiled up at him and found his eyes on hers. They sent a wave of weakness through her but she wouldn't succumb, she'd remain strong and she turned her gaze away.

As planned they were called to the banquet at six. She had overseen the seating and had placed herself and Margaret either side of their father who headed the table. William was next to her, the Earl's brother next to Margaret. Melbroke was on Margaret's side but farther down the table. The servants brought in one dish after the another. Goose, beef, venison, capons. Some roasted, some marinated and stewed. There were fricassees of rabbit and pigeon and a variety of vegetables cut into shapes of animals and birds. Red wine was served in silver jugs and the meal ended with sweet custards and comfits.

The Earl made a short speech, applause greeted the news of his second grandchild and glasses were raised to the King, family and friends. On cue the entertainments began back out on the lawns, the music struck up again and the men, eager to stretch their legs, began drifting back into the grounds.

All evening Melbroke had regularly looked in Frances' direction. He was not unaware of her decisions. No gown, no place near her at the table, not a glance in his direction during the meal. He would not be deterred. He had decided tonight was the night. He would tell her of his feelings. He was tired of not knowing. Tired of living between potential ecstasy and possible pain. If it were to be pain then best he knew it soon.

He was waiting for her as she left the dining room. "Would you care for some fresh air Lady Frances?" She nodded and they strolled into the gardens. They made small talk as he steered her away from the guests and round to the blind side of the house.

"So, you stayed in France for quite a while in the end?"

"The King gave me many tasks then I tried to track down Jasper, I want to clear my name of this ridiculous murder charge."

"Did you find him?"

"No. He appears to have gone into hiding."

"You've been very busy then?"

"Yes, busy and thinking about us."

She looked up at him. "Us?"

His deep brown eyes, now shining with love, met her gaze. "You must surely know how I feel about you?"

She turned away. "You are talking about lust again. O please, no more of that." She smiled, tried to laugh but it felt false. "I know you lust after me, you've made that perfectly clear since first we met."

He took a step in front of her, stopping her tracks. "No, I am not talking about lust." His voice softened, he lifted her chin so her nervous eyes were his. She could see the tenderness, it disarmed her but she was powerless to look away. "I'm talking about love. I love you, Frances."

A kind of giddiness threatened to overcome her, something like a nervous laugh left her lips. She was glad when he took her upper arms, he didn't know it but he was supporting her. "I love you." The urgency in his face was turning to pain as she didn't respond. It was exactly what she wanted to hear but something deep within her, something vulnerable and untrusting, made her disbelieve him.

"No," she said, pushing him away, freeing herself from his grip. "You'll say anything. You think me beholden to you because you saved me in the barn. Do you think me so weak that I'll succumb to your words of seduction?" He was shocked to the core.

"Frances, I'm telling you I love you." He was stunned at her hostility.

"You don't believe in love, you told me so in the carriage to Blean. You're just tricking me," she scoffed. "You think me a fool!"

"I didn't realize you still think so little of me. I thought your anger and hostility toward me were in the past."

"Why? Because I let you kiss me afore you left for France?"

"Because you told me so, because we seemed to be getting on so much better and yes...because you let me kiss you."

"One kiss and I'm yours, is that it."

Her words stabbed him like daggers. His heart ached but his pride was kicking in now.

"Madam, I have clearly misunderstood the situation. With your permission I shall rest Galahad for a few more hours then we shall leave at dawn." He turned on his heel and left her standing alone in the garden. He grabbed two flasks of wine and went to his room. His anger was his master. Damn you Frances. He wished he'd never met her. Never allowed his heart to become so vulnerable. He pushed open the window, he needed air. He threw himself on the bed and drank.

He had broken his own vow that he would never love a woman, never trust love. He was right! She had thrown it back in his face. A woman will destroy you if you let them, he chided himself. Stop being so weak! Forget her!

Frances stayed at the party, mixing with guests, trying to smile, trying to be the good hostess but when it was time for them to leave, she was glad. Her head throbbed and her emotions were getting the better of her. She needed her room. She needed peace and time to think.

She threw herself on to her bed and re-ran their conversation over and over. She had longed to hear him say he loved her but something stopped her from believing him. Fear? Distrust? Memories that were poisoning her reasoning? Events that had so shaken her she even mistrusted her own feelings? She didn't know the answers to the myriad of questions that were flooding her thoughts. She made one decision though. She would go to the stables at dawn and talk with him again.

AT FIRST light she lifted herself wearily off her bed. She hadn't undressed and had slumbered lightly atop the covers, making herself wake up regularly, worried that she would miss the dawn.

It was still difficult to clearly see when she arrived at the stables but the white of Lunar stood out and she knew the huge, dark mass beside her was Galahad.

"What are you doing here?" The booming voice was his. He walked Galahad into the courtyard and used the growing light of dawn to begin saddling up.

"I wanted to check Galahad was still here." What a stupid thing to say!

"Well, as you can see he is but we'll be gone in a moment. I'll soon be away from here, you'll soon be rid of me."

"I don't want to be rid of you."

"I certainly feel that you do and I won't stay where I'm not wanted. Now please, if you've anything else to say, say it and get it over. Has been a tortuous night, I've many miles ahead of me."

"You are making this very difficult for me."

"I'm making it difficult for you!" His voice was raised. In exasperation he threw back his head. He turned to her, hands on his hips. "What do you want of me, Frances?" He was angry and glaring. "What exactly do you want?" His face was stern, his eyes fiery all tenderness gone, his demeanour ungiving, harsh.

"Absolutely nothing my Lord," she said, gathering up her skirts, wishing she hadn't come. She turned and ran back to the house. "Travel safely," she called, hoping her voice didn't betray the ache that tore at her very being.

From a front window she stood and watched him leave. An upright figure on his black charger. The sky was moody. Large grey clouds against the lightening sky were pregnant with rain, threatening and unyielding. The breeze played with Galahad's tail and every so often Melbroke leaned forward and patted the beast's broad neck. She couldn't take her eyes off him and little did she know that he was thinking of Madeleine, now deeply regretting he hadn't stayed with her, thinking he would again soon for he would make new tracks back to Paris as soon as possible.

Suddenly he slew Galahad to the left, jumped him across a low, broad hedge, turned a half circle and began trotting him back to the stables. Relief flooded through her and she ran to the stables arriving just as he dismounted.

"You came back."

"You are very observant."

"Why have you come back?"

"Please, have some kindness. I did hear correctly? You did say you didn't want rid of me?"

"Yes I did."

"Then what do you want?"

"I thought we had become friends."

"Friends!" He fired the word at her as if it were an insult. "I've told you I love you and my God, how I now regret that." He unsaddled Galahad and turned to her, full square and scoffed. "I can hardly bring myself to look at you. With every fibre of my being I love you and you want to be friends!" He lay the saddle where the groom would find it and began walking to the house.

"Where are you going?"

"Back to my room. I've remembered your father wants to meet with me this morning."

"You didn't come back for me?"

"No, madam, I came back for your father."

It was time for contemplation and all the nuns were in their cells.

Some shared, Magdala didn't. At least not any more. One of the few advantages of long service was a cell of her own, although sometimes, including today, it felt like solitary confinement.

"Look into your hearts," Mother Esme had urged them all. "Where you see dark let there be light."

Magdala used to see a lot of dark. When first she came here she was bursting with anger and pride and hatred. Hatred for her brother who had taken her from her home by threat of death to her son. Anger at her husband for not fighting him. Pride in her beautiful son, still a boy when last she saw him.

All those fierce but negative feelings had worn her out. As had the tears when her brother had shocked her to the core with his plan to put her in a nunnery. "You should never have married him! You are a traitor to our family, our country and our cause."

She hadn't meant to fall in love with the wrong man. Handsome, striking, tender, wonderful but from the wrong family, the wrong side of the political Plantagenet divide. Yes, her father had been horrified at first but then he and her mother had met her beloved and they, too, grew to love him. Permission was granted for their nuptials. Her brother, always mean in spirit, unkind, ungiving, had refused to attend. While their father lived he could do nothing but when their father died he came for her. To punish her!

Not for the first time she lowered herself to her knees and asked for God's help. Her brother had given her the gift to better understand forgiveness, she knew she should be grateful for that but it was hard.

The life she now led had been sanctified but she hadn't. Her fellow nuns had consecrated themselves to a life of poverty, chastity and obedience. A life of regular observance. God had called them and it shone from their eyes. They magnified the Lord with their love and their pure beautiful voices. Most, although not all, radiated their love for Him. They were at peace. At one with all things spiritual. Magdala was not.

She was still full of questions, her heart still back in the secular world. Was her husband still alive? How was her son? Had he married? Was she a grandmother? Did anyone out there know, or care, where she was? Most days she fought it, today she couldn't. Over-tiredness from so much planting and Esme's insistence on extra prayer, had led to little sleep and it was undermining her usual resolve.

Tears filled her eyes. Selfish, self-centred, self-pitying tears. Her heart today had much black in it. She would struggle to find light today.

Chapter Fifteen

SHE COULD HAVE done without the morning trip into Canterbury but she'd had appointments that couldn't be broken at short notice so despite a throbbing head, exhaustion from a sleepless night and low morale, she had seen to her commitments. She was glad when she turned Lunar back up Blean's drive.

Galahad had gone when she'd collected Lunar, presumably he'd had his meeting with her father and left. Normally she would have taken the carriage but she wanted to ride. Wanted the freedom. Wanted to be able to scream with no one hearing her. Wanted to fight with the wind and win, it was all she could win at the moment. He was gone and her heart was heavy as stone.

"Frances! At last," her father snapped. He was in his study, she had been summoned to him immediately upon her return. He was irritable, tense, concerned. It filled the room. She kissed his cheek and turned. The back of a familiar figure stood in the long window, looking out. A tall figure, his hair loose over his collar. Her heart stopped. Shock weakened her. She was wrong then, he hadn't gone. She looked for a chair.

"Come sit here, by me," her father ordered. She happily obeyed. Melbroke spun round and set his gaze upon her. Set his gaze upon the neat-netted hair under the small hat with its feathery plumes, the tight bodice of her riding dress, the short jacket that led his eye to the elegant skirt, the dainty boot and the delicate hands that now lay in her lap.

Somehow she managed to speak. "Lord Melbroke, I thought you had left us." He didn't reply, just walked to the chair opposite and sat down, one booted ankle on the other knee. She averted her eyes.

His steady, determined gaze burnt into her. She could feel the heat, her skin tingled, her breathing shallowed. Nature forced her to take a deep in-breath, he must have noticed. Must have realized she was uncomfortable. Eventually she had to look up, he made her, forced her to look into his face. Stern, ungiving, unforgiving. He was sitting with his elbows on the chair's arms, his hands clenched under his chin. His knuckles were near-white. His eyes seemed to burn with anger, his jaw rigid. He was giving her no quarter. She turned away, pain groaned through her.

"Frances, my dear, I have a sorry tale to tell. I've got myself into some trouble, Melbroke is going to help."

She looked at her father then at Melbroke. "What's happened?"

Melbroke rose. "That's it," said the Earl. "You explain Melbroke, I'm very tired by it all."

Melbroke turned to Frances and began the tale.

"The King is building up his armies, he needs iron for cannon, swords and such like. Kent is believed to be rich in iron ore, money has already been made and last year your father asked a

London expert to examine the Blean lands, take soil samples, to see if he could assist his King."

She was listening intently, her eyes going from Melbroke to her father and back again.

"The expert identified a large plot on the northern boundary, said it was rich in iron ore. On the strength of this your father invested heavily in building an iron works, a furnace with an adjacent forge. Once completed he put out word that the land and works were up for lease."

The Earl turned to his daughter. "I didn't want to get involved with extracting iron myself but I want to support the King and anyway I'd be a fool to ignore a way for the estate to make more money. I thought it was a good risk to take, to make money and let someone else do all the work. Thought I was being clever!" He scoffed at himself, slapped his thigh in anger. For the moment he wouldn't tell them about Grinstead, Frances had a lot to take in.

Concern crossed her face. "'Tis those two rough men, isn't it? They've something to do with this?" The Earl nodded but bid her listen to Melbroke.

"The men you refer to, the Harwykes, have paid your father a handsome sum to lease the land and they've been digging for several weeks."

"I've not seen or heard anything," said a puzzled Frances.

"'Tis way over the other side," explained her father, waving his arm in a northerly direction. "Well away from the house and the estate's main activities. That's what's so good about it. They enter the land from the other side, they don't come anywhere near the house. It seemed ideal."

"The problem that has arisen," continued Melbroke, now pacing the room, "is that they've found no iron and are now accusing your father of cheating them."

"Can they do that?"

"Yes. The Earl gave them a report confirming there was ore. They say it is a lie. They've had their own survey done, without your father's knowledge and indeed without his permission." He turned to the Earl: "Can't believe that's lawful, we need to look into that." He turned back to Frances: "Their surveyor says there is no iron ore on the land and never has been."

"Can't you just give them their money back?"

"I've offered that," said the Earl. "They just laughed in me face. They accuse me of fraud and theft, they want to take me to court." Anxiety was ravaging the old man's face. "Melbroke and William are going to help sort this out. I'm sorry you have to be burdened with this, my dear but they both felt you and Margaret should be told. They are probably right," he said, rising from his chair. The three dogs were immediately alert. "'Tis your name, your inheritance after all. Now if you don't mind, I need a nap." He left the room, his shoulders rounder than usual, his step slower, the dogs bounding ahead.

Frances sat quietly for a while, the information whirling in her thoughts. Melbroke was back at the window, looking out, his broad back again toward her.

"Thank you," she said, quietly

He spun round. "'Tis my pleasure to help your father. He is, as you told me, a grand person. I couldn't refuse him."

"Yes, thank you for that but also for saying Margaret and I should be told."

"It would have been wrong not to have told you. There will be a lot of activity in this house over coming weeks, meetings, discussions and the like. You would have realized something was afoot. Secrets lead to lies and like misunderstandings they cause pain."

His barbed words found their mark. Quietly she asked: "Margaret knows already?" He nodded. "So, what happens next?"

"Two things. But first I need to make it clear that my helping your father does not mean I feel you beholden to me." He was raising his voice. "Is that clear?" He was standing over her. His anger filled the room. She nodded.

"You will oblige me with an answer."

"Yes," she said, quietly, "'tis clear." She kept her gaze to her lap.

"Good. It is an affront to me that you suggest I have done anything with the sole purpose of placing you under a debt to me that must be repaid...in any way."

She did not respond. She couldn't, his anger had reduced her.

He sat on the chair opposite. "Now, with that understood I am happy to outline my plans. Firstly, I will need to find out more about these men? Who are they? Where did their money really come from? What is their experience in iron prospecting and mining? What do they stand to gain by lying? And why?"

"You have seen the report that father commissioned? 'Tis genuine? Father hasn't made a terrible mistake?" She forced herself to re-find her confidence but still she couldn't meet his eyes.

"I haven't yet seen the report. But your father's expert is the best in the business, he came personally from London to Blean, he didn't send an underling. 'Tis unreasonable to think he made a mistake. Your father acted with integrity, he could do no more than trust the expert's opinion. If anyone has made a mistake 'tis the surveyor, not your father, although I doubt that."

"That's a good thing surely. As you say, experts don't usually make mistakes."

"Indeed. Not only do they have specialist experience but

they also have their reputations to think about."

"You said there were two things needed to be done?"

"The second is to discover who did the report for these men. What kind of expert is he? Does he even exist?"

"You obviously believe these men are up to something. Trying to trick father?"

"Definitely. But what and why?"

"Do you have any experience in iron ore?" She asked incredulously, believing she knew the answer.

"None at all. But fortunately I have a lot of experience with life and the things people get up to."

"And William is going to help?"

"The move to Greenwich occupies him, he will be away quite a bit but he is there if I need him. I think together we will sort this out and protect your father."

"And I'm here, too," she urged, managing to look him in the face for the first time since his rebuke. "Please allow me to assist. I want to."

"Have you met these men?"

"I've seen them but not spoken to them. They were most undesirable, untrustworthy types. I took an instant dislike to them."

"So did your father. Seems he should have acted on his instincts." Melbroke thought for a few moments. "Could you face another trip into Canterbury tomorrow morning?" She nodded.

"We'll ride in. But not with your horse, she's not strong enough. I want you keeping up with me. Tell the groom to prepare a stronger horse."

"I'll take father's, I've ridden him regularly, I can handle him."

"Good." He bowed and left. He wasn't going to indulge in small pleasantries. His pride, his anger, his heart weren't ready for that. He was being forced by circumstance to remain in a house he had intended to leave and never set foot in again. Her co-operation could be useful, he wouldn't shun that. From now on though he would not be playing the courting game, he would remain in control of every situation whether she liked it or not.

THE OFFICES of lawyer George Jarrett were down a narrow side street near the cathedral. Frances led the way.

"May I introduce Lord Melbroke, a family friend."

The lawyer bowed and bid them both sit. He reclaimed his wooden armchair behind the huge, heavily carved oak desk that was covered with piles of parchment and vellum. Each pile was supported by a sculpted piece of wood to stop them from tumbling on to the floor. A large wooden bird with a spiteful beak on one side, a prowling wild cat on the other. Between the piles Jarrett sat like a wise owl looking at his guests. His face opaque white, blue veins tracing patterns around his temples, eyes grey, his demeanour mirroring both cat and bird. His white, boney fingers lay atop his desk. He waited unblinking.

Melbroke began. "The Earl of Blean finds himself in some trouble, we need your assistance."

The lawyer's eyebrows lifted queryingly.

"Earlier this year you drew up a lease for a parcel of the Blean estate."

"To be used in iron exploration," the lawyer, nodded. "Yes, I remember."

"That is correct. Except now the leasees are claiming there is no iron ore and are threatening the Earl with court action. The Earl has asked me to speak with you on his behalf in this matter."

Melbroke handed over the Earl's letter of authority.

"Goodness gracious," the lawyer mumbled, pushing the letter, unread, to one side. "But the Earl hired a top London expert. It was all very professional, I read the report myself." He scuffled around in the piles of documents lining the perimeter of his room. Bundles wrapped in ribbon, bundle upon bundle, all in perfect order to him but chaotic to the onlooker. He quickly fetched out the one he needed.

"Here we are," he said, perusing the pages. "The lease was granted on a parcel of land called Pensel for three years with an option to renew for a further two. Then the land reverts back to the Earl. They paid handsomely, didn't quibble, didn't try and beat the Earl down on price. All went very smoothy."

Melbroke asked: "The men that signed the lease, they had lawyers acting for them?"

"No, my Lord, they did not. And a lot of concern it caused me. It was two men, brothers...yes, here we are," he said, rapidly turning parchment with a boney finger. "Arthur and Samuel Harwyke of Faversham."

"Tell me," asked Frances, "did they always wear black, with peaked hats and leather gaiters tied with bows at the front."

"Yes, my Lady, that's them."

"These are the men that now threaten my father, they've been to the house."

"They were difficult to deal with," continued Jarrett. "I felt they were constantly deferring to someone else. They never seemed sure of themselves. Shifty."

"Advise me," requested Melbroke, "wouldn't a leasee have had their own survey done at the time, before they committed to a three-year contract and to such a large amount of money?"

"Well, my Lord, I must confess iron prospecting isn't one of my specialist areas but certainly in other areas, such as property and estate leasing, that would certainly be the case."

"Even to me it would seem to be a sensible thing to do."

"Quite. I know a lawyer in the Weald who specializes in iron prospecting. There is more of it going on over there. I would be happy to write to him on your behalf."

"Please yes, that would be very helpful but wait a few days," Melbroke said, standing in readiness to leave. Frances and the lawyer followed suit. "We are going to make more investigations and may have more questions for you to ask."

Back in the narrow lane they walked silently to the horses, the only noise Melbroke's boots on cobble. "Do you know Faversham? Is it far?"

"'Tis about ten miles from here," she replied.

"Can you ride there now?"

She nodded.

"Do you need me to assist you on to your horse?"

She looked around. There were no mounting steps or block, many a road had them carved into a wall, this narrow lane did not. With reluctance she nodded. She had no choice. "If you would be so kind."

He put his hands around her waist and lifted her on to the horse's back.

FAVERSHAM WAS busy. Hot sun was back after yesterday's clouds. The streets were full of folk buying or selling. The mud roads were dust-dry and beggars of all ages sat, some laying horizontally, crying for alms. People jostled and side-stepped each other. Hawkers mingled selling wares from baskets and an old man with a humpback turned a pig on a spit, its smell catching many an empty stomach. Children batted balls and played with hoops. Men in ale-sleep slumped in corners snoring, others played dice in groups.

The scene looked innocent enough but of course it wasn't. Busy streets never are, villainy always thrives. Melbroke turned to Frances. "You put your arm through mine and you stay by me at all times," he commanded. He checked his boot for his dagger and the street for dark corners. In the distance pigeons flew, soaring and squabbling over midden heaps.

"How do we find where they live?" She hadn't visited Faversham for some time, it was busier than she remembered.

"We ask someone."

He led her down what seemed to be the main road. "Would you recognize them again if you saw them?"

"Definitely."

At the end of the busy road they came to a cross roads, to the right a well-trodden, narrow, winding path led down to a row of tatty, straw-roofed cottages. Outside the one closest to the mill they could see an old, rotund woman taking the sun. They headed toward her. She sat on a low stool, her eyes closed, a mass of pink and white daises bobbing around her feet. She was sucking on a pipe of herbs, the scent travelled up the road toward them. A skimpy sleeveless dress stretched across her overweight body, a sleeveless jerkin of rabbit pelts revealed flabby, weathered arms. Her face was gnarled, her mouth gummy, her body labouring under its years. Her eyes opened as they approached.

"Please, don't rise," said Melbroke as she tried. Her attempt was obviously a difficult task.

"Thank you m'Lord, me bones ain't what they woz," she said, pushing the pipe into the corner of her mouth. Frances watched as its smoke curled back into her face, turning her hair into a smoking, grey thatch.

"We are trying to find the Harwyke brothers, Samuel and

Arthur, would you know where they live?"

"Not in Faversham m'Lord. Not no more. Not for many a year."

"Oh?"

"They woz here, born and bred on the other side of market. Parents both dead for a good few year, brothers left, don't know where they went. Wrong uns frew and frew. No trade, no skills. Crook'd as the day is long. I'd have no truck wiv 'em, told me boys to keep well away." She flicked her pipe-free hand in the air as she spoke, the tops of her arms flapping. "Wrong uns frew and frew."

"Thank you, you have been most helpful," he said.

"Afore you go m'Lord, could you help me up? I should go inside now, got me jobs to do." Frances saw a twinkle in the women's eye.

"Certainly," he said, putting his arms around her and lifting her upwards. The woman giggled. "Been a long while since such a strong, handsome man had his hands on me, I can tell you," she said, giggling, showing her toothless mouth.

Melbroke escorted her to the open door that hung within wattle walls. "Would m'Lord like to come in?"

"With regret, my urgent business demands I leave."

"Shame, another time, mayhap."

He gave her a brief bow out of respect for her age. Frances grinned, mockingly as they walked away. "Just fall at your feet don't they! Everywhere you go women just throw themselves at you!"

He struggled to stifle a grin. "Be quiet and hold my arm."

THEY WERE walking back along the main road when suddenly Frances stopped. She snatched off her hat and net allowing her hair to tumble down over her shoulders. She ran her fingers through her locks to bush them out, she pinched her cheeks to make them pinker.

"What on earth are you doing?"

"Quick. Hold these," she said, handing him her gloves and jewellery, "'tis your turn to be quiet." She quickly removed her expensive riding jacket and pushed the sleeves of her dress up her arms to above her elbows. She tucked the front hem of her skirt into her waist, revealing her underskirts.

"Do I look like a doxy?"

"Not in the slightest."

"Well, I shall have to risk it."

Before he could stop her she was walking across the road to an inn, her curls bouncing, her hips swaying in seductive fashion.

"Frances," he shouted, his eyes glued to those hips. "Get back here. Now!"

She ignored him and headed inside the inn. It was gloomy and noisy. The stench of ale and beer hit her senses. The air was stale, a mix of human smells, dog smells and cooked-food smells that hadn't collided with fresh air for goodness how long. Thousands of particles of dust danced in the few sunbeams that streamed into the room. It took her eyes a moment to become accustomed to the dingy scene. The inn was packed to bursting. Some sitting on low stools, most standing. Various men called out: "Hello darling, want a drink?" "Want a plunging?"

Melbroke by now was also in the inn, angry beyond measure. She looked around, had to stand on tiptoe to see above and around heads and when her eyes fell upon the man in her sights she took a deep breath, thought of her father's plight and boldly went straight to him. "Skoose me mister," she said, in as common a voice as she could muster, "I 'ope I ain't disturbing you."

He turned to face her. His eyes lit up. "Well, 'allo my beauty," he drooled, putting down his ale, "you can disturb me any time you like." An arm went to her waist and pulled her to him. Melbroke stiffened and moved closer.

"Which part of me would you like to disturb first?"

She giggled playfully, put one hand on his shoulder and with the other teasingly twirled his greasy, straggly hair. Melbroke couldn't believe what he was seeing.

"Well actually," she said, flirtily, "'tis your gaiters wot caught my eye."

"My gaiters! Well I can have them off mighty fast lass. Why don't we go in the back, there's all sorts of things I can have off mighty fast," he said, running his hand along the upper line of her bodice." Melbroke stepped even closer. What was she doing!

"They are very unusual, I've never seen such handsome gaiters," she giggled. "Where did you buy 'em?"

"Up the road, Josiah Penn made 'em."

"My bruvver would love a pair.'

The man stood up, pulled her roughly against his body. "Let's go in the back and mayhap you can earn the money to buy him a pair." He pushed her hair back off her shoulders and ogled her beautiful, naked neck. He was just about to plunge his face toward it when Melbroke grabbed her arm. "Annie, what have I told you about coming into places like this."

The man froze. "My Lord?"

"She's one of my servant girls, I won't have her come into places like this."

Melbroke took her arm with an iron grip and dragged her from the inn. Outside he stood staring at her, so candescent with rage he couldn't speak. He wanted to grab her shoulders and shake her. She quietly pulled down her sleeves, released her skirt, replaced her jewellery and slipped back into her coat.

"You stupid, stupid woman," he blasted at her.

"I need to get home, have a bath, wash that man and those smells off me," she said, quietly, now shaking from her experience.

"Had you no thought as to what could have happened in there?" He was shouting now.

"I knew you were close by."

"And supposing he'd had ten friends? Twenty friends? You assume I can fight off a hundred men? They'd all of had you. One at a time."

He grabbed her upper arms and glared into her face. "And you take my protection too much for granted." There was panic in her eyes, he had frightened her to the core. It had been his intention to rant but now her vulnerability was affecting him. For a brief second his desire to hold her close nearly overcame him but he fought it. She yanked herself away from him, turned to the gutter and retched. She thought she may be sick but wasn't. She was now shaking badly. The realization of what she'd just done was hitting her, the blood had drained from her face and she was trembling uncontrollably.

"Good," he said, still angry and unsympathetic to her condition. "Please tell me there was a purpose to all that. And where did you learn to behave like a harlot?"

"I did what was necessary."

"Explain yourself Frances and quickly."

She retched again, dabbed her mouth and tidied down her clothes.

"Come on, explain!"

"I saw that man walk into the inn, he was wearing exactly the same gaiters, the ones with the bows, as the two men we are seeking."

"But to put yourself at such risk, you stupid, stupid..."

"I did it for father and anyway I knew you were only a few steps away, I believed I was perfectly safe."

"You weren't! And why should I fight one man for you let alone an inn full?"

She didn't answer, she had none.

"You should have told me, I would have spoken with him."

"Why would he talk to you?" She looked at him in disbelief. "Why should he assist someone of the rank he probably loathes and despises. He wouldn't have spoken to me normally, it was good fortune he didn't notice my gown was silk."

"He was way past noticing what fabric your gown was made of! So were the other men who were watching."

"My way was effective and quick."

He paced silently as she arranged her hair back into its net and replaced her hat.

"So what did you find out?"

"The gaiters were made just up the road from here. The cordwainer should know his customers surely, mayhap even have an address for them?"

"You certainly have a habit of nearly getting yourself raped," he said, snappily. His anger made him want to be brutal with her, to ram home some commonsense. "And don't assume, madam, that I will make a habit of saving you."

As she gazed at him so his image dimmed, his voice quietened. Darkness crept in from the edges and by the time it met in the middle she had fainted. He just managed to grab her before her head hit the cobbles. He had seen a respectable inn back near the mill. He threw her over his shoulder and with receding anger mixed with a growing admiration he strode to its comfort.

Chapter Sixteen

IT WAS JUST after dawn, a few days later, when the constable's staff banged into the Blean House front door. The occupants were just awakening. Gates rushed to the commotion.

"Open up," boomed the Sheriff, pushing his way past the steward. "I must see the Earl, immediately."

Upstairs both Melbroke and Frances had heard the noise and had hastily left their beds. Frances, barefoot, hair loose, long robe billowing, ran down the stairs. "Gates, what on earth is going on?"

"My Lady, the Sheriff is demanding to see the Earl."

"Immediately, if you please." The Sheriff stood stiff backed, chest pumped, stern faced, authoritative. Frances smiled graciously and kept her decorum.

"Gentlemen, follow me, we'll go to my father's study." Gates turned to fetch the Earl. Once inside the study, the door closed, she released her anger. "How dare you burst into our home like this! You forget your rank sir, you are beholden to my father for your station, think on that before you show such discourtesy."

The door banged open, it was Melbroke, fully dressed. "Lady Frances speaks well Sheriff. Look to your rank and remember with whom you deal."

"I know my rank, my Lord," he said bowing. "And I know with whom I deal, his Lordship being an Earl and you being a cousin of the King and all. 'Tis why I waited 'til daylight. As to my station, I am the law officer for the County of Kent. I have duties and responsibilities vested in me which I would hope people of your rank," and he bowed to them both again, "would not prohibit me from carrying out."

Three dogs rushed into the room, followed by a flustered Earl. "By hell's burning fires, what on earth do you want, man?"

Frances tightened her robe and left the men to their business, her hair catching the morning sun, the Sheriff again bowing, Melbroke watching.

"Come on man, what do you want?" The Earl was rattled, hungry, he wanted rid of this intruder.

"Serious allegations have been made against your Lordship. Very serious."

"Get on with it man. What allegations?"

Melbroke stood silently waiting for the inevitable for both he and the Earl, knew what was coming.

"Arthur and Samuel Harwyke of Faversham have accused your Lordship of fraud and theft with regard iron ore extraction."

"Yes, yes," said the Earl, waving his hand dismissively. "I know all about that. Absolute rubbish and I've got the paperwork to prove it." He flopped into a chair, the dogs took their places around him.

"You know?" The Sheriff's jaw dropped, his eyes widened.

The Earl emitted a long, irritable sigh.

Melbroke stepped in. "Indeed we do." He proffered a chair, his gesture was ignored. "I have been trying to assist the Earl in this matter. Been trying to get to the bottom of these allegations, at the moment I am at the early stages and can tell you little. But if you care to visit George Jarrett, lawyer in Canterbury, he has a copy of the survey the Earl commissioned. It is by a top London expert and is emphatic about the presence of ore."

"But the Harwykes have dug, toiled for days they tell me and no ore! Say they've been tricked." Hands on hips, the Sheriff held his ground. "They allege extortion!"

"And you allege you have intelligence, you clay-brained pumpion!" The Earl was forward in his chair, his face red, his manner angry.

The Sheriff also was now red and angry. Offended! Not sure how to deal with insults from an Earl. Melbroke ignored the Earl's intervention and continued.

"We are aware of their claims," he said, calmly, gesturing for a second time to a chair. This time it was taken. He needed the Sheriff's co-operation on another matter, he did not want this becoming hostile. "They've made their allegations directly to the Earl. They were menacing and abrasive. If they call here again they will not be admitted."

The Sheriff shuffled, gathered his robe of office around him. "But they say they've had their own survey done and that it confirms there is no ore! They claim the Earl deliberately lied! That he stole their money!"

Melbroke pulled a heavy, carved chair nearer to the Sheriff and sat by him. He would talk to him man-to-man, share a confidence, gain his trust. "We are aware of all this. Lawyer Jarrett advises that no surveyor of repute would do such a thing without the landowner's permission. It would be illegal. No one sought the Earl's permission which means either they used an unprofessional and probably unqualified surveyor or they had no survey done at all. In short Sheriff, they are lying."

All wind had now gone from the Sheriff's sails. He shuffled in his chair, fiddled with his cuffs. "I will ask to see their survey my Lord."

"Good idea Sheriff and if it exists mayhap we can be allowed a copy."

"I will look into it and may I say I am glad to hear what you say my Lords. 'Tis no pleasure for me to have to come to Blean in this manner but I am obliged to investigate such allegations." His rigid back had noticeably relaxed, his bumptious confidence now depleted, his haughty air gone.

"The Earl understands," said Melbroke, "as do I." The Earl quietly huffed. Melbroke smiled. The meeting was ending on a courteous note, Melbroke was making sure of that. "Allow me to show you out," he said, softly, his raised arm signalling it was time for Malins to leave. "And please deal with me in this matter or Lord Runmore or Mr Jarrett," he explained, as they strolled along the hallway. "The Earl is elderly and tired, he has asked us to act for him."

"Very good my Lord but you realize that if this comes to anything it is the Earl I will need a statement from and possibly have to arrest."

"It won't come to that, I am sure."

The two men walked into the fresh air of a fine June morning. "'Tis a perfect day Sheriff, don't you think, for a ride into Canterbury?"

"Yes, yes my Lord. Have no fear, I shall be seeing lawyer Jarrett later today."

"And Sheriff afore you leave, what of your attempts to speak with Lord Jasper, the Marquis de Champagne? Is he still accusing me of murder?"

"Colleagues in London, Kent and Surrey are looking for him but he seems to have vanished."

"Indeed. When I was in Paris I looked for him at the French Court, no one has seen him there for many a month. And until he is found I still have this outrageous allegation hanging over me?"

"'Fraid so my Lord but I have read the statements yourself, Lady Blean and Lord Runmore have made. I am happy with those. But I don't understand why the Marquis would make such an allegation if it weren't true. Why?"

That, you will never know, thought Melbroke as he headed back into the house.

DURING THE afternoon Melbroke took his chance to speak privately with the Earl. William and Margaret hadn't yet fully removed from Richmond and Jasper's mother, the Marchioness, was only a few miles away from them at Mortlake. Did Melbroke have the Earl's permission, he asked, to write to William and request that Lady Margaret, on behalf of the family, pay the Marchioness a visit? Unofficially as it were. Woman to woman. A member of the extended family that was so nearly united with the Marchioness' paying her respects and offering support. Would the Earl permit it?

His request had taken the Earl by surprise. "Why? For what real purpose?"

"To try and establish if the mother knows where her son is."

"This murder allegation business?"

"Yes, my Lord."

The Earl gave his permission and Melbroke spent time in his room writing to William. Several times, through his window, he saw Frances in the gardens with her dog. He was resigned now to her only wanting friendship. It wouldn't do for him and as soon as this 'iron ore' business were sorted he would go for good. Then William's words came flooding back: she loves you, she just doesn't realize it. He shook his head in exasperation and put his concentration back on the task in hand.

He was just about to give Gates the letter for the next post-horse when a messenger galloped up the drive carrying two letters, both for him. The first was from lawyer Jarrett. It informed Melbroke that on re-reading the documentation connected to the iron ore lease he, Jarrett, had been reminded that the Earl had offered the Harwykes a cheaper deal. He was prepared to reduce the annual cost of the lease in exchange for a percentage of the profits. The brothers had dismissed the offer out of hand.

"It is a second proof that the Earl believed iron ore to exist but it also occurs to me," the letter continued, "that it suggests that the Harwykes knew there would be no profits. Seems they successfully connived to make the Earl take an awful lot of money FROM them." The capital letters for the word 'from' indicated the lawyer's growing suspicions, they concurred with Melbroke's. Good point Jarrett, good point.

The second letter was from the Sheriff. Apparently Jasper had now produced a witness to the murder. A farmer was saying he had seen a defenceless man of the Marquis' description being stabbed by a tall, well-built man of Melbroke's description. The farmer had seen the Sheriff of Surrey, a statement was in the process of being prepared and would be with Sheriff Malins in a matter of days. "I shall need to speak with you, do not leave Blean," the Sheriff's letter instructed.

Melbroke screwed up the letter, his face ashen with shock and rage. Jasper's evil was deepening, he had obviously paid a farmer to commit purgery but why take him to the Surrey Sheriff? To gain time, mayhap? Why? As to Malins giving him orders! That sent another wave of a different kind of anger through him. He would leave Blean as and when he chose, not before, not later. He had got to find the damnable Jasper, that was now more imperative than ever.

FRANCES WAS in the saddle and ready to go when Melbroke blocked her way. "Off to Canterbury again?" His enquiry was mere courtesy he had no real interest, his angry thoughts were still upon the Sheriff's missive. He'd found her leaving the stables as he'd ventured out for a stroll to cool his temper. He was looking up at her, the sun behind her head making him shield his eyes.

"No, I'm going up to Pensel, I want to see this iron ore extraction, see what's been going on." Suddenly his interest was back.

"O no you're not! Not on your own you're not!" He grabbed Lunar's bridle.

"Let go."

"Absolutely not. It could be dangerous, those men could be up there."

"This is my home, my land, my horse. I will go where I please. And anyway, you told me I should not assume your protection! Will you please let go of the reins!"

"No." He turned Lunar around and steered her back to the stables.

Frances was fuming. She couldn't jump down without

risking injury, she was under his control, she didn't like it! Back at the stables he tied Lunar to a post and bid the groom saddle up Galahad quickly.

"Now we will both go to Pensel," he said, mounting his horse and signalling to the groom to untie Lunar.

"One minute I'm scolded for taking your protection for granted now you are insisting I have it," she snapped. "You are a most infuriating man! Truth is I don't need your protection. You assume a role that is not yours. I didn't need protecting before you came into my life why should I need it now."

"Yes, that's right. About to marry a man who would probably have been violent toward you, I seem to remember. Pretend to be a doxy in a tavern full of lusty men! All very sensible!"

"I haven't asked you to protect me, my Lord."

"Don't flatter yourself, madam, I do this for your father." And anyway, he was thinking, going to Pensel is a good idea. He was inwardly smiling. She's an intelligent woman, he mused but he wasn't about to tell her that.

He allowed Frances to lead the way and cantered at her speed. It was a lovely summer's early evening. The air was balmy, the sun still warm. Creatures fluttered and buzzed and flitted, swooped and sang. Kent was alive. At its best. He lived in the confines of a palace, it was a good life but the freedom here was better. He let her ride in front of him, her neat, erect figure stealing his gaze.

They arrived more quickly than Melbroke had expected and he was surprised when she brought Lunar to a standstill and dismounted, stepping on to a fallen trunk. They were in a clearing, a few late bluebells still swayed, a distant brook gurgled. Melbroke jumped from his horse.

"You stay by me at all times," he ordered. "No running off. No repeat of last time, do you hear me?"

"Here we go again!"

"I mean it. Or I shall have to put you on a rein!" Her eyes flashed. Just let him try!

They wandered between the trees for quite a while, everything seemed as it should. The foundry stood silent, waiting for action. There was an eeriness in the emptiness of the place, a sadness as if it were neglected. Back on their horses they extended their search area. Rooks took flight from their ash-top homes, shrieking their disapproval harshly as their territory was invaded. They came upon the remains of a poacher's bonfire, a pile of rabbit bones in its ashes. Melbroke grabbed a fallen, sturdy branch and began sweeping the undergrowth. Within moments he found pits, some shallow, some deeper, up to five feet of so. As he widened his search, more pits revealed themselves. More and more, like a rash on the landscape.

"They've been mining then," she said, sadly. "They've minded and found no ore."

"But where are the shafts? They should have been digging deep shafts, anything up to twenty-five feet, mayhap even deeper. I'm no expert but I know it should be deeper than this. This isn't proper mining, this is just scratching the surface."

"What does it mean? I don't understand."

Melbroke knew exactly what it meant. The Harwykes had put on a show but hadn't seriously excavated. Why? Why do all this? That he didn't know. He would keep his counsel for now but this trip to Pensel had been very productive.

"Why pay father all that money and then not mine properly? I don't understand."

"Nor I." He was though, seeing conspiracy clearer and clearer. As yet he had no proof. That was his next task.

She watched him as he led the way from Pensel. Through

the trees, ducking the low branches, warning her of brambles, jumping the occasional low thicket and waiting to be sure she jumped safely. He cut a fine figure on a horse. His military bearing excelled. Straight back, relaxed shoulders, strong legs controlling a powerful stallion that towered above Lunar. She followed behind safe and happy, it was how he made her feel.

IT WAS after dark, the house had settled for the night, Frances was gently dozing when she heard a man's footfall pass her door. Down the stairs it went and across the tiled hallway. At the window she waited. A few moments later the same tall, elegant figure on his usual large, black stallion walked down the main drive. Melbroke was going out.

Was he bored? Was life at Blean not exciting enough? Was he looking for the brighter lights of Canterbury, the inns, the wenches? She tortured herself for a while with these thoughts, tossed on her feather bedding, her head pounding until at last sleep released her.

A HEARTY plate of food sat before him. "Good morning," Melbroke beamed, as she made her way to the large table. He was breaking his fast in good spirits. He looked contented, his face aglow with something she took to be satisfaction. For her part she knew she looked pale, exhausted after a night of shallow sleep. Her spirits were low. He returned to his food.

"Has father been down yet?"

"Been and gone. He's an early bird today."

"And you, my Lord, were a late bird, I think. I heard you go out, must have been toward midnight?"

"I hope I didn't disturb you, I tried to disturb no one."

"I wasn't asleep, I heard your horse's hooves on the drive. So, did you get the merriment you sought? Did Canterbury fulfil your needs?"

"O yes. Very much so."

Her heart sunk. She pushed her plate away from her, its few morsels of food untouched.

"Not hungry?"

"No, I slept badly, I have a headache this morning." She poured herself water. It had been drawn this morn from Blean's own well, it was cool and soothing with a hint of mint from the fresh leaves that bobbed atop the jug.

"I'm sorry to hear that," he said, "I, on the other hand, had a wonderful night. I shall go again tonight and probably tomorrow."

She felt sick to the pit of her stomach. She pushed her chair back from the table and made to leave.

"Would you not like to hear what I did?"

"Why on earth would I want to hear that? I've had enough of Canterbury's inns to last me a life time. Pretending to be a doxy was one thing, hearing about your exploits with them is quite something else."

"If you care to sit down," he replied, struggling to smother a grin, "I will tell you what I did and it isn't what you assume." A smile overcame him and his face beamed. Would William say she was showing signs of jealously? He mused happily.

She sat, tried to eat a little bread and waited for him to speak.

"I went to Canterbury, to the address Josiah Penn gave us. The cordwainer who made the gaiters?"

"I know who Josiah Penn is!" Tiredness was turning to irritability.

"I found it quite easily," he continued, quietly. "A small stone hovel, single story. The Harwyke brothers were there, I saw them through the window. They were drinking beer, had been for some time."

"Didn't they see you?"

"They were busy with wenches, not their wives I think, probably whores. They were too pre-occupied to spot me."

"Why is this important?"

"Because now I know for sure where they live. They have a life there. Hopefully, unlike damned Jasper, they won't be vanishing before I've dealt with them!"

"Dealt with them! What do you mean? Surely you just tell the Sheriff and he deals with them."

"Absolutely not! If the Sheriff is involved it becomes official too soon. It could lead to legal proceedings, court, that's the last thing your father needs. I want to deal with them privately, put the fear of God into them so they leave your father alone, leave Kent and hopefully leave the country!" He was angry now, his voice raised as his clenched fist slammed the table. Immediately he apologized.

"I should not have displayed my anger," he said, "but to think that two such ne'er-do-wells can threaten a good man like your father, an Earl to boot, makes my blood boil."

His genuine concern for her father touched her. He was a good man, she had come to realize that, he had just confirmed it again.

"I shall go again over the next few days. I shall watch their movements. I shall also write to William and ask him to return to Blean, I shall need his assistance on the night I confront them."

"Why?

"Well, they won't obey like lambs! There will almost

certainly be a fight."

"Two against two," she said quietly, her heart quaking at the thought of him being injured again - or worse.

WILLIAM ARRIVED with his family and entourage of servants. Margaret, her pregnancy advancing, settled them as usual in the east wing and sent word she would be resting for the remainder of the evening. She would not be joining the family for supper. She would catch up with Frances and her news on the morrow.

Melbroke had concluded his reconnaissance, was paying three youths to watch the property in shifts and to send urgent message should the Harwyke brothers appear to be quitting the house. He had spent the first few hours after William's arrival closeted in the study with his friend, hearing his news, going over events and outlining his plan. When he emerged he was a mix of fury and concern.

"Lady Frances, a word if you please," he summoned, heading through the hall toward the terrace, his boots hitting the tiled floor angrily. It was her cue to follow.

Once outside he turned, hands on hips and confronted her.

"What's happened? What's the matter?" She asked gingerly, fear now dominating her, she not knowing why.

"Lady Margaret, at my bidding, visited the Marchioness. My hope had been that she could lead the conversation round to Jasper and the Marchioness would reveal where he is. With that information I could then visit him, get him to drop this ridiculous murder allegation and clear my name before it became Court gossip." His words were stern, cold, laced with import she didn't understand.

She stood stunned. He was overflowing with rage, she felt it was all aimed at her. "What is this to do with me?"

"While the Marchioness doesn't know where Jasper is, she was able to tell your sister that he is very busy with his new project - iron ore extraction!" He was rigid with anger. His jaw set, his face flushed. "There's a lot of money to be made apparently! Especially in Kent! She says that you told Pierre all about it."

"No! Never!"

"She says, you told Pierre that your father was looking to lease land." He was pacing now, up and down the terrace, his boots scraping the stone but keeping his glare on her constant.

"'Tis not true."

"You told her, apparently, that your father was hoping to find some novices in iron, men who didn't know what they were about so he could cut an advantageous deal and make huge profits."

"Nonsense! I said no such thing."

He strode right up to her, towered over her and looked directly into her eyes. "Is this anything to do with you, Frances? Do you have any part in this?"

Now anger was claiming her: "How dare you!" She returned his glare and took a step back. She wanted more space between them. She put her hands over her eyes in despair. He was accusing her of conspiring against her father! "How dare you!" She was now raising her own voice. She glared at him, her lip quivering, the insult raging through her. She raised her right hand and lashed out to strike his face. He pulled back, she missed and he caught her wrist. He was glowering at her, hard and severe. For a second they stood motionless, like a statue, anger commanding them.

"I've said nothing," she ventured, trying in vain to free her wrist. "I didn't know father was involved in iron ore, I knew nothing to tell. And anyway I wouldn't. Nor would father act in that way. I wouldn't hurt father!" Her anger had turned to misery. Her eyes glistened. "I wouldn't," she said, agony now etched on her face.

She wriggled her arm and he tightened his grip. His eyes were penetrating hers, trying to see into her mind. She gazed back, she had nothing to hide, she was not guilty of these accusations. He didn't want to believe ill of her but he had to be sure. He'd needed to see her reaction.

"You were part of that family for a year, could you have accidentally said something?"

"No! I didn't know anything about father's plans. It was you who told me the other week. I didn't know..."

She sensed his grip slacken, she tried to release her wrist but his fingers re-tightened. He stood staring deep into her eyes. His mind was racing. His emotions felt shot to pieces. His jaw was clenched with rage. She could hear his heavy breathing.

"I tire of this Frances. One moment I'm perfect then you want rid of me. You nurse me with such tenderness then you are so cruel I can scarce believe it. I declare my heart and you dismiss it as being of no consequence. You think me so shallow I think only of lust. You complain of my protection yet use it when it suits. I tire of all this, it is at an end. No more. I withdraw my declaration of love. I want no more of this."

His words crashed into her head as if they were bells in a belfry and she were locked inside. Her head was spinning, she wanted to answer each of his accusations but the power of reason had drained from her. In her despair all she could manage was: "You're hurting me."

He pushed his mouth into the palm of the hand he held and kissed it. He then tossed it back to her, turned and stormed back into the house.

She went to the stone bench and sat down. Her wrist was throbbing in competition with her head. She lowered her face into her hands determined not to weep, although she felt like it. She would not cry, not for him, never again!

From a window Melbroke watched her. His anger had not receded but he did believe she had nothing to do with telling the Marquis about iron ore. Why would the Marchioness say such things? Or did her sons lie to her? Was Jasper, mayhap even Pierre, behind all this? His head was spinning with possibilities. A Marquis involved in crime! Everything else he had said to Frances he meant. His heart ached but he was a man of truth and he had said his fill.

William strolled in and joined him at the window. He saw Frances on the bench outside and realized Melbroke had been watching her. "Something happened?"

"'Tis over, dear friend. There's nothing between Frances and myself nor ever will be."

With Mother Esme's grudging permission Brother Thomas called on Magdala before his busy day began. An elderly nun, bent double over her psalms, was charged to chaperone. The monastery's senior apothecary knew Magdala from their furtive talks but maintained the distant dignity of a stranger.

Magdala had been abed for two days. She was experiencing a recurrence of the severe pain in her abdomen and couldn't eat. She was pale and weak and had been unable to resist the sleep that stole her from her duties. The Brother knelt by her bed and examined her over her habit but its folds and thickness were a hindrance. He used his furrowed brow and slight shake of the head to indicate to Magdala that he could not properly do his job. She understood and quickly bid their chaperone to fetch Brother Thomas a stool. In the few seconds they had she lifted her habit and lay covered only by her thin cotton shift.

Thomas' deft, light fingers quickly pressed and pushed. He'd been a married man before his calling, a woman's body was no stranger to him and his touch was considerate and modest. It told him all he needed and at the sound of the returning nun's sandals scraping the stone corridor he pulled Magdala's habit back into place and went to his medicine case.

"I would speak with my patient alone," he said, after making a few notes. "Alone Sister. Immediately."

Angrily the elderly Sister departed again but left the door wide open and stood in the corridor, out of earshot but with both man and woman in her sights. Evil would not reign on her watch! She would do nothing that could engender Mother's wrath.

Brother Thomas told Magdala what she already knew. She had a growth. A lump which he would monitor for size but for which he could do little more, save offer pain relief. This she accepted gladly. He would call again in one week unless she needed him before. He had looked tenderly into her eyes before he left and touched her hand. "I am so sorry, Sister," he had said softly.

"Don't be," she'd replied, " I long to be away from here." He smiled, he knew she'd never had the calling. He understood.

Chapter Seventeen

28th June, 1515
The King's birthday

THE INVITATION HAD arrived tied in purple ribbon with the King's seal and delivered by the King's own messenger. It had caused much excitement. Two days of pageant, songs, masques, dancing and feasting. The Earl had been reluctant to accept. It was too close to the Champagne tragedy. Frances was still in mourning. Would it be fair to re-engage her with those at Court who would have been feasting on the story? He was struggling with the iron ore allegations. Life was miserable, did he want two days of socializing?

"Father, please, it will do me good," she had implored, trying not to reveal how shallow her mourning actually was. "I've got to face the Court at some time." At every possible moment she campaigned. He grew snappy with her. Tired of her persistence. In the end he surrendered, unaware as to the true reason for her eagerness.

Melbroke had left early the morning after their argument, so early she hadn't seen him again. His departure was partly to get away from her, to deal with his feelings in private but also to make sure the Sheriff didn't bring his power to bear. If the farmer's statement appeared genuine he may arrest the Lord who needed his freedom to prove his innocence. He was back on the trail of Jasper and this time he'd got to find him.

Frances was sure Melbroke would be at the festivities. As the King's cousin he was bound to be. Every day since his departure had been a labour of heartache and torment. Every waking moment he had been in her thoughts, she couldn't rid her mind of him yet every thought stole her very breath.

The family would stay with William and Margaret in their new apartment in Greenwich Palace which meant they would be in the thick of things. Dressmakers were summoned to Blean bringing with them bolts of taffeta, damask and silks. One of Blean's many guest rooms was turned into a fitting room for the sisters and was quickly littered with cottons, ribbons, boxes of pearls, crystals and gems. There were head and hair adornments to think about, shoes, jewellery. Next door, tailors for the men drew and amended sketches, measured backs, chests, legs and so on. The Earl and William needed to fit the bill, too.

Urgency was in the air, so too, vanity. For the irritable Earl and resigned William it was a necessary evil, for the sisters it was heaven. The days passed in a frenzy of fittings and refittings, of train lengths, sleeve design, fabric choices and decorations. There were day and evening gowns to be considered, cloaks in case the wind off the Thames was chilly, sun shades in case the sun burned down.

"We're going to need a convoy of carts at this rate," the

Earl moaned each morning as, breaking his fast, he listened to the girls still talking about their latest plans. "Don't forget the blasted lot has all got to be transported to the Palace."

THEY TRAVELLED to Greenwich the day before the festivities began and already the place was packed. The usually busy Thames was now covered by a swarm of boats, large and small, bedecked for the occasion, glinting and bobbing on the impressive waterway. Some had musicians on board, practising for the morrow; others fluttered with flags and pennons. They wove in and out of each other with deft experience and Frances couldn't help but think, not for the first time, that the Thames must be the most beautiful river in the world.

The streets were already filling with folk who'd travelled in from the surrounding counties. From Kent, Surrey, Essex, Hertfordshire and beyond. They'd ridden, carted, even walked. All eager to be at the front of the crowds to get a good look at their monarch, his queen and the processions. The day was Henry's twenty-fourth birthday in the year of the thirtieth anniversary of his father winning the battle of Bosworth, taking the Crown and beginning the Tudor dynasty. The whole country had been commanded to celebrate, his realm was obeying, his capital filling up.

He always celebrated his birthday somewhere in England. He would take his entourage around the country so all had the chance to see his splendour and power. This year Queen Katherine was pregnant again and with four lost children behind them Henry was taking no chances. This year Katherine would not have the burden of travel.

The red rose of Lancaster could be seen everywhere,

so too Queen Katherine's pomegranate, the sign of fertility and abundance but it was the Tudor rose, the amalgamation of the Lancastrian red and Tudor white, that stole the show. Frances could see it on flags, on wood, on walls, on clothing, even painted on hands and cheeks.

There was an air of excitement which filtered contagiously into their carriage as the horses were forced to slow down and negotiate the chaos. An Earl and his two daughters drank in the atmosphere; William had gone ahead on horseback.

The crowds didn't know who the Bleans were but they saw the colours fluttering off the carriage and the crest on the doors. It told them they were aristocracy and great whoops and cheers greeted them as they negotiated their way through the crowd. "God save the King" someone shouted. "God bless King Harri" called another, referring to the late King. Frances was thrilled. She had been away from Court too long, she was glad to be back and when she turned to Margaret, her hands protectively on her swollen belly as the carriage swayed and jogged, she could see she was, too. She couldn't see either of them permanently living at Blean.

A THUNDEROUS booming sound awoke Frances with a start the next morning. It reverberated around not just her room, nor the palace but the whole area. It seemed to shake her very bed, it certainly shook her. No sooner had her ears accustomed themselves to the deafening roar and the birds resettled on their branches, than another came then another then another. From her window all looked as normal. Folk were scuttling busily about their business, a few couples promenaded arm in arm, gardeners were already about their work and the gentle sun of morning shone invitingly down on another beautiful Beltane day. It was only later she learned the noise had come from cannon, ignited by gunpowder to spew a heavy stone ball through a long barrel. On the battlefield it killed men in large numbers, today it was just powder with no ball. Today this death machine signalled celebration.

The first day was spent watching the street procession. Their Majesties began their journey from Westminster, where they had been guests of Cardinal Wolsey in his fine house York Place. The Royal Barge then carried them down the Thames to Greenwich from where, on horseback, they processed through the streets to the Palace. Both looked magnificent. The Queen was resplendent in purple silk and yards of ermine curled around her. She had been called the most beautiful creature in the world and today she more than lived up to that. By her side the King, strong, handsome, confident, glittered like a god from mythology as the sun caught the scores of precious stones that adorned him.

The noise that surrounded them was deafening, the excitement contagious and Frances cheered along with everyone else. The Bleans were on a high wooden platform, one of many that had been erected along the procession's path. She was above the heads of the crowds and had a perfect view. Her eyes scanned constantly, she was probably the only person not fixated on just watching the royal couple. Suddenly she saw the man she had really come to see. He was in the entourage, two rows back from his cousin and slightly to the right, the side farthest from her. Her heart lurched.

He too was resplendent, wearing black and silver that caught the sun. Around his erect shoulders lay the golden Melbroke chain and Galahad was looking blacker and shinier than he'd ever been, so long had he been groomed. Melbroke's eyes were constantly looking around, left then right, sometimes he turned behind, watching the crowd. His face was intense, concentrating, not allowing the moment to stray his thoughts. Then she saw the large sword that hung in a bejewelled scabbard from his side and the King's badge on his hat and on Galahad's flank. So, he was a body guard. Close because he was a relative but there too for his fighting prowess.

He wasn't the only one. Outside of his immediate royal grouping was another contingent of guards. All sporting the Tudor green and white, broadcasting their presence, bragging their strength. Their Majesties were well encircled by protection - a recognition that not everyone in the realm had yet forgotten Richard, the last Plantagenet King.

He didn't look up. Didn't see her but she watched him until he was out of view.

THE SISTERS rested in the afternoon. The Earl and William were presented to the King and hoped for some hawking. As the sun began to set Annie laid out Frances' new rose pink gown. A heavy silk creation with a woven swirling pattern that laid over numerous red-wine underskirts. The long sleeves were wide at the wrist, turned back with pink satin which also trimmed the square neckline. Around her waist she wore the girdle of Blean pearls with more pearls adorning the headdress that framed her face. Her long hair was loosely plaited with more pearls tucked into the folds. Around her neck hung her mother's rubies.

With her family by her side she entered Greenwich's enormous banqueting hall. Thousands of buttermilk candles welcomed them. Some in circles hanging from the ceiling; others in bunches on the walls and in dozens of smaller candelabra that decorated the tables. Standing haphazardly around were tall metal candelabra, over six foot, with layers of candles sitting like church steeples. Each one was in the charge of two servants, their job to move them to where they were needed. The hall was a dance of shadows and shapes, of glitter and shimmer and silks.

Melody from the musicians filled their ears, the candles' warmth greeted their skin, the tables already heaving with morsels stimulated their palates. Slowly the queue edged forward, the Earl's irritability mounting with every second he was forced to wait. His injured leg throbbed, the other ached under the burden.

"Saw Melbroke earlier," he whispered, leaning into Frances, aware of nearby ears. "Been in France again apparently, trying to find the damnable Marquis."

"Did he?" She too kept her voice low.

"No but he's got spies out, has done for weeks, no news yet. The blasted churl seems to have evaporated into thin air. Shame this murder allegation can't do the same."

"Will he be here tonight?"

"Of course," he snapped, frowning. "He's the King's cousin. Of course he'll be here daughter!" She knew his legs were paining so ignored his irritability. She saw William speaking to an usher who on understanding Margaret's condition called the family forward so they could be seated without further waiting.

"Thank the Lord," the Earl said, easing himself into a chair. "Well done, William. You must keep Margaret permanently with child, comes in very useful for an old man."

"I'll do my best, my Lord," he said, grinning and kissing Margaret's cheek as she looked aghast.

Hundreds of guests were being seated and Frances looked anxiously around. Her attention was drawn to a stunningly attractive redhead, wearing rich cream with an onyx girdle. Everyone was looking at her, so orange was her hair, so Celtic-pale her skin, so deep green her eyes. She slipped her arm through the arm of the man who was accompanying her and Frances' insides nearly left her. It was Melbroke. He was smiling happily, settling her at their table, adjusting the redhead's chair, pouring her wine, seeing to her every need. He looked so happy and strong and bold and so comfortable in her company. Frances gasped for breath and looked away.

Course after course was laid before them, Frances lost count at ten. Fish pasties, meat pies, mutton, venison, swan, blackbirds, wild boar. Some stewed, some pickled, others roasted or seared. Followed by custards, tarts, fritters. Comfits and marchpane sat in brightly coloured glass bowls. Wines from Bordeaux and Gascony flowed then Malmsey, all set off, well past midnight, by the King's favourite sweet liqueur hypocras, which Venetian merchants brought from the Levant.

Melbroke didn't glance her way once, not once during the six hours of feasting. He was attentive to the redhead, seeing to her every need, helping her take vegetables from dishes, picking up her fallen napkin. They talked and laughed and he looked triumphant! It ruined Frances' evening but she wouldn't show it. Immediately after the hypocras the Earl and Margaret indicated their desire for their beds, she was glad. Others were also now taking their leave and the Earl joined the group waiting to bid farewell to their Majesties. She watched proudly as the King greeted her father with great affection, embracing him warmly, smiling radiantly. She couldn't help but think what hard work being a King must be. William joined Melbroke's table.

THE NEXT day found the sisters strolling around the grounds enjoying the myriad of events that had been arranged. Jesters, jugglers, men on poles so tall they towered above the world. Frances had wanted to ask William about the redhead but didn't.

She resigned herself to the fact she had lost him. Her foolishness had cost her dear. She would regret it for the rest of her life.

Tonight was a masque followed by dancing. Her spirits were low and she was looking forward to neither but for the family's sake she would act. She had after all, made a huge fuss to be here. She dressed in a gown of lavender lace and adorned her hair and neck with amethysts. Margaret didn't want to dance, her father couldn't, so she would oblige William but apart from him she hoped no one would approach her.

Once again all eyes were on the redhead who again was accompanied by her dashing suitor. Tonight she was in crimson and looked magnificent. Melbroke danced with her and only her, all evening. He spoke briefly to William in passing but otherwise made no attempt to converse with the Bleans.

Back in her room her strength dissolved and she allowed the tears to pour from her. She had been so stupid! So stupid! Her life had turned on the spin of a few words, her words. Silly, ignorant, uncaring, disrespectful words that now she regretted more than she could begin to explain.

She'd wiped her face before Annie arrived to disrobe her and was forced into artificial small talk about the lovely evening she'd had. She climbed into her bed as if it were a refuge from the world and pulled the linen over her head. Here she would hide, 'til morning at least, from the painful world that now surrounded her and where only in sleep could her aching heart and tortured mind find something resembling peace.

Chapter Eighteen

Blean House, July, 1515

MARGARET LOOKED PALE and anxious. "They've taken trays into the study," she said, as they gathered for the midday meal. It was a few days after their return from the celebrations and life was taking a turn for the worse.

"They go tonight!" She was addressing her father as Frances entered. His hand was gently squeezing hers. His face also drawn.

"Who goes where?" Frances flapped open her napkin.

"Anything could happen!" Margaret's head fell into her hands as she fought back tears of fear. Frances looked to her father.

"Alban's here," he said, his voice noticeably quieter than usual. "He's eager to act against the Harwyke brothers in case they flee Canterbury. He's had someone watching them, they're still here, he wants to act now."

"Alban's here?" She knew her face flushed but Margaret and the Earl were too immersed in their concerns for William to notice.

The Earl nodded. "He came in the night. Wants to keep his presence secret until he can prove to the Sheriff that he is innocent of the charges and that Jasper has plotted against him."

"He'll get that proof tonight?"

"He hopes to."

The threats on the Earl had become intolerable, a constant barrage of unpleasant letters, accusations and malice. Finally the demand came - pay money now and avoid a court case and scandal. The Harwykes wanted a small fortune. Never the kind to acquiesce to blackmail or bullying he had spoken with Melbroke at the celebrations and he'd agreed to return to Blean. The plot was reaching its climax, action was needed now.

Despite Melbroke's desire to never see Frances again he would not let down the Earl. He and William would deal with the Harwykes and free the Earl from the intolerable position he was now in. He'd have to hunt down Jasper on his own, he couldn't rely on the Sheriff's men, they could take an eternity. That would be his next mission, then he'd speak to his cousin and see where his orders took him. Hopefully, far away from Blean.

Frances now understood, indeed shared, the fear on Margaret's face and she took on the role of re-assurer. Melbroke and William were good swordsmen, she said. They were trained, experienced, the brothers weren't. The Earl said the same. Everything would be fine they both insisted, privately praying to God they were right. Margaret's anxious face revealed the inefficiency of their intent. She didn't want reassuring words, she just wanted an end to the whole business. She left the table without eating and went to lay down.

"Gates is with them," said the Earl to Frances, uncharacteristically subdued. "Apparently they've got a role for him. I've given me permission to all their plans even if they don't share them with me. It seemed the least I could do given I caused all this by seeing gold in the ground and letting it tempt me."

"Father you can't blame yourself! You weren't to know the men were evildoers." Frances rubbed the back of his old hand that lay so helplessly on the table. Mayhap not but blame himself he would.

The afternoon found Blean House busy. Melbroke and William were not seen but their presence was very much felt. The atmosphere was tense, the air thickened. A helplessness hung in the corridors, a surrender to a fate that all knew they were powerless to influence, even less so to control. Post-horse messengers came and went. Gates assumed a manly dominance that he rarely had the opportunity to display. The grooms were preparing horses and Margaret played half-heartedly with her son, Geoffrey, in the nursery.

Everyone was desirous of normal. They wanted the day over and life back to its usual rhythm but Frances was no longer sure what her normal was. By constantly being in her thoughts Melbroke had become a part of her life, that was now her norm. So too, the hollowness at the very centre of her being, a hollowness that never left her.

The hours of the afternoon passed painfully slowly as she relived their conversations, re-enacted scenes. She pained as she remembered his harsh words, his loving words, her words, her phrases. Fitfully she traced and retraced her actions, her responses.

His words at their last encounter, many of them she knew to be true, had made her look to herself. She was not used to this but then much of what was associated with this handsome man, she was not used to. It disturbed her but in this particular regard she knew the discomfort to be honest.

Also true was the fact that when she nursed him she had done it securely and confidently, why was that? Deep down she knew the answer - because she could view him as brother. His drug-induced sleep rendered him inactive. He was unable to touch her heart, arouse her body, upset her emotions. Had her heart been stone then? Were her emotions too precious to be disturbed? Was she too proud to have her body aroused? He'd had the courage to confess his emotions. He had confidence where she had none and to say this was because she was inexperienced was not good enough. Slowly, in loneliness and pain, she was beginning to read herself.

She pulled a wrap around her shoulders and strolled out into the grounds. Everywhere was quiet save scuffling in the trees and the occasional splash on the stream. She visited the horses and stood for a while stroking Galahad. She liked him being there, close to Lunar, part of Blean.

The sun was catching the white stone of the family mausoleum that nestled in a shallow vale near the lake and she found herself drawn toward it. She visited regularly and today she particularly needed its peace. She pushed open the heavy door and entered the oasis of silence with a welcome acceptance of the calm that always lived here. She allowed it to embrace her. It was chilly but soothing. Completely re-assuring in its quiet and stillness. A place away from the world, a place that reminded her of our brief time on this earth and how one day even she would be here. Her father's tomb was already waiting, next to her mother who lay in an ornate sarcophagus which as always was brushed and cobweb free, like all the Blean ancestors in this place.

She sat, as she had done so many times before, on the low

ledge that ran around the outside of her mother's tomb. It was hard and unkindly cold and she allowed her head to flop backwards against the harsh, carved stone. She had been eleven when her mother had died but her memory was as if it were yesterday. She could clearly see her round face with the blue eyes she had inherited. Still remember her voice, the softness of the skirts she had clung to and the tiny waist her arms had encircled.

"What shall I do mama?" She spoke out loud to the empty chamber. "I've been such a fool." Silence. She was at the edge of the known fabric of her life; the unknown frightened her. She needed her mother's wise words now as never before. A single sunbeam powered in through the open door and she saw a tiny mouse scurry across its spotlight. Life in this place of death, this place of memory and love, it pleased her. "I'm scared mama and I don't know what of. Why do I feel like this?" No tears now, she had cried them all. She was low and unhappy, angry with herself and confused.

She closed her eyes and fancied she could smell her mother's perfume. She was looking up into those loving eyes, her mother's arms were about her. They were in the nursery and the world was safe and uncomplicated. "You're in love you silly goose," came the voice.

"It frightens me so."

"Of what? What are you frightened of?"

For several minutes Frances sat silently, her mind blank, her heart racing. "Of him touching me, taking my will, overwhelming me." She finally confessed out loud to the emptiness.

"That's what love is my darling, giving yourself to the man you love, heart and soul and body."

"It frightens me."

"You are taking a step into the unknown, my dear one. All

women feel like this, all women have to get over this fear but you must let your love for him overshadow your fears. Don't you want to lay with him, love him, always be by his side, have his children?"

Frances couldn't give her response out loud this time. Emotions were all but choking her. She nodded. A smile crept on to her lips.

"So, what you really need to ask yourself is how would you feel if you never saw him again."

"I wouldn't want to live."

"Then find your courage. Listen to your heart. Release fear, embrace love, trust him."

"'Tis too late, I've lost him." Her words echoed helplessly around the cold space.

"'Tis never too late. Tell him how you feel."

"I'm scared his feelings have changed."

"Release fear, embrace love, trust him..." and slowly the voice faded away back into the folds of memory. She sat for a few moments, her eyes closed, those words going around in her mind: release fear, embrace love.

A calm descended upon her and after a few moments she opened her eyes to the gloom of the mausoleum. Yes, she finally accepted it, could fight it no more. She was in love. She must be!

It was true that when she was close to him her heart raced; that the thought of not being with him was so intense it pained her to breathe. When he protected her and despite her objections, she felt safe and happy, yet when he had declared his love she had rejected him. Why! It was right under her nose but she had been denying it. She was scared. Not of him, no, not at all of him. She was frightened of her own feelings and where they would lead. Nervous too of the physical of which he had so much experience and she had none. Scared of the emotional. Petrified she could control neither. Release fear, embrace love. The words rang in her ears.

She was an innocent, this was all so new to her. She had never felt like this with Pierre. That she now realized had been friendship. She was in control of that. There was no passion, even Queen Katherine had realized that. What she felt now was something quite different. This could never be friendship. A certain dashing Lord had known that. Now she did, too.

THE EVENING meal was an uncomfortable affair with the Earl increasingly agitated as the men's departure grew closer. Margaret and Frances were pale, wan and worried. Melbroke and William by contrast were exuberant and in need of a substantial meal. They were happy, buoyant, on top of their plans, eager to get going, the adrenalin racing. They ate large, hearty meals, everyone else picked at morsels.

"My Lord," said William, trying to inject some lightness into the mood, "Margaret and I thought we would stay at Blean until the baby is born."

"Wonderful," beamed the Earl, happy to have something to smile about.

"And you Melbroke? Do you have plans, you are welcome to stay here as long as you like."

"I thank my Lord but I shall leave tonight."

"Tonight? Really?" Frances gasped, the words slipping from her before she could prevent them.

"Assuming all goes well, my Lord, which I am confident it will," he continued, without acknowledging her, "I shall ride straight to Dover and head for France on the morrow." It wasn't true but he wanted to make it clear to a certain pair of ears that she wouldn't be seeing him again.

"I'm saddened to hear that."

"Yes, my Lord, so am I but there is nothing at Blean to keep me here now. Other things call."

Frances felt weak. Was the redhead calling him? She waited a few seconds while she composed herself, took a sip of wine and stood to leave. "You must excuse me gentlemen, I have things to do in my room. Please don't get up, don't disturb your meal." A few steps from the table she looked back. "So Lord Melbroke, this will be the last time I see you."

"Indeed my Lady," he said, standing.

"I trust tonight will be successful and I thank you for all the help you have given me and my family."

"An honour and my pleasure," he said, tipping his head but not meeting her eyes.

"What time do you set off?"

"Ten o'clock."

"May God keep you safe," she said, her cracking voice just managing to rise above a whisper.

She returned to her room in a profound state of shock. Her behaviour over past months had brought her to this. Her very soul ached. She had pushed away a handsome, gallant, brave, generous man from fear and stupidity and jealousy. Yes, jealousy too, of his past exploits. She had come to understand things too late. Too late!

THE EARL had given William the key to the armoury and had bid them both choose any weapons they needed. Their daily swords, the ones they oft wore to defend themselves on the roads, were adequate but the Earl had a collection of heavier, longer, broader, battle swords and they were gladdened by what they found. Melbroke chose three of different sizes and lengths and three daggers. His intention, back in his room, was to spend a little time in private testing them as to weight and balance. All regularly met the whetstone, their sharpness was not of concern.

He'd just heard the nine o'clock bell when his door, with no knock of announcement, opened. Frances entered and closed it behind her.

"What are you doing? You shouldn't be in here!"

"I must speak with you, 'tis urgent. Everyone is downstairs, they don't know I'm here."

"Not worried I'll ravish you then," he scoffed, sarcastically, continuing his work. "Lust is, according to you, the only thing I ever think about." He made a sudden, sharp step toward her. She held her ground. He threw his head back in a mocking laugh. "Don't take my manners for granted, madam."

"I am truly sorry for that remark, it was stupid. I deeply regret it. I now know you to be a gentleman."

"Don't rely on my honour either. You in my room with a bed and a closed door, I might not be able to control myself."

"Please, Alban, don't mock me."

"So 'tis Alban now! I am honoured!" He continued with his work, not looking at her, concentrating on what he was doing. "What do you want? I've a demanding night ahead of me. Say it and go."

She could hardly breathe, her heart was pounding, her mouth dry. "May I have a sip of wine?" She had noticed a flask on a side table.

"No. Say what you want and go. Get on with it, time's passing."

His anger, annoyance, irritation with her were hers to be

felt. He was making no attempt to hide them. She had decided she had nothing to lose, or at least, only her pride. Given the stakes that was worth risking. This reception she hadn't anticipated and her courage was waning. For a brief second she thought to leave but immediately re-strengthened her will and determined not to be the coward. *Release fear, embrace love.* She took a deep breath.

"I can't have you risking injury and possibly even your life, yet again, for a member of the Blean family without telling you..." She broke off, ran her tongue around her dry lips and swallowed hard. "I need to tell you something."

"And this need of yours, it must take precedence right now, must it? It can't wait?"

"It cannot."

"Then get on with it."

"I want to tell you...*release fear, embrace love*...I want to tell you that...that I love you." She lowered her eyes to the ground unable to look at him. Her heart was in her throat, she could feel blood pounding in her head. He stopped what he was doing and turned toward her. He perched himself on the edge of the table and folded his arms across his chest. "O really," he said, haughtily.

"I love you. I think I always have, I've been fighting it." Once she'd started her words tumbled out, she couldn't stop them. "I was muddled, nervous, frightened of your reputation. I thought I was just your latest challenge. And then the barn and Pierre dying, then the apothecary said you might die and I thought I would if you did and then you said you loved me and I couldn't believe it." Her words were racing. "I rejected you, I've been so stupid, I've hurt you and you probably don't love me any more but I couldn't let you go tonight without telling you."

"Frances, stop talking."

"Yes, my time must be up. I'll go." She made for the door.

"Frances, stop. Stop!"

She froze. After a few seconds she turned to face him. He was standing now, looking at her. He still looked stern but the mocking eyes had gone. "Come here."

She was caught like a rabbit in the light of the lamp. Her body felt weak, her chest tight. Her heart pounding. How her legs carried her to him she didn't know. She stopped two paces away, her body trembling. "Come closer," he commanded. As she stepped forward the air between them thickened, the tension was almost unbearable, it was ravaging her senses, her legs were weak as if an invisible force were draining all the strength from muscle and bone.

"What do you want, Frances? What do you actually want of me?" His voice was softer now, his eyes enquiring.

"I want you. I love you," she said, still looking down, unable to look into his face.

"Frances, look at me," he said softly, tilting her chin upwards. His deep chestnut eyes were searching hers and he was forcing her to receive them. The harshness had gone, they were soft and they were roving her face. The tension was unbearable and she closed her eyes in the hope the darkness would bring relief. He kissed her forehead, her cheeks, her neck, her ears, her throat. Between kisses he kept asking: "Are you sure?... Are you truly sure?... Are you really sure?" She could hardly speak but each time managed to utter a whisper. "Yes...I'm truly sure...I'm sure... Yes...I'm really sure." He made her say it a dozen times as his light kisses ignited her skin sending little trills of pleasure shooting all over her body.

At last he very gently placed his lips on hers. She gasped as delight tingled through her. As soon as he felt her responding, opening her lips for him, he entered her mouth, stole her words of love and took them into himself, the words he had for so long been longing to hear. He claimed her mouth as his, kissed her sweetly, passionately. Her world was spinning, even the floor seemed to sway. She reached for his shoulders for support and he crushed her to him, stealing her breath, her will.

He groaned like a man released from purgatory. When he broke the kiss so they could gasp for air, she just kept uttering: "I love you, I love you," until his lips descended on hers again and she was back in a world that was spinning and rolling and drifting her toward the heavens.

Suddenly her feet were off the ground and she was in his arms. He laid her on the bed and sat next to her. He looked at her lips, ruby red from arousal. He ran a finger over them, she opened them slightly and he bent and kissed her again, pushing her head into the pillow. She felt the weight of him on her, pinning her down. His hands ran over her dress, feeling her contours, setting her alight.

A bang on the door startled them. "Alban, what are you doing? 'Tis time to go." It was an impatient William.

"I'll be right there, Will. One minute, I'll meet you downstairs."

"I have to go," he groaned. She nodded.

He stood up, took her two hands and pulled her off the bed and into his arms. One last brief kiss and his attention was back with his final selection of weapons. He secured his sword belt, rammed the blade into its sheath, put one dagger into each boot, another in his belt. "Time to go."

She wanted to ask him about the redhead but was still frightened of his answer and anyway this wasn't the moment. She could see his body girding itself for the night's task. She could see the haste in his eyes, the desire to get going. "You haven't said you still love me," she said, her eyes appealing as he stood in the open doorway.

"Alban, come on," William called.

"Do you still love me? Have I left it too late?" There was desperation in her voice and on her face. He glanced back briefly as if holding her image to memory. Something was stopping him from responding.

"Alban! God's wounds man, what are you doing! Come on!"

"I have to go."

One more glance and he was gone.

AT EXACTLY ten o'clock three horsemen trotted their horses down the drive. Melbroke and William on their own mounts, Gates on a borrowed, gentle horse that the groom had especially chosen for a man whose riding skills were a memory of his youth, although he had spent time this day re-acquainting himself with life in the saddle.

The moon was high, the sky an endless, deep blue velvet, the air heavy and scented as a warm English summer night can be. They reined left at the Blean gates and headed for Canterbury. Their mission in detail in their minds, their confidence solid, their courage high.

In the house two women and an elderly man worried. The three agreed to catch some sleep with a view to rising again at one in the morning. Surely the nightmare would be over by then? Surely!

The Earl and Margaret retired to their rooms and laid atop their beds. Frances did not. With her maid's help she quickly prepared for her own mission. They tightly netted her hair and got her into a plain, dark riding habit. Tiptoeing down the back stairs, she exited the house at the rear and made her way to the stables.

A strong, dark bay stood saddled and waiting, she having secretly prepared him earlier. He swished his black tail as she approached and she shushed him as he snorted. She led him down the grass verge of the drive and only when she was on the mud track that ran by the side of the Blean estate did she mount.

She and the horse were practically invisible but so were the men. She knew the route they would take. She assumed because the inexperienced horseman Gates was with them, that they wouldn't gallop. Her father and William and almost certainly Melbroke too, could put their ear to the ground and tell how far away hoof beats were. She did not possess such skill. She would have to rely on the feminine gifts of intuition, discernment and submission to the way of things. For a while she galloped, the thudding hooves and the hoots of owls the only sounds on this starlit night. As soon as her instincts told her she was only some fifteen minutes or so behind she dropped into a canter and followed the track under the light of the moon.

Magdala was back in the herb garden. The apothecary's pain relief was good, she had felt it working almost immediately and today she felt strong enough to dig and plant. She knew that if her lump grew her days were numbered but somewhere, deep within her consciousness, she knew that anyway. Much of what she planted now she may not see being cut and turned into cures. She didn't mind, she would work for as long as she could. Being useful was all she had left. She would cherish her tasks and give thanks for the richness and pains of her life.

As the bell for Vespers and evening prayer rang out her helpers left. Magdala lingered 'til the coast was clear. The monastery's head gardener had sent a request for seedlings. Could she help him with anything on his long list? She had most of them aplenty and when her fellow nuns went off to light the lamps she slipped away to meet him.

The gate had been opened when she arrived. "Quick! Here," he called urgently, beckoning her from behind the trunk of the huge oak on the monks' side of the wall.

"I'm glad to see you up and about Sister, Brother Thomas confided in me that you are ill."

"Yes, Brother, the Lord calls me soon."

"I hope you don't mind him telling me."

"Not at all, I know you and he are close."

"We are Sister. Twenty years we have served God together which is why I worry about him."

"He's ill too?" There was alarm in her voice.

"Not yet Sister but I fear illness lurks. His weight increases daily, his breathing is bad and his workload too demanding. It is tiring him out."

"God will protect him Brother," she gently chided, "don't lose your faith!"

"He is too conscientious, that's his trouble. Visiting patients at all hours. Putting his own need for sleep second. He answers God's call to serve with a zeal that is incomparable."

"We must ask our Lord to make haste to save him."

He caught her tender smile. "Ignore me sister. I am angry on behalf of my dear Brother. Over a dozen people he sees on some days, travelling between homes then facing a queue on his return. Then the patients think they know better than he and that makes him so angry he shakes and cannot sleep for head pain, so great is his dedication."

She furrowed her brow questioningly.

"He was visiting the Earl over in Blean, he had a guest with a seriously infected sword wound. Bad fever. Could have died. Seven in the morning and seven again at night he visited, saved his life, then the patient pulled rank and argued about his treatment."

"Pulled rank?"

"Cousin of the King apparently, thought he knew better than a mere monk."

"Did he recover?"

"Yes, he recovered. A strong fighting man, about thirty years of age. He survived to fight another day and then no doubt another Brother Thomas, somewhere else in the world, will wear himself out to save him."

"Cousin of the King?" Magdala allowed her tired frame to lean back against the tree. "Who was he?"

"Melrose, Pembroke, something like that, can't remember."

"Is he still there, at Blean?"

"No idea Sister. Why are you interested?"

"Oh nothing. Just wondering if Brother Thomas was still riding to Blean everyday."

"No, he's not, thank goodness." The monk took her tray of seedlings. "Bless you Sister. Take care of yourself. Remember God has his plans for us all, 'tis not for us to understand them, just endure them. He may have more in store for you yet."

I hope so, she thought quietly, I truly hope so. She turned away from the monk as he jangled his keys. She darted back through the gate unseen and he locked her in again. This time as the key turned her heart was soaring. Joy was possibly hers.

Chapter Nineteen

THE HARWYKE'S RAMSHACKLE cottage was, as usual, the only one in this enclave of Canterbury's outskirts that was still alight at this time of night. Its glassless windows shone as invasions into the black night. The brothers had returned from the inns with female company and the frolicking was already underway when Melbroke, William and Gates arrived.

Melbroke had everything planned in finest detail. Even where they could tether their horses unseen had been thought of. The three walked stealthily around the stone detached hovel, Melbroke encouraging the others, in whispered tones, to get their bearings. He checked the outer doors - bolted as usual. Merriment from the inside filtered out with the alcohol-fuelled giggling and raucous laughter far out-pitching any noise they may make.

William noted the door he was to break down. He nodded his understanding to his friend. Gates was shown where he was to stand on guard, whistle in hand, to warn if anyone approached.

He was nervous but in control. Melbroke was concerned that the whores, having been thrown out of the house, may run for re-inforcements, Gates knew his task and would perform it with his usual diligence.

On the given signal, the first blow of Gates' whistle, Melbroke kicked open the front door exactly as William kicked in the back. Gates was the first to enter from the front. He grabbed the wenches, the upper arm of each in a vice-grip and dragged them off the premises. They were off their backs and in the road so quickly that their tongues had no time to garland lewd language nor their feet and elbows time to jab and kick. Gates told them to 'shove off' in no uncertain manner and watched as they staggered, somewhat dazed, back in the direction of town and other customers. He then positioned himself, as instructed, outside the front door watching both ways for any activity, whistle at the ready.

Melbroke and William had already drawn their swords. "So," shouted Melbroke, as he crashed in. He'd lost the element of surprise, he was relying on power. He and William were twice the size of these men. Taller, broader, fiercer. They were battled hardened with scars to prove it. "You seek to ruin the Earl of Blean do you!"

The two brothers, startled and half clad, backed against a wall. They could see their exits were blocked and their eyes darted like cornered animals as they moved from Melbroke to William and back again. As if telepathically connected they both rushed to the bedroom and returned armed with identical short, stubby swords. Melbroke had allowed that, he wanted them to fight, this wasn't a slaughter expedition. He wanted them to put up a fight so that he and William could win fair and square. It would satisfy him and the Sheriff.

The Harwykes had no time to see to their dishevelled

clothes before Melbroke and William were upon them. Their tunics and shirts were undone, revealing scrawny little chests. Closer now, Melbroke could see they were thin men but not wiry; their shoulders and arms were not those of swordsmen. In theory he and William were much stronger but sharp blades in the hands of any man, even a child, are dangerous. Neither he nor William were complacent.

The rooms were small with too much furniture. Lit wall sconces sent shadows dancing, deceiving the eye. Both fighting men quickly checked their surroundings, got a bearing on distance, height, width, ratio of walls to furniture, space that was good, space that was too confined. There was far too much of the latter! Their training, their experience kicked in. Their blood-rush was under control. They were ready for whatever these wretches threw at them.

FRANCES HAD arrived in the locale and was looking for the men's horses. Instead she saw Gates. She dismounted a few hundred feet from him and tethered her horse behind a curtain of willow. From the horse's back she untied the mightily heavy sword that some unaccountable sixth sense had insisted she bring and using the strength of both arms and hands, hugged it close to her body. She moved as stealthily as possible, using shrubs and trees as cover and gingerly moved toward the house that Gates was guarding.

Several times she trod on twigs that snapped, she wasn't trained for this kind of thing, neither was Gates and he didn't hear. The noise from the house was now even louder and harsher. Men shouted and swords clanged and furniture smashed. She successfully avoided Gates' attention, crept around the back and watched through a gap in the tatty curtains.

Melbroke was dealing with the taller and older of the two

brothers, sword in one hand, dagger in the other. William had the shorter, obsequious one. It was the two Lords who were throwing furniture out of the way, all of it cheap, most of it snapping like tinder on impact with the walls. Swords were clashing, grating, iron on iron. The horrific sound put the fear of God into Frances. Her heart was in her mouth as curses rang and sparks flew.

The brothers' short, cheap swords, were no match for the heavier weapons of the two Lords who, very quickly, had the upper hand. Just at that moment Gates' whistle blew again and he ran into hiding. Frances crept around to the front of the house, hugging the wall, keeping in the shadows but determined to see what was going on. She was just in time to see a thin, reed of a man enter through the front door. She raced back to her window and resumed her position, the heavy sword propped against the wall beside her.

Tall, thin, with greasy blonde hair hanging lank, half hiding his face, he was startled at what he found. He'd only come visiting, expecting some fun with the whores and now he was in a sword fight! He was unarmed, not that it would have made much difference, he was no fighter. His weak chest, narrow shoulders, thin legs set him apart from the warrior. Samuel Harwyke threw him a dagger and shouted: "Don't just stand there, do something!"

As the tall brother turned his attention for half a second to the incoming man Melbroke struck. Caught him square in the middle of the abdomen. Blood immediately soaked his shirt, in an instant the hands that clutched his stomach were dripping scarlet. The blood drained from his face, the strength from his body, his legs buckled. He fell to the earth-packed ground in a wail of disbelief. Melbroke was on him in a flash and dragged him into the bedroom and out of the way. As the brother continued to wail Melbroke tied his hands behind his back and swiftly returned to aid William who was now fighting two men.

William had knocked the shorter brother's sword from his hand. He in turn had instantly grabbed a flaming torch from its sconce and was waving it furiously in William's face. He could feel its heat on his skin and he ducked and dived to avoid being burnt. The limitations of the small room, the fact William's back was so quickly against a wall, was making it hard to dodge the flame and several times it was perilously close.

Melbroke took the skinny incomer who had retrieved the fallen, short sword from the floor. Clearly untrained and totally unaware of how to use it, he was waving it about like an axe. His lank hair whipped around his boney features. The long tendrils for fingers of both hands clutched at the hilt 'til they were white with strain. He was though, light on his feet so what he lacked in skill he made up for in agility. Melbroke blocked and charged, only to be faced with dance-like movements as his opponent skipped behind tables, threw stools and shouted: "Salaud! Qui etre tu, salaud?"

"Bastard am I," shouted back Melbroke, surprised to discover his opponent was French. "Never mind who I am, who are you?" No answer came as he parried, teased and goaded. Constantly manoeuvring for the upper hand, not giving this thin Frenchman any quarter, he moved across the room then back again, chasing the Frenchman wherever he went, giving him no leeway, no rest, no time to think or plan. He was facing untrained instinct and it had to crack soon!

Melbroke was just trying an upward thrust to the chest with his dagger when the Frenchman's sword caught him. The broad side of the blade slammed the back of his left hand, had it been the sharp side it would have cut his hand in two. The pain was intense and forced Melbroke to release the dagger which fell to the floor. It was immediately picked up by the brother with the flame. Melbroke quickly reached for another of his daggers while William now faced a dagger and flame.

Frances was watching intently. Just at that moment the remaining brother, successfully avoiding William's sword, thrust the flame into William's chest and rammed it home. It caught his doublet, set the fabric aflame and William was forced to beat flames with his left hand while still using his right to fight with his sword. Frances ran to where she knew Gates was hiding.

"Don't ask any questions Gates, just give me your hat." Gates was flabbergasted to see her. His jaw dropped. "Your hat! Now!"

She ran to the water butt, dunked the hat until full to the brim and rushed in the front door. She darted around the back of Melbroke and threw the water over William's chest.

"God dammit woman, get out of here! Now!" Melbroke shouted, aghast at her presence. "Now!"

William, now wet but at least not on fire, began to get the better of his opponent. He brought his sword down on the man's right hand and severed it at the wrist. The roar of a wild animal filled the small room, the man's dagger thumped to the ground, so too, the torch which William quickly stamped on. He dragged the man into the bedroom, pulled his arms behind him and tied them at the elbows. He propped him next to his brother.

Only the third, skinny man was left and he had enough sense to realize he couldn't take on two powerful swordsmen. He backed against a wall, threw his sword to the ground and raised his hands in surrender. Melbroke and William dropped their swords and rested their own bodies against the wall. For a few unguarded seconds, they panted hard, tried to catch their breath and closed their eyes. It was over! Done!

Another blast from Gates' whistle came seconds too late. "Well now gentleman, thought you'd won? A bit presumptuous

I believe." They looked up and another tall, this time effeminate, man in velvet and silk, was at the door. Lord Jasper, Marquis de Champagne was smirking a triumphant grin. "Did you really think my brother and I would let you get away with theft!" In their few off-guarded seconds the Frenchman had gathered up the weapons. Melbroke and William were now unarmed. Frances raced to the tree where she had left the heavy sword and raced back to the hovel.

"Alban," she cried, rushing into the devastated room. She held the sheath toward him and he yanked out the blade.

"Get out! Go! Now!"

Lord Jasper didn't stay to fight. He opted for the easier option and chased after Frances. He caught her easily from behind, wrapped his arms about hers so they were pinned to her sides and dragged her, screaming and aimlessly kicking, toward his horse. He hit her violently about the head, knocked her unconscious and threw her over the beast's neck. Melbroke had raced to the hovel door and saw the horse gallop off. "Jasper's taken Frances," he shouted to William, "don't kill the Frenchman, we need him alive!"

Gates having read the situation had run to the horses and had Galahad untied and ready for Melbroke to jump straight on to.

It only took a few seconds for William to overpower the now, even more startled Frenchman, who begged for his life as William trussed him tightly. At that moment the Sheriff and four constables burst into the room.

"Lord Melbroke, an explanation if you please," demanded the Sheriff, who, having received a note from Melbroke earlier in the day, had arrived at exactly the time requested.

"He's not here, I'm afraid Sheriff," said William, exhaustion slowing his speech. "You'll have to make do with me."

The Sheriff looked around at the chaos, the room's blood-splattered contents now only fit for a bonfire. His eye settled aghast on a severed hand. He strolled over to the three men, sitting in a row, tied and beaten. "God's wounds! What has been going on?"

"Allow me to catch my breath," said William, still panting, "and I will tell you everything." He bent over, put his hands on his knees and inhaled deeply.

The Sheriff, with a constable, checked the two brothers. The one with the severed hand had bled profusely and was unconscious in a crimson pool. The other with the internal injury was dead. The Frenchman was shaking with fear and although bloodied was not badly injured.

"Sheriff," began William, "two of the men in the other room are Samuel and Arthur Harwyke. Mayhap you recognize them. They are the men who presented themselves as a consortium wishing to invest in iron ore, they are nothing of the sort. They are just two villainous miscreants whom the Marquis de Champagne hired."

"The Marquis? Involved?"

"Not just involved, organizing it!"

"Organizing what?"

"Blackmail!"

"Judas' eyes!" The Sheriff could scarce believe what he was hearing. "This is all most confusing."

"Not really Sheriff. It was but now things are becoming clearer."

" Explain, if you please, m'Lord."

"This night we have discovered that it was Lords Pierre and Jasper who were behind the Harwykes. They reduced themselves to blackmailer in order to trick money out of the Earl and used the brothers, presumably paid them, to hide behind."

"No! Surely not!" The Sheriff was incredulous. The

aristocracy was far from perfect but it wasn't usually cowardly.

"With his brother dead," William continued, "Jasper has been carrying on alone. They thought the Earl, wishing to avoid scandal and defend his reputation, would pay to have the charges of fraud and theft dropped. They made their blackmail demand some days back, the Earl was not prepared to submit. We'll probably discover that the murder allegation against Lord Melbroke falls into the same devious category."

"He's been blackmailed, too?"

"Not yet, 'twas only a matter of time."

"So! You came tonight to murder the Harwykes!" The Sheriff stood face on to William, his eyes now glaring.

"Certainly not! We came to talk to them. Try to reason. Threaten them with law mayhap but not the sword. They set upon us." William would seek forgiveness for this lie in the Blean chapel later! "We thought they were acting alone, the involvement of two Marquises is as much a shock to us as to you."

"But why? Why would the Marquises blackmail anyone?"

"God alone knows. But Lord Melbroke will get to the bottom of this, have no fear Sheriff, this story isn't over yet!"

The Sheriff walked over to Arthur Harwyke and nudged his shoulder. His head fell to one side. His outer jacket and doublet were soaked with blood and red trickles ran from his mouth. Melbroke's blade had caught a main artery, death would have been quick. The other brother, the one with the severed hand, groaned when the Sheriff kicked him. Life was ebbing from him. The Frenchman, quaking and shaking, begged. "Mon seigneur, mon seigneur, je suis innocent. Vraiment, je suis innocent."

The Sheriff turned to William. "What's a bloody Frenchy doing here?"

"No idea. But he isn't innocent, he joined in the fighting,

helped the Harwyke brothers."

"And where is Lord Melbroke?"

"He's gone after Lord Jasper..."

"The Marquis was here!"

"Oh yes. He's kidnapped Lady Frances. Lord Melbroke has taken chase."

"Good Lord!" The Sheriff paled. The Earl's daughter taken! He could only but begin to imagine the dressing down he would get.

"What was a woman doing here?"

"You may well ask. We most certainly did not bring her with us!"

A constable called from the bedroom: "The brother with the severed 'and is dead. Bled to death." He scraped his blood-wet shoes on some rushes.

"You'd better not die," said the Sheriff, lodging his boot in the Frenchman's ribs, "I want a full statement from you, hopefully voluntarily but one way or another I will get it!" He was bending down now, shouting in the Frenchman's ear. "Do you hear?" Another boot, this time to the man's groin. A pitiful scream tore around the room. "Oui, oui."

The Sheriff turned back to William. "I shall need full statements from yourself and Lord Melbroke also from your steward whom I saw outside."

"Of course Sheriff but may I ask that it wait. We have to find Lady Frances. That must surely be our priority now?" The pain in his chest was also worsening, he knew the burn needed attention, he wanted to get back to Blean and Margaret.

The Sheriff nodded. "Leave it with me m'Lord, I have my contacts, ne'er-do-wells in my pay, they all seem to know each other."

"Good, I would like to return to Blean. Someone must tell the Earl."

The Sheriff straightened his back, tried to bring authority to his shocked face. The variety of life his position gave him was one of the things he enjoyed about his work. This night, though, took some beating. Two Lords of the realm, one a cousin of the King, fighting a French Marquis in the dead of night, an Earl's daughter kidnapped, two violent deaths and a trussed-up Frenchy, were not in his usual day's work. He needed to assimilate the situation, plan his strategy. He settled for: "Please tell the Earl that I am personally overseeing his daughter's rescue and that everything possible is being done."

William nodded. That will really put his mind at rest, he was thinking.

THE WINDOWS of Blean House were twinkling as William, Gates and Frances' empty-saddled horse, trotted up the drive. The house had not settled this night, its lights still burned and it looked like a lantern against a black canopy. There was tension in the withdrawing room as father-in-law and wife counted the moments. It was past one. Surely they couldn't all have been killed? Surely there would be word soon? Then they heard what they had been waiting for. Voices in the hallway. William calling for Margaret; Gates instructing staff.

Margaret fell into her husband's arms, tears of joy and relief streaming down her cheeks. "You're burnt!"

"'Tis nothing, a torch caught me, 'tis nothing." In truth it was more than nothing, it was aching like hell and it needed treatment.

The Earl was on his feet. "Gates, tell me daughter you've

returned, request she join us." The steward didn't move, his eyes turning to William's. The Earl stuttered. "What's the matter, man?"

William rescued Gates. "My Lord, I have mixed news," he said, lowering himself painfully into a chair. He had to sit, the ache of his chest had spread all around his body, his back was now complaining. "In one respect the evening went very well. Both the brothers are dead."

"Thank the Lord," said the Earl, allowing his own strained body to flop back into a chair. "There's more my Lord, please brace yourself for a shock."

"What? What's happened? And where's Melbroke?" Suddenly he'd realized Melbroke wasn't in the room. Alarm bathed his face, his eyes darting from William to Gates and back again.

"Alban is well. My news concerns Frances."

"Frances? What you talking about! She's upstairs!"

"Sadly not, my Lord. She followed us, we had no idea. As you can imagine both Melbroke and myself were, are, very angry."

"What's happened?" The Earl and Margaret spoke in unison.

"She's been taken."

"Taken?" The Earl was forward in his chair, his white hair picking up the glow of the low fire that burned to the side of his chair, his face suddenly haggard, his eyes alarmed. William went on.

"Lord Jasper turned up, turns out he's behind all of this."

"Jasper?"

"He grabbed Frances and sped off with her. Alban took chase. He'll find her, have no fear of that, he will find her."

"Jasper's involved! Taken Frances! God help us." He was pacing now, his old hands cradling the crown of his head. "Why? Why?"

"The Marquises were determined to get money out of you,

my Lord, they've failed, now I expect Jasper will want money for Frances."

"The Marquises behind the blackmail? Now kidnap? Can't believe it!" He was still pacing, back and forth. Margaret and William remained silent as the old man assimilated the new situation he found himself in. "If that man lays one finger on me daughter I shall personally kill him, weak heart or no."

"I think you may find Melbroke will beat you to it."

IT WAS the cold water splashing against her face that brought Frances round. "Wake up whore," the angry voice snarled.

She was on the floor, propped against a harsh, cold wall. Her hands and ankles were tied. Her head was sore and throbbing. She was on smelly rushes, the room was dark, small, stale and stunk of ale. There was no air, no window. She had no idea where she was. She looked around. Jasper was sitting on a stool to her right. The meagre light from just one candle revealed the hatred blazing from his usually featureless eyes.

"Because of you whore, I have lost my brother!"

She was confused, fear soared through her but she wouldn't show it. "Pierre brought his death upon himself."

"Liar!" He screeched into her face, grabbing her chin in a vice-like grip. "You were unfaithful, you betrayed him. You broke his heart. He had to fight the fornicator, he was obliged to. It was a matter of honour."

Days back she would have insisted that Melbroke had forced himself upon her. Now she didn't. She didn't want to blacken the name of the man she had come to love. She was wiser now. Now, she understood love, realized its passion, its hold, its demands.

"Pierre didn't love me, I realize that now."

The Marquis cracked a shallow, bitter laugh. "Of course he didn't, you stupid woman. He was marrying you for the Blean money. You would become Marchioness, he would become wealthy. It was a fair exchange. A deal. You thought he loved you?"

"You just said I broke his heart?"

"Yes, because he trusted you. He thought you were a Lady, he would have treated you well, given you respect, loved the children you bore him. He thought you would do your duty and he would do his. Love? No. He wanted a dutiful wealthy wife, that was all."

She remained silent, taking all this in wasn't easy but in a way it lifted some of her guilt. She was glad Pierre hadn't loved her, at least she hadn't got that burden to carry for the rest of her life.

"What are you going to do with me?"

"Sell you."

"Sell me!"

"To the highest bidder. Melbroke or your father," he tormented, "who will it be do you think? Which one wants you the most? Which one will pay the most?"

She kept quiet. That he didn't intend killing her at least gave some respite in this hell hole.

"At least give me a chair to sit on," she asked, her body increasingly aware of the cold, damp floor.

"A lady would be given a chair, you're no lady, the floor will do just fine," he snarled. He placed the candle in the middle of the floor and left. She heard a bar go across the door. She was thirsty, scared, cold. The side of her head was pounding, tender to her touch and the ache was spreading into her eyes. Her wrists were already sore from the rope that grazed them.

She looked around her damp, dark prison. The candle's

glow hardly went to the perimeter even though it was a small room. It was bare, save some sacking in one corner and a huge lump of something in the other. As she watched, the lump appeared to move. She thought she heard a groan and tried to train her eyes more narrowly. Yes, it moved!

She heard another groan. It was female. A very large woman, dressed in dark colours, her head slumped forward so Frances could see no face, her gown right over her legs. She could see no patches of pale skin which would have helped her determine shape but it was definitely a woman. She could see the outline of matronly breasts and the glint of something shiny on her head. The figure was on a low wooden bench, her back against the wall. Who was she?

MELBROKE RODE around for two hours but the night was black. A gibbous moon had been smothered by cloud and the darkness became another enemy. The sweat from the fight had turned his hair into damp rats' tails. He hooked them behind his ears. While the moon had shone he'd followed the kidnapper's trail but the hoof marks had led into forest and tracking became impossible. He had shouted Frances' name in the vain hope she may be able to call back but the night remained silent. She was unconscious he assumed but he was trying anything.

That he hadn't told her he loved her was now haunting him. He hadn't been able to bring himself to say it a second time. Why? Had her rejection stung more than he realized? Did he now doubt his love for her? He was in turmoil as he chided himself. All he knew for certain was that he'd got to find her, get her to safety. If anything happened to her now...

He lent forward, stroked Galahad's mane and resigning to

failure this night, turned him back to Blean.

She was at the gate at five in the morning. Her note had asked Brother Thomas to meet her there and he was already waiting. Today it was locked, neither of them had authority for the key but they could talk through its grille.

"Sister, how are you? And why here?"

"Brother, I am as well as can be expected. I wanted to see you not for the health of my body but for my mind."

The apothecary looked puzzled. He had brought more pain-killing medicine and handed it through the bars.

"I need your help on another matter."

"Anything my dear soul," he smiled "anything." He knew her pain would worsen, soon there would be little he could do. If he could help her now, he wouldn't hesitate.

"I have to rely on your integrity. May I do this without burdening you?"

The fat monk nodded.

"You've been treating a man at Blean House, a lord, cousin of the King, I believe?"

The monk nodded again. "Yes, a Lord Melbroke."

Magdala, gripped the grille. "Do you know his Christian name?"

"Yes, I heard him called Alban."

"Are you sure, Brother?"

"Positive, I remember thinking how wonderful to be named after our first English martyr."

Magdala paled. She allowed her head to rest against the grille, her knuckles now white from their gripping.

"Sister, what is wrong?"

"I think I may know him, someone from my past."

He could see pain on her face and joy in her eyes. "What would you have me do, Sister?"

"Ask him to visit me?" Her eyes were wide now, appealing. Moist, beautiful and tender. "Will you do that, Brother?"

Again the generous, benign face smiled down upon her. "Of course. And if he has left Blean I will endeavour to find where you can contact him. I can see 'tis important."

They blessed each other and Thomas left. Magdala walked back to her herbs and sank to her knees in glory to God. She allowed the tears to stream down her face. Very soon her knees had wet patches from the morning's dew and her breasts were damp from her tears.

Chapter Twenty

MELBROKE RETURNED TO Blean full of anguish and fury and in need of the warmth of the hearth. There was no more he could do in the darkness of night where only wolves prowled and owls hunted and bats flew. He could hunt no more but at daybreak his search would resume. His ride back to the house alone had been a torture, his thoughts racing, his heart paining. Why on earth had she followed him? Insufferable woman! Insufferable, beautiful, wonderful woman! Jasper had her now. If he touched her, he would kill him. I might do that anyway, he was thinking, as he led Galahad toward the stables.

Margaret had tended William's burns as best she could and was now abed. The apothecary had been sent for. William slumbered alone in the withdrawing room, awaiting his friend's return. Like all the family, he was drawn, exhausted, worried to death. The slam of the iron handle on the sturdy oak door and then heavy steps entering the room snapped him back to reality. "Alban?" His voice was full of urgency.

"I haven't got her," Melbroke said, striding to the fire. "It was impossible in the black of night. I'll have to wait for dawn."

"We'll search together."

"And me," said the Earl, entering the room, having heard Melbroke's return. "Three's better than two."

"No, my Lord, please, no," said William. "We could be in the saddle for many hours, you must consider your heart. Your daughters would never forgive us if anything happened to you."

"God's hooks! Am I too old to do anything these days!" He poured three wines. "I can't just sit and wait. God only knows what's happening to Frances."

Melbroke too was racked with such thoughts. He looked out of the window, the glass reflecting back his hopelessness. No sign yet of dawn.

"My Lord, perhaps you can help with this? A Frenchman turned up at the Harwykes' hovel."

"A Frenchman? What did he look like?"

"Tall, thin, scrawny, scraggy blonde hair. Spoke good English but with a strong accent."

"Good Lord! Sounds like me under-founder at Grinstead, Pascal Blanc."

"Grinstead?" Both Lords asked together.

"Yes, Grinstead!" The Earl fidgeted uncomfortably, slamming one fist into the other palm. He looked at the two younger men, his face riven with guilt. "Don't look at me like that! I am allowed a life, even though I'm half dead. Grinstead was me first."

"First what?" Again two voices were in unison.

"First iron works. It was that one's success that got me thinking of extending to me own lands."

"Is it a secret?" William asked, quite aghast that no one knew.

"No one lets me do anything these days! Always on about me heart, the girls fussing around me." He was tired, worried, irritable, it was showing. "It was set up eighteen months ago, I kept it to meself. No 'tis not a secret, just didn't broadcast it." He swigged back some wine, his face flustered, his tired body back in its chair.

"What do you know of Pascal Blanc?" Melbroke moved from the fire to a soft chair near the Earl.

"Not a lot. The French are ahead of us in iron production, me founder Bellowes thought some French expertise would be a good idea. Blanc advised on the Blean works, oversaw the building."

"Well he's in custody now," said William. "Seemed very close to the Harwykes, was prepared to fight alongside them."

The Earl's face paled, tormented anew. "It was Blanc who brought the Harwykes to me! He said he'd put word out in the Weald and they had come forward. Mayhap the blaggard's a liar."

He certainly is, thought Melbroke, keeping his own counsel, not wanting to add to the Earl's distress.

THE LUMP in the corner stretched herself and groaned back to life. Her eyes, wide and startled. She looked about her and finally settled on Frances. "Who are you?"

The two women gazed at each other, neither recognizing the other. Frances could see tear stains on the chubby cheeks. Small eyes sank into the folds of her round face, small cupid lips sat above a dimpled chin. It was a homely face, benign and Frances guessed that it was usually a contented face.

"I'm Lady Frances, daughter of the Earl of Blean. Who

are you?"

The woman heaved a sigh of great relief. "I's Alys. Praise the Lord! Now mayhap someone will come..." and her eyes closed again.

"What do you mean? You know me?" Frances called across the gloom several times. The woman didn't respond. "Please Alys, wake up," she called, her voice bouncing off the walls of the empty chamber. "Wake up, talk to me!"

"I's Alys," the woman repeated, her words slurring. "He likes me apple pies..."

"Who does? What are you talking about?"

The woman's head slumped back on to her ample bosom.

"Alys, wake up. Who likes apple pies? What are you talking about?"

"Your father...likes me pies."

"You know my father!"

With that the woman was drawn back into her drug-induced state. Jasper had given her a narcotic drink when she wouldn't stop screaming. It was actually a blessing. She was a highly strung woman and couldn't have coped with the situation. Frances on the other hand was made of fierier stuff. She began using her fingers to work the rope that tied her ankles. If Jasper came back she would kick him and run for the door. That was her plan. She had to have a plan or she would go mad in this dark hell hole.

BROTHER THOMAS arrived at Blean just as the sky was beginning to lighten. The dark canopy was giving way to vermillion streaks that heralded the new day. Melbroke was eager to get searching but William had shown him his chest and he could see it needed treating. So too, Melbroke's left hand which was now throbbing from the blow from the sword. It had swollen considerably, his fingers were now stiff and unbending.

The apothecary was irritable at being summoned in the early hours but grateful for the use of the Blean carriage which had been sent to collect him. He tended both men in a ground-floor ante-room. William's chest took priority. As always, Brother Thomas was tender but still William winced. Areas of his chest were raw and inflamed, the tissue now swelling and very painful. Brother Thomas smeared the area with a thick salve and applied bandage. It would need to be changed regularly with salve regularly re-applied. The monk wished to speak with Lady Runmore. William left to fetch her.

Happily finding himself on his own with his second patient the monk ventured: "My Lord, may I have a private word with you? 'Tis urgent."

Melbroke, his hand throbbing as the monk prodded and flexed, was intrigued. "You may, be quick."

"There is an elderly nun at the convent in Canterbury who would like to talk with you," he said, smearing the hand with arnica liniment to draw out the bruising.

"What on earth for?"

"I am sworn to secrecy m'Lord, I have promised to say nothing but as God is my witness I can assure m'Lord that 'tis of the utmost importance." The monk was now winding bandage around the hand, rendering it virtually unusable.

"I already have matters of the utmost importance to deal with Brother, can't this nun wait? And have you really got to do that?"

"Yes, m'Lord I have, unless your Lordship, as before, wishes to take his health into his own hands." The monk glared, Melbroke resigned himself.

"The nun is soon to meet her maker. 'Tis important you visit the convent as soon as possible."

"What on earth can a nun have to say to me?"

The monk remained silent as he tied a sling over Melbroke's shoulder and fed his patient's arm into it. Rescuing Frances was Melbroke's priority right now. "Tell the nun I will visit her once my current urgent business has been resolved."

The apothecary smiled, bowed and left just as the Earl entered the room. "My Lord," Melbroke said, turning to him. "This isn't exactly the perfect moment but I wish to thank you most sincerely for the welcome you have given me into your household..."

"No need for any of that formality young man," the Earl said, waving a hand dismissively. "I confess I have come to rely on you, you have been a grand friend to this family."

He would miss the Earl. He would miss all of them but he needed to get away. Clear his thoughts. He had come to believe that it was a blessing that Frances had rejected him and that he hadn't responded to her later declaration of love. Something had stopped him, something deep within him. He was about to make a terrible mistake, he felt. He was glad he could very soon get away.

He didn't trust love, never had. What was it anyway? Some mystical state where two people believed something magical had happened between them. What nonsense! What he knew of love always brought pain. On the other hand, he couldn't deny the feelings Frances aroused in him. He was confused and yes, fearful. Fearful of the pain he had seen in his cuckolded father. Fearful of risking again the agony of his childhood when love had been so unexpectedly snatched from him. Fearful of becoming unaccustomed to loneliness only to have to navigate it anew.

Frances believed in it, mayhap it was right for her, not for him. She was a beautiful, lovely woman, she deserved better than he. She would find love again, she would soon be someone else's wife. He would forget her and she him. He would avoid the risk. 'Twas best this way.

"Thank you, my Lord. As soon as we get Frances home safely, hopefully that will be today, I shall then take my leave."

"You are truly intent on leaving?"

"As I said before, there is nothing to keep me in Kent any longer. I shall see the King and head wherever he sends me."

"I shall be very sad to see you go Alban, we all will." Melbroke managed a half-smile but inwardly he was far from smiling. He would return to Madeleine and her like. He would forget the breathtaking nineteen-year-old from Kent with her bewitching blue pools for eyes, her hair like an angel and spirit like a vixen. He would get his life back on its proper track!

The monk was talking to Margaret in the hallway as William returned. "Have I missed anything?"

"Nothing at all," said the Earl. "Now go, the pair of you and bring my daughter back to me."

DAWN HAD broken. Vermilion had waned to gentle pink and the air was fresh and clean as the two men resumed the search.

"The Frenchman's the answer to all this," Melbroke said, as he and William made their way back to their horses. "There's no point in us riding around the countryside when that Frenchy probably knows where Jasper would take her."

"Agreed," said William. "To Canterbury then and the Sheriff's cells."

The bandage on Melbroke's left hand was protective but along with the painful swelling, it rendered the hand unusable in a fight. He thought he may, with difficulty, be able to hold a cudgel or axe but he couldn't be deft with a dagger. His sword arm was strong but if it came to fighting and he assumed it would, he liked a weapon in both hands. Before he'd left the house he'd taken a small axe from the Earl's armoury, it was now tucked safely into his belt. With his good hand he checked Galahad's girth, mounted and gripped the reins. "Let's go," he called to William and the two men trotted into the pink world of sunrise, the deed in hand in sharp contrast to the beautiful world that blessed it.

AN ASHEN Gates, himself unable to sleep under the agonizing circumstances, was back in his work clothes and ready for the new day when the banging began. It started loud, forceful, strong but over a matter of seconds became feeble and weak. Laying on the great stone step, immediately outside the front door, he found an exhausted, middle-aged, fat man gasping for breath, his face swollen, his belly wobbling as his chest heaved in and out.

"His Lordship please! 'Tis Bellowes. I must see him," he cried, in anguish. The Earl had heard the banging and had descended the stairs.

"Bring him in Gates, there's a good fellow."

"But who is he my Lord?"

"Never mind who he is, just bring him in. To me study. Now!"

Gates lifted the man from behind, hooking his arms under the armpits and helping him to his feet. Bellowes' breathing was calming, his strength slowly returning. He'd had a long ride from Grinstead. His body wasn't up to such exertion, especially not on top of a sleepless night and all the worry he now carried. Gates supported him to the study where the Earl had already poured brandy.

"Get this down you, Bellowes. What on earth is this all about?"

"They's tak'n m'wife. Snatched Alys. Threatened to kill me." Bellowes sank into the chair the Earl offered, his body shaking.

"Who man? Who's taken her?"

"Complete strangers m'Lord. Burst into our house yesterday morning, just afore I was leaving for the foundry. Said they'd kill her if I did anything, told anyone. Just grabbed her, dragged her away screaming. I was helpless m'lord, helpless." Tears filled his eyes. He was shaking from head to toe, the brandy in his glass rocked. "And I've done the most terrible thing. By the grace of Our Lady I swear I didn't mean to."

"Calm down man. Take your drink. Calm yourself!"

Bellowes knocked back the brandy and gratefully took another. The warmth of the high-summer sun that poured into the room, the alcohol, the imposing reassurance that was the House of Blean, began to soothe him. Eventually he continued. "I agonized all day m'Lord, all night, not knowing what to do. Then I reckoned they might kill her anyway. But I didn't know who to turn to then I thought of you m'Lord, I hope you don't..."

"'Course I don't mind Bellowes." The Earl went to the window and looked out. This was too much of a coincidence! His daughter snatched, now his founder's wife as well. He didn't believe in coincidence! Seemed only fair to reveal all to Bellowes, well, some of it! He sat down opposite his founder. "We're amidst a drama of our own Bellowes. Me daughter's been taken, too."

"Your daughter, m'Lord?"

"Yes, some hours back, in the middle of the night." He didn't intend telling Bellowes the reckless situation his daughter had put herself in! "Me son-in-law and a family friend are out looking for her now. So's the Sheriff, not that I've much faith in his band of useless constables."

A new wave of confusion tremored through Bellowes, a new anxiety etching his usually contented features. Was this good news or bad? Was Alys the safer for it? And given what he'd done, was he safe? He couldn't decide. Tell all though, he now must. "M'Lord, there is more. I've hesitated, forgive me, because I'm thinking of my beloved Alys' safety but if the Sheriff is already involved..."

The Earl poured himself a second brandy, Bellowes a third and returned to his seat. "Go on man. From the beginning."

"Two evenings ago Pascal Blanc didn't turn up for his nightshift, I couldn't leave until he arrived, I was getting very annoyed. Eventually I lost patience and began searching through his papers to find his home address. I intended sending a message. Was he ill? Where was he?"

"And?"

"I found this m'Lord." Bellowes pulled a parchment from within his tunic, its edges now crumpled from the ride.

The Earl had no sooner begun reading than he was on his feet. "God's mercy! I've been trussed up like a goose for roasting! What the hellfire is going on here!" He slammed down the document. He was candescant with rage, his hands slightly shaking as he took on the reality that now lay before him.

It was the London surveyor's January report. Its seal broken, its contents well fingered. It categorically stated that there was no iron ore at Blean, that it was not suitable for mining and that he did not recommend the wasting of any time, effort or money on what would be an expensive and futile venture. The Earl read it again and waving it in the air, he turned to Bellowes. "Blanc had this!"

"Indeed m'Lord, hidden away in a leather pouch. He arrived just as I was opening it, he snatched it from me, pushed me against the wall. He shouted viciously, told me to say nothing or I would be a dead man. But there's more m'Lord, 'tis terrible! Terrible!"

The Earl pushed open a window, let in some fresh air, his antennae twitching, his anger at near boiling point.

"He got the document back?"

"At first he did," Bellowes said, his face contorted with anxiety, his hands again shaking. He sipped his brandy. "I've done a terrible thing m'Lord, may God forgive me." His eyes turned upwards and he crossed himself.

"Get on with it man! What's so damn terrible?"

"I had no idea what the document was about, I hadn't had a chance to read it but I had glimpsed your name. It nagged at me, after all, what was Blanc doing with it? So, I pretended to leave but after ten minutes or so I crept back and hit him over the head. I took the document m'Lord, while Blanc lay slumped on the floor."

His whole body was again shaking, his belly and triple chins wobbling in rhythm. "I think I killed him, m'Lord. Killed him! I ran from that place like a bat out of hell, I can tell you. Then at dawn men came and took Alys. I've done this to her! I've done it!" His head sunk into his cupped hands, his voice cracked.

The Earl strode to his founder and slapped his back, trying to offer some kind of reassurance. Bellowes looked up: "Sorry m'Lord, I should have come earlier, might have saved your daughter."

"No it wouldn't Bellowes, it wouldn't. And no you haven't murdered Blanc, sorry to say. He's very much alive and been kicking, although he is now in the Sheriff's cells in Canterbury."

"You mean I didn't...O thank the Lord." Relief flooded his

being as he relaxed back into his chair and closed his eyes. "Been arrested? What for?"

The Earl ignored the question and lifted the brandy flask from the sill where it had been warming in the sun. "You've been extremely brave," he said, "very brave indeed. We'll find yer wife, have no fear," he said, pouring two more drinks.

The men sat in silence. Around the Earl's feet the dogs stirred, outside the open window birds sang. The day was warming up. Both men were thinking about their women who had been kidnapped, how their ageing hearts would break if anything happened to them, how life would never be the same, how they should have better protected them. After a while the Earl asked: "The men who took yer wife, didn't they ask for the report to be handed back?"

"I denied I'd got it. They didn't believe me, slapped me around a bit but I just kept denying it. They said they'd kill Alys and me if I were lying."

"Well done, Bellowes! Excellent thinking. The document is very valuable evidence, you've absolutely done the right thing. They won't touch you here and we'll find yer wife. Have no fear, we'll find her."

Bellowes couldn't respond to the praise, his heart was too heavy, his fears too great.

"At last we're getting somewhere," said the Earl, thinking aloud, thinking also that actually things were getting even more confused.

Bellowes allowed the amber tincture to bathe his mouth then let it burn its way down his throat. He had no idea what was truly going on. He would trust the Earl. He had never let him down before.

PASCAL BLANC was lying in a corner unconscious when Melbroke and William arrived at the Sheriff's cells. His face was battered, his clothes splattered with blood. Sheriff Malins was absent so both Lords assumed the constables had enjoyed their sport with a Frenchy.

Melbroke yanked him up off the floor, pinned him against the wall and slapped his face with his good hand. "Come on you whoreson. Where is she? Talk to me." His hand flicked from one side of the man's face to the other, one slap after the other. Frenchy didn't respond.

"Bring water," William yelled and Melbroke stood back as a constable threw a bucket of cold water over Blanc. He slowly slipped down the wall, groaning. His thin shirt couldn't conceal his weak, narrow chest. Now saturated he looked like an underfed partridge, all small and insignificant with no substance on the bone. He raised his tied hands and wiped his dripping face on his cuffs. He opened his eyes and on seeing William and Melbroke tried to back himself further against the wall.

"Non, non, mon seigneur, je suis innocent."

"Speak English you cur. Innocent? I don't think so," and Melbroke's foot met his stomach. The Frenchman gasped, doubled over, drew up his knees and wretched between them. Blood-stained liquid fell from his mouth. He'd obviously been hit many times since his custody.

"You want more of this? You want to hang you wretch?" Melbroke lifted him back into a standing position, his one good hand ample for the weight of this wafer of a man. He propped him against the wall. "If they kill the Lady of Blean you will hang. The King's my cousin, I shall make sure of it you morceau de merde." The Frenchman was shaking from head to toe. "Non, non, I kill no one."

"You are part of the gang, part of this evil conspiracy. If she dies, you die."

Another blow to his stomach and a punch to his jaw forced him to raise his hands. "No more, monsieur, I beg."

"Then tell me, you dung-smeared pig. Where would that piece of girlie-reed take her?"

"Mayhap to ze inn on Dover road. No more, I beg," he cried, raising his tied hands to defend his head. "They are friends with ze man who runs it."

"Which inn?"

"On ze left from Canterbury. Le Soleil, I think. Please don't tell them I told you."

Melbroke's good hand smashed his mouth hard and viciously. "You don't make bargains you whoreson. If I save her you may live, you get nothing more." Blanc spat out a tooth. A trickle of blood ran down his chin. With that the Lords left.

"Do you know The Sun Inn?" Melbroke asked William, as they mounted their horses.

"'Fraid so. 'Tis a whorehouse, a terrible place."

Sweet Jesus, please protect her until I get there, Melbroke pleaded as he and William spurred their horses into a gallop and headed for the Dover road. As they gathered speed Melbroke yanked off his sling and threw it away.

Chapter Twenty-one

SOMETIME DURING THE night the two women were moved from The Sun Inn and were gone by the time Melbroke and William arrived. It was a filthy place, in every way. Whores of all ages were gathered around a large grimy pot of something indistinguishable, taking sustenance with dry bread and small ale.

Two huge, bull-built men had thrown Frances and Alys, like bundles of baggage, on to the back of a horse-drawn cart. The Marquis and another man had held down a woozy Alys as they forced her, yet again, to drink more liquid but Frances they couldn't force. Once again she had kicked and struggled as she refused to be adulterated with what she correctly assumed to be drugged wine. Her desperate thirst would have to go unsated. Her face, hair and bodice were soaked by the cheap red liquid adding to her discomfort but unconscious she was not. That she was not having! They gagged her instead.

The cart ride had been painful. With hands and feet tied she was unable to steady herself and she'd rolled like a marble, banging on one side of the cart then the other, as it took bends at a pace. By the time they arrived at the destination she was even more bruised. Her face was grazed, the tight gag cutting the sides of her mouth. When the cart stopped and the voices returned she was lifted by strong arms and shoved into a new prison. The unconscious Alys was dragged, heels scraping on the stoney ground and tossed into a corner.

MELBROKE WAS off his horse first and threw his reins to William. "Guard the horses, someone'll have them, this place is a den of cutpurses."

This was a quiet time of day for the usually busy Sun. Scrawny chickens pecked at gravel. Rooks in a nearby tree squawked. Inside, stale stench hit Melbroke's senses. Somewhere in the distance a chopper came down on today's carcass. The rhythmic action beating like a drum. Wooden stools were scattered around. Dozens of pottery and pewter beakers lay discarded, not yet washed for the new day's business. The air was thick from the smell of woodsmoke, the dead fire having spewed itself as much into the room as up the dirty chimney. Around the hearth lay discarded, muddy boots, drying while their owners pleasured themselves. Drunken men still snored in corners, some stirred, some looked dead to the world.

Melbroke could feel the axe handle digging into his thigh, it gave him comfort, so too the sword's hilt which he held with his good right hand. Ready, just in case. In one corner a couple lay in ale-sleep, legs intwined in a mass of dirty clothes. The woman's eyes opened, she raised her eyebrows in expectation as she looked to Melbroke, hoping he was her next customer. They paid well, the men in silk.

He averted his gaze from her naked, ample breasts and made his way down a long, dark corridor. Each door he kicked open, sword at the ready. Satisfied neither Frances nor enemy were on the ground floor he went upstairs. The stairs got narrower, the ceiling lower and he was forced to stoop. It was hotter up here, there was no ventilation and it smelt of sweat and sex. Again he systematically worked along the miserable corridor. Some rooms were empty, the night's bedding in piles on the floor; in others wenches were washing, readying themselves for their next sessions, making no attempt at decency as their door burst open. No Frances though.

He went out the back and found a squalid yard, more emaciated chickens, a scruffy cockerel, discarded barrels, a haphazard pile of part-chopped fire wood. In one corner stood a large stone building with a tatty sieve of a thatch that a gale could easily steal away. The door was locked but the old, weathered wood soon yielded under the strength of his shoulder.

It was empty save some well-worn brooms and a long, low bench seat, one of its legs broken. A dented, pewter mug lay by its side, some of its contents now on the floor. He picked up the mug, it smelt strange. The stub of a candle had been kicked into a corner. He walked around, skirted the room's edges looking for something out of place, something that could give a clue that Frances had been here. Then he saw it. His eyes fell upon a coarse, screwed-up spider's web, on closer inspection it was a woman's riding net. Would a whore have a riding net?

He took the net to his face and fancied it smelt of Frances. He had just pushed it into his pocket when a vicious blow to the back of his skull sent him reeling. A flash of lightening seared across his eyes, his legs went under him, the world spun, he could feel himself crumbling and then blackness.

Outside William waited. What on earth was taking Melbroke so long? He'd walked the horses round to the stables at the back intending to tether them among the others already there. They would make good camouflage, he thought. What he found horrified and angered him. The stables were a disgrace. Cramped, dirty, dark, smelly. Both his horse and Galahad snorted and bucked. He tethered them among trees. Money from horses and women! Both treated with contempt!

Taking a small dagger from his belt he ventured into the gloom of the inn. "'E went out back," the whore with the ample bosom called, running her hopeful eye over the second man in silk.

"He's not in the stables," he called back.

"Try the ale store."

He bowed. "Thank you mistress." She smiled and blushed. Courtesy was not what she was used to.

William found Melbroke on the floor. He was just beginning to stir. "Someone got me from behind," he mumbled, bringing his hand to his head and feeling the damp of blood which now trickled down his neck. "Feels as though my skull's been split by an axe."

"I can confirm that it hasn't. From behind Melbroke! Really! Basic training that, you idiot!"

"God, the pain's excruciating."

With William's help he got to his feet, slumped against a wall and waited until dizziness passed. A wave of nausea swept though him as his head pounded like a smithy's hammer. The whore entered the storeroom, leaving the door wide open and allowing shafts of morning sun to lighten the miserable place. Melbroke turned his now sensitive eyes away from the sudden light, the head movement making him dizzy again. "You looking for two wimmin?"

"We're looking for one. Were there two here?" William asked.

The wench nodded and both men could now see that she was hardly out of childhood, fair and pretty. "One young woman, kept kicking and screaming and another older, fat woman."

"The younger woman could be the lady we seek," Melbroke said, the words banging his skull as he spoke them. "Where are they now?"

"No idea. Heard a cart go in the night and the two woz gone by daybreak when I come to look."

"So they were in this storeroom?"

The girl nodded. "Tied up like chickens, they woz. The older woman seemed to be unconscious."

"Tell me, please," said Melbroke, showing her the riding net, "do any of you girls wear a thing like this?"

"Hardly sir, that's for riding, we don't 'ave 'orses, we walks."

"You've been very helpful," said William, stepping forward and putting a coin in her hand.

"Yous welcome sir, anytime you wants to call back just ask for Jane."

"We most certainly will," he said bowing. The girl giggled and blushed again. Being bowed to was also not what she was used to. She turned and left with care, clinging on to her skirt and the eggs she had just gathered that lay in its folds.

Initially, Melbroke argued when William suggested they should return to Blean so he could rest. He didn't want to lay down, he wanted to push on and find Frances but when he walked out into the morning's fresh air and full sunshine, weakness tremored through his legs. His head continued to feel as though it were under the blacksmith's hammer. He had no choice, he was forced to drop all objection. He would return to Blean, take a painkilling draft, rest until after the midday meal and resume the search in the afternoon.

"The hair net was a sign for us," he said, mounting Galahad with uncustomary difficulty. "She was trying to leave a trail."

"I realize that but in what direction did they take her?"

"Don't know but she had little with her, I expect she'll leave a boot next."

"Rest Melbroke, you need rest. We'll look for boots later."

HER TIED hands had just been flexible enough to pull down the dirty rag of a gag that had grooved her face. She was on a mud floor, propped against a cold, damp wall. Her ankles were tied so tightly it hurt to move her legs or feet even slightly. She had never seen such a place. It was a large building, part stone, part wood. About half had a covering roof, the rest was open to the sky. It was cold and bleak but she could smell fresh air and through the open roof she could see the tops of tall trees. The silence was eerie and made a shudder of fear travel through her. The sky, pitch black when she arrived was now soft blue and somehow offering a comfort which she grasped. The new day's sun was bringing some warmth but she was desperately thirsty and now very hungry.

What looked like a huge hearth was at one end. It was above her level of vision, she couldn't see into it but above it a chimney rose up to the ceiling and beyond. It was definitely something that held fire. Around its edge a parapet of brick was supporting an array of black, heavy implements. Spiteful, sharp, pointed, hammer-like, metallic. Weapons or tools? She had no idea.

At the other end there was a mighty wooden beam, the size of which she had never seen before. From one end hung a gigantic lump of metal, bigger than her father's heavy safe, square but chiselled into a ridge along one side. It looked like an enormous hammer big enough to knock down a house. It would certainly kill whoever it landed on. She shuddered again and turned her thoughts away from the possibility that she may be in a torture chamber. She'd heard of the one at the Tower and she imagined it could very well look like this.

Alys was a few feet from her, slumped against the wall. She had been gently snoring for hours, the rhythm was strangely re-assuring but now its regularity was changing. Was she coming round?

"Wake up. Whoever you are, wake up!"

Suddenly Alys coughed. Her chest heaved slowly as she repeatedly gasped for air. She was choking. She opened her eyes wide as the coughing increased and she tried to manoeuvre her large trusted-up frame to ease the discomfort. Very quickly her body was shaking vigorously as she struggled for air. Her face reddened, her eyes turned watery as she heaved again and again. Her tied hands extended to the beaker of liquid by her side.

"No!" Frances called. "Don't drink that. They're drugging you."

The woman's puzzled eyes turned to Frances but she heeded her words and bent her body double in an attempt to stop the coughing. Slowly she regained control and the heaving and coughing subsided.

"Are you all right?"

"Hardly," she croaked, looking around her. "All this dust must have caught me throat. You say they're drugging me?"

"Definitely. I've refused the liquid and I'm not unconscious."

"Satan's henchmen," the woman snapped, more herself now, the herbal influence having worn off.

"Who are you?" Frances asked again.

"I's Alys Bellowes. My husband is the founder at Grinstead

iron works."

"So how do you know my father?"

"'Cos he visits regular, every month, I prepares him food. He's a good eater, likes me food I can tell you. Very partial to..."

"Never mind all that," Frances interrupted, slightly offended that this stranger was familiar with her father. "Why does he visit?"

"'Cos he owns it."

"Owns what?"

"Iron works, of course."

Stunned, Frances rested her head back against the cold wall. That's where he was on those days when he went missing!

BACK AT Blean Margaret tended William's chest. It was still red, inflamed and weeping. She smeared on the ointment the apothecary had left and replaced the bandage. She also tended Melbroke's head. She gave them both a painkilling draught, not as strong as the apothecary could provide but it would suffice.

Having heard Bellowes' story and read the surveyor's genuine report it was now obvious to Melbroke that the plot of Pierre and Jasper was deeper, nastier and longer in the planning than he had realized. Jasper had clearly taken both Frances and Alys Bellowes. The whole outrageous business was about the iron works and in relieving the Earl of as much money as they could. Even poor Bellowes may now be asked to provide a few extra coins! It was as if revenge on Melbroke was an opportunistic side issue, albeit a very dangerous one.

"We need to see that churl Frenchman again," he urged William, as they were eating. "Really put the fear of God into him this time. She's not at The Sun and he's the only person who may know where else Jasper's taken her."

William nodded. "We can't ride aimlessly around Kent looking for ladies' boots, that's for sure."

WHEN THEY arrived back in Canterbury, Pascal Blanc could not be questioned, by order of the Sheriff. He was regularly coughing up blood, was in agonizing pain and slipping in and out of consciousness.

"God's wounds man," Melbroke had barked at the senior constable, "do you not care for Lady Frances' safety?"

To prove he did and knowing the Earl would be told of events, he allowed Melbroke to look into Blanc's cell. He was clearly unconscious and of no use for Melbroke's purposes. The two men left in thwarted mood.

"You now go to lawyer Jarrett," Melbroke suggested to William. "Ask him to send a message post haste to the surveyor. We need confirmation of his negative advice and we need to know how a report could be altered."

"What are you going to do?"

"I've a personal matter, it won't take long. I'll meet you back at The Sun in two hours, the innkeeper may have returned. We need to have a nice little talk with him," he grinned and snarled, both at the same time. "Get Jarrett to also ask the surveyor what company of post-horses he used."

William waved his acknowledgement and the two men went about their business, a light drizzle further dampening their already low spirits.

Melbroke went straight to meet Brother Thomas. He'd sent

message earlier this day that this afternoon would suit his plans and the two of them now stood at the convent's main door. His heart was strangely apprehensive, his mind swinging between curious and irritated. He was unarmed as seemed befitting. The monk banged the metal knocker against its knob, cutting into the afternoon's stillness.

While they waited in silence for what seemed an age Melbroke glanced around. In the distance he could hear wood pigeons cooing, mayhap a woodpecker hammering. The sun was catching the drops of mossy damp on the high convent wall, making them shine like jewels. An air of peace that he wasn't used to pervaded, he pulled back his shoulders and drew in the sweet, tranquil air. He wasn't sure how he felt about God. Not after what he'd witnessed: the greed of Court, the carnage of the battlefield, the treachery of man - and woman. A tight bundle of butterflies flittered past, red squirrels played chase atop the wall. An insect buzzed around his head, he let it live.

"We may have trouble with the Mother Superior, one by the name of Esme, a cold woman. Just follow my lead, my Lord." Melbroke nodded.

A nun pulled back the wooden covering of the grille and peered through. Recognizing the monk she opened the door but when she saw the large, imposing figure of a second man she made quickly to close it. Men did not enter here. Brother Thomas was an exception. Not only a monk, he was a medical man. All others were banned. Melbroke's foot jammed her intention.

"Sister," said the monk, smiling, "Lord Melbroke is on urgent business. You will let us in or answer to the King."

For a few seconds she hesitated. Her fear of the Bishop, who would not want her thwarting the King, proved to be greater than her fear of Mother Esme and she stood aside, indicating with outstretched arm that they should enter. She kept her eyes to the ground as Melbroke passed, as if even looking upon him were a sin.

The monk led Melbroke straight to Magdala's cell where she waited, her heart pounding, the pain in her abdomen quelled by a recent dose of painkiller. Brother Thomas had told her Alban was coming; she was ready.

"You only have a few moments," the monk said. "The nun is bound to go for Esme. Be quick," he urged, as he left them to their privacy and set himself as sentry in the corridor outside.

"Sister, you asked to see me," he began, aware that the woman couldn't take her eyes off him.

"This situation is not ideal," she began. "I would have liked to get to know you first, as it is I am forced to come straight out with it."

"Please do, Sister."

"Alban, I am your mother," and with that she stretched out her trembling arms.

"You are mistaken," he said indignantly, remaining rooted to where he stood. "My mother is dead. She is dead! What nonsense is this?"

"I am not dead Alban, although sadly I may soon be. Ask me any questions you may have, so I can prove who I am."

"Nonsense. I am leaving," and he turned back to the door.

"Please, Albie," she called. "Please stay."

A knife stabbed his heart. It had been twenty years since anyone had called him Albie, his mother always did. It was a trick!

"You must have known my mother. Who are you? A distant relative mayhap, a servant?"

"Ask me, anything, please."

He thought for a moment, his back still toward her. Then he turned. "What was the colour of my first horse?"

"It was a bay. You called him Freckles because he had lots of small white markings."

"How old was I when you left?"

"Ten. You'd not long had your birthday which is June 22nd, the feast day of St Alban.

"What did my father collect?"

"Gold pocket sundials. He had dozens of them in his study. His favourite was the one I bought him for our tenth wedding anniversary, it has our initials entwined around its edge."

Alban's heart raced, his mind in turmoil. He raked his hand through his thick hair as he stared at the ground in deep thought.

"If you are my mother you would know if I have any marks on my body."

"You have a brown birthmark, the shape of a dog's head, on the back of your left thigh."

He was shocked to his core. He looked up and straight into the eyes of the woman whose own eyes were now dewy and shining with happiness. He fetched out the small sundial from his pocket and showed it to her. The old nun broke down and reached to clasp it. He jerked it away. "Yes, that is it my dear, dear son. You've kept it all these years!"

"What other feature does this dial have?"

"It has ten diamonds embedded in its base..."

Before she could finish the door banged open and in the gap stood a very angry Mother Esme. The lowering sun behind her creating a golden aura around her. She looked like an angel but all who knew her, knew better.

"Sister, go to the chapel at once, prostrate yourself on the floor and beg our Lord for forgiveness?"

"She will do no such thing," Alban's voice boomed, as he stepped out from the shadow of the door."

"And you Sir, will leave this nunnery immediately."

"No. But you Mother will hold your tongue. I am visiting my mother who is sick. Perhaps some Christian compassion runs somewhere within you Mother?"

Esme looked at Melbroke, then Magdala, then back again. "Mother?"

"Yes. Mother. Widow of an Earl, related by marriage to the King. In future you will give her the respect she deserves."

Brother Thomas winced. Esme was not used to being spoken to in this fashion. Sister Magdala married? A mother?

"We have only just been reunited so if you would be so kind as to leave us, we would be most grateful." Melbroke bowed, indicating it was her moment to leave. Esme didn't move, her face frowning, her eyes cold. He continued: "Would it be rash of me to assume that there is some Christian kindness in you?" He asked sarcastically, signalling again to the open door.

Esme mumbled something inaudible, turned on her heel and swept away.

Alban turned to his mother who was now standing, her arms again open toward him. This time he walked over and took her in his arms. He held her tightly. For the first time in twenty years mother and son embraced. The mother wept until exhaustion overtook her. The son fought his emotions as questions piled up in his mind.

The next morning the Bishop received two letters. One from Brother Thomas outlining events. The other from Mother Esme reporting Melbroke's forced entry into her convent. Knowing Lord Melbroke's pedigree he filed Mother's letter at the bottom of his ever-growing pile.

Chapter Twenty-two

ANOTHER COIN IN the same pretty wench's palm got a message to the innkeeper of The Sun alerting him to trouble in the stables. Horses were whinnying, threatening to trample on each other, he was told. He was busy, The Sun's main business was hotting up but the message tore him from his work. It got him running and as soon as he entered the stable William grabbed him, yanked his arms behind him, crushed him face-front against a wall and tied his hands.

"Now then, cur," Melbroke growled, turning him round. "Where did you take them?" His sharp blade played the man's neck. No answer. "I don't recommend you play games with me you dung-smeared mangehound. Open that sour little mouth of yours and speak. Unless you'd like it cut a little wider, would that make talking easier? Mayhap it would," he teased, running the blade into the corners of the man's now trembling lips. Melbroke took his mouth to the man's ear and bellowed: "Speak! Now!"

"The Blean crossroads," he gasped, shaking. "I was told to take 'em there."

"Then where?"

"I was met by a man, didn't know 'im, wiv an accent, not English. 'E took the cart from there."

"And what did you do with the young woman while she was here? Did you touch her, you milk-livered foot-licker? Did you lay even one of your grubby fingers upon her?"

"No, no, truly sir, I never did."

"Did anyone touch her?"

"Don't know but I did nuffin', I just takes rent for rooms. Two men what brought her rented the beer store. They tried to make her drink wine but she refused, they roughed 'er up a bit."

"Is she injured?"

"Not that I noticed."

"Not that you noticed!" Melbroke hissed, digging the blade into the man's neck. The flesh yielded, registering pain on the contorted face. "You mean you didn't look at her?"

"No, I never."

"Liar. She was beautiful wasn't she?"

"No, Sir, truly. She was none of my business. And anyway I's surrounded by that sort of thing all day, if I needs a woman there's plenty here."

Melbroke gazed into the man's face not sure what to believe. It could be true. He could be lying. He pressed the knife deeper, broke the skin and watched as a ball of blood oozed down the man's neck, adding stain to the already filthy shirt.

"Where was she being taken?"

"Truly, I don't know," the man replied, now shaking from head to toe.

"If you want to live man, you'll tell us," William shouted,

crushing the man harder against the wall, the side of his face now grazing on rough stone. "Your friends aren't going to save you, no one's going to save your putrid hide."

"They wasn't friends, just customers."

Melbroke took his good hand down to the man's groin and twisted harshly. The man screeched in agony, his face turning into an ugly gargoyle.

"Please...I knows no more." He gasped, the pain was stealing his breath, he could hardly speak. "If I knew I'd tell. Honest. But I's don't."

Melbroke had no more dices to roll. This man was his last lead. "Think man," he snarled, keeping his grip tight. "Did these men mention anywhere, anywhere at all?"

The landlord's body heaved with pain. He could hardly think for it but after a few excruciating seconds his eyes lit in hope. "I heard them referring to an iron works," he whispered, his eyes appealing to Melbroke's. "Nearby mayhap, that's all I can fink, honest, m'Lord, honest." With that tears of pain and fear began to flow from his eyes.

"The lady in question is the daughter of an Earl, if one hair on her head has been damaged, you will pay. You and all the others. It will be my personal mission to see you hanged. Do you understand me?" The man nodded vigorously, Melbroke's vice-like grip to his groin still controlling him. "And if that pretty wench who gave you our message has one bruise, one mark on her body, you'll see my knife again. Understand me?" Again he nodded vigorously.

"And this," Melbroke snarled, giving one more twist, "is for your attack on me. From the back, eh coward?" The man didn't deny it as the grip to his groin again seared unbearable pain through his body. Melbroke and William finally released him. He doubled over, his legs so weak he collapsed to his knees, hands still tied.

"Remember me, cur. If I ever hear that you've hurt or mistreated a woman again, whore or not, you'll have me to deal with." Melbroke bellowed, kicking the man over on to the dung-littered floor. "And do something about these stables, employ an ostler you stinking puttock, horses shouldn't be in such disgraceful conditions."

The man remained silent. Fear and pain had the better of him. By the time he had the strength to look up Melbroke and William were gone. They both assumed the ironworks in question was Pensel, the Earl's own works in the northern reaches of his estate. It had to be! Melbroke knew the way. Suddenly he felt elated, soon he would have a certain courageous, infuriating little vixen back with her pack.

BELLOWES, HAVING drunk far too much brandy was resting in one of Blean's many guest rooms. He was strewn unceremoniously across the bed, his boots still on, just as Gates had thrown him. The Earl was slumbering in his study, one ear alert for the knock on the door that would bring the ransom demand.

He'd been thinking about his wife and how like her Frances had become. Every time fears for his daughter's safety swept through him he raised his glass to his wife in heaven. "Keep her safe my sweet, keep her safe," he'd say, out loud to the empty room, swallowing hard to remove the lump of emotion that felt like iron in his throat. His heart jumped when he heard the bang on the door and he was on his feet in seconds. Melbroke and William entered.

"Any news?"

"Yes my Lord," said Melbroke, smiling for the first time in what seemed an age. "We're on to them. Means, there'll be no ransom note and we'll have to act quickly." Melbroke rightly assumed that the innkeeper, having knocked him out, would have hastily gone to his cohorts and warned them. "But we know where she is. She's being held captive at Pensel, we believe Bellowes' wife is with her."

"Good grief! Good God! So close to us! Right, well we must go..."

"No, my Lord," interrupted William, putting a sympathetic hand on his father-in-law's shoulder. "You know that would not be wise."

The Earl sighed. "Lucifer's curses! This growing old is a trial and no mistake. All right," he huffed, "I'll play the woman and sit here and wait."

THE NOISE outside had been going on for quite a while. She could hear several men's voices and passed some time trying to differentiate and count them. She thought three, mayhap four. Jasper's she recognized, the others' she didn't. Then she could smell food, her stomach yearned. Her mouth was now so dry from thirst it felt as though her tongue had swollen. She was also experiencing sudden, short bouts of dizziness.

Then came the scraping and dragging and the sound of heavy things being dropped from a great height. Intermittently there was heaving and the sound of boots on cold stone and orders being given and men calling. Each sound stabbed her still-aching head. Then the strange noise came. Roaring, strong, relentless. Then the acrid smell, the like she had never known. So pungent it caught her breath and she coughed to clear her throat.

Alys grew more fearful. "What are they doing?" Panic was in the fat woman's eyes and Frances had to confess that she had no idea.

Two strange men, built like bulls with huge shoulders and massive, grimy hands fetched them just as the sun was inching to the horizon. They picked up the rotund Alys by her shoulders and feet and in sheer fright she collapsed into a limp, shaking, lump. She was taken into the adjoining forest and tied securely to a tree.

"And you, bitch," Jasper hurled at Frances, his shrew-like face pressing up against hers, "are going to meet your maker."

"I thought you were going to sell me?"

"Seems no one wants to buy you."

"I don't believe you, my father would certainly have paid a ransom," she said, her mind racing. Wouldn't Alban too? Mayhap he didn't love her after all. Mayhap whatever love he'd had turned to hate when she rejected him. She forced her mind away from such thoughts, her survival was paramount and suddenly a different agony was drowning her.

"Nope. Neither your father nor your poxy lover want you back," he growled, managing a sneer of contempt as his growl turned to a hollow laugh. "Seems you're not worth anything to anyone, certainly not to me."

Panic was setting in. Jasper took a short knife to slash the rope that held her ankles. "What are you going to do with me?" He ignored her. He pulled her roughly from the floor and shoved her outside. She staggered and nearly fell. She looked around. Now she knew what the noise and smell were about. An imposing stone tower, at least twenty foot tall was belching out smoke and soot and occasional sparks. The roar of the flames raging on the inside was deafening. It was the Pensel iron works. So close to home, yet so far.

"I've got this dilemma, you see," he mocked sarcastically, grabbing her from behind, his hands like iron grips on her shoulders, his mouth against her ear. "I've got this huge furnace over here, all burning and ready to go but I've got no iron ore to throw into it

’cos I was tricked. The flames are hungry, you’ll have to do.”

Frances had never seen the usually effete Jasper so fired up. Suddenly his usual weak body had found its strength.

“You’re not going to to...”

“Well yes, I am actually,” he hissed, roughly turning her around so she faced him, his eyes more piercing than ever. “You have wrecked my family. My brother is dead, our finances in ruin, we’ve had to sell our lands and all because of you, bitch,” he snarled, his hot, foul breath forcing her to turn her face away. He grabbed it back. “Turn away from me would you, the whore who likes being touched by anyone. Got fussy all of a sudden have you,” and with that he planted his mouth on hers. With all her energy she slammed a knee into his crotch sending him reeling. She grabbed her moment and ran.

THE ACRID smell and thunderous noise surrounded Melbroke and William as they approached Pensel. They galloped to within a few hundred yards then dismounted. They checked their weapons. Melbroke ran his sword several times in and out of its scabbard to check its ease for quick use. He tried to flex his injured hand, it was a little easier but only a little. His head still ached but Margaret’s draught was largely quelling the pain. He checked his boots for knives, pushed the small axe even more firmly into his belt. William made similar checks. Then they headed into the trees, using the noise of the furnace as the destiny they headed toward.

They had to tread carefully. The afternoon sun was struggling with the trees’ thick canopy and very little light reached the forest floor. Each man broke off a long tree branch and used it to test the ground as, with care, they made their way over the deep undergrowth. Before each step they prodded between fern and bramble, checking for firmness and for the cruel animal traps that could abound in a place like this. Every so often an animal would call a warning to its clan or a bird would screech its alarm as two humans invaded its territory.

Slowly the clearing came into view and they stopped to survey the situation. The furnace was close to a hill and a long wooden walkway ran from the hill's side to the open mouth at the top of the furnace. Steps had been gouged into the hillside and reinforced with wooden treads so that whoever was feeding the furnace could easily go up the hillside, along the walkway to its mouth.

Today, as Melbroke and William watched, it was two huge bull-like men who moved with great urgency, taking it in turns to lumber huge baskets of wood and charcoal. Up and down they worked, their hard, bulging thighs and calves negotiating the steep steps two at a time. As they tipped their baskets into the furnace's mouth they jumped back as it belched sooty smoke and sparks. They had been at their work for some time and already their faces were blackened, their huge hands, too.

For a few seconds Melbroke and William watched from the darkness of the trees. The cover was good, it gave them time to study the scene. Suddenly their thoughts were invaded by a human voice. It sounded like a cry for help and it rang through the trees again and again.

"Did you hear that?"

William nodded. "Where from?"

"Over here," Melbroke called, having already turned to their right.

Alys Bellowes, her eyes now well accustomed to the forest gloom, had seen the two well-dressed, elegant men and decided to risk calling. They were by her side in seconds. Her plump body was well trussed to the tree, her double chins quivered as she spoke, her grey hair curled around her forehead, her hazel eyes were round and strained, her chin dimpled - all just as Bellowes had described.

"Are you Alys Bellowes?" Melbroke asked tenderly, smiling his friendship, hopefully convincing her that all was now well. She nodded. "I is. And pray who are you?"

William took his knife and began cutting her from the tree. "I am Lord Runmore, son-in-law of the Earl of Blean."

"Heaven be praised," she whispered to herself, rubbing her wrists then her ankles to restore circulation.

"I am Lord Melbroke but please, is the Lady Frances here?"

"She is my Lord. Last I saw her she was in that building over there," and she pointed to the forge. With the men's help she made it to her feet.

"Please, take yourself deeper into the forest and wait," Melbroke said, holding her firm as she found again the use of her numb legs. "This situation is going to turn very nasty, take yourself to safety until 'tis over."

She nodded. "I understands my Lords, I shall do as you bids and no mistake."

FRANCES HAD only made a few paces before Jasper grabbed her from behind and wrestled her to the ground, forcing her face down, her head against the still-hot stones of the men's fire where only minutes earlier they had been cooking rabbit. The stones banged and grazed her forehead.

He straddled her waist and laughed haughtily. "Now, this is a nice position we find ourselves in, isn't it? Shame Pierre, your beloved, never got this close." He began running his hands over her back and up over her neck. She felt his weight lessen slightly as he leant forward to nuzzle her hair, she quickly lifted her bottom and nearly succeeded in pushing him off. She was just turning on to her hip when he regained his balance, grabbed her arms and savagely turned her over, slamming her back on to the ground and re-straddling her. "An even better position," he snarled, leering over her.

"Jasper, this isn't you," she said, desperately trying to appeal to the gentleman within. "You don't behave like this."

"Neither did my brother but look what you drove him to! Perhaps I should take my revenge in his name." And with that he lifted her head up to his, licked her lips, then threw her head back down again. It caught the edge of a boulder and suddenly she knew no more. He had knocked her unconscious for a second time. Perfect, he thought, no more trouble from you and with that he hoisted her over his shoulder and headed for the furnace.

He was just turning on to the high, wooden walkway when Melbroke and William spotted him. They'd been to the forge and found it empty, save one of her boots. "She's still trying to help us," Melbroke said, looking all around for more trails.

Then a noise, coming from above his head, made him turn to the furnace. "Look!" He pointed to the walkway, twenty feet in the air. "He's got her up there." He was having to shout in competition with the furnace. "She's slung over his shoulder, see how the sun catches her hair. 'Tis Frances all right!" With that he made to race to the steps in the hillside. Suddenly, two giants of men appeared from behind the charcoal store and second guessing his intention, barred his way. William was by Melbroke's side in a flash.

"Which one are you taking?" William shouted, a dagger already in his hand.

"Neither," screeched back Melbroke, his eyes flitting from

the men to the Marquis who was getting closer to the furnace's mouth by the second. "He's going to throw Frances into the furnace, I've got to get to her. Can you take them both?"

"Yes but help me get them away from the steps."

With that both Lords drew their swords, the bulls drew daggers from the back of their belts and slowly the four faced each other, two on two. Stoney eyes glared, unblinking, intense. Rigid jaws, set foreheads. The bulls growled like trussed dogs, the Lords remained calm, instinct kicking in. They jabbed and teased, the bulls responded with clumsy thrusts, unaware they were being manipulated. As soon as Melbroke and William had successful turned them in a circle and the steps were clear, Melbroke thrust his sword back into its sheath and raced up the hillside's steps to the walkway.

William immediately turned and ran into the forest. The two men, not trained fighters and with no battle strategy, followed him. Good, he thought, looking behind and seeing they hadn't the sense to divide and follow a quarry each. Both bulls tore into the forest after William who could now use the trees as cover.

Melbroke was up the hillside and on to the walkway in seconds and could see that Frances was showing not a flicker of life. His heart leapt. Was she dead? Was Jasper destroying the evidence?

"What have you done to her, you whoreson," he screeched.

The Marquis turned on the spot. "Get back or I'll kill you, too."

Melbroke edged toward Jasper slowly, the heat of the furnace touching his skin. A hostile world above another. A roaring lion threatening to kill; smokey air ready to choke; a narrow walkway that could be a wire. One small step at a time. He didn't want a fight, it could be perilous, not least for Frances, if she were still alive. A fall from this height would certainly kill her should the Marquis drop or throw her. The mouth of the furnace was belching again, the heat intensified. She'd be ashes in no time if he succeeded in his intent.

"'Tis all right Jasper," he yelled, trying to beat the noise of the furnace. "I just want to talk."

"Talk! You're the last person I want to talk to!"

Even across the distance between them Melbroke could read his disdain. "If you fight, you die and your mother loses her only remaining son. Would you do that to her?"

"Take me for a fool! If I live I shall be executed anyway."

"Why? You've not raped nor killed anyone...have you?" Melbroke was almost frightened of the answer.

"None of your business," the now hoarse voice shouted back. "But if I live it will mean I killed you!"

Melbroke struggled to reassure. He was inching his way along the walkway very slowly but there was still a big gap between them. "You're only guilty of conspiring to defraud at the moment. Don't add murder!"

"You're the King's cousin," Jasper howled. "You'd have your way."

"I wouldn't want an innocent man executed. I promise you that."

Jasper stood rigid, staring at him, thinking, the relentless noise bruising his ears, the finale of this moment his to decide. Melbroke sensed the weakness. "Give me Lady Frances," he pleaded. "If she is alive, you won't die. You have my word."

"Trust you? I don't think so!"

"You have no choice. Test my patience much longer and I shall run my sword through you." Melbroke yanked his weapon from its sheath. He could see hesitation in the Marquis' demeanour, he grabbed his chance. "Step twelve paces forward and lay her down," he ordered, his voice now grating in his throat, "then return back to where you are now."

"And I will live?"

"If she's alive, yes, you have my word. Twelve paces. Now!"

For a few more seconds the Marquis agonized. The furnace belched its anger, sooty smoke swirled around his shrew-like features. Melbroke was on tenterhooks, searching for a sign of life in Frances but seeing none. After what seemed an eternity the Marquis walked towards Melbroke, stopped halfway and lay Frances down, as he'd been commanded.

IN THE forest William, using the trees as cover, had successfully dispatched one of the men who had fought like a raging beast. The power of his body had been colossal, his weight alone had almost beaten William but in the end his lumbering had been his downfall and the experienced swordsman won the day. He now lay like a fallen stag in the undergrowth.

The second man was just as heavy and had backed off when a blow from William's sword had almost severed his forearm. He was bleeding profusely but seeing the demise of his friend he was now facing William anew, vengeance firing him, a long blade in each hand. Rage was making him act madly and he kept surging toward William, prepared it seemed to risk William's sword to his torso. He too lumbered, his bovine frame denying him agility, he was no real threat to William but he was trying to take him alive, for the Sheriff.

In a sudden unexpected move the man lunged forward, caught William's sword arm making him drop the weapon and lose his balance. As he fell backwards and knowing the forest would give him a soft landing, he pulled a knife from his belt and before his attacker realized what was happening, he thrust it upwards into the groin that was hovering above him. If 'tis good enough for the Romans, William said to himself, knowing that severing a groin artery was one of their preferred methods of killing, 'tis good enough for me! The bull collapsed to his knees, William rolled over so as not to be crushed and within seconds was on his feet, his sword back in his hand. Sadly, there would now be two dead witnesses.

MELBROKE CARRIED Frances back down to the ground. At one point she groaned, his heart soared but she remained semi-unconscious. He laid her on the lower slope of the hill and waited for Jasper to descend. The Marquis took his time. He stood for quite a while on the walkway, occasionally collapsing his head into his hands. It crossed Melbroke's mind that mayhap he was going to throw himself off but he didn't. In due course he slowly made his way back across the walkway to the hill then down the treads. His shoulders rounded, his feet heavy. It was the walk of a defeated man.

When Melbroke's face was level with the Marquis' chest he grabbed him and suspending him in mid-air thrust him against one of the enormous sturdy oak supports of the walkway. His injured hand protested vigorously, the pain scorched up his arm but his adrenalin was overloading and gave him strength.

"I am a man of honour you scab of hell," he hissed at Jasper's startled face, "unlike any man in your miserable family. Now, this is the deal..."

"You don't know what honour is you philandering dog," Jasper spat back, his eyes darting in angry defeat. "There's no deal, I care not what happens to me now."

Melbroke slammed the Marquis' back repeatedly against the oak beam. "Be quiet you querulous ninny. You get on your horse and you ride to France, right now, do you understand me?"

Jasper stared back blankly.

"Do you understand?"

The Marquis nodded. He was bewildered. He had assumed he would be handed over to a sheriff.

"I said you won't die and I will keep my word but you leave England now and you never return. Never! Do you understand?"

"You're letting me go?" The defeated man was astounded.

"No, never! I shall never forget what you have done. Never forget what you put the Earl through and his family! And me! Never! You will never be a free man, the stain of guilt will always be upon you. But if you never set foot in England again at least you will keep your pathetic life. Do you understand?" Again he jabbed the flimsy body repeatedly against the harsh, oak prop.

"I understand," Jasper hissed, his head dropping on to his chest.

"As soon as you get to France you write to the Kent Sheriff and withdraw this ridiculous accusation of murder. Do you understand?" The Marquis nodded.

"Say it cur," demanded Melbroke.

"I understand," came the whisper.

There was so much more Melbroke wanted to say but he didn't want to waste time. His priority now was getting Frances safely home. He threw the Marquis into the air and watched him land several feet away. For a few seconds he twisted on the ground, groaning.

"You know what you've got to do," Melbroke shouted.

The Marquis picked himself up and made for his horse.

"If I ever see you in England or learn that you are here, I

shall kill you. Do you understand?"

The Marquis didn't turn, nor speak, he just raised his arm in a defeated, accepting manner. Melbroke watched as he mounted his horse and turned it away from the sun toward the East. He was heading for Dover. Good!

WILLIAM ESCORTED a weeping Alys Bellowes out of the forest and joined Melbroke who was sitting by Frances' side, stroking her forehead, encouraging her to speak. She groaned from time to time, turned her head on the soft grass but never fully regained consciousness. He could see the gash on her head, the dried blood, her matted hair. There were scratches and emerging bruises on her face, raw welts around her wrists and ankles that bled occasionally. She had struggled, it made him proud! It also increased his hatred of those concerned, including himself. "She's been knocked unconscious," he said, looking up at William who was now standing over them. "You all right?"

"Yes, fine. The two men aren't though, they're both dead."

"Good."

"I thought a witness might have come in handy?"

"As far as I'm concerned the fewer witnesses the better. Everyone's dead now except the wretched Frenchman Blanc and the Marquis who I've told never to set foot in England again on pain of his life."

"Blanc's no trouble, he doesn't know the bigger picture. He only knows about the iron works."

"Exactly, we can use the greasy quisling to make sure the two Marquises names are truly blackened, as they damn well should be. He'll say what we tell him the weakling, he will actually be useful."

Melbroke looked around the iron works, weighing up their current situation. One unconscious woman, one near-hysterical woman, his injured hand now throbbing mercilessly and a sinking sun. A cart stood in a corner. "Could you drive that back to Blean House?"

"Put the women in it you mean?"

"Yes, my hand's too painful to manage either on my horse. And anyway Frances needs help as soon as possible. I'll go straight to Canterbury for the apothecary, you take them back to Blean,"

"Agreed," said William, lifting Frances and carrying her to the cart, Alys Bellowes following like a terrified duckling scampering behind its mother.

Sitting next to his mother, he asked: "Why did you leave us?" They were both on the side of her low, hard bed. "I saw you ride off with another man, a stranger. Your lover?"

"You saw?"

Her face drained. She hadn't known. "No! Not my lover! I loved your father Albie, loved him!" She squeezed her son's hands in new pain. She'd not known he'd been at a window, not known she had left a little boy with thoughts of betrayal.

"Then who was he? And why?"

"My brother Hugh, my mean, ungiving, heartless brother. You had never met him because he would have nothing to do with us. My family were Yorkists Albie, I'm sorry you never knew that but it wasn't something to broadcast in those days. Not when you've fallen in love with the enemy, as I had. Your father was a faithful Lancastrian..."

The son nodded. "Yes and proud of it."

"Indeed and I was proud of him. My parents accepted the

situation and in due course gave us their blessing but my brother never did. He held it against me, refused to attend our wedding. As far as he was concerned it was the worst thing I could have done, he saw it as a personal betrayal."

"He put you in here?"

She nodded, tears now glistening in the candlelight. "Lancastrian thugs, certainly not men Harri Tudor would have been associated with, raped Hugh's wife then murdered her. He took out his grief and hatred of all Lancastrians on me, his traitor sister. Why should I be happy with my Lancastrian husband when his loyal Yorkist wife was no more? He came that night and took me away."

"But why didn't father fight him? Why!"

"Because you would have been killed if he did. Hugh would have slit your throat."

Alban threw back his head and looked at the dark, miserable ceiling.

She gripped his hands. "We both acted to save our dear, beloved son. Your father was not a weak man, Albie, never think that. He was strong and generous. He loved you. He did what he had to, to save you. We both did."

They sat quietly together both reeling as they considered the brutality that had crossed their family, their lives. Such misery had been rife across the land with Lancastrian and Yorkist slaughtering, raping, maiming each other, be it on the battlefield or in the towns and villages. The wars had ripped families apart and at that bleak, misty dawn it ripped apart theirs.

Alban's heart ached but these were sweet words that began to answer so many questions. Words he never thought he'd ever hear.

"I have lived all these years believing you abandoned us, that you preferred another man to father, that we meant nothing to you," he said, swallowing back emotion.

"Never. I have loved you and your father every day of my life. I have never stopped loving you." She cupped his face in her hands. "I have held your faces in my mind's eye all this time but of course, I didn't know what you now looked like. I've remembered you as a boy but what a fine man you are, your father is very proud of you, I am sure?"

"Father died when I was 16. I think from heartbreak, he never got over you leaving."

She hung her head low and emitted a few soft cries as she allowed the tears to tumble. She would never see him again, then. Not in this life. "Life is so painful, Albie. Be sure to take whatever happiness you can. Grab it with both hands."

The dying day turned to night as they sat together, sometimes holding hands, sometimes he with his arms around her. Occasionally one would speak, sometimes the other. Occasionally Alban lifted his hand to his mother's cheek and stroked her soft skin. Her eyes sparkled with love and he recognized their warmth. He had oft wondered if dying wouldn't have been preferable to the loneliness and abandonment he had lived with since he was ten. Now, though, a small voice in his head reminded him that if that had been the case he wouldn't now be experiencing such joy.

As the rising moon lit the tiny cell, they smiled. Together they would discover each other again, for however long God gave them.

Chapter Twenty-three

BROTHER THOMAS ARRIVED under an artist's sky. The day's light was sinking in beauty and cyan was turning to violet as the sun's golden rays made a halo in the sky.

"Brother, you are becoming quite a regular visitor," Gates joked, on seeing him once again at Blean's door.

"Indeed I am. And as a regular may I be so bold as to ask for a glass of wine, it has been a demanding day."

The monk shuffled in, his body weary, his breathing heavy. Summer heat was not his friend and the past days had been getting hotter.

"Indeed Brother, his Lordship insists."

The apothecary examined Frances by soft candlelight. She was slowly regaining consciousness although still drifting fitfully in and out. He advised bed rest for the foreseeable future, a poultice for the head wound and liniment for the bruising. He would also leave a potion for pain for when she regained full consciousness.

Margaret had tended the raw grazing on her wrists and ankles, bed linen now hiding them from his view. Brother Thomas was told the patient had fallen from a horse. He left something for shock. Her father and sister were by her bedside. He would return on the morrow.

He re-examined William's chest. It was still very inflamed, still raw in parts and causing distress which the patient hid. The Brother applied more unguent, a fresh bandage and warned that there would almost certainly be scaring. He left new supplies for Margaret to apply thrice daily, more painkilling draught and something to steady the patient's sudden bouts of shivering.

He hadn't asked how the injury occurred, it wasn't his place to pry but his experience shouted 'fighting'. He also left fresh remedies for Melbroke who had dallied in Canterbury and was also under the monk's shadow of 'fighting'. He drank his wine and welcomed the few morsels of food that came with it. Within the hour he was heading back into the evening, early stars now decorating the canopy above.

He stood for a moment and took the warm air, surveyed the scene. The magnificent house, the shapes of the landscape looming up from the rich Kent soil, the snake of a silver stream heading to the coast. He thanked the Lord for steering his journey away from battlefields to this beauty. He felt blessed as his nostrils caught the scent of roses and woodbine, his habit swaying in the welcome, gentle breeze. As he mounted the second of his two dun horses - he had two so as not to continually burden just one with his enormous weight - he wondered how Sister Magdala and her son were getting on. They too had been blessed. God was indeed great.

Upstairs in the house the Bellowes had been reunited. They also had an apothecary's remedy for shock and sleep, Brother Thomas having been told they had been robbed on their way to

Blean. Laying in each other's chubby arms they were now sleeping like children.

The mother asked: "Not married Albie?"

"No. I saw how father suffered, I believed you had caused it by betraying him. I saw how his pining for you cut short his life, I hated you for it, I vowed I would never let a woman treat me that way."

She cupped a hand over his angry fist. Stroked it. She understood his fury; recognized it. They were sitting by her small wooden table. Mother Esme had allowed a second stool be taken to her cell, now she realized a cousin of the King would be visiting.

"My dear son. Love is all that matters. Without love we are all hollow shells. Love enriches everything."

She looked deep into his face and smiled. "I don't believe a good looking man like you isn't popular," she teased. He grinned, averting his eyes from hers. "No modesty Albie, Brother Thomas has told me of your reputation!" She lifted her eyebrows in tender disapproval.

"Good Lord, can a man have no secrets from his mother?"

"Not any more it seems," she said, laughingly poking his chest. "No one special then?"

"I saw women as fair game. If they wanted some fun, so did I. I had no intention of letting any of them get a hold over me." He stopped and looked down into their clasped hands.

"But?"

"Until now. But still I'm not sure."

"Go on."

"She is wonderful, beautiful. My heart was full of love for her. My feelings overcame my reason and I told her so."

"And?"

"She rejected me."

"And you saw that as a second woman hurting you? First your mother then the woman you love."

He nodded. "The agony on father's face came crashing back. I felt I couldn't risk it, couldn't risk such hurt."

"Dearest Albie," she said, turning his chin toward her, reclaiming his eyes. "Women are tender creatures. Your reputation may have bewildered her. She wouldn't have known whether to believe you were being honest with her. Do you think she loves you?"

He nodded. "Later she told me she did...but O, I don't know..." His gaze went to the tiny window, he could see only sky.

"You must take a risk," she urged, squeezing his hand. "You must! If you truly love her and she loves you, you can't let this slip away."

She ran her hands over his strong chest, his arms, his shoulders. "Look how strong God has made you. You fight for your King without a second thought but Albie, life is a battle, too. The difference is that in life it is surrender that is the conqueror. Victory isn't about winning, 'tis about accepting and trusting. I have lived for twenty years with a broken heart, my dear son, the pain is indescribable."

"I know, I already know."

"'Tis true Albie, that you can only lose what you have but what kind of life would it be to have nothing. You have to trust. You must trust your love and learn to trust hers. If you truly love each other then 'tis God's will."

"Mayhap I'm afraid to love."

She nodded. "'Tis understandable because you didn't know the truth about me but now you do. I didn't abandon you, my dear son, I was taken from you. Don't let my brother win Albie. Be happy. For me, be happy."

There was an urgency in her eyes as she looked up into his. She clung to his arm and rested her head on his shoulder. "It wasn't love that caused your father's pain, nor mine. It was loss of love. We were wonderfully happy together, it was the loss that was unbearable. Don't lose her, don't inflict more pain upon yourself that you will never be free of."

Her words rang true. He knew they did. He also now realized how brave Frances had been in visiting his room, speaking to him as she had. O, how he now wished he had responded. Fool! Fool! He smiled and kissed his mother's cheek. "I shall bring her to meet you. If she still wants me!"

"I pray she will. Make it soon, I long to meet her."

For a few moments he held her. Embraced the soft, comforting figure that once he hated but now loved. He helped her lay down and pulled the wafer-thin blanket over her. She shouldn't be living like this, he was thinking as he moved the candle so it didn't shine in her eyes. He kissed her forehead as she drifted into a deep, contented sleep. New-found happiness saw to that, so to Brother Thomas who was slowly increasing the strength of her painkilling draught.

NEVER HAD Blean House been such a welcome sight and Melbroke smiled the broadest of grins as he turned into its long driveway. He went straight to Frances' room. "How is she?"

The Earl grunted and stood up. "Outside!" The two men regrouped on the gallery. "What's been done to her? How did she get into this state?"

"She is as we found her, surely William has explained?"

The Earl nodded. "He has. But 'tis most unsatisfactory. Do we know if she's been..."

"No, I'm sure not," he interjected, his stomach sickening at even the thought. "For all his myriad faults I don't think Jasper has it in him to do that."

"What about the other men, two enormous buggers William says."

"They wouldn't have acted without the Marquis' permission."

"But her clothes are torn, there are marks on her legs and arms, she's been manhandled as well as tied up!"

"According to the landlord of The Sun, the place where they first kept her, she put up a struggle. They tried to give her drugged wine, to keep her quiet, she refused to drink it. Kicked and punched apparently."

"That's my girl! Always has had spirit," the Earl smiled, relief palpable on his face. "And is this business all over? For pity's sake tell me it is!"

"Not quite my Lord. We need to know why all this has happened. Why were you cheated? Why was Pierre and latterly his brother, so determined to ruin you?"

"Well, why? Come on, spit it out."

"I hope to be able to make everything clear very soon but I must ask for your continued patience, I want to be sure of my facts. I have more information on its way to me."

The Earl looked deflated. "Very well, I can wait, getting used to the infernal waiting game! I just want Frances well, that's my priority right now." He made to go back into her bedchamber.

"My Lord, one other thing," Melbroke said, leaning toward the Earl's ear. "May I have a private word with you?"

"My study. In an hour. And by the by, thank you," he said, slapping the young Lord's back. "Thank you for all you've done and for bringing her back safely. I don't know what I'd have done without you and William. Two fine men and no mistake."

A certain guilt filled Melbroke's thoughts as he headed for the hot bath Gates had arranged. He was partly to blame after all, for some of it at least.

EXACTLY ONE hour later saw a changed man entering the Earl's study. Being reunited with his mother had done that. He hadn't been abandoned. He hadn't grown up unloved. His mother hadn't deserted his father for another man. Suddenly his heart had lost a tightness that had been with him for so long he thought it normal. Suddenly he felt free. He, life, the world, had changed. Suddenly it was a kinder, richer place. As his mother had said, God had brought them back together, he must honour Him by being the strong man He had made him. He would take his mother's advice and trust his newly-found heart.

Unfamiliar nerves were in the pit of his stomach for he knew the Earl to be a stickler for protocol and procedure. He didn't want to put a foot wrong. The Earl was behind his desk, Melbroke approached and bowed.

"What do you want? I'm tired, get on with it," the Earl ordered, shuffling some untidy parchments into a pile.

"My Lord, I come to ask for the hand of Lady Frances in marriage."

The Earl looked up, astonishment on his face. "I had no idea you and she were..."

"We aren't my Lord. I confess, there was a time when I wasn't sure she even liked me but I can no longer deny my feelings and I seek your permission to speak with her." He was saying words he never dreamt he would ever utter. For strength he kept his mother's face in his mind's eye.

The Earl stood up and walked around his desk toward Melbroke. "Your family's first class, the Bleans would be honoured to be united with the Melbrokes..."

The nervous Lord nodded a shallow bow, sensing that a 'but' was coming. He was right. His reputation went before him. He'd a scandalous past and he knew the Earl knew. "You've the reputation of a rakehell, how do we know we can trust you?"

Melbroke shuffled, ran his fingers around the pleated shirt collar that he now wished he'd instructed his tailor to make looser. He was uncomfortable, he knew the Earl spoke the truth. A silence filled the room as the Earl waited.

"I have never loved before," Melbroke said quietly, realizing the future happiness of his life spun on this moment. "My pursuit of lust was hollow and meaningless, I realize that now. I shall never return to those ways."

He had spent time, as he'd soaked his aching body, in anticipating a father's questions. He'd shaped his replies carefully but now the moment was here it was far more difficult than he'd imagined. He coughed, cleared his throat. "I love your daughter. I shall honour and cherish her and any family we may have. I shall never betray her." He meant every word and could only pray that his sincerity rang clear.

Blean remained silent, watching the shadows from the candelabra on his desk flicker over his papers. Melbroke shuffled. The Earl looked up into the taller man's eyes, held his gaze as if trying to search the young Lord's soul.

"Me wife and I married for love, Melbroke. My slate wasn't exactly clean. I do understand the sentiments you have expressed. Love changes everything." For a few moments he didn't speak. Melbroke's heart was thumping. Eventually the old man smiled. "The Alban I have got to know over past months is a fine man," he said, slapping both Melbroke's upper arms hard. "I shall hold you to the words you have just spoken and trust that you truly mean them."

"I do my Lord."

"I give the permission you seek but I won't tell me daughter whom she should marry. It must be her choice. If she wants you as husband you will have me blessing."

"Thank you, my Lord," said a relieved Melbroke, bowing low, "'tis all I ask."

"Now go," said the Earl. "I need sleep and plenty of it."

Just as Melbroke opened the door the Earl called out. "I take it this means you won't be leaving us on the morrow...for France?"

"No, my Lord. I hope I will never be leaving."

ON A beach near Dover a beaten brother kicked stone. Beaten, distraught, desolate. His life at its nadir; his name blackened; his future bleak. In the dark of the midnight hour he stood with the flame he had taken from the inn where he awaited the boat that would take him to exile. He could see little. The moon was hidden by cloud, his torch illuminating just the few feet around him. The tide was high, too high, its undercurrents too unpredictable. The captain wouldn't be sailing yet. The thud of waves on shingle filled his ears. Sleep wouldn't be his this miserable night.

He had only what he stood up in. That and the little money he'd gained by selling his horse and its paraphernalia. Once in France he would write the most difficult letter of his life. To his mother in Mortlake. He would tell of his failure, his humiliation, his crimes. He would tell her that the family name was ruined and what they still owned would need to be sold to pay off remaining debts.

That she may never wish to see him again was a certainty to him. He knew himself not to be loveable, not even likeable. Possibly, now, not even by his mother.

Shingle flew into the air as he rammed his boot into a drift. Flew high and landed like a cackling crone. His foot bore his anger while indignation began to fill his mind. His raging thoughts began to take new form. There was another world the other side of the blackness he now stared in to. Plenty of wealthy, single women there, even widows. France would be his salvation, not this miserable dank country with its stews and ales and mists that sapped the very life force. Mayhap he would model himself on Pierre. Improve his sword arm, become a better horseman, copy his brother's skills in small talk, discover music and dance. There again, mayhap not. Pierre had natural strength and much charm. He had neither.

All he had were his title and his wits. They would have to work for him. They would be his salvation. He would get to France and make new plans. This time next year he would have a wife. She may not be pretty. She may be the one woman no one else wanted but by hell's pains she would be wealthy. He would sell the status of Marchioness to the fullest pockets and one day he would laugh again.

Chapter Twenty-four

LAWYER JARRETT HAD several pieces of news when Melbroke visited him in Canterbury a few days later. Together they shed the final pieces of light on the why, who and when of what had been going on.

Firstly, the London surveyor had responded immediately to Jarrett's request for clarification. He confirmed that the negative report was the correct one and his urgent missive revealed a professional man now angrily concerned for his own reputation. He requested the lawyer urgently appraise him of how his accurate report could have been changed. He also gave the name of the post-horse company he had employed. It was based in Southwark.

Jarrett was preparing his reply, explaining that it had to be assumed the reports had been switched somewhere between Southwark and Canterbury, when Melbroke arrived. Over small ale the two men discussed the situation as the noonday sun bore down on the cathedral city and the temperature in Jarrett's office rose to near unbearable.

It was obvious to Melbroke who was behind the switch. Lord Pierre. He'd wanted to trick the Earl into a contract then sue him for fraud and theft when no iron was found. Melbroke even doubted the wisdom of spending more time and energy in bothering to find out exactly how it was done.

The bona fide report, they knew, travelled in a post-horse saddlebag from Southwark to Canterbury in January, on Twelfth Night to be precise. Someone was probably paid to steal it and replace it with the forgery. No, he'd leave it there. No need to lose a rider his job or sully the reputation of a perfectly good post-horse company.

Secondly, Jarrett had a reply from France to the investigations that Melbroke had commissioned him to make some weeks earlier. Melbroke's friend, Lord Hal, part of the English delegation in Paris, had given him the name of a good French investigative lawyer and he'd had Jarrett write to him. The 'why' of all this had always been baffling.

Why attack the Earl? Why wish to rob him of his reputation and standing in English society? Why ruin him? The surveyor's report predated Melbroke's visits to Frances' rooms at Richmond Palace, so it couldn't just be about romantic revenge. That had come later. There had to be more. The searches in France were to provide the final answers.

Jarrett explained: "When the old Marquis died he left the family in deep financial troubles. He had been a feckless man who put pleasure afore responsibility. He drank, gambled, took expensive mistresses. Pierre, the new Marquis, inherited a lot of problems."

"And he thought to marry himself out of them!" Melbroke interrupted the lawyer's flow as a flash of sudden illumination filled his thoughts.

"Exactly," said Jarrett. "The Earl's daughter became his target." Anger was rising within Melbroke as he sipped the ale Jarrett's man had brought. July was sticky and clammy, this day hinted at a storm, neither man was comfortable. The small window allowed some air but little circulated in this stuffy room with its walls of parchment and vellum piles and dust of years. He was grateful for the drink and emptied it quickly.

Jarrett knocked a small bell for replenishments and continued: "He chose his bride carefully. Not just titled, wealthy and pleasing on the eye but she had no brothers. All the Blean wealth would be divided between her and her sister."

"What a perfect plan. Dastardly but perfect. And heaven knows what fate might have befallen the Runmores and their children. Why stop at half the money!"

"Quite."

Melbroke stood. Went to the window for air. His brow glistening. "And to think it was my family Jasper accused of financial ruin! It was his all along!"

"There's something else. Lord Hal made some local enquiries of his own, made a point of discovering what gossip there was about the family."

"And?"

"Lord Pierre was not the new Marquis, Jasper was."

"Good Lord!"

"Pierre was seven years older than Jasper. He was the Marchioness' son by her first marriage. Two years after her husband's death she married the then Marquis, they had a son, Jasper, the weak, unattractive one."

"And they swapped roles because the handsome Pierre would secure a better bride and a better financial outcome would result."

"In the absence of any other explanation we must assume that. And the old Marquis didn't die last year he died two years ago, so they've been plotting for a long while."

"Christ's pains!" Melbroke reclaimed his chair and sipped more ale. He took a few moments to mull over the new information. "They must have been really desperate if Jasper was prepared to relinquish his title to his half-brother."

"Indeed. The lawyer in Paris has confirmed that the Marchioness has already sold most of her lands, they would seem to be struggling to hold on to the house."

"They would have bled Lady Frances dry."

"It doesn't bare thinking about my Lord. The whole family would have been ruined, possibly even been in personal danger." The potential ramifications of the plot, had it succeeded, were indeed horrendous. "What I don't understand," continued Jarrett, "is why they would accuse you of murder?"

Melbroke stood to leave, scraping his chair on the floor. Only himself, Frances, William and Margaret knew the reason for that and he had no intentions of increasing the number. "No idea, Jarrett. Mayhap it was simply that the plot was failing, Pierre was dead, Jasper was struggling to cope alone. Mayhap he just lashed out in anyway he could. 'Twill blow over, I'm not too worried about it. Not now."

THE PAST week had seen Frances much recovered despite the draining heatwave and over-protective flapping from her father. Brother Thomas, sweating like the pigs he loved to eat, had called daily. No one in the house knew that he also brought messages and gifts from mother to son. Her first gift had been her wedding ring. A gold band with a large inset ruby that had been taken from her on entry to the convent. She had demanded Mother Esme return it and Mother, now aware of Magdala's status, did so immediately.

"Your calling was obviously divine providence Sister," Mother had insisted, on handing back the ring. Magdala's eyebrows lifted questioningly. "The ruby, represents the blood of Christ, He brought you to us."

Magdala didn't reply. It was human revenge that brought me here, she was thinking, there was nothing divine about it! Esme would never know the truth.

It seemed an age since Frances had plucked up every ounce of her courage and told Alban she loved him. Now he'd gone again. He was in London and she was worried. Now almost fully recovered, her thoughts returned to the fact he hadn't said he still loved her. The sinking feeling in the pit of her stomach was back. Was he with the redhead? The thought she may have lost him haunted her. She kept telling herself to put him out of her mind, that he knew where she was if he wanted to talk with her but she couldn't. Again he was stealing her every waking moment.

Margaret and her father had kept a bedside vigil. Before he left Melbroke had called in briefly from time to time but there had been no chance for them to speak privately. She didn't even know if, when, he was returning from London.

Today she was up and fully dressed. The high-summer sun beckoned. The hot days spoke to her of freedom and she wanted to be back in the world enjoying life. From her window she could take in the heavy air, see the bees droning lazily around the flowers, see the ducks on their river squabbling with visiting geese. The water was lower than usual, the dry mud on the sides was caked solid and as the water dropped so the Blean birds became more territorial. Like the land, they wanted rain. The world seemed very still, as though it were sleeping by order of the sun. She wanted to go see for herself. She would take her first ride out, a gentle canter, nothing too strenuous.

Knowing her father wouldn't approve she left the house via the kitchen and was in the stables preparing Lunar when the thud of hooves on hard sun-scorched ground caught her ear. It was Melbroke. He was back!

He swung a high-booted leg over his mount's neck and slid gracefully from the polished saddle. She watched as he led a steaming Galahad through the stable door. She watched as he stroked the horse's head and mumbled soothing words. She watched as he removed the saddle, led Galahad to shade and fetched a net of fresh hay. She watched and weakened. He appeared not to notice her. Her heart was pounding so loudly she thought he must hear it. When he strode to leave she called: "Alban. How are you?"

He turned on the spot and gazed at her. "You're up? Out of bed? You intend riding? Are you sure?"

"I'm sure. I've been going crazy with boredom."

"Now you know how I felt," he said, smiling as he walked toward her. She threw Lunar's saddle over the animal's back.

"Let me do that," he said, taking control, noticing how pale she still looked. His closeness shortened her breath and she took a step back. He bent down to deal with the straps and the sun shone on his thick, chestnut hair, tied back off his face today by black chord. She wanted to reach out and touch him but she didn't. Instead she turned away and took a deep breath. When she turned back he was right by her side, his eyes searching for hers. After what seemed an eternity he stepped even closer and took her in his arms. She pulled back. His face cracked with pain. "You said you loved me. Didn't you mean it?"

"It doesn't matter what I meant, you have your redhead now."

"What are you talking about?" He sighed, throwing his head back in the desperation that she, yet again, sent soaring through his veins.

"The beautiful redhead at the King's celebrations, you couldn't tear yourself away from her."

"Yes, she is very beautiful and yes, I was by her side nearly all of the time..."

"I would understand," she interrupted, "if you had fallen in love with her, what man wouldn't."

"Frances, stop this," he said, clasping her upper arms. "She is the King's current mistress, she was new to Court, I was charged with taking care of her. It was all part of my punishment for dallying here with you for so long. I was King's body guard and then nurse maid! On duty all day! She is nothing to me."

"So if she weren't the King's, you would want her?"

"Stop this. Now! Stop!" His eyes tore into hers. "There's only one thing in the world that matters to me, you said you loved me, did you truly mean it? God's mercy Frances, tell me, I can take this torture no longer!"

"I meant it, of course I meant it," she chided, pulling herself out of his grip. She moved away, his touch weakened her, she needed to keep distance between them. "'Tis you that doesn't love me any more. You didn't say it. You've hardly visited me."

"No more!" He moved quickly back by her side. "No more of this nonsense. I love you with every fibre of my being, I've told you that." He grabbed hold of her and pulled her to him. His mouth was covering hers before she could utter another word and his intensity overcame her. *Release fear, embrace love...*She allowed the words to sweep away any lingering doubt as she surrendered into the place where she wanted to spend the rest of her life. The kiss was long and passionate, his woody smell drowned her senses, his strength overcame hers, they welded into one and her heart sang.

Somewhere in the distance she could hear blackbirds singing, Lunar was scuffing her feet, her father was barking orders. Somewhere else a world was going about its business but right now her world stood still in a glorious embrace that only they could share. Eventually he broke the spell: "Marry me Frances, marry me?"

Her eyes glistened as she looked up into his deep, dark, soft eyes. Her emotions were overflowing, she nodded and wrapped her arms even more tightly around him. He pulled her away: "Please Frances, I need to hear you say it. Will you be my wife?"

"Yes Alban, yes, I will marry you. Yes, yes, yes..." and he needed no more. His lips descended on hers again, his arms enveloped her. Unable to move she was drowning in love and happiness.

They stood holding each other for a few minutes, he kissing her face, feeling her body yield to his. Such softness after so much fighting, so much pain.

"Hadn't you better ask father?"

"Already have."

"What did he say?"

"That if you would take me he would give his blessing."

"I happen to know that he holds you in very high regard."

"And I him but not nearly as much as I do his beautiful, wonderful daughter." And his lips were hers again and their bodies swayed in unison in the afternoon sun that pushed its way through the broad stable door.

William had to cough four times before they heard him. "I assume this means you two have finally realized you love each other."

"Frances has just consented to be my wife."

"Alleluia! Well done you ol' devil," he said, embracing his friend. "And do I have my Lord's permission to kiss the cheek of my sister-in-law?"

"You do my Lord," said Alban, radiant at the sudden ownership he had of the woman he loved.

"You'll need to ask the King," William reminded him.

"Already done that. 'Twas why I went to London," he said grinning, pulling Frances back into his arms. "Went through hell for you, madam," he said, tapping her nose. "Had to stand in a corridor for two days before the King would see me. He was still in foul mood, still holding my late departure to France against me. Threatened to imprison me for lying to his majesty."

"What?" She gasped, anguish in her eyes.

"He decided my injuries were fabricated so I could stay here with you. 'Twas only my arm's fresh scar that saved the day. That and the intervention of the Archbishop of York."

"Wolsey was there?" William was surprised.

"O yes, he's always there these days. Calmed the waters though, told the King his cousin had done good works in France. I was grateful to him for once."

"So, my friend, you've the permission you need?"

Melbroke nodded and beamed.

"I see my Lord has it all organized," Frances teased, looking up into his face.

"Yes, your Lord has," he grinned, "which reminds me. When we are married, your Lord, who by the way has now saved your life twice, says there will be no more of this reckless streak of yours. No more fights, no more midnight outings. Your Lord expects you to obey him."

"O, of course Alban dear, of course," she said, her face alight with happiness. "But don't forget it was my reckless streak that brought the extra sword to the Harwykes' hovel, that threw water and saved William, that got us the name of the cordwainer and gave me the courage to visit your room and tell you I love you."

"Enough, enough!" She was right, he knew that and loved her for it. He would have the last word though. "No riding today, my Lady, 'tis too soon."

As they strolled back to the house William asked. "Will the King be at the wedding?"

"Don't know. He's still not pleased with me, things aren't quite back to normal. I hope so. At least I'm not in the Tower!"

THE FAMILY and Gates gathered in the withdrawing room to hear Melbroke's explanation of events. "About bloody time," the Earl mumbled, as he settled into his favourite chair, his three dogs around him. In his usual way Melbroke's account was succinct, orderly, clear. He told them everything except his history with Frances, only four people would ever know that.

"What a relief," the old man said, allowing his head to loll against the richly-carved chairback, "'tis really over." He swung his legs on to a cushioned stool, one of the dogs rested its chin on his thigh.

"The Marchioness was in on the plot?" Frances asked, quietly. "She must have been, if she agreed that Pierre could claim to be the new Marquis."

Alban nodded. "I'm afraid so. Seems she wasn't the person you thought she was either."

"I can't believe it. She was so lovely, so kind."

"You were her salvation, that's why she was good to you."

"What a terrible family," grunted the Earl. "The whole bloody lot of them. Took me in, fool that I am."

"People do desperate things at desperate times," said Frances, trying to find some Christian charity. "Who knows what any of us might do?"

"You are being too kind," her father snapped. "Me, I'm riddled with guilt that I didn't realize. I was giving them me daughter, happily entrusting you to them," he said, raising his two arms in a helpless gesture towards Frances. "What a fool I've been."

Silence weighed heavy as all present assimilated the news. Everyone, including little Geoffrey and the child Margaret now carried, could have been ruined if the plot had run its course.

"So, not satisfied with the dowry he would have received," an ashen William asked, his arm protectively around Margaret, "Pierre, well the whole family, wanted more...lots more, as soon as possible. They couldn't wait for Frances to inherit."

Melbroke nodded.

"They are drowning in debt, the claimants are taking everything, they saw blackmail as a quick solution. They'd have hoped none of your family would have found out, of course. They were hiding behind the Harwykes. They could have succeeded in blackmail and Pierre could still have married into the family, with potentially even more wealth available to him."

A wave of nausea enveloped Frances, she held on to the arms of her chair. Melbroke continued: "The Champagnes involvement was not intended to be revealed. Me killing Pierre ruined all that, changed the plans completely. Suddenly there was no marriage, no long term future. Then, Jasper came up with the contemptible idea of accusing me of murder, hoping I'd pay to drop the ludicrous charge. More money for them!"

"Then they took Alys Bellowes," Frances added, "poor, poor woman"

"To threaten Bellowes mainly, stop him talking but Jasper

may well have asked for money for her return."

The Earl who had been sitting quietly, taking it all in, was full of contempt and making no effort to hide it. "Let Satan have 'em! The sooner the better!"

The shock of the realization would take a while for them all to deal with. Silence filled the room as five devastated, enraged, pitying souls assimilated how they had been manipulated. How close they had come to disaster, ruin, even death. After a while Melbroke cleared his throat. "Actually my Lord, there's been another, happier development."

The Earl looked up, anger still his master. Frances crossed the room to be by Alban's side. "My Lord, Lady Frances has graciously consented to be my wife."

The father slapped his thigh and almost jumped from his chair. The dog whimpered in objection. "Wonderful! Well done, Alban. Had every faith in you." Margaret hugged her sister. "Gates," bellowed the Earl, "some of the best wine, as soon as you can and some sugar sweets to go with it. Tell cook we'll feast tonight. Let's put this awful business behind us and concentrate on the future. That damnable family can't ruin that now, thank the Lord."

FRANCES HAD a teasing glint in her eyes. "A one-year betrothal then?" They were walking the dogs in the soft, evening light, the Earl having retired, exhausted but happy, straight after the celebratory meal. He was expecting the best night's sleep he'd had in quite a while. The air was still warm and heavy but the dogs were full of energy and the couple watched them bound in and out of the river, scaring the ducks and sending them flying upward and away. Alban stopped dead in his tracks. "One year!"

"I think father may assume that."

"I can't wait one year, not even one week," he insisted.

"A wedding takes a little longer than one week to arrange, my love."

"One month then. With great difficulty I could wait one month."

She slipped her arm back into his and they continued on. "Whatever father says just agree with him. I will talk him round later. And be prepared for him to rant on about your reputation, all your women."

"He already has." Alban took a step in front of her, stopping her in her tracks. He held her by the tops of her arms squeezing her to him. "Frances, I swear to you there are no other women," he said, looking earnestly into her eyes. "None. Never again. You are the only woman for me. If it makes you happy to know I have been with no other woman for months, not since my heart decided to go into turmoil over you." He was grinning from ear to ear. "You changed me, even against my own will, you changed me."

"Not even when you were in France recently?"

"Not even then. I confess I thought about it but I didn't. I've been haunted by this beautiful face," he said, stroking her cheek, "night and day for months. All I want is you," he said, pulling her closer, "and the sooner the better."

"I've thought about you, too, all the time. And I'm sorry I lied to you."

"What about?"

"I did like you coming to my rooms at Richmond, that's why I had to flee. I did want you and I knew if you came to my bedchamber you would overwhelm me."

"Now she tells me!" He grinned again but this time only for a second. A seriousness befell him. "What I was doing was wrong, so very, very wrong but if I'm honest, I am glad of it."

"You are?"

"Of course. If I hadn't been the reason why you fled I wouldn't have felt duty bound to chase after you and I would never have realized I loved you."

"If you put it like that..."

"Let me overwhelm you tonight?" He gathered her into his arms and kissed her neck, her ears, her hair.

She shook her head and blushed. "That blush of yours is going to be the death of me," he groaned. "And why can't I? We are betrothed."

"But not yet married."

"It had better not be a year!"

The stool was rickety but Frances didn't notice. "My lady," she said, sitting opposite Magdala who was perched on the side of her cot. "Alban and I would like you to move to Blean House, spend your last months with us."

Magdala beamed, happiness radiating from her face. "Call me Elizabeth, 'tis my real name."

"Please, Elizabeth, will you come?"

For a moment the old nun looked into her lap, the events of past years racing through her mind. Slowly she shook her head. "No my dear, I will stay here. 'Tis where God brought me, it has been my home and is where I shall be buried."

Alban stepped forward. "Mother, please. At least think about it. We can give you so much more comfort. A decent bed for a start," he said, kicking the leg of her shabby resting place.

"Life is not about comfort Albie. This bed does its job. This blanket warms me, the plain food feeds me, my habit covers me. I have everything I need. Life is about love, it is the only thing that matters in the end," she said, reaching out to take a hand of each of them.

"Finding you Albie and knowing that you have found true love with this beautiful young woman, is all the comfort I need. I shall die happily now. I have peace and contentment, you have both given me that."

"You will come to the wedding?" Frances urged.

"O yes, I would like that," she said, cupping Frances' face in her gentle hands. "You are most beautiful my dear, I can see why you've tamed him."

"Mother!"

"I know all about his reputation," Frances said, smiling.

"And he's explained why he disrespected women so, why he couldn't trust his heart to love?"

"Yes, he's explained everything. I understand now."

Chapter Twenty-five

THE EARL INSISTED on a six-month betrothal. "You can't marry a different man in the same year as you were meant to marry the first," he'd snapped at Frances. "And you Alban, will just have to control yourself!"

It was a muggy afternoon, there was thunder in the air, an uncanny sense of expectancy was gathering as the sky darkened, demanding candles be lit in the house. The couple were seeking fresh air as they strolled, arm in arm, by the river after the midday meal. They were staying close to the house, expecting the menacing sky to open at any moment. Even butterflies and midges were having trouble flying high today. Even the birds were quiet. Alban and Frances were quiet too, both deep in thought. He reminding himself he must keep the King informed about the wedding, Frances thinking about her maid's health. "Something wrong? You are very quiet," he asked.

"'Tis nothing. Annie has a terrible head cold, that's all."

"I'm sorry to hear that..."

"You don't have to feign interest," she laughed, squeezing his arm. "I'm concerned about father and Margaret, don't want them catching it, not in their conditions, nor any of us come to that. I've given her leave of duties for two days so she can stay abed and fully recover."

He didn't reply, his thoughts having taken a different turn. Smiley scampered to them, tail wagging, little legs working in a blur, coat wet, face happy. Melbroke hurled a small branch into the river, the dog turned on the spot and took chase. "So, if someone came to your room tonight not a soul in the world would know?"

"No! It doesn't mean that at all," she argued urgently, jabbing his upper arm. "Father would definitely know."

"How?"

"Believe me, he knows everything that goes on." She stood in front of him. "No Alban, no!"

He called Smiley to heel as he steered her back to the house. He was walking on air, his arm around her waist, kissing her hair, plans already in train. He had no intention of waiting six months!

"You make very free with me daughter," bellowed Lord Blean, from behind.

The couple turned around. "O father, really," appealed Frances, "we are betrothed."

"No, Frances," said Alban, "your father is right. I have been presumptuous. I am in the wrong." He bowed low, giving deference to the man soon to be his father-in-law. "My humblest apologies, Sir."

The Earl slapped Alban on the back. "I'm not made of stone Alban, I was young once but not in front of me and definitely not in front of the servants."

"Father you are supposed to be resting."

"Been thinking, want to speak with you both." He turned to Alban. "Frances tells me your mother's not long for this world, sorry to hear that, very sorry."

"Sadly not. Mayhap just a few more months."

"Can't deprive her of her son's wedding. Not after everything Frances has told me. Just been reunited I understand?" Alban nodded. "Your father was a fine man, didn't know him personally but knew of him. Fought valiantly against the Yorkists. Shame he's not here but your mother is. I've changed me mind due to the extenuating circumstances. One month, the wedding in one month. That do you?"

He didn't wait for an answer and headed toward the kitchen. "My study in one hour. Bring Margaret," he called, as he clicked his fingers and three panting dogs gathered around his ankles heading for food. "We'll start making plans. Got to get the invitations out. Be thinking what you want, who you want, where you want it, all the usual rigmarole."

Alban and Frances looked at each other, both smiling radiantly. He wrapped his arms around her just as the first clap of thunder cracked the sky above them. Suddenly 'twas urgent, there was much to do.

SHERIFF MALINS arrived unexpectedly as the family was talking guest list, food, entertainment, music, order of service, transport and so on. The groom's cousin would be invited but stay elsewhere, Blean couldn't cope with the royal entourage. That was assuming the King agreed to attend, things between them were still frosty. The groom's and bride's other relatives would stay in the house. There would be some forty guests, they were keeping it small, it felt appropriate given the year's events. The cathedral as the venue was dismissed for the same reason. The service would be in Blean's own chapel.

"You must ask your mother if she has guests she wishes to invite," the Earl instructed Alban. He nodded gratefully. "And bring her to Blean soon, want to get to know her."

Gates ushered in an uncomfortable Malins. He shuffled, kept clearing his throat and his hand shook as he accepted the wine Gates poured for him. "There's been a development, a most unfortunate development, I'm afraid."

"Get on with it man!"

"Two days ago the King's men came and took away Pascal Blanc. I had no say, couldn't protect him."

"Protect him!" Alban was on his feet. "Protect him! The man's a criminal."

"He was entitled to fair trial m'Lord, at least in my book he was."

"Get on with it man!" The Earl barked, he didn't want this subject back in his house.

"He was taken to the Tower and tortured. He's dead."

Alban was still on his feet, although now a little subdued. "I confess this may be my doing. I told the King what had been going on here. I didn't realize he would take action, I didn't ask him to but he was obviously trying to assist the Earl whom he knows to be a loyal supporter."

"That's as maybe m'Lord but I don't like it."

"I'm sure we'll all make a bloody note of that!" The Earl barked again. "Have you lost your senses man. He and his cohorts were out to ruin me, take me lands, me money, me reputation. They tried to kill me daughter. You expect me to feel sorry for him?"

Malins stayed silent, his eyes on the floor. After a long

pause he continued. "Under torture he revealed Blanc was not his real name."

"So who he?"

"He claimed to be the Marquis' brother."

"The Marchioness had three sons?" Frances was shocked.

"Seems so."

"Not true," scoffed the Earl. "He knew all about iron production, the blaggard's lying."

"His identity has been confirmed by the Marchioness. He studied the subject in preparation for the deceit, apparently."

"She never mentioned him," said Frances, quietly.

Alban could see the pain of having been deceived back in her eyes. "She wouldn't, would she! He was the one that was to deal with your father face to face. They needed to keep him hidden."

"They were truly desperate," she uttered, in shocked whisper.

"Desperate and bloody evil," hissed the Earl, slapping the side of the nearest dog who responded by laying his chin on the old man's knee.

The Sheriff continued: "I am tying up the loose ends. The bodies of the Harwyke brothers were formally identified by a neighbour, a respectable merchant, who confirmed they were a pair of good-for-nothings, always causing noise and disturbance in the area, frequently whoring and getting into fights. The Canterbury constables' records show they have been held for a series of petty crimes over many years. Do anything for money, it seems."

"Now there's a surprise," quipped Alban, sitting on the window seat, his eyes closed, welcoming the sun on his back.

"As to Lord Jasper, I'm ashamed to admit I can't find him, all leads have run cold. He's vanished."

Alban's attention was back. He sat forward, the better to

listen.

"But I have received a letter from him withdrawing the murder charge," Malins continued, turning to face the accused who was now standing. "It came via a Dover post-horse company. The Marquis has withdrawn all his accusations against your Lordship. That he was in Dover probably means he is now abroad."

"You are probably right," agreed Melbroke, mightily happy at what he was hearing.

"And I feel," the Sheriff continued, "that your theory is correct. Lords Pierre, Jasper and Pascal hired the Harwykes to do their dirty work, intending, possibly but not definitely, to come in the for the kill, so to speak, when it got to the blackmail stage. Pierre was the brains and after his death his two brothers continued alone, veering from the original plot, getting involved in kidnap, murder allegations and the rest. It all started going wrong when Pierre was killed, his death was the beginning of their end."

"Your summary is excellent," said Alban, flattering the man.

"The Harwykes heard you were making enquiries about them and called you to their home in order to rid themselves of a problem. It is they who had murderous intent not yourselves." He nodded a bow to Melbroke and William.

"Again, you are correct, Sheriff," said William, inwardly breathing a great sigh of relief. Both Lords knowing the Sheriff would never know the whole story. They certainly didn't intend telling him.

Malins turned back to Melbroke: "Your name has not been besmirched m'Lord, no formal documents of murder were served by my office, 'tis as if the matter never happened."

The Earl was on his feet. "Good. Now, time for you to leave Malins, we're planning a wedding."

"Oh?"

"Me daughter and Lord Melbroke, just become betrothed."

Malins offered his congratulations and turned to leave. He had much paperwork to see to. He was nervous, his dealings had never brought him so close to the King before nor had he ever had to provide documentation explaining why a French nobleman was beaten to near-death in his cells and then tortured to death in the Tower of London. It would be easy to put a foot wrong and he had intended asking the King's cousin for advice. This clearly wasn't the moment, he would have to cope alone. Shoulders slumped, he headed for his horse, the air now fresher after the storm but his burdens heavier than ever.

LATER, AFTER the family had retired for the night Alban shaved. He had no intentions of waiting even a month. With wine and goblet he trod stealthily down the stairs to Frances' room, listening for footfall, for voices, making sure no one saw what he was about. The house was still. He didn't knock, he went straight in and closed the door quietly behind him.

There she was. By her dressing table, her hair catching the candlelight. When she heard the door she turned and stood up. "No!"

"Yes, Frances, yes," and he walked straight to her. She could see the urgency in his face, the passion in his eyes. She saw the sigh that went through him as he looked at her, the need in his gaze. Her flimsy gown emphasized her curves. Her slender waist, the round of her hips, the swell of her breasts.

Even under silk her skin tingled as his eyes roamed her. Already she trembled. Already he was affecting her. *Release fear, embrace love...*

"No! Father would be angry." She took a step back from him, he instantly caught her. "Sweeting, you are too beautiful." Now he had his arms about her she froze. She couldn't talk, she was too tense. He kissed her tenderly, she couldn't respond. The soft voluptuousness of her caught his breath. His hands slid easily over the silk as he roamed her contours, down and round and down again. "Your father will never know."

She shook her head and tried to remove his hands that now cupped her face. "I'm not leaving Frances, I know you want me. I'm going to love you tonight, sweetheart."

She didn't move. She didn't signal yes or no. She was frozen to the spot, imprisoned in the moment, struggling with her emotions, her body's sensations, his closeness, his desire, his hot breath on her cheek.

"I should be a virgin on our wedding night," she managed to whisper.

"This is our wedding night," and he covered her mouth with his so she could object no more.

He had vowed to himself he would take her gently, slowly. They had all night, there was no rush. He would move at a speed that suited her. Tonight was the first night of their life together, it would set the scene forever, he was determined to make it a scene she enjoyed and wanted more of.

"Let me love you," he whispered, again and again as he brushed his lips on hers. Once again she felt like the rabbit in the lamp but this time the lurcher was claiming her. Her heart was pounding, she could hear it in her ears. She could hardly breathe. She stood passively. She couldn't fight, didn't even have the strength now to say 'no'. He had drained her body of its own will. *Release fear, embrace love...*

His hands were supporting the back of her head, buried

in her hair, toying with its curls, as he slowly kissed every feature of her face. He could feel the tension in her body. Could feel her trembling. Somewhere from a hundred miles away she could hear his voice saying: "Relax, sweeting, relax."

He told her he loved her over and over and then brought his lips back to hers. Suddenly she was soaring again, the two of them spinning in a void, being carried away from Earth toward the sun. Her hands went up to his shoulders, she needed something to cling on to as she melted into him.

He slipped the gown off her shoulders and returned his lips to her soft, sweet-perfumed skin. He journeyed over her neck, her throat and she threw back her head and gasped as sensations she couldn't name travelled through her.

He opened her silky gown a little further, took a step back and looked at her. She waited for his touch but it didn't come. The breasts he had gazed upon at Richmond were finally his. They were beautiful, perfect and he groaned as he gently pulled the gown back over her shoulders to cover her. His own arousal was mounting too fast. He needed to quell his own need if he were to stick to his intent of taking all the time in the world. He took her hand and led her to the bed.

"Come," he said, "drink some wine while I undress."

She lay on the bed watching him. It only took a few seconds and he was back by her side, naked but for his shirt. "You have never touched a man before? Never seen a man's body?" She shook her head. "I thought you would like to become acquainted with me, before..."

"Yes," she whispered, nodding. She had accepted the inevitable now. He would love her tonight, she couldn't stop him. Didn't want to. He lay back on the bed. "Explore me Frances, explore me," and he closed his eyes as her fingers tentatively began their journey.

She started at his shoulders and arms, ran her hands over their strength, their power. The shoulders and limbs of a fighting man who had fought for her, risked himself to save her honour and her life. Muscles like iron. She moved to his chest, slid the palms of her hands over him, made tiny circles with the tips of her fingers as she moved down and round. She closed her eyes as she explored and pushed and stroked. The thin shirt denied her little and his strong body was exciting her.

Down to his abdomen, taut but yielding under her touch. Next his thighs, strong, solid as trees. She heard him take a sharp intake of breath as she began tracing their shape. When she tentatively touched the bulge that was larger than her cupped hand, he grasped her arm. "Stop, no more," he growled, his voice raspy with desire.

He pulled his shirt over his head and threw it to the floor. Completely naked now. His body gleamed in the candlelight. She was mesmerized by ripple of muscle and sinew as he moved, the wispy dark hair that carpeted his chest, the sheer size of him. So strong and yet so tender. He undid the tie of her gown and released her arms from its sleeves. She lay naked now, exposed, vulnerable. Her hand searched for the robe, she wanted to cover herself, he realized and stole her hand and kissed it. "Sweetheart, let me look at your beauty."

He began exploring her, kissing, licking, working his magic over her. The sensations that flew through her were almost too much to bear. She could feel the bed beneath her but it was as if it weren't really there. Her skin tingled, her body rolled in welcome at his touch. His fingers were gently stroking, teasing her senses, setting her alight. Any last semblance of resistance had long dissolved in the heat as she surrendered to the pleasure he brought her.

His own need was now great, could wait no longer. "Are you ready for me?" She nodded.

"I'll be as gentle as I can." And for a moment she tensed again, preparing herself for she knew not what. A warm sensation was followed by a brief discomfort which lasted a mere second. Pleasure followed. Warm, then hot, then all consuming. A pleasure that she could never have imagined. She felt him moving, slowly, rhythmically. Her hips seemed to know what to do and she began to move with him. A heat within her was mounting, sending wave after wave of a sweet, unbearable sensation. To the very edge of her being it soared. She gasped and groaned as his rhythm increased and the heat began to turn into an inferno.

He watched her, her eyes closed, hips moving with him, head twisting on the pillow. She was drowning, her very soul was his, she wanted to be in this state of surrender forever. The inferno raged and turned into a fireball that ripped through her. She screamed out, called his name, gasping for air.

He growled the growl of the conqueror, the loving conqueror, whose own body was on fire. They soared together in their zenith of passion, an ecstasy she had only dreamed of was hers. Slowly, very slowly, the heat began to wane and together, they quietened.

He laid his head by hers on the pillow, her arms wrapped around him, feeling his weight, the dampness of his back. Together they calmed, caught their breath, felt their sated bodies sing. Eventually he lifted off and lay on his side, facing her. He waited. He saw a tear trickle to the pillow. After a while he said: "Sweetheart. Say something."

She didn't respond, couldn't, she was overcome with emotion. Overcome with the after-hum that lingered like soft moonlight after the boiling sun. He pulled her closer, stroked her hair, her face. "Frances. Please. Say something."

"I was right." she said quietly, rolling her body to him so they lay facing each other.

"You were?"

"You did overwhelm me."

"And that was good?"

"It was wonderful," she smiled. "My Lord needs flattery?" She teased as she kissed his nose.

"I need to know I gave pleasure to the woman I love."

"O yes, Alban, you did that."

"So, why the tears?"

"Because I'm so happy."

He reached for the wine and they sipped from the shared goblet. He pulled the covers over them and Frances snuggled into the security of his body. You were right mama, you were right.

"I hope you're not too sleepy," he said, "I intend overwhelming you again in a minute."

Earlier that evening Brother Thomas heard Magdala's story. Such good friends had they become she decided to tell him the truth.

"There was a family feud, between my husband and my brother. My brother won."

"Your brother put you in here?"

"Yes," she nodded. "'Twas...is...my punishment for loving a Lancastrian."

The apothecary said nothing. He'd seen enough of the darkness of men's hearts. Enough of physical carnage on the battlefield. He'd seen families ripped apart, pregnant women killed, old men tortured. Nothing shocked him any more but his heart pained for this gentle woman.

"The wedding is in one month," she smiled. "Can you keep me alive for that?"

"Your time isn't that soon Sister, you've a few months yet."

She relaxed and closed her eyes. "I'm invited to spend a few days before the wedding at Blean House, to be part of the excitement."

"I can treat you there, I will make sure you enjoy every moment."

She took his hand in hers, it was an affection they had come to allow themselves to share. For a few moments they sat in silence.

"This isn't what Christ would have wanted, Sister," he said, trying to soothe her as he dabbed the dampness from her brow. She was having a bad day. Sometimes the pain was too much and today the heat wasn't helping. Mother Esme had summoned him, now she knew Magdala's status she was to receive better treatment, it seemed.

"I know. I have come to understand the love and peace of Christ but my heart has ached everyday for the love of my husband and son."

"Love is God's gift, so is pain. You have been truly blessed."

She smiled, more uncertain than he.

Chapter Twenty-six

SEVERAL PASSIONATE HOURS later Frances fell asleep in Alban's arms as he continued drinking and thinking. Never could he have imagined back in the spring, when he'd hurled himself on to Galahad and taken chase across Kent, that he was galloping into such a beautiful new world. A world of miracles and wonder. A brand new world to him. A territory he had never traversed, nor thought he ever would. What a year it had been!

He'd been accused of murder and been a murderer's intended victim. He'd fought two Marquises and slain one of them. He'd revealed the wicked intent of one mother while discovering the true story of his own. His future had been empty, now his path was rich. He'd been living the life of the philanderer, now all he wanted was fidelity.

He'd saved Frances from rape and murder and from herself at times! She had wrecked his emotions with her smile, her sapphire eyes, her scorn, her anger. Where once she hated and despised him, now she loved him. Where once she had to force herself to share a carriage, now she shared his bed. She had given herself so sweetly, he could never doubt love again.

Thank goodness he threatened to leave and go to France. It had been his last throw of the dice. If William had been wrong about her feelings for him then he'd be on the other side of the Channel tonight, laying with goodness knows who. An empty, meaningless night of sex. As it was William had been right. Frances did love him and she couldn't let him go. He shuddered at what a gamble that had been and then looked down at the whirl of golden waves laying on his chest and thanked God for bringing her to him.

In four weeks they would marry, their life together stretched before them like a stream in dappled sunlight and he realized he was happier right now than he had ever been. He finished the flask of wine, snuffed the candle and drifted into a sleep of deep contentment that no other woman had ever given him.

IT MAY have been the servants' movements in the outside corridor that awoke him. It may have been the distant chiming of a church bell announcing the six o'clock. It was far more likely it was Frances gently rolling him on to his back that did it. She propped herself on one elbow and began playing with his thick chestnut hair. She bent down and kissed his head, then nuzzled her face into the side of his neck and teased his ear with her tongue. She moved her lips in kisses across and down his chest. She ran her hands all over him. "Stop pretending you're still asleep," she whispered.

"Madam, you are wanton!"

"O well, if you're not up to it," she giggled. "I shall be understanding, you are, after all, eleven years older than me." She swung her legs off the bed, making to get up.

"I haven't given you permission to leave," he said, grinning and pulling her back. He rolled her over so she was under him and gazed into her intoxicating eyes. "I think I could force myself again, if you absolutely insist."

"This time yesterday," she laughed, "I was an innocent! 'Tis all your fault. Look what you've turned me into!" She nudged him on to his back, smiling and looking down into his gaze.

He met her smile. "I love you my Lady of Blean. I love you more than I could ever have imagined."

Her lips brushed his. "Now, you my Lord, are going to do what I say."

"Am I indeed."

"Yes. Firstly, no touching."

"What!"

"I withdraw my permission for you to touch me."

"And why is that?"

"Because," she said seriously, sitting up. "I want to love you." She knelt between his legs. "Remember no touching."

She gazed at him. He was magnificent. His mouth soft and sensual. His jaw strong. His forehead wide, high and intelligent. He watched her looking at him, it was more tantalizing than he could have dreamt.

He raised his arms to hold her. She pushed them back.

"No! No touching."

"Now you command me, madam?"

"I do. Behave!"

He closed his eyes as she kissed him gently on the lips. She lifted his hands and kissed every finger, taking the tip of each into her mouth. She stroked his arm, kissed its length, then went to his other side and did the same. Between kisses, she told him how she loved him, how magnificent he was, how he was delicious to touch, beautiful to taste. He watched her, his heart aching. She was adoring him, he had never been so loved. Twice he tried to hold her, twice she scolded him. Scores more kisses dusted his skin as she worked over his neck, chest, abdomen. Scores of soft, loving kisses, all over him.

This was commanding every ounce of self control he could muster and he was losing. By the time she got to the top of his thighs his arousal was complete.

"Well, well, my Lord. Seems your age isn't a hindrance after all."

"Lady of Blean, you will pay for this," he laughed.

"Shush! I haven't finished with you."

She took her attention to the very core of him. She could hear him groaning. "No more, this is torture. You are definitely wanton," he said, gasping.

"You're absolutely right," she teased, moving away, grinning, making to leave the bed. "I shouldn't be doing this. A well brought-up Lady, unmarried, an Earl's daughter and all, I really shouldn't be so forward, I ought to stop."

His hands grabbed the tops of her arms. He flipped her back on to the bed and pinned her down by her wrists. "'Tis too late for that," he beamed, "your reputation's already in tatters."

Just then they heard the Earl's dogs barking below their window. He was up and about!

"I can't trust you to be quiet, my little wanton" he said, coaxing her over on to her front so she could bury her face in the pillow. Now he knelt between her legs, his lips skimming her back, his fingers exploring her, her back arching in sheer pleasure. She cried in a kind of agony of delight. "Pillow," he commanded and she sunk her cries further into its feathers.

Together they moved, slowly at first, soft and strong. She

knew him now, knew the feel of him and not for the first time this night she wondered if she would truly live through so much passion. The rhythm quickened, the inferno was back. He held his mouth tightly closed as the crescendo came and together they again soared like summer swallows in the sky before plummeting downwards back to earth.

Quickly he grabbed a spare pillow, covered his face and let free the emotions he had been holding in. He kissed her back then lay beside her, his legs still covering hers. After a while he began stroking her hair. "I think it's official," he whispered, as he twirled waves around his fingers. "My Lady of Blean is definitely a wanton hussy."

"Aren't you the lucky one."

"I am indeed."

For a short while they slumbered, then the church bell sounded again. Seven o'clock.

"How on earth do I get out of here without being seen?" He was already up and dressing. "There's too many people in the corridors, I can hear them."

"Out the window."

"What!"

"There's an old, sturdy hazel right outside, its branches press against the wall. 'Tis what I used to do as a child, as a short cut to the gardens."

"This how all your men leave?"

"Usually," she said, slipping into a silk robe. "Only one fell and broke his neck, I told father he was a thief."

"Come here you," he said, pulling her to him. "Come here, this is the last time I can touch you for four weeks." He ran his hands over her back, cupped her buttocks and pulled her close. "Stop," she said, "and go."

"Stop and go. Madam your commands are becoming confusing."

"Go, go, go," and she opened the window. She looked all around, no dogs no father, no servants.

"Quick, the coast is clear.'

He looked down and saw one particularly strong branch that would possibly hold his weight. "Come break your fast soon, my sweet." And with that he squeezed through the window, lowered himself on to the tree, swung on the branch and jumped down on to the grass below just as three mastiffs bounded around the corner. Seeing him they began to bark and jump with excitement.

"Just out for a stroll Alban?" The Earl had turned the corner of the house just seconds behind his dogs.

"Yes, my Lord, a stroll afore breaking my fast."

"Good show."

FRANCES WAS the last to arrive downstairs. She had quickly bathed and washed her hair which now hung, still damp, behind a head-dress and under a silken snood. She looked fresh and very happy. She took a chair between Alban and her father who, as always, sat at the head of the table. She helped herself to sliced meats, cheese and plenty of cook's freshly baked bread. There was freshly churned herbed butter, boiled eggs, salted fish and the Earl's favourite, a large dish of sprats.

"Good morning, my dear," said the Earl. "I hope you slept well, nothing disturbed you I hope?"

"Thank you father, I slept well."

"Positively glowing, isn't she Margaret? Never seen her look so glowing."

"And you Melbroke? You on the other hand look a little

peaky. Didn't you get much sleep? Disturbed night was it?"

Alban's heart sunk. He knows! And he's back to calling me Melbroke. How on earth can he know?

The Earl continued: "I nearly chopped down that hazel last year, Melbroke. Good job I didn't, don't you think?"

Alban was too stunned to reply, he stopped eating.

"It gives shade to the house at the height of summer although it does drop a lot of leaves, especially if it gets a good shaking. Didn't you notice, Melbroke? A lot of broken twig and leaves around your feet?"

William, sitting opposite Alban, was beginning to understand that this conversation was loaded. He raised his eyebrows questioningly to Alban. When the Earl had finished his sprats he slammed down his napkin, stood up and made for the door. "Library, Melbroke. Now!"

Alban turned to Frances: "He knows."

"Told you he would!"

"He definitely knows something," butted-in a grinning William, "and he's angry. I can but guess what it is."

"Hell's teeth," said Alban, pushing his still full plate away from him.

MORNING SUN was pouring into the large library. The Earl ignored Melbroke's entrance. Both men stayed silent. The Earl pacing, making him wait.

"Do you think me stupid, Melbroke," he eventually asked. It was rhetorical, he didn't want an answer nor did he want Alban to speak. He raised a hand to bar him. "Did you think I wouldn't know what you were about under me daughter's window, unshaven, dishevelled and with half a tree all around you. You've disappointed me, Melbroke. You've been welcomed into me home, nursed back to health, supported when accusations were made against you and how do you repay me? By insulting me."

"My Lord..."

"Don't speak! Don't even try to talk your way out of this one. You've insulted me, offended the Blean name. Me daughter won't now be a maiden on her wedding day, her mother would be heartbroken, thank goodness she's not here to see this." Alban remained silent as instructed.

The Earl went to his favourite window and looked out at what was destined to be another glorious summer's day. His hands, linked behind his back, churned in anger. Alban stood frozen to the spot, dread in his heart and head. After what seemed an interminable age the Earl spun round on the spot. "Well, did she enjoy it?"

"My Lord?" Alban was somewhat taken aback.

"Lost your use of the English language now? 'Tis a simple enough question. When you were pleasuring yourself with me daughter did you pleasure her? Was she happy with you? I want me girls happy."

Alban shuffled and cleared his throat. "She certainly gave me the impression that she was happy. Very happy, actually." The Earl flashed a glare, as if to say 'that'll do'.

"If you betray her, break her heart, hurt her in any way, I shall set the dogs on you. D'you hear? They'll go for your throat and liver, 'twill be a nasty death."

"They'll have to get in the queue, my Lord."

"Eh? What d'you say?"

"Lady Margaret has threatened me death by slow, agonizing poisoning and William will pin me to a tree with his sword and leave me to die under a hot midday sun."

"Looks like you'll have to behave yourself then."

"I have no intentions of not, m'Lord and not because of the plans for my death but because I love your daughter with every fibre of my body."

The Earl remained silent as did Alban. Slowly a grin crossed the old man's face. "I know you do Alban. You're a good man. And I can see she loves you."

"My Lord, I deeply apologize for offending you. If there is anything I can do..."

"Just make sure I've a third grandchild on the way by Christmas. Do that and you're forgiven. Now go."

"I'll do my very best." He bowed low and turned for the door making sure he concealed a very broad smile. He went straight back to an anxious Frances.

"Has he thrown you out of the house?"

"No, no. He accused me of insulting him, offending the Blean name and so on." He put his arms about her waist. "He asked if you enjoyed it, I said you gave me the impression that you did." A deep blush rushed to her cheeks and down her neck. As always a little thrill went through him. "He also said that I could only redeem my disgraceful behaviour by making sure he had a third grandchild on the way by Christmas. You, my sweetling, are going to have a very busy wedding night and the next day and the next night and the next..."

His lips lowered on hers then he lifted her up and spun her round. "Now let's get back to the food, I have to build up my energy."

WHEN SHE returned to her bedchamber later that day she found a small box and a love letter on her dressing table. The box contained a pair of sapphire earrings to match her eyes. Single stones in gold which he had retrieved from the cache of his mother's jewels that he kept at Richmond Palace. Her jewellery box was all he'd had of his mother, something had made him keep it, although he had rarely looked into it. How glad he now was that he could share it. The letter professed his undying love and devotion. 'I ask only,' it ended, 'that you allow me to love and serve you until God takes the last breath of my body.'

Magdala sat on the grass watching the August clouds make flimsy cobwebs in the sky. Groups of birds were swooping, they'd be going soon. Occasionally leaves drifted down, autumn was nudging in. Contentment was hers this day. The apothecaries shelves were full. Her remaining herbs would soon be cut back for drying and the nuns' winter store would be full and promising. Her work was done and she was glad. No cure could save her now but they could save others. A note from Mother instructed her to sit next to her at meals from now on - she had been promoted, it seemed. It made her smile. Such shallowness.

Had she more life within her she may have asked her son to find her brother but there was no time. She could forgive him without meeting him, indeed already had. Part of her, though, would like to know that he and his children were well but it was not to be. It would be the last deprivation of her life. She was comfortable with deprivation, it had become her friend.

She assumed a baby may already be on the way. If her son were like his father then it could well be. Hopefully, that would be confirmed before she died. She wouldn't meet her grandchild but she could imagine. Alban's strength, Frances' beauty. A child born in love, as Alban had been. She shuddered as her thoughts reminded her of how badly wrong life can go.

This evening she was to have a pre-supper meeting with Esme in her office. She was to join the inner circle, be privy to convent decisions and plans. She didn't seek it. She wanted to be left alone with her new-found joy but it was Esme's desire so it had to be. She would smile and offer her thoughts and be kind when Esme was harsh and uncaring. Perhaps her last task on this Earth was to make Esme smile. It certainly wasn't to soften her heart, that was a far too big a task. Even God hadn't managed that one. A smile would be an achievement. Why not, she thought. One more ambition afore I go home.

Chapter Twenty-seven

Blean House, late-August, 1515

THE NEXT FEW weeks saw much nuptial activity. The wedding gown was hanging in the hope all creases would fall. The fine silk was fragile, it would be wise to avoid pressing. A multitude of underskirts were washed and aired. Throughout the house silver was polished, furniture buffed, carpets cleaned. Gates checked the wine stock and organized entertainment; cook thought menus and arranged temporary extra help; the housekeeper filled the guest rooms with sweet smelling herbs and organized flowers for the house and chapel.

To Alban's relief and delight a missive arrived from Court: his cousin would be attending. Forgiveness it seemed had come just in time.

Mid-afternoon, a few days before the wedding, two tired horses trundled up the Blean drive. Gates was the first to hear their snorting so made his way outside. They were pulling a small carriage. Dirty, down-at-heel, made even shabbier by the mud that had spat from the ground on its long journey to Blean. The sides were covered in it, the horses' hooves caked with it. August was proving to be a contrary month, burning sun and sudden, heavy rain. Meagre upholstery would have given an uncomfortable ride for its single occupant. It pulled to a halt and the coachman descended.

"The Marchioness de Champagne," he said, his words well-rehearsed, "most sincerely apologizes for arriving unexpectedly but respectfully begs an audience with the Earl of Blean and Lady Frances." He shuffled uncomfortably, such formalities were not part of a driver's job.

Gates knew his master well enough. He would not refuse her, despite what she'd been party to. She was a marchioness, she had not been arrested for any crime and he would give her due deference. He indicated this would be acceptable and the man helped the Lady gingerly descend.

As on her one previous visit the Marchioness couldn't help but be impressed by the house, its grounds, the elaborate hall she was shown through and the drawing room in which she now sat. Last time, she was here to celebrate, now she was shrouded in grief. She gladly sipped the refreshment Gates arranged. Her body, sore from the ride, she allowed to sink into sumptuous cushions. She looked about her. The house sang of history, tradition, wealth. All of which she once had. Now she had sadness and shock and anger. She'd lost two sons to violence, a third was carrying the shame of all three. Her wrecked nerves jumped as the door banged open and the Earl, with Frances, entered.

Father and daughter were both taken aback by the visit. The atmosphere was tense. The humbled Marchioness, now on her feet, her bones still aching, her self-respect rock bottom, struggled to maintain some dignity. "I wanted to see you both again," she began, "to apologize for all that has happened." She ran her hands over her coat, straightening imaginary creases. "I am leaving England for good. I travel via Dover, I was so close to Blean I chanced that you would be here."

Neither the Earl nor Frances spoke. They waited. Eventually she continued, sitting now in the chair the Earl had indicated. Father and daughter also sat. "I wish to apologize for my sons, apologize to both of you. The Sheriff has told me of their crimes, their attempt to blackmail you to raise money...and the rest." She lowered her eyes and dabbed them. "I am so ashamed."

"But you were party to their schemes, don't deny it," challenged the Earl, his face reddened, his eyes thunderous. "We know you agreed that Pierre should claim to be your husband's heir when in fact Jasper was. You lied, to all of us." He was on his feet again, staring angrily down at her. "You lied and tricked us."

"Yes. And I regret it most deeply. We were desperate. My husband was not a good man, he was selfish and unkind. The debts were not my sons' fault, they were trying to help their mother, to protect me. Securing a beneficial marriage for Pierre could have been the answer to all our problems. You are good people, to my dying day I will regret that deception."

For a second time the door banged open. "Jasper would have seen me executed!" All eyes turned to the striking, formidable frame of Melbroke. His eyes were harsh as he glared at her. "Were there no depths to which your sons would not sink?"

"You had your revenge, my Lord. You killed Pierre, I believe." The Marchioness had never before met this Lord but her intuition knew him to be Melbroke.

"With deep regret I have to admit that is true but revenge was not my motive."

An uncomfortable atmosphere filled the room. The Marchioness stiffened her back, lifted her chin. "My sons were trying to protect their mother. Their behaviour was unforgivable but they didn't deserve to die. It all got out of hand."

Both Earl and Melbroke held their tongues. Got out of hand! Both correctly assumed that she didn't know all the facts. Didn't know how far her sons were prepared to go nor just how evil they were. Didn't know they planned to completely ruin the Earl, take his money to themselves and possibly, over time, kill all his living relatives. She didn't know that in effect they planned to take the Blean estate.

Sitting before them was a broken woman, in grief. Her eyes red from tears, her face puffy, her status gone, her future bleak. They had no need to add to her woes. The Sheriff, like them it seemed, had also seen room for a little kindness. He clearly hadn't arrested her, all thought she had been lucky there. He too, like those with whom she now conversed, saw no advantage in adding to her tragic plight.

The Marchioness turned to Frances and tried a smile. "Richmond is alive with talk of your marriage to Lord Melbroke."

"I didn't know," she said, looking to her lap, grateful that she didn't have to listen to it.

"Did you love Lord Melbroke before Pierre died?"

"No, my Lady, we have only, in recent months, discovered our feelings for each other."

"I find that difficult to believe."

Melbroke stepped forward. "We care not what you believe. The truth is as you are being told it."

"You didn't love Pierre?" The mother kept her eyes on Frances and away from Melbroke. She could avoid his eyes but not his anger. It stifled her.

"I know now I did not," Frances answered. "I am trying to remember the good things about your son but 'tis all very painful. He was not the man you all made him to be and that you also had a third son kept secret as part of the deception, is very difficult to deal with at the moment."

"I understand."

"Do you?" Frances snapped, "I doubt it!" It was not her way but she was struggling with both sorrow and anger and momentarily the latter won. "And what about all those times you and I sat together? I thought we had become friends but all the time you were lying to me, using me and my family, plotting against us." Distress filled her voice, her eyes moistened.

"Frances dear, I did grow to love you, I was happy for you and Pierre..."

Frances raised her hand, bid the older woman stop. "No more, I can talk about this no more. Whatever you say now I cannot believe. I am struggling with Christian understanding and pity, I hope to be able to look more kindly upon you and your sons one day but for now I cannot."

"I care not for myself," the Marchioness continued, her eyes now full of tears, "but please try and look kindly upon my sons, especially Jasper who now has to struggle on alone."

Melbroke paced toward her, his heels banging, his temper explosive. "Your son," he said, towering over her, "has his freedom, be grateful for that! He should have had a blade to his neck!"

"O, he'll be dead soon enough," the mother said, standing to try and meet his piercing gaze. "His own health will see to that."

"He's dying?" Frances asked, incredulously.

The Marchioness nodded and brushed more tears from her cheek. "He has the same problem of shakes and sweats that his uncle had, he died very young. I have been advised that Jasper almost certainly will, too. I shall have no sons then." Her head sunk on to her chest and for a moment she covered her face with her hands.

Frances couldn't stop pity from filling her heart and had to fight the urge to comfort the woman.

"It was the original reason," the Marchioness went on, sinking back on to her chair, "why we agreed to say Pierre was the new marquis. If it were left to Jasper the line would almost certainly die out. Pierre could produce heirs. Jasper probably cannot."

"You think that justifies everything?" Melbroke glared at her, his fists clenched by his sides, desperately trying to hang on to some degree of civility. "You think that makes what you all did acceptable?"

"No, my Lord. I do not," she bristled. "'Tis, however, the reason why 'twas done. Surely we are all entitled to protect ourselves."

"Lucifer's nails," the Earl boomed, "I've had enough of this. 'Tis time for you to leave."

Just at that moment the drawing room door creaked open and a woman with a serene face, beautiful eyes and wearing a nun's habit, entered. "I'm so sorry, I didn't realize you had a guest."

"We haven't Elizabeth, she's just leaving," said the Earl.

The Marchioness stood. Similar in age and height the two women looked at each other, not sure how to respond to the sudden meeting. Melbroke took control. "Mother," he said, putting a protective arm around her shoulders, "this is the Marchioness de Champagne. She visits en route to Dover."

Elizabeth smiled kindly. "A pleasure to meet you, my Lady." Her eyes were tender, happiness radiating from her face.

The Marchioness stiffened in anger and envy. "O, 'tis my

replacement! 'Tis you," she hissed, pointing a rigid finger, "you who will be Frances' mother-by-law! I wasn't expecting a nun!" She threw back her head in mocking laughter.

Elizabeth stepped back, such anger she was not used to. It withered her. She allowed her son to pull her into him. "That will do," he retorted, angrily. "You have no place here now. As the Earl has said, 'tis time for you to leave."

The Marchioness scoffed as she acknowledged her cue. "Mayhap it was your family that tricked us!" She smirked accusingly, her face distorted in disdain.

"Leave! Now!" The Earl boomed. "Now!"

All four ushered her through the door being held open by Gates. No one spoke. No one wanted to. Just before reaching the main door the Marchioness turned swiftly, sharply, hatred in her eyes. A low grating noise emitted from her throat, her cheeks screwed together and she spat at Elizabeth with as much venom and strength as she could muster.

The slimy projectile was aimed at her face but Alban pulled his mother back and it fell way short of its mark. It splattered on to the tiled floor. All stood in horror. An elderly woman, a widow, related by marriage to the French aristocracy reduced to tavern tactics, shamed them all. Melbroke stood rigid, glowering but silent. They all did. Gates coughed to break the pregnant silence and the woman picked up her skirts and rustled out of their lives.

"Got out of hand!" Alban hissed, as the carriage pulled away and Elizabeth quietly whispered a request to God. "Ease her heart," she appealed, "give her peace." Her son had told her a little of what had been going on but by no means all of it. She didn't want to know. She had her son back, that was all that mattered and however many weeks God was content to give her, she just wanted to enjoy them. The past had gone, she would share the joy of the newlyweds, if only for a little while.

Alban's clenched fist slammed into the palm of the other. "When I think what that family has put us all through..." His thoughts and words tapered off as he wrapped his arms protectively around Frances.

"Please no more." Her eyes sparkled with emotion as she gazed up at him. "She doesn't know the whole truth and I'm glad. She's been through enough. Her life is in pieces, ours is just beginning. We've come through it, let's concentrate on putting it behind us and just think about our future."

They stood and watched the Marchioness disappear from their lives. Frances was right, he knew.

THEIR MAJESTIES arrived just minutes before the ceremony was to begin and only seconds after an overweight apothecary puffed to his seat. A murmur swept through the chapel as all guests stood to bow or curtsy. A lone harpist played a selection of music as candles flickered and wisps of sweet incense floated around all who waited for the service to begin.

The groom, his chest tight, as near to nerves as he had ever been in his life, waited at the chapel door. He'd been out riding earlier. He'd needed a fast gallop, the wind around his head, the thrill of a few jumps to help abate the unfamiliar tension that coursed through him.

"What on earth's the matter with you?" William had mocked. "Anyone would think you'd never taken a woman before."

"I've never taken a wife," he'd said. "I keep thinking 'tis all too good to be true, that something will happen at the last moment to whisk her away."

"Classic wedding nerves. Believe me, I know."

He shuffled from one foot to the other as minutes felt like long, endless hours. Then he saw her. His breath was snatched from him as his eyes fell upon the vision that walked toward him. She was wearing his gown. The soft blue silk from Paris with its bodice and tight sleeves covered in hundreds of tiny crystals. Her multitudinous underskirts emphasized her slender waist. The wide, square neckline showed off her beauty to perfection. The naked slope of her shoulders, her elegant neck, the ooze of breasts just above the bodice line. Atop her loose, tumbling hair sat a delicate hoop of fresh flowers that she and Elizabeth had picked together earlier this day. Little dots of blue peaked out between the roses and carnations. Starflower, the same colour as the bride's eyes, placed especially by Elizabeth to bring joy.

Frances looked like a celestial being as she walked toward him, sparkling brighter than a starlit sky as the candles danced on the crystals and her hair glinted in golden shafts. Closer now, he saw she was wearing his betrothal gift, his mother's sapphire earrings. He swallowed back the lump in his throat and stepped forward to greet her. "You've taken my breath away," he said softly, taking her hand and leading her in.

Together they knelt before the altar and the priest began the service. At the given moment Alban lifted her left hand and placed his mother's gold and ruby ring on to her finger. "God the Father," he said softly, as he slid it on, then off, her index finger. "God the Son," as he did the same on her middle finger, slipping it finally on to her third finger with "God the Holy Ghost." Frances gasped when she saw it. The ruby, as large as a hip, was part-sunk into the shoulders of gold and glowed on her finger. "Thank you," she mouthed to his eagerly awaiting gaze. Elizabeth's eyes glistened.

Ceremony over, he led her from the chapel, along the flower-lined corridors, to the dining hall. The servants had gathered in the main hall and clapped and threw flower petals as they passed. At last Alban's nerves dissipated. For a few brief moments he had her to himself before the guests caught up with them. "You wore my gown and I thought you didn't like it."

"I was saving it, especially for today."

"Saving it! You mean you knew we would marry?"

"I hoped we would," she beamed.

In joyous laughter he threw back his head, as much in release of pent-up nerves as at the subtle manipulation of the female race. "You look so beautiful sweetheart, I shall remember this image for the rest of my life." His lips gently brushed hers.

The guests were joining them, more clapping, more petals and seeds for fertility, showered upon them. The music was playing and chatter was circulating. The Earl kissed his daughter's cheek and slapped Alban on the back. "Their Majesties wish to speak with you then take their leave for Dover Castle."

Alban led Frances to his cousin. The King smiled, welcomingly. "Do I have the groom's permission to kiss his bride?"

"You do cousin."

The King kissed her hands as he lifted her from her curtsy. It was the first time she had been this close to her monarch. "So, this is the beauty that kept you from me for so long."

"Alban was seriously ill, Your Grace," she said. She felt Melbroke's nudge. She ceased speaking and lowered her eyes.

"Don't keep her from us Alban, I expect you both to dine with us."

Queen Katherine embraced her as the two men exchanged a few words. "You have discovered passion my dear?" Frances blushed. "I can see that you have. Good. Take the summer to be with your handsome husband, when next you come to Court speak with me. We are related now, not so formal in future. Visit me, I need people I can trust."

❁

TO FRANCES' embarrassment everyone began clapping and banging the tables when she and Alban made to leave. They had hoped that by leaving the feast before all the courses had been served, they would be able to slip away quietly. It was not to be. She had though, insisted there would be no public bedding ceremony. She had heard with horror the stories that had circulated the Court when the King's younger sister had wed the fifty-something King of France. The wedding night was a rowdy spectacle, apparently, with onlookers filling the room and peeping through the curtains of the four-poster as the King indulged himself in his new bride. Traditional custom it may be but it would not be happening at Blean!

She had though, allowed the priest to bless the bed. It was a private affair just after dawn as the cool of the morning welcomed the excitement of the wedding day. Just herself, Alban and close family. The priest, sprinkling the bed with holy water asked God to grant the couple fertility and Frances safe delivery. The significance of the latter, given so many brides didn't see their first wedding anniversary, was lost on none of the participants.

The guests with eagle eyes had alerted the others when Alban took Frances' hand and whispered: "'Tis time, sweetheart." They saw the couple stand and they jumped to the right conclusion. Word spread in a buzz. Hands clapped; fists banged tables; cheers rang out. Frances blushed scarlet and Alban raised a hand in mock appreciation. As they mounted the stairs so the guests followed, clapping, whistling, jeering. Saucy remarks rang around their ears. Too much wine had encouraged uncharacteristic lewdness. When they got to the first bend in the stairs Alban acted. Frances continued up to what was now 'their' room, while he turned and addressed them.

"Thank you," he shouted, using his hands to try and calm

them down. "Thank you all for being here today, for witnessing our marriage, for your gifts and good wishes but please, if you don't mind, I would like to be alone now with my wife."

Whistles and jeers greeted that remark but he concentrated on the sense of delight flooding through him as he used the word 'wife' for the first time.

"Yes, come on everyone," said William who, having done his share of whistling, was now aiding Alban. "We've had our fun." He herded them back down the stairs to port, brandy and sweet pies. Thank goodness there's only forty of them, Alban was thinking as he bounded up the stairs, two at a time.

Frances turned to face him as he entered. "Have they gone?" He could see the anxiety on her face. He nodded. Maid Annie had filled the room with bowls of sweet-smelling rose petals. She had sprinkled the linen with perfumed oils and hung pomanders of aromatic spices. The light was soft, the air sweet. It heightened their senses.

Alban made no secret of what was uppermost in his mind. His eyes glowed like a wild animal's. Even across the width of the room he managed to make the air between them tense, unbreathable. He tossed his sleeveless, velvet coat over a chair. Its pale fur trim caught the sun as it cascaded to the floor.

"Has been a wonderful day," she said, her senses reacting as he strode toward her.

"Small talk later. You know what I want," he said, his eyes full of lust and longing and love. He took the wine goblet from her hand and placed it on a table. Despite knowing him already, or mayhap because she did know, she was nervous again. She felt herself tremble at his closeness as she anticipated what was to come and her chest tightened as her body responded with little thrills of memory.

"Trembling Frances?"

"I told you, you overwhelm me."

"Good," he said, removing the flowers from her head. He knelt and removed her shoes. He ran his hands under her skirts and stroked the silkiness of her stockings. She stood submissively, starting slightly as his fingers strayed to the naked skin above making her heart pound in anticipation. He stood up and ran his fingers through her hair, cupping the back of her head and gently, sweetly lowering his lips on to hers. He brushed her lips back and forth then slipped away to a sensual exploration of her neck, her ears, her throat, making her sigh and weaken as he gently stole her will.

"I want to worship you," he said huskily, the need rising in him, his eyes afire. "How do I get you out of this gown?"

"You don't, I'll do it."

He crossed the room and sat on a chair to watch her. Under his close, loving scrutiny, his eyes boring into her, she untied the laces that held the sleeves and peeled them off. She unhooked the bodice, then released the skirt. She looked at him, he nodded, it was her cue to carry on. She slipped out of one underskirt, then the next, then the next. Layer upon layer of flounces and frills, their perfume wafting around him, making him inwardly groan. At last she arrived at the final chemise. Just a thin layer of cotton now between her and nakedness.

The guests were drifting out into the gardens and chatter filtered through their open window. They could hear music from the lutes, the recorders and bells and away in the distance there was laughter, presumably the entertainments were under way. They'd be lighting the torches soon and fruit confits would circulate along with an array of liqueurs. Alban and Frances had everything they wanted in this room. Love for each other. Hope for their future.

Dreams of joy to come.

He could see the shape of her waiting for his touch. Wanting him. He couldn't see her inner yearning, her longing but she could see his. His face, his eyes, his occasional deep growl of need could hide nothing. Nor was he trying to.

He nodded again. She slipped the straps off her shoulders and the chemise fell to the floor. She bent to untie the blue ribbons that held her silk stockings just above the knee.

"Leave them."

His eyes roamed her nakedness, she watched them as they scanned her, her skin tingling in their wake. He walked around her, ran his fingers lightly across her back, kissed her shoulders, ran his hands round and over her hips. She closed her eyes but the darkness somehow increased her vulnerability, made her aware of the air on her skin, his throbbing presence just inches away. She opened them again and in those few seconds he had all but undressed.

His green doublet, with its huge, puffed sleeves slashed to reveal red silk, was on the floor. Green and red - the Melbroke colours. Its jewels of emerald and ruby, along with cut jet, glinted in the candlelight. His bejewelled hat he'd tossed on to the bed and she just caught him pulling his silk shirt over his head.

He stood before her now, naked, magnificent. Boasting his arousal, allowing her to look at him, making sure that she did. His skin caught the glow of the setting sun as it filled the room with its redness. He looked like an ancient warrior, invincible, possessing what he knew was his. He picked her up in his arms and lay her on the bed. His lips took hers at last. Possessively, eagerly, hungrily.

"Now my Lady of Blean," he said, taking a long plume from his hat, "what games shall we play?"

"Lady Melbroke now," she managed to whisper.

"In our bed, my sweet one, you will always be my Lady of Blean."

Epilogue

ELIZABETH HAD JUST one Christmas with her new-found family. She died as the snowdrops pushed through the iron-hard earth and the old year gave way to the new. She was buried after a small service in Blean's chapel. Mother Esme attended, although not actually invited and on the front row of pews a large monk dabbed his eyes. He later planted starflower around her grave.

Before her death Elizabeth had felt her grandchild kicking in Frances' belly and pronounced it was a girl. She was correct. Another Elizabeth entered the world a few months later, mother and child both perfectly healthy. Margaret's second child was another son and all three children shared the nursery while a second wing was added to Blean House for the Melbrokes. Alban, always an agent for his King, agreed to help William run the Blean estate, both men becoming vital support to the ageing Earl whose heart ticks on.

The small group stood silently as the coffin was lowered

into the convent ground on a cold but bright February morning. Brother Thomas and a few fellow monks chanted softly alongside the nuns who had shared 'Magdala's' life for so many years. Just the Earl, the Runmores, Frances and Alban remembered - and always will - the lovely lady with the bright eyes and beautiful smile. The end had healed her wounds, she had returned to happiness and hope and had died with her son holding her hand.

The priest's voice cut into the crisp morning air as he intoned sacred Latin verse and as the coffin met its resting place Alban's hand found the golden sundial in his pocket. He grasped it tightly, swallowed back a rising emotion and found his thoughts wandering to his spiteful uncle...Mayhap that story isn't over yet.

A second book featuring the King's cousin, Alban, Lord Melbroke, and Frances, will follow. Meanwhile, readers may wish to stay in touch with them and other characters from this book on the Tudor Blog at www.WillowPondPress.co.uk/Tudor-Blog

Historical Note

The dedication, investment and risk-taking nature of men like this novel's Earl of Blean brought profit to them, employment to Kent and Sussex and strength to Henry's arm. The Wealden iron industry flourished. Some one hundred furnaces and forges churned out the iron the King had demanded and for decades the Weald was dominated by its noise, smell, smoke, hammering and roaring furnaces. Future military campaigns and future monarchs came to reply upon it. Queen Elizabeth I - Henry's daughter by Anne Boleyn - faced continual threats from Spain during her reign and England's naval success against the 1588 Spanish Armada was in part due to Wealden cannon.

To this day the area abounds with references to its illustrious past: minepit wood, hammer stream, forge lane and so on. Looking today at the peaceful, beautiful, undulating countryside of this area it is difficult to imagine that heavy industry once existed here and its country lanes were once busy highways for wagons laden with this precious treasure that was to play such a vital role in England's safety and history.

Also happening in 1515...

• Archbishop of York, Thomas Wolsey, a man of humble origins, became Lord Chancellor of England and a Cardinal of Rome. He also took over a private house on the banks of the Thames and turned it into a lavish bishop's palace. Hampton Court was later taken from him by King Henry who turned it into one of the most magnificent royal palaces in Europe which it remains to this day.

• In Portugal, people marvelled at the first rhinoceros they had ever seen. It was sent as a gift from India to their King. A strange beast - it caused a stir!

• At Cambridge University, England, a magnificent fan vault ceiling, a miracle of master stonemasonry was completed in King's College Chapel. To this day it remains the world's largest.

• In Mexico, the Aztecs were supreme. Little did they know that the Spanish were coming and they were doomed.

• In China, Ming emperors were living a life of outstanding luxury and decadence. The Mings have gone but their pots remain. In Hong Kong in 2014 a small cup was sold at auction for £20 million.

• In Germany, a little girl with political destiny was born. Anne of Cleves was to be Henry VIII's fourth wife, The marriage lasted six months, it was not consummated and she was never crowned queen. She cleverly kept his friendship and her head!

Acknowledgements

To the people below I offer my sincerest thanks for their help in the researching, editing, design and production of this book.

• *To Wealden iron expert*, lecturer and author Jeremy Hodgkinson for allowing me to interview him at length and for checking my 'iron' accuracy. His books "The Wealden Iron Industry" and "British Cast-Iron Firebacks" are available from www.hodgers.com/books

• *To fellow journalist*, broadcaster and author, Mary Atkinson, who helped with the 'first read' and editing of this book. Her encouragement, support, skills and the many hours she gave leave me in her debt. I can but wish her every success with her own project: "Story Massage for Children: Once Upon a Touch". Book, DVD and more information from www.storymassage.co.uk

• *To artist* Norman Leevers who diverted his attention from his usual work in oils to create the cover of this book. He comes to book illustration from art teaching, ceramics and landscape and knowing his commitment to exhibitions and galleries I very much appreciate the time and creative touch that he gave. Contactable on: 01985 216780 or via the publisher

• *To IT specialist* Robert Brown without whose skills this paperback and the ebook version, would never have seen daylight. Contactable on help@x-Mac.co.uk

About the Author

Mela Ells is a Londoner and has been a national magazine and newspaper journalist for over thirty years. She has been a feature writer, reporter, fiction writer and occasional broadcaster. *Tudor Hugger-Mugger* is her fourth book and is set in a period of history that intrigues her. For seventeen years she lived a stone's throw from Hampton Court Palace, her house being on land that many Tudors, including their monarchs, walked and galloped over. Their ghosts became her neighbours, they drew her into this fascinating period of English history which is now her joy to use as the back-drop to her mystery-romances.